Praise for *Do Tell*

'A wonderful, provocative novel about the way time changes how we
see the world. Edie O'Dare is a failed Hollywood actress who
reinvents herself as a gossip columnist in order to keep a roof over
her head, only to discover that this is the job she's good at. Like our
intrepid narrator, *Do Tell* manages to be both funny and substantive,
breezy and wise. I stepped into the stream of the narrative and didn't
look up until I came to the last page'
Ann Patchett, bestselling author of *The Dutch House*

'Gossip columnist Edie O'Dare has enemies and sources, but no
friends in a Golden Age Hollywood whose gleam is tarnished by
exploitation, cruelty and betrayal. Like a latter-day Cecil B. DeMille,
Lindsay Lynch deftly directs her large cast of morally complex
characters to illuminate issues of fame and notoriety as relevant now
as they were almost a century ago'
Geraldine Brooks, *New York Times* bestselling author of *Horse*

'There is little more alluring than the promise of secrets, and *Do Tell*
is full of them – glamorous, tawdry, and human. Lindsay Lynch has
created a rich portrait of the lives of early Hollywood's beautiful
puppets and those holding their strings'
Emma Straub, *New York Times* bestselling author of
This Time Tomorrow

'In *Do Tell* Lindsay Lynch takes a glance back at golden-age
Hollywood and captures the fizzy magic, the secret lives, and the
deep, destructive misogyny within the industry's DNA. This is a wry,
entertaining, and incisive debut'
Lily King, *New York Times* bestselling author of *Writers & Lovers*

'This dazzling novel is a riveting exposé of the dream factory which
will surprise readers at every turn. You won't be able to put it down'
Adriana Trigiani, *New York Times* bestselling author of
The Good Left Undone

'*Do Tell* is an absolute marvel: page-turning yet thought-provoking, historical in its setting yet contemporary in its concerns. With a keen eye for period detail, Lindsay Lynch explores how the power of secrets were the secret to power in Hollywood's Golden Age. The result is a deeply moving, immensely satisfying blockbuster of a debut novel'
Anthony Marra, *New York Times* bestselling author of *Mercury Pictures Presents*

'Lindsay Lynch has written a novel so thoroughly immersive, I looked up from its pages disoriented — confused not to find myself amid the couture gowns and hushed secrets of old Hollywood. I'll tell every reader I know: I adored *Do Tell*'
Mary Laura Philpott, bestselling author of *Bomb Shelter: Love, Time, and Other Explosives*

'*Do Tell* is a glittering riot of a debut filled with tantalizing gossip, lavish parties and an insider's glimpse into a bygone era of Hollywood glamour. Lindsay Lynch brings the studio system to life with these unforgettable yet deeply complicated characters whose lives are caught at the crossroads of power and truth telling. This is a novel you won't want to miss'
Kali Fajardo-Anstine, bestselling author of *Woman of Light* and *Sabrina & Corina*

'An electric novel about power and complicity in the Golden Age of Hollywood told through the eyes of Edith O'Dare, a narrator as fearsome as she is fallible. In *Do Tell*, Lindsay Lynch masterfully uncovers a world in which gossip is currency and image is everything, laying bare the devastating consequences of secrets told and untold. Enthralling and utterly relevant'
Jenny Tinghui Zhang, international bestselling author of *Four Treasures of the Sky*

DO TELL

A Novel

LINDSAY LYNCH

HODDER &
STOUGHTON

First published in Great Britain in 2023 by Hodder & Stoughton
An Hachette UK company

I

Copyright © Lindsay Lynch 2023

The right of Lindsay Lynch to be identified as the Author of the Work has been asserted by
her in accordance with the Copyright, Designs and Patents Act 1988.

A CIP catalogue record for this title is available from the British Library

Hardback ISBN 978 1 399 70737 4
Trade Paperback ISBN 978 1 399 70738 1
eBook ISBN 978 1 399 70739 8

Typeset in Fournier MT Std

Printed and bound in Great Britain by Clays Ltd, Elcograf S.p.A.

Hodder & Stoughton policy is to use papers that are natural, renewable and recyclable
products and made from wood grown in sustainable forests. The logging and
manufacturing processes are expected to conform to the environmental regulations of the
country of origin.

Hodder & Stoughton Ltd
Carmelite House
50 Victoria Embankment
London EC4Y 0DZ

www.hodder.co.uk

FOR MY PARENTS

Cast

EDITH O'DARE	*Actress, gossip columnist*
SEBASTIAN O'SHAUGHNESSY	*Novelist, brother of Edith*
AUGUSTAN CHARTERS	*FWM publicist*
CHARLES LANDRIEU	*FWM actor, frequently portrays outlaws*
NELL PARKER	*FWM actress, engaged to Charles Landrieu*
FREDDY CLARKE	*FWM actor, frequently portrays heroes*
ROLF JUNGER	*FWM director, notable for his Westerns*
THOMAS BRODBECK	*Studio chief at FWM Studios*
MARGY PRESCOTT	*FWM actress, married to Hal Bingham*
HAL BINGHAM	*FWM actor, married to Margy Prescott*
SOPHIE MELROSE	*FWM newcomer*
INES MARQUIS	*Heiress, primary stockholder in FWM Studios*
POPPY ST. JOHN	*Rival gossip columnist*
BAIRD DEWITT	*MGM actor, known for character work*
JEANETTE MANNING	*FWM actress, comedienne*

~ 1 ~

ONE

The last time I saw Charles Landrieu in Los Angeles, he told me I had gotten everything wrong.

"Everything?" I asked him.

Everything.

It wasn't the first time someone had leveled this accusation against me and I was certain it wouldn't be the last.

Actors talk so much– not enough people focus on the things they won't say.

So I did. I built my career in silences and averted glances, paying attention to who missed work, who skipped parties. I asked why, and when no one answered, I filled in the blanks myself.

The day I talked with Charles, I considered asking him to give me whatever he believed to be the correct story. To tell me what I had missed. By that time, he was blacklisted from every studio in Hollywood; he had nothing to lose.

But he didn't want to talk. He paced around my living room and made reference to a party we'd all been at before the war—he had every reason to remember it well; it was his engagement party. That was all he had to say. Charles Landrieu was done talking for a while.

I told him to gain ten pounds and join the army. He did.

Let's talk about the night in question, the night I allegedly ruined a life or two, or three: Thomas Brodbeck's party celebrating the engagement of FWM Studios stars Charles Landrieu and Nell Parker, August 1939.

The guest list included a group of people whose lives would be altered by that night: Charles and Nell; Augustan Charters and myself; Margy Prescott and her notably absent husband, Hal Bingham; and Sophie Melrose, a young actress who only wanted to go to her first Hollywood party. Finally, there was the man who had not been invited but arrived anyway: Freddy Clarke.

When I told my brother, Seb, we'd be stopping at a party that night, I might have intentionally withheld some details. It was his first day in Los Angeles, so the name Thomas Brodbeck meant little to him. There wasn't any reason why Sebastian O'Shaughnessy, darling of the New York literati, should have had any idea who the FWM studio chief was, or even what a studio chief did. As soon as I began listing the names of actors and actresses, though, Seb understood.

"We won't have to stay long?" he asked.

"An hour at the most, not even that," I said. I told him we had to say hello to Brodbeck and congratulate Charles and Nell on their pretend engagement. Public appearances like these were part of my contract with the studio.

I had convinced Seb to move to Hollywood on the pretense that I was a moderately successful actress who could land him a job screenwriting.

The thing is, I really was a moderately successful actress who could land him a job screenwriting. My only omission to my brother was that I had only three months left on my contract and FWM Studios didn't renew contracts for *moderately* successful actresses.

"Anyway, you have to talk to Augustan," I said as I poured us each a glass of whiskey—mine on the rocks, his straight.

"I don't know who that is."

"You'll love him," I lied. "He runs all the things at FWM that no one else has the time to run. I already told him you'd be there. He's excited to meet you. I'm certain he can get you a job."

As I began going up the stairs to change into my dress, Seb demanded that I wait a goddamn minute. Seb still had a heavy accent from our years growing up in Boston. His voice went up as he spoke to me, and for a moment I saw the young boy he had once been—the lanky awkwardness of his posture and the redness in his pale cheeks. Though we regularly wrote each other, I hadn't seen him in person for a long time. Between the two of us, I was the one who could afford to travel, and I hadn't left California since the early thirties. I'd talked about it in my letters to him, swearing that I'd take the time off to visit. But the time off never came.

"You told me I already *had* a job," he said.

I shook my head and pursed my lips. "I wouldn't have said that."

Seb went over to his worn-down briefcase by the front door and began rummaging through it. He produced a handwritten letter. He went over to the couch and smoothed the letter out on the coffee table. I watched as he bent over it, carefully running his finger along each line.

"There," he said, pointing to the letter. "In your own words, one week ago: 'If you come to Hollywood, you'll have a job.'"

I nodded and leaned against the banister. "Yes, you *will* have a job. Look at you—college graduate, one novel published already. You're very employable! That's why we're going to the party."

"I took out my savings to come here, Edie," he said. "I got rid of everything I had!"

"And I'm sure the mattress that lived on your floor is happy to begin anew in a dumpster somewhere."

I looked at Seb sitting in my living room, his red hair standing on end and his shirt wrinkled. He'd arrived from the train station only a few hours earlier.

"I don't suppose you have a suit?" I asked.

· · ·

Seb was not amused when I came down the stairs fifteen minutes later in a gown. The gown was on loan from a friend in the FWM costuming department; it was intended to be worn by Carla Longworth in an upcoming romantic drama, but she'd rejected the fabric choice, said the tulle made her look too wide. I wasn't sure how wide the tulle made me look, and frankly didn't care—it wasn't as though I was in the running to be the most beautiful woman at that party. Anyone from the studio would be able to identify the dress for what it was, but I could see Seb doing mental calculations of its worth. That's how it had always been with me and Seb; after a childhood of scarcity, we could never stop appraising what was in front of us.

Even if I had told Seb the gown wasn't mine, he still would have resented me for making him go to a party underdressed. He spent the entire car ride over picking at his sleeves and smoothing out his trousers.

"Trust me," I said. "They'll think it's very *New York* of you. That kind of credibility gets people jobs."

"Humiliating is what it is."

"Well, I'd hate for you to discover the kinds of getups actresses have to wear to be employed here."

When we pulled up in front of the Bel Air mansion, Seb refused to get out of the car. I told him I'd drag him by his ear if I had to. I'd done it a hundred times when we were children, and I would do it again.

I watched Seb's face as he took in the mansion, the way his mouth turned down at the corners and his eyes grew wide. While I assumed he'd seen his share of wealthy estates on the East Coast, I couldn't imagine any of them had prepared him for what Los Angeles had to offer. Thomas Brodbeck's house had been built in the twenties, all tiled floors and high ceilings. Anything that could be gilded was gilded, from the molding along the walls to the railings on the staircases. He imported plants from around

CIVICA

Issued

Branch: South Dublin Lucan
Date: 24/10/2023   Time: 12:18 PI
Name: Correos, Babie
D: D4000000354161

ITEM(S)   DUE DATI

to tell : a novel................. 06 Nov 202
SD200000047759
Item Value: €17.48

How you see us................. 06 Nov 202
SD200000052751
Item Value: €14.77

Total value of item(s): €32.25
Your current loan(s): ?
Your current reservation(s): 0
Your current active request(s): 0

To renew your items please log onto My
Account on the OPAC at
https://southdublin.spydus.ie

Thank you for using your local library

the world: palms, orchids, birds-of-paradise. Even the staff was adorned with gold buttons and a fresh flower for every lapel.

Five years ago, he would've toned it all down; it was poor taste to be wealthy while the rest of the country was devastated. But the thirties were nearly over. As we crept closer and closer to a new decade, there was a promise of fleeting abundance—everyone figured they could take advantage of it as long as it lasted.

We hadn't made it five feet inside before a glass of champagne appeared next to me and I heard a voice in my ear, smooth and low.

"Do me a kindness and murder me, would you? I trust you'll make it discreet and relatively painless."

I turned and saw Augustan looking elegant in a tuxedo. He was always a sharp dresser: one of those men who took care that their pocket squares complemented their ties, that their hair was neatly combed back, that their shoes were sent over from Italy. The real beauty of it was how he never drew attention to himself. It wasn't Augustan's place to be noticed. His traits were mostly unremarkable—he was of average height, with dull brown hair and pale gray eyes. It was only in spending excessive time with him that I ever noticed the care he put into the details.

Before I had the chance to introduce Sebastian to him, Augustan directed me into the foyer, his hand firm against the small of my back. I left poor Seb standing alone next to the doorway with nothing more than a wave and a mouthed apology.

Chief of publicity was Augustan's real title. He could be seen in the background of every FWM party and premiere, where he kept a watchful eye on the actors and actresses. Most of his time was spent managing the A-list of FWM Studios—among his treasured wards were Freddy Clarke, Nell Parker, and Charles Landrieu.

During my time as an actress, I was neither precious nor destructive enough to merit Augustan's care. My handler was an old man named Horace, who always smelled of sardines. I only ever heard from him during my first two years under contract—every few months he called to tell me I had to do a photo shoot to celebrate whatever holiday was closest. He once had me stand half naked in front of a forest backdrop with a photo crew for an hour. It wasn't until I saw my picture in *Screenland* that I realized we were honoring Arbor Day.

My friendship with Augustan was forged at an upscale party while looking for an escaped monkey from the host's private zoo. We took a bottle of gin, a large net that was originally intended to fish leaves out of the backyard pool, and some galoshes from the hunting room. Augustan joked about taking a musket, but I told him nobody likes a dead monkey. ("You mean nobody likes a dead actress," he replied. "Which, I have to tell you, statistically speaking? They really do.") For three hours, we took turns swinging the net at miscellaneous bushes and shrubs while we complained about every person we hated in Hollywood, from the actors to the executives. Nothing forms a bond quicker than discovering a subject of mutual loathing, and we had several. We never did find that monkey. Monkeys can live a long time, decades even; I like to imagine it's still wandering somewhere around Orange County.

As my acting roles waned, my confidence with Augustan grew. We started arriving at parties together, and before long we started occasionally leaving together as well. Augustan and I had a mutual understanding that neither of us would ever put too much stock into the fact that we had shared a bed here and there.

I don't like to deploy the word *snitch,* so let's say I became an unofficial publicity associate. Actresses sneaking into their costars' dressing rooms, men who couldn't hold both their liquor and their tongues, set crews talking about unions—that was the kind of information Augustan valued, so I made certain I always had stories on hand.

I knew plenty of failed actresses who rode out the remainder of their contracts sitting in whatever hotel room or apartment the studio paid for, eating burgers and fries with reckless abandon until it was time for them to go back to the midwestern towns they came from. I'm sure all of them found nice husbands with nice paychecks and their time spent in Hollywood became nothing more than a benign anecdote for cocktail parties.

Turns out I'm not the benign-anecdote-for-cocktail-parties kind of woman.

Augustan began explaining that the newly engaged couple, Charles Landrieu and Nell Parker, had the chemistry of a soda bottle left open in the sun for too long.

"They only just got off location," he said. "Traveled overnight from Arizona and then it was straight into this. I'll be lucky if they remain conscious through the dessert course."

Augustan continued with his grievances: The actor Freddy Clarke had weaseled his way into the party despite having been banned from any festivities at Brodbeck's estate a few months ago. The hors d'oeuvres weren't properly chilled and tasted sour. Someone had been pestering him about meeting a second-rate novelist for a screenwriting job.

I hit his arm with my clutch. "That was *me*. And he's a very first-rate novelist!"

Augustan scoffed. "Is he Hemingway?"

"No," I said, "but he'll do a damn fine job adapting Hemingway, which you and I both know is more than anyone can say for Hemingway himself."

All this time, Augustan had been leading me toward the back of the room, where Charles and Nell stood at the end of a large winding staircase, with a crowd of reporters pooled around them. Every minute or so, the bulbs flashed, illuminating Charles and Nell as he held an arm around her waist and she turned to look up at him lovingly.

The two made for a nice contrast: Nell's pale tone and white-blond hair against Charles's tan skin ("Spanish heritage," Augustan liked to assure people). Charles was clean-shaven that night, his curly black hair oiled back so it wouldn't obscure his blue eyes. Next to him, Nell was wearing a gold-embellished Schiaparelli in white. The dress looked loose on her, but I had also heard that she had all her dresses tailored to make her appear even smaller than she already was. When it came to Nell's appearance, there were never any mistakes. If that woman so much as had a hair out of place, I could be certain it was done on purpose.

In spite of Nell's efforts, the last time Augustan polled the public for adjectives they'd use to describe her, she got *charming, pleasant,* and *fair.* Hardly the qualifications for a leading lady in a major studio.

So, what did Augustan do? He paired her with the adjectives *fiery* and *gritty.* Said one housewife from Des Moines: "He looks like he would toss a girl onto a couch, but not without asking politely for permission first."

Charles Landrieu.

He was still a fresh face then. Back around '36, the director Rolf Junger pulled a young man named Émile Arceneaux off the stunt lot. One of Rolf's secondary actors had quit just days before they were scheduled to go on location for a Western. He needed a cheap and easy replacement, so he went through FWM's available stuntmen and pulled whichever ones were the best looking.

Émile's screen test has long since been filmed over, but I heard it was an absolute disaster. His Louisiana accent was so thick, nobody could understand a word he said. Émile would've been left doing stunts for the rest of his days if it hadn't been for someone telling him the cameras weren't rolling anymore and catching a reel of him giving, apparently, the world's most charming apology in the low baritone voice that would garner him fan letters by the hundreds over the course of the next year.

The name Émile would never do—too feminine for any man in Hollywood—and no one had any idea how to pronounce his last name. But he had a photogenic smile and a nice laugh. He knew his blocking and wasn't nervous around a camera. The men at FWM Studios decided they could work with that.

Ultimately, all it took was a year's worth of speech therapy and a pair of cowboy boots to create Charles Landrieu.

Nell took all the questions from her place on the stairs, never raising her voice above its soft lilt. As she talked, I watched the reporters inch closer and closer to her, until they were practically at her feet. She carried on as if she didn't notice, talking down to them about how she and Charles were hoping to set a wedding date as soon as possible, but, oh, how busy their schedules were!

Next to her, Charles became distracted every few moments, his eyes traveling around the room, or settling on the floor in front of him. Whenever he did this, Nell called him back by squeezing his biceps and smiling up at him, at which point Charles would kiss her cheek and say something vague but charming.

Before their arranged engagement, Charles and Nell did two films together. Prior to that, Nell had been playing the innocent sweetheart, and she usually ended up with the all-American type: blond, blue-eyed, perfect white teeth. All those housewives and their ilk went wild when Nell was suddenly in the arms of a foul-mouthed, dark, handsome bandit. And so, for her subsequent films, Nell *constantly* found herself in the arms of a foulmouthed, dark, handsome bandit.

Their latest was a Western, *The Sure Shot*. As the press built up around Charles and Nell, so did the budget for *The Sure Shot*. It was the first film Rolf Junger had been allowed to direct in Technicolor. He was given free rein with location—production was based in Arizona, but he'd been designated plenty of trucks and equipment to capture as many vistas as he wanted. The plot wasn't anything special: Charles was cast as a cowboy arrested for smuggling goods across the border, and Nell was the sheriff's daughter. They become infatuated with each other. Charles's character dies in his moment of redemption, when he saves the sheriff from an Apache attack. As far as audiences were concerned, the plot paled in comparison to the prospect of seeing Charles and Nell together again, in full color.

Augustan wanted Nell's name on the top of the "Best of" lists in the next year. Everyone assumed that was about how long her engagement to Charles would last.

As for Charles, he simply wanted a role where he wouldn't die before the end of the reel.

Augustan's hand was at my elbow. "I *suppose* we ought to congratulate the happy couple," he said grimly, gesturing toward them.

Augustan and I walked across a room filled with the most beautiful people in America, in the prime of their lives.

In all my time among them, the thing that never ceased to shock me about these people was how little excess they carried—excess skin, excess fat, excess hair. The level of curation was astounding. They were, all of them, exemplary creatures.

I suppose this was part of why I clung to Augustan. He had a gap tooth, front and center. Sometimes it caused him to whistle when he had too much to drink. He could afford to fix it, and yet he didn't. For all his attention to detail, I always believed it was the one thing he kept for himself.

For my part, I'd been a beauty when I started out: thick red hair, alabaster skin, a trim figure. Over the course of seven years, my skin hadn't held and my natural waist had gone from a twenty-four to a disappointing twenty-seven. One too many encounters with a hot iron caused portions of my hair to dry out and defy any treatment from the latest creams and gels. I learned to be very nifty with a set of hairpins and hoped gravity would be on my side any given day.

And I knew our stars had flaws, too; but I also knew that Freddy Clarke was once coached to smile so he showed more teeth on his left side, and his lopsided grin became part of his signature look. We like our stars to have flaws, but we like them to have the *right* flaws—the crooked smile that reminds you of a boy back home, or a beauty mark you might see in a daguerreotype of your grandmother when she was young and beautiful.

There's an art to knowing which flaws are acceptable, the careful line between something that inspires empathy and something that inspires derision or judgment. Men like Augustan seemed to know instinctively where that line was.

"Are you getting tired of spitting that champagne back into your glass yet?" Augustan asked Charles in a low voice when we approached him and Nell on the stairs.

The reporters had dispersed, leaving the two stars to relax for a moment. I watched Nell put her weight on Charles's shoulder while she rolled her ankle under her gown. Charles let out a breath as he looked down at his full glass of champagne.

Charles smiled widely, and I was close enough to hear him tell Augustan in explicit terms what to do with himself.

It had taken me a late night and a full bottle of reserve port to convince Augustan to give me the story on Charles's intervention.

A few months before, all I saw was a note in the papers that Charles was taking time off for "exhaustion."

Augustan wasn't the type to encourage sobriety in anyone, but he was the unfortunate soul sent to check on Charles after he didn't show up to work one day. He found Charles's empty car crashed into a tree nearly half a mile away from his home. Inside the house, Charles was sitting fully clothed in a bathtub of cold water, mumbling in Creole.

After Augustan hauled him out of the tub, Charles collapsed in his bedroom and spent the next three days going through full withdrawal. The studio doctor came by at some point to patch him up. Charles had supposedly been teetotaling ever since, though I was certain I had seen him slip up a few times.

That night, I could see the strain in Charles's smile. His hands shook slightly when he lit his cigarette. He already had a reputation for reclusiveness—he purchased a ranch shortly after sign-ing a generous seven-year contract with FWM. With his salary, he could have bought a place on the beach like everyone else, but he chose the desert. The ranch was well outside the city, with enough land to keep retired film horses (a marketable quirk that Augus-tan didn't even have to invent for him). He dutifully attended parties when Augustan told him to, but he was rarely seen in the social clubs.

Charles had never been a talker at parties. Most people, I think, assumed as soon as he spoke with his slow accent that he was dim. I suspected he was quite the opposite.

Augustan and I parted ways, leaving Nell and Charles in the foyer, while I scouted the party for Sebastian's head of red hair—it was an O'Shaughnessy family trait; every one of my five siblings had it.

When I was under contract with FWM Studios, they changed my last name to O'Dare, fixed my teeth, scrubbed away any trace of a Boston accent, but no one was allowed to dye my hair. Some-one in publicity had declared it my trademark. Unfortunately, whoever was handling a young woman named Margarita Cansino at Fox had the same idea. She didn't keep her name, either—no one remembers my red hair, but they certainly remember Rita Hayworth's.

When I didn't see Seb anywhere, I started asking around. I stopped a few waiters and checked with the bartender. No one on the waitstaff had seen a redheaded man.

Instead, I found Freddy Clarke lounging on a divan.

Freddy got himself banned from Brodbeck's parties earlier that year, after he drank half the bar and challenged Charles to a fist-fight in the back garden.

At first, we all thought it was a real laugh to watch two of FWM's leading men go up against each other—Freddy's roles usu-ally entailed waving swords and kicking down doors to save the day, while Charles was more likely to be shooting someone from horseback.

Some people swore Charles threw the first punch, but only after Freddy taunted him (in all my searching, no one has been able to specify what Freddy said). Augustan thought that he saw Charles laugh at Freddy when his back was turned. Others maintained that Freddy and Charles each took a swig of whiskey and then squared up in more of a gentleman's agreement.

It seemed gentlemanly for the first few minutes. Freddy bested Charles in height and weight, but Charles was quick on his feet. They got a few good punches in and then Charles tried to step out. But Freddy was relentless. From what I could see, it looked like Charles threw himself onto the ground to call the whole thing off.

Freddy claimed he broke one of Charles's ribs. Both men were out of work for two days. The papers called it a "set-related injury."

"Did you bribe the doorman?" I asked Freddy. I perched myself on the back of his divan and placed a hand on his shoulder to get his attention.

Every month, one of the papers printed a popularity ranking of Hollywood actors and actresses. This was, of course, very healthy for their egos.

That summer, Freddy had claimed the number-one spot for four consecutive months. Freddy, with his coiffed dark blond hair and crooked smile, was regularly cast for swashbucklers, war heroes, and princes. He played Robin Hood five years ago and established himself as Hollywood's most devilishly handsome protagonist. His fan mail was delivered in buckets.

He briefly pinched my cheek and shook his head.

"I'm a plus-one," he said. There was that smile.

Not his wife's plus-one, I assumed. Nineteen-year-old Bunny Clarke was a rare sight at Hollywood parties. It was a fast wedding (and, to be frank, a fast marriage, but I'm getting ahead of myself), at which plenty of attendees claimed they could see a tightness in

Bunny's wedding gown, right around her waist. No one was surprised when their baby happened to be born two months early.

Freddy gestured across the room to the actress Jeanette Manning, known at the time for being the top comedienne on FWM's roster.

I leaned in closer, thinking I'd do some light teasing. "Did you bribe *her?*"

Freddy sneered and told me he was going to get another drink. So much for that.

"Don't hit anyone on your way out!" I called after him.

A member of Brodbeck's staff announced that dinner would be served shortly, so I began making the rounds for Seb. I imagined him locked in a coat closet somewhere, drinking a stolen bottle of liquor and cursing my name.

It wasn't a coat closet but the library. He was perusing the shelves when I found him.

"Don't tell me you came in here to check if the pages are cut," I said.

"They are and I did not. I wanted to be somewhere quiet," he explained. "Mr. Whatshisname has surprisingly good taste."

I explained to him that it was more likely one of Brodbeck's assistants had good taste. A few years ago, there was a story going around that Brodbeck had hired a woman to read him new literary manuscripts while he worked in his office. It puzzled everyone until we learned that Selznick had bought the rights to *Gone with the Wind* within a month of the book's publication.

"Maybe we'll get invited back and you can sneak your book in here, hmm?" I said before shepherding him out of the library so we could eat.

For dinner, Seb and I were placed at a table with Augustan, one of his publicity cronies, and the director Rolf Junger and his wife. Augustan and the crony were busy talking shop to each other. Rolf had also just arrived back from filming on location; his exhaustion showed as he conversed in German with his wife. She would make a soft-spoken comment and he would bark a one-word reply. I didn't need to speak German to understand that the conversation wasn't cordial and that I wanted nothing to do with it.

We were served beef Wellington with a side of sautéed mushrooms. The meat was gamy, and Augustan wouldn't give me a second to introduce Seb to him. He was busy arguing over the casting for a remake of *The Mark of Zorro*.

Seb looked visibly uncomfortable. He was the only man not wearing a tuxedo. He sat as though he might be attempting to become a part of his chair.

I spoke to him in a low voice. "Do you really think anyone in this room is paying attention to you?"

He didn't reply as he glanced around. Over the din of glasses clinking and silverware hitting plates, people were talking and laughing.

"I'm not saying it to be cruel," I continued. "One of the best things I did for myself here was become invisible. See that man over there?" I nodded toward an actor sitting a few tables away. "I've been in three films with him. We had scenes! Dialogue! A few months ago on set, he mistook me for a makeup artist and explained in detail that a rash had developed on his face. He asked if I would make certain it stayed covered up before he went home to his wife. It didn't take me long to sort out which of his costars he was sneaking away with."

I left out the part where I sold that story to a journalist for twenty dollars.

"If you asked him or anyone else in this room, they'd swear up and down that nobody knows their secrets. There are real benefits to being nobody."

Midway through dinner, we were interrupted by the late appearance of the young actresses Sophie Melrose and Margy Prescott. They burst into the dining room in a loud fit of giggles, clutching each other's hands. Margy had the staff add an extra two chairs at Freddy's already full table. They practically ate their food off their laps.

I'd seen Sophie only once or twice before then. She was about to be placed under contract at the age of sixteen. Her father was a midwestern auto tycoon, Markham Auto Parts. She'd given herself a new last name, Melrose, before any studio could do it for her. Her father permitted her to live in Los Angeles with an old aunt so she could pursue an acting career. Getting cast in *The Sure Shot* was supposed to be Sophie's breakthrough. She played Nell's younger sister and had a few scenes causing trouble for Charles's bandit in jail. It was the kind of role that launched careers—as long as she landed a few snappy lines, she could set herself up to be the next Loretta Young.

Margy had "taken the girl under her wing," as Augustan liked to put it. Not sure what a twenty-two-year-old newlywed actress was going to teach her, but it wasn't my job to worry about it.

Now, wondering why Margy's new husband wasn't with her at the party—that was my job.

I hadn't noticed Thomas Brodbeck, our host, that night until he stood to make a speech. He was one of those men who could do that—you wouldn't see him until he wanted you to. Went from being the human equivalent of dated wallpaper to the man who ran one of the biggest studios in Hollywood.

"We're here to celebrate two young people whose love goes straight to the heart . . . a bit like a *sure shot*."

Pause for laughs.

Of course, this was all extended promotion for the film.

After Brodbeck finished his speech, the guests began growing jittery, switching tables, waiting for the next portion of the night.

Margy and Sophie accosted poor Charles while he was trying to get a glass of water from the bar. He took a step back each time Sophie leaned in toward him. Margy made no effort to stop the girl from making a fool of herself in front of the whole room. If anything, Margy was holding back laughter. Some role model.

Margy ("That's with a hard *g*," she'd remind people) was a former Kentucky pageant queen with a passion for horseback riding. She had a wide smile and sharp facial features, which had helped her win Miss Kentucky, and then, as predicted by Augustan when he picked her from a lineup of queens, translated beautifully on-screen. She was offered a contract within a few months of arriving in Hollywood. She and Charles rose through the ranks of the studio around the same time—they both had to take speech lessons to de-southern their tongues. They used to show up to parties and premieres together, always making too much of a fuss about their relationship being friendly and nothing more.

When Margy walked by my table, she looked at it with her nose turned up. I couldn't tell if the sneer was intended for me. Word was going around the studio that I had something to do with Margy's getting snubbed in Poppy St. John's column for the *Examiner*.

Poppy had maintained a monopoly on Hollywood gossip since the late twenties. As movie theaters began cropping up in every corner of the country, so, too, did the voice of Poppy St. John—by the mid-thirties, she was syndicated in nearly every major paper across America. A mention in Poppy's column, the "Tinseltown Tattler," could make a career. I know this because I never got one.

Neither had Margy at the time. It was clear she had her eye on the column when she married Hal Bingham. Their elopement was an expertly rigged scandal. Last spring, Margy and Hal went to Wyoming to film the Western *Afterglow*. They were joined by Charles, the film's third costar. After filming wrapped, the three of them made a detour in Nevada, where Hal and Margy got married in a church off the interstate, with Charles as their witness. A studio-approved photographer happened to be there for the ceremony. An anonymous call was placed to Poppy with the exclusive news.

It was a secret to exactly no one that, in addition to providing Augustan with the chatter of FWM Studios, I also moonlighted as Poppy St. John's favorite source. The same week that Margy and Hal eloped, I handed Poppy a story on the birth of Freddy's daughter, including an interview with his wife, Bunny. Margy didn't stand a chance.

She had not spoken to me since.

I looked across the room and saw Sophie rushing away from the table, her face pale and sickly. Her gown clung awkwardly to her as she tried to walk quickly along the edges of the room. Meanwhile, Margy was now sitting with Charles, her arm draped casually over the back of his chair as they talked, and took no notice of Sophie. I excused myself from my table—leaving Seb, once again, to fend for himself—and followed after her.

I stood outside the bathroom and gave the door a soft knock with my knuckles.

"Are you all right?" I asked.

I heard a small voice: "Margy? That you?"

I leaned against the door and cooed, "Margy's busy talking to Charles; I don't think she saw you leave."

"Can . . . can you go get her?" There was a quiver in her voice, followed by sniffling.

"Why don't you let me in? I'm a great help at these sorts of things."

I heard a small hum, which I took as a yes. I opened the door and there was Sophie, kneeling over the toilet. A few strands of blond hair were stuck by perspiration to her forehead and neck, and I could see the discoloration in her pale silk gown along the neckline. I looked at the skirt of the dress bunched around her knees and my first concern was how wrinkled it would be when she stood up.

I told her my name was Edie as I joined her on the floor. I held her hair and rubbed her back while she released the contents of her stomach into Thomas Brodbeck's gilded toilet bowl.

"Too much champagne?" I asked.

Sophie paused for a moment before lifting her head and wiping her mouth. There was a smear of pink lipstick across her cheek. Her mascara had held up, but her eyes were red and watery. She confessed to me that she wasn't used to the "hard stuff." I presumed that meant alcohol.

Then she started crying. She was one of those girls who can't breathe when they cry.

"It's"—she sobbed—"just—so—embarrassing."

I reassured her that no one had seen her run off, and promised that we'd get her put back together. I gave her a towel to dry her hands with—she was dangerously close to wiping them on her skirt and ruining what I knew was a very expensive gown. For a brief moment, I caught her hands in mine, and I was reminded of my younger sisters, the softness of their palms and fingers whenever I had to hold their hands.

"By the time the dancing starts, you'll have forgotten this even happened!" I swore.

I ran a hand towel under some warm water and wiped off her lipstick. With her hair unpinned and half her face makeup-free, Sophie looked five years younger. I could see how rounded her cheeks were, the natural plumpness of her lips, and the puffiness around her jaw. Instead of an intoxicated young actress on the ground, I now saw a sixteen-year-old girl.

She remained on the floor while I took a seat on a plush stool and instructed her to move so I could fix her hair. She settled in front of me, facing away; I could feel her uneven breaths against my knees. I repinned her hair as best as I could, trying to re-create the meticulous rolls at the top of her head. I had been left to do my own hair for the last few years under contract; I'd gotten fairly good at it, and Sophie's hair was easier to tame than mine.

"See," I said, "it's going to be fine. You'll have a wonderful rest of your night, won't you?"

For a moment, she turned to me and smiled, but then she broke back down into sobs when I asked where her clutch was so I could help with her makeup. She didn't know. I found my own lipstick and told her she could keep it. The bright shade of orange-pink wasn't right for her skin tone, but it was something.

"You're lovely," she said when she stopped sobbing. "Just lovely."

And then I left her there. In the months and years to come, I'd think about that moment a lot, replaying it in my head with different outcomes—sometimes in these imaginings, I lead Sophie back to the party and hand her off to Margy for the night, or I drive her home myself and sit in the car until she's shut her front door behind her.

Before I left the bathroom, she told me she was fine. Why I believed her, I'll never know. I didn't think she would go wandering by herself after that. In the worst of my imaginings, that's what I see: Sophie, alone in any of the mansion's empty, half-lit rooms.

By that time, the party had cleared out of the dining room. Music was playing on the back terrace, so I walked toward the noise. Outside, the whole terrace was lit up with candles, from the floor to the pool in the yard. The sun was beginning to set, giving everything a violet hue. Even as it got darker, the summer heat was relentless. In the languorous night, guests began to discard their jackets and shawls, roll up their sleeves, remove their shoes.

It took me only a moment to find Augustan. We danced; it was our custom to steer each other around the room so we could check on everyone else. Nearby, Charles was dancing with Margy.

I gave Augustan's shoulder a tap and asked him where Margy's new husband was.

"Not tonight, Edie," he said.

Whenever Augustan would say something like this to me, I usually dropped it. But that night I saw the way Margy rested her cheek against Charles's shoulder. They had slowed to the point where their dance was closer to an embrace. He spoke into her ear and her grip tightened around his shoulder. Looking at the way their hands were clasped close to their chests, I decided I would get my information elsewhere.

I looked again for Seb's red hair. The whole purpose of my inviting him all the way to the West Coast was so that I could keep an eye on him—I'd done a botched job of it so far. As I searched, I thought of the letters I'd received from one of his writer friends back in New York. There were concerns about Seb's health. Too much drinking, days spent in isolation, a burgeoning pill habit. I'd written back with the suggestion of bringing him to California in the hope that sunshine and a steady job would do him good.

I finally spotted Seb drinking in the gardens with a few men I recognized as screenwriters on the FWM payroll. Now that most of the men at the party had removed their jackets, his suit no longer stood out in the crowd. I could see that the men were engrossed in some story or another that Seb was telling. My brother wasn't a tall man, but when he got into the thick of a retelling, he could become the largest presence in a room. He looked as happy as I'd seen him since his arrival, so I left him to it.

These parties usually involved someone jumping into the pool before the end of the night. This time it was Margy skipping down the steps of the veranda and tossing her drink over her shoulder—the glass shattered across the outdoor tiling. She gave one dangerous look to the crowd behind her and then, with a loud hoot, jumped into the water fully clothed. Her dress billowed out in the water, creating an emerald ring around her. She pulled a pin out of her hair and dipped her head back.

A member of the staff scrambled to clear away the broken glass before the rest of party went jumping in after her.

Charles was sitting at an empty table. He seemed unaware that it was odd for him to be alone, just sat back in his chair and gazed out at the party as he smoked. He looked healthier than I'd ever seen him—sobriety suited him; his tan skin glowed and his dark hair shone, though that could also easily be attributed to someone from the studio having polished him up for the party—but there was something exhausted in his overall demeanor. A slight hunch in his shoulders, his face downcast.

I caught his eye and he waved me over.

"No swimming?" I asked him.

He flicked ashes into his champagne glass and laughed softly. "You can tell Poppy St. John that I'm being very respectable."

Poppy's readers had been avidly following Charles's love life for the last year or so, during which time he'd grown used to me pestering him. Poppy didn't care to interact with him directly. She never liked any of the Hollywood rogues—too much drinking and fighting for her taste. I, on the other hand, found them all terribly amusing.

I sat next to him and pulled a hand-rolled cigarette from my clutch. I'd learned which actors and actresses had a taste for reefer and presumed Charles was still one of them.

A genuine smile spread across his face when I handed it him. He dropped his own cigarette into the glass and lit the new one. He arched his neck back as he exhaled smoke.

"How're you enjoying your new engagement?" I asked.

He leaned in, resting his elbows against the table, and lowered his voice. "You know, as a boy growing up in Louisiana," he drawled, "I always dreamed that someday I would be contractually obligated to date one of the most beautiful women in Hollywood."

"We should all be so fortunate," I said with a laugh.

He handed the cigarette back to me. "Any big plans before your early retirement?"

I exhaled as I spoke. "I might give the acting thing another shot." My attempts at a straight face were feeble; I could feel my cheeks rounding. "Maybe I'll try out a Western. What do you think, cowboy?"

He smiled and shook his head. I pressed on. "How's about it, you, me—hell, we could get Margy and Hal, the whole gang."

I looked down the stairs at the pool, where Margy was calling out for more people to get in the water.

At the mention of Margy and Hal, Charles sighed and loosened his bow tie.

"I know what you're doing," he said flatly.

I was shameless. "I would've thought Hal would be here. Weren't you the best man at their wedding?"

There were stories floating around about the shoot for Charles's last picture, *Afterglow*, because the three costars—Charles, Hal, and Margy—got on uncommonly well. Usually when the studio ships off two cowboys to location, they end up at each other's throats, measuring who's got the bigger role.

Instead, they all got on so well that Hal and Margy made that nice big show of eloping before they got back to California.

I paid a cameraman to tell me what had happened in Wyoming and I got nothing. He told me the three of them boozed up plenty, but there didn't seem to be any fighting or flirting. One foot on the ground, Code-proper the whole time!

Script supervisor: same story.

So I was suspicious; sue me.

Charles appeared unfazed by my bringing up the wedding. In his drinking days, it would've been easy for me. One time, I got him to go on a twenty-minute tirade about the casting for *Gone with the Wind*—all I had to do was mention the fact that Vivien Leigh was British. Poppy loved that story.

"If I remember correctly, you were in an accident shortly after the wedding," I mused, blowing smoke.

"Good Lord, Edie," he said. He was still smiling, but I could feel his patience waning.

I smiled and lightly tapped the glass table with my nails. "It's just an observation! Augustan said you crashed your car. That's too bad."

Charles sat back in his chair and crossed his arms. The sleepy look he usually wore was gone; he narrowed his eyes and set his jaw. I'd only ever seen him look like that on camera, usually before he shot an officer of the law.

"We all get loose sometimes."

"Loose enough to never drink again?" I asked with a nod toward his glass of champagne, now so full with discarded cigarette butts that it nearly overflowed.

Charles stared at me and I knew I'd lost him. He took one of the half-empty glasses of champagne sitting on the table and swallowed its contents in one gulp.

Hear me out: No man who spent a portion of his early career doing stunts is likely to crash his car into a tree in the middle of the day, I don't care how drunk or doped up he might've been. There was something he wasn't telling me.

I took my drink and wandered to the top of the steps, where I could see the party below.

Nell was lying on a chaise lounge and Augustan sat by her feet. This languid Nell was new to me—she usually kept herself alert. I'd seen actresses fall apart before and it wasn't like that with Nell. When she spoke, her words weren't slurred. Her makeup remained fresh on her face. She seemed like one of those dolls whose eyes open and close when you lay her down.

Margy was swimming laps in her slip—her gown had been discarded and draped on one of the lounge chairs. She was like that, on-screen and off. It was always *a hoot* when Margy was around. She was joined in the pool by a few others but mostly kept to herself. No funny business, as far I could tell.

Charles was still sitting at his table, now talking to Rolf, the director originally responsible for Charles's current position in Hollywood. Rolf had directed Charles multiple times by then, including *The Sure Shot* and *Afterglow*. He had a reputation for being one of Hollywood's rougher directors. His abuses were regularly overlooked by the studio because his lush Westerns never failed to bring in audiences and gross profits. Rolf had no tolerance for weak ladies or men who couldn't conceivably beat him in a fist-fight. Charles already had an athletic build, which had endured years of being hit by things when he was a stunt double, and he didn't seem shaken by being yelled at. For better or for worse, Charles was Rolf's current pick among the leading men of FWM.

Thomas Brodbeck was talking with one of his lesser Augustans on the veranda. He had a whole troop of them, all young and well-dressed men with honeyed voices and wide smiles. The lowest of them spent their time scouting train depots for pretty faces and pert chests. A subsection of them was dedicated to inventing sanitized backstories for the pretty faces and pert chests: "Veronica grew up on a farm outside Topeka, Kansas, where she had a pet chicken named Billy." And then the real Augustan had the task of making sure America never forgot that Veronica was a sweet girl from Topeka, Kansas, when she got caught sitting too cozily with her married film director.

I went down to the pool to join the riffraff.

I removed my shoes and gathered the hem of my dress to sit by the pool.

"I don't think the boys in costuming will be very happy to hear about how you've treated their gown," Augustan said from behind me.

He sat next to me and carefully set his glass down at the edge of the pool. He smiled grimly and I understood that he wanted to rile me up—every other woman at that party was likely wearing a dress hand-tailored to her form. My tulle gown looked completely out of season next to the sleek designs worn by women like Margy.

"Costuming loves me," I said with a pointed stare. "I don't think *anyone* at FWM will miss me more than George." George Wynette was the head designer for FWM and one of my favorite peers to gossip with.

"I'm sure he'll be inconsolable," Augustan said flatly. "We've got three months and four days to find out, don't we?"

Of course Augustan knew the exact day my contract was up. I put my feet in the pool and kicked water at him. He was unmoved by my provocations.

"Enough about your ruined film career," he continued with a swat of his hand. "You won't believe who I saw inside."

I told him I had already seen and spoken to Freddy Clarke, no surprises there. He shook his head. "Old news; Freddy's gone and put himself to bed somewhere upstairs. I'm talking about the *Marquess.*"

The Marquess was Ines Marquis, the twenty-three-year-old surprise inheritor of FWM's primary stockholdings. Her uncle, Nico Marquis, was the original *M* of FWM Studios: Feldman, Westing, and Marquis. Back in the early twenties, Saul Feldman had the investment money, J. D. Westing had the film cameras, and Nico Marquis had the theaters.

Ines had been whisked away from Paris earlier that summer, after Nico suffered a heart attack and died on a studio lot. With no children or family to speak of, Nico left roughly ten million dollars in stockholdings to his niece, a French stenographer who barely spoke English.

Ines refused to attend board meetings and was rarely seen at parties or film openings. My understanding was that she spent most of her time in the family mansion, depleting the wine reserves and reading obscure foreign poetry in her bathtub.

"Our Marquess was sitting in the kitchen eating pastries and talking to some nobody in a secondhand suit."

As soon as Augustan had said the word *Marquess,* three different conversations stopped around us. In her short time in Hollywood, Ines Marquis had become something of a myth around the FWM Studios lots.

For my part, I was more concerned with the nobody in the

cheap suit. Seb wouldn't have a clue who Ines was, and I had a feeling she wasn't likely to tell him.

Within moments, Margy swam over to our end of the pool and insisted that Ines was a foreign spy. Another woman said she was a Communist. I continued to splash the water with my feet as Augustan formulated diplomatic responses.

At some point, Charles came down to the pool and was toasted as the "man of the hour." He held his hands up and explained that he was only there to attend to his fiancée, who was currently drifting in and out of sleep on a chaise. He gave everyone a parting salute before lifting Nell in his arms.

Margy let out a provocative whoop as he left with her. She rested her elbows against the side of the pool and I watched her track Charles's movements all the way back up to the house.

We all knew that Charles would carry Nell upstairs to one of the empty bedrooms. He'd sit with her while she fell asleep, if need be. After that, he'd probably go find a different bedroom to sleep in. I knew a number of people who were experts at tracking which guests shuffled between bedrooms at parties like these—not once had anyone seen Charles and Nell wake up together.

While I'll admit their on-screen romances were impressive, Charles and Nell did very little to be convincing when they had to put on the act after hours.

It was after midnight when Sophie Melrose appeared in the gardens. At first, I didn't even see her emerge from the darkness. There was an odd quiet as everyone around the pool began listening to the sound of footsteps in the garden and the shape of Sophie came into focus.

With her head down, Sophie trod carefully through the bushes to get to the pool, though there was a path a few feet away from her. As she walked, her gown caught on some branches. She stumbled and continued until the branches broke behind her, small bits dangling from the fabric. The hem of her dress and her bare feet were covered with freshly cut grass. Her dress was wrinkled, the silk fabric puckered along the lines of the bias cut, and one of her sleeves was slipping from her shoulder.

A few people called out her name; she made no response.

She climbed up onto the diving board and for a moment looked poised to do a swan dive. Her makeup was smudged and her hair had once again become unpinned, so a few loose blond curls fell over her shoulders. She stood in front of us, her back straight and her chin held high, as though she were looking at an audience in the far distance. Instead of diving off the board, she sat on the edge of it. The ends of her dress trailed in the water and her feet were submerged, clumps of grass floating around them.

Glances were exchanged among all of us around the pool before Margy took up the call and swam over to the board.

Margy rested her arms against the tip of the board and talked to Sophie in hushed tones. Sophie looked even more like a child in front of Margy, whose elegant angles were on full display as she swam around.

"She just took a walk," Margy announced to everyone.

Sophie remained in her place, even as Margy beckoned her into the pool, told her she'd have a swell time in the water. The look on Sophie's face was blank—not sad, just somewhere else.

Sophie continued to sit on the board in silence. We all tried to carry on with the party and talk around her, but there was no doubt that something had shifted. Finally, a woman I recognized from the FWM payroll announced that she would be driving home and pointedly offered a ride to anyone who might need it. Without saying anything further, she walked over to the diving board and gently took Sophie's arm. She exchanged a few words with Margy and then left with Sophie.

Shortly afterward, someone came by the pool to report that Grant Hastings was singing inside, should anyone like to join. Various rooms in Brodbeck's mansion were lit up, including the parlor, where a small group could be seen crowding a piano.

There were only six or seven of us left around the pool, and Margy seemed to be getting tired of swimming laps.

I gave Augustan a look and nodded. It was time to leave the party, let the guests drink and sing far away from our scrutiny.

I've always enjoyed watching people show themselves home from a party in the late hours of the night—everyone remembers that they have beds of their own that they ought to be sleeping in, and that those beds are often occupied by husbands or wives who might be wondering what's kept them all night.

I asked Augustan to help me find Ines, who I assumed was somewhere in the house with my brother. Everyone was leaving the pool, pulling plush robes and towels from the pool house nearby, wrapping up before going back inside.

Augustan led me toward the kitchen, where he'd last seen Ines. He was accountable for making sure that she got home safely; one time he'd let her out of his sight at a party downtown and she'd sneaked away to a seedy jazz club down the street. (Poppy wasted no time writing that the Marquess was a wild French bohemian intent on corrupting American values—mostly because I told her that the Marquess was a wild French bohemian intent on corrupting American values.)

Staff members were going along the halls, attempting to clear away the party. Augustan waved them off each time they tried to ask us if we needed anything.

In the midst of people darting in and out of the kitchen, I saw Sebastian and Ines. They were talking loudly as they ate the remaining desserts from a nearby platter and took turns drinking from a bottle of champagne. Seb's hands flew about when he talked, as they always did when he was excited about something. Neither of them took any note of the uniformed man trying to take the tray away from them to clean it.

Ines Marquis was the best-dressed woman at a party where no one even saw her. She sat on a kitchen counter in a periwinkle gown of close-fitted silk. She was beautiful in the way the French are—high cheekbones and thick dark hair.

"*Bonjour,* mademoiselle," Augustan called out loudly in over-enunciated French.

Ines straightened and smiled, beckoning us over. There was something sardonic in her smile, as though she were in on a private joke with herself.

She mimed looking at a watch on her wrist, which was adorned only with diamonds. "Did I miss the party?" she asked.

Augustan offered his arm and helped Ines down from the counter. "Of course not; the party missed you, *cherie.*"

When I walked up to Seb, he leaned toward me.

"She's read my book," he whispered. The bafflement in his voice was barely concealed.

It turned out my scheme to introduce Seb to Augustan was entirely unnecessary; thanks to Ines, he would be hired at FWM Studios the next day.

After explaining who Ines was, I spent the car ride home talking Sebastian down from any fantasies he might have about running away to France with a multimillionaire. The entire drive, he couldn't sit still as he asked me a hundred questions about Ines and the Marquis family.

"She's here for life unless she sells her stocks," I explained. "And there's an army of studio lawyers hired to make certain she can't do that, barring some form of global catastrophe."

The sun was nearly up by the time we got back to my house. Sebastian stumbled to the cramped guest room and collapsed fully clothed onto the bed.

I left a full glass of water on Seb's nightstand and shut his door before I went back down to the living room. I had to make a phone call to Poppy St. John.

"Please tell me everyone misbehaved," she said. Her voice was perfectly alert—she regularly woke at an ungodly hour to read the morning papers.

I explained to her about Freddy sneaking into the party, but she was disappointed to hear that he hadn't caused any sort of commotion. When I brought up Margy's absent husband, Poppy cut me off.

"No one cares about Hal Bingham," she said.

Then I offered up the intoxicated young actress I'd seen in the bathroom. Poppy liked that well enough.

In her next column, Poppy wrote, "We were all very jealous of FWM newcomer Sophie Melrose's pale blue Dior gown—though perhaps she needn't have spilled her drink on it so many times! Good thing she was able to clean herself off in the powder room. We're glad the gal had a *good time*."

How were any of us supposed to know her words would later be used in a court of law?

TWO

In 1931, I wrote in to a contest. It was sponsored by Miss Appleton's Hair and Beauty Care. "Live Like a Hollywood Star for a Week!" I was nineteen.

Applicants had to write an essay about what a week in Hollywood would mean to them. Naturally, I made the entire thing up. My family was poor, but not the kind of poor that the good people of Miss Appleton's Hair and Beauty Care wanted to deal with, so in my letter I gave my parents a raise and nixed two of my five siblings. My father became a manager at a soap factory and my mother stayed home to care for her children. I borrowed some old issues of *Photoplay* and *Screenland* from one of our neighbors, who was an avid collector. I searched for every advertisement for Miss Appleton's and wrote down the names of the actresses featured in them so I could cite them as my favorite actresses in Hollywood. Finally, I sold a pair of my old shoes, which were supposed to go to my younger sister, to pay for a headshot. The picture would run with an article announcing the winner of the contest.

At every train station during the three-day trip out to Los Angeles, I saw my smiling face in the newspapers: "Miss Edith O'Shaughnessy of Boston, Massachusetts, wins the trip of a lifetime!" Alongside an ad for Appleton's was the picture of me, grainy from being reprinted in the paper—it wasn't even clear how much care I'd taken to arrange my hair just right. The brief accompanying ad copy included all the lies I told about myself.

My week spent living like a Hollywood star involved trolley

tours around Paramount and MGM Studios. I was permitted to
be a hundred feet away from Norma Shearer while she filmed a
scene on a closed lot. That was fine; what was even better was Miss
Appleton's put me up in a decent hotel and let me order food to
be sent to my room. It was the only time in my life I'd ever ordered
one of everything. I still remember the taste of the ice-cream sun-
dae I ate while sprawled on my bed in a hotel robe and slippers.
On my last day, I went to FWM Studios and had my face made up
by the same woman who regularly worked on Nell Parker and Jeanette Manning. She trained my curls into a neat wave and pinned
them for me. I was loaned a few dresses from the costume department and then sent over to a studio where I'd get to have my picture taken.

Everyone was perfectly respectful. The man behind the camera
coached me on how to tilt my head and angle my shoulders. They
let me try three different dresses and a nice woman told me which
jewelry looked best with each one. The dresses weren't even particularly nice, but I'll never forget how I felt when I put them on.
Growing up, I had gone straight from wearing children's clothes
to housedresses—there had never been a time when I dressed to
feel beautiful. When I saw myself in the mirror with my face and
hair made up, wearing a gown pinned along the back to show-
case my every curve, I didn't feel just beautiful; I felt promising, as
though I was worth so much more than my life had offered those
past nineteen years.

At one point during the photo shoot, I looked over at the Miss
Appleton's representative charged with handling me for the week
and asked her when I'd be signing my contract. I was only joking,
but she looked up from her magazine, gave me the once-over, and
told me my chances would never be better than they were at that
moment.

Part of my contest winnings was a year's supply of Miss Appleton's
Hair and Beauty Care products, which I sold for three months'
rent in a ladies' boardinghouse. I never took my train ride back

to Boston. When I called home to break the news, I couldn't get through to either of my parents, who were perpetually out working. My mother had barely been on speaking terms with me for the past year anyway—not since I helped Seb leave for college. I had to leave a message with my sister Jillian. I lied and said I'd be back in a month or so. I told her to keep an eye on our sisters until I got back.

Every month, I called and I lied. It went on until, eventually, my sisters were given instructions not to accept calls from me anymore.

Over seven years later, I was still in Hollywood and getting my makeup done so I could say a few lines to Nell. A month had passed since she wrapped *The Sure Shot* with Charles, and she was already in the thick of a new shoot—a war drama, *Stars Over Calcutta,* with Freddy. He was playing a British major stationed in India. Nell's character was caught in a love triangle between him and her dull diplomat fiancé.

When I arrived on set, they were filming a scene in which Freddy had to grasp Nell and nearly—but not yet!—kiss her. (Freddy was consistently ranked the Best Kisser in Hollywood that year.) They were brightly lit in a city alleyway, Nell pressed against the wall, while Freddy stood with one hand positioned by her head. He had about half a foot on her heightwise; the military uniform only added to his imposing stature. She seemed small, but Nell always had a sturdiness to her. She was a master at clenching her jaw and putting a hand on her hip in a way that said to men, Don't you dare—but I might not mind if you did.

When the scene was called, I caught Nell's eye. She walked over to me, rubbing her neck where Freddy had held it. She struggled to sit down comfortably while wearing a heavy dress with a corset and layers of fabric.

"Remind me, do you fall in love with him before or after he saves the day?" I asked Nell.

"*Before.* I give him the confidence to go save the British forces," she said with a bored wave of her hand.

I looked over at Freddy as he was walking off the set.

"We thank you for your service, Major Clarke!" I called with a salute. He didn't acknowledge me and stalked off toward his dressing room.

"He's been like that the whole goddamn shoot," Nell said in a low voice. "I usually wouldn't mind, but it's becoming unprofessional."

Nell had been in the industry for over a decade by that point; she was a few years into her second seven-year contract. Her mother had been a Ziegfeld girl and her father did stage work in New York. They went to California for themselves. Winnie Parker was a nonstarter, though Jack Parker did get work for a while before dying of a heart attack at forty.

Someone had to make the move to California worthwhile. So Nell started at age ten, doing bit parts—"girl crying in street," "dancing girl," things like that. Her mother went into debt to put Nell in acting classes. She did well, signed a contract at fifteen, and was even briefly sent to England to study with Laurence Olivier.

When she came back, she was supposed to be the next award draw for FWM. They put her in a Joan of Arc drama, but the whole mess lost thousands. She hadn't been cast in a film where she wasn't accompanied by a strong male costar since.

The first time the studio put her opposite Charles, it was for *Billy the Kid.* Augustan told me she nearly threw a fit after she was cast with him, because she knew that he had originally been a stuntman.

It went on to be the fifth-highest-grossing film of that year—no surprise when Nell quickly changed her tune about Charles.

We were called onto the set. I was supposed to be playing someone's wife welcoming Nell's character to Calcutta.

Gideon Wright was waiting for us, shifting his weight from foot to foot as he stood behind the cameras. Gideon primarily directed period films for FWM. I had worked with him a number of times; he was well mannered and patient. He liked my red hair, and my figure was good for carrying the extravagant costuming he favored. That day, I was corseted up in Victorian lace and wheeled around on a rickshaw by two young men wearing dark makeup and turbans.

Of everyone at FWM, Nell was easily one of the best actresses to work with. She had a healthy detachment from her roles. One minute, she could be sitting calmly in her chair, waiting for her cue, and the next she could conjure up tears and screams—she'd snap out of it as soon as the camera stopped rolling. It was unnerving to watch. But it made her, above all things, efficient.

We went through our scene in less than an hour before Freddy was called back. The air immediately changed upon his return. Everyone at FWM knew what Freddy was like on set. He had originally been discovered while touring the boxing circuit as an undergraduate at Michigan and was never formally trained as an actor—certainly not in the way that Nell was. In spite of this, he lacked the humility of a novice. His rise to fame had been so quick that by the time anyone at FWM thought to offer him an acting coach, he was too entrenched in his image as *the* Freddy Clarke to suffer the embarrassment of remedial lessons.

While I was on set with him that day, Freddy responded to Gideon's requests with a childish resentment. When asked to alter how he delivered his lines, he would say them the exact same way and insist that he was changing his tone. I'd seen him do it before—it put directors in the awkward position of finding infinite ways to rephrase their requests or risk telling Freddy that he was wrong. Some of them had no tolerance for it; the director Wesley Vaughn worked with Freddy once and found the experience so infuriating that he spent the next two years exclusively helming

Westerns (over his four decades of film acting, which continued into the 1960s, Freddy Clarke never once played a cowboy).

Nell was right about Freddy's sour mood. Gideon told him he didn't seem connected to Nell ("She's the girl you're not supposed to fall in love with, which is, of course, why you're going to do exactly that!"), but Freddy was lost when it came to the concept of longing. Instead, he roughly grabbed Nell's arm and pulled her to him. Nell let out a yelp of surprise, which she quickly hid with a stilted laugh. Her eyes remained fixed where Freddy held her arm.

"How about that?" he said. "Connected now?"

It was a relief to rid myself of my dress and makeup for the day. I always loved running my hands over my face after removing the layers of blush and concealer, free of concern that I might smudge everything. I hate to think of the number of times I went to scratch an itch on my cheek, only to discover I'd somehow ruined my entire face, much to the chagrin of the makeup artists who were tasked with putting me back together. After washing everything off, I sometimes got lost in the act of stretching and poking at my skin, clearing away every crease that the makeup might have gotten caught in, until I could see my face for what it was.

Augustan once let me see the notes from my initial screen test—I bribed him with a bar of his favorite dark chocolate and a story about an actress falling over at a party. I was originally given a chance at an FWM contract because of my voice and my figure; apparently, the men in the screening room that day thought my voice was "sultry" and my figure was "well defined." My point of comparison was Myrna Loy.

Once under contract, every actor is assigned a type: dramatic actor, comedienne, swashbuckler, that sort of thing. Sometimes it takes a few tries to figure it out. Charles did exactly one contemporary film early on and the powers that be decided they preferred him strictly pre–twentieth century. Some of us had a strong enough presence to transcend type—Nell was always allowed to work across genres and time periods.

I spent my first two years under contract wearing flimsy dresses and making double entendres. I wasn't the primary character, only the person they put in the room to make the primary character look more reasonable. That was about as far as a sultry voice and a well-defined figure could take a girl.

On my way out of the studio, I saw Charles. He was riding a horse around the lots between takes—the popular rumor was that he did it to annoy Freddy, who was supposedly afraid of horses. As he rode, he seemed to be on the lookout for someone. His black hat was pulled low over his eyes, but I could see his head turn as he scanned the crowd.

Charles was playing a reformed outlaw. Outlaws with hearts of gold were his bread and butter. The only thing America liked more than watching Charles Landrieu die on-screen was seeing him atone for past sins.

He gave me a "Howdy" when I caught up to him. He didn't stop the horse, but it wasn't walking all that quickly. My breath caught when I saw a streak of blood going down his cheek, but as I got closer, I realized it was all fake. The area around his left eye had also been painted purple and blue.

I kept pace with him and said, "I'll bet the tour groups love it when you do this." Lo and behold, there was a trolley filled with people waving from down the alleyway.

"I could go get Nell and really give them something to yell about," he said with a smile. He tipped his hat at the trolley and kept riding.

The papers were delighted with Charles and Nell's engagement. The pairing was hailed as an exciting match and their pictures from the party at Brodbeck's were set to appear in all the magazines. According to Augustan, the fan mail for both had tripled in the weeks since the party. Nell was up to ninth on that month's Best Actress list.

"I just saw her," I said. "She's preoccupied with her surly costar."

"One of the doubles over there told me Freddy damn near bayoneted him the other day," Charles said.

In what could have been an awkward situation, Charles managed to stay in the good graces of his former coworkers on set. If anything, the stuntmen were more loyal to him now that he was speaking on camera. Once again, I put forth my case that Charles was one of the sharper men in Hollywood—he was regularly informed about what was happening on any given set, at FWM Studios and beyond.

"I heard the news about Zorro," I said. Charles had been up for a remake of Douglas Fairbanks's Zorro film. The role went to Edward Percival, FWM's most recent acquisition from Broadway.

"It's a shame; I'm already wearing half the costume." He sighed. He had on a faded black jacket, with a bandanna hanging around his neck. All the studio would have to do would be to switch out his chaps and cowboy boots.

"I doubt that *anyone* was worried about the Zorro part—it's Don Diego that might've been a challenge. No one here can imagine you doing the bolero in a bejeweled jacket."

When it came down to it, the studio was more comfortable teaching a fop like Edward how to be tough than teaching someone like Charles how to be foppish.

He began riding back to his lot, where members of the crew were doing lighting tests on a mechanical horse-drawn carriage. A mural of a desert was rigged to move behind it. Charles jumped off the horse and one of the ladies in makeup ushered him away while a studio hand took the horse. In an hour, Charles would climb on top of the carriage as it rocked and he would use a wooden pistol to shoot down whichever man had wronged him this time.

In that same span of time, four lots down, Edward Percival would fracture his ankle while doing a complicated tap dance number. Doctors would declare him unable to do any serious physical activity for the upcoming months, bolero dancing and sword fighting included.

Nell and Freddy would wrap up a scene in which Freddy's character snatched Nell's off her horse. She would hit him with her gloves and he would taunt her until she confessed that she enjoyed it.

Margy was working on a society comedy with her husband, Hal, three lots down. The two would be chasing a Jack Russell terrier around a restaurant. In a bit of calculated choreography, they'd find themselves in each other's arms after the dog slipped past them under a table.

Augustan would be sitting in Brodbeck's office to discuss what to do with replacing Edward in the role of Don Diego Vega. Augustan's choice was Charles, while Brodbeck had an affinity for Victor Perez. They'd cut cards for it; whoever drew the higher card got their man—Augustan would get a queen and Brodbeck a five.

Sophie Melrose would stop me as I went to my car and hand me a letter intended for Poppy St. John. In that letter, Sophie explained that on the night of August 2, 1939, she went to a party at FWM studio chief Thomas Brodbeck's house. That, in the middle of the party, the actor Freddy Clarke persuaded her to go upstairs with him so she could take a nap. He shut her in a room and forced her to perform sexual acts against her will. That her father, Sidney Markham, owner of the national chain Markham Auto Parts, would hire lawyers on her behalf and press charges.

Sophie had recognized me from the party. After she read Poppy's column detailing her bathroom exploits, she pieced together that I was the only person who had seen her in there that night. From there, it wouldn't be difficult to confirm that I was Poppy's source—most everyone at FWM knew it already.

She approached me by saying that she wasn't angry at me for telling Poppy about our encounter. When she spoke, her voice was steady and practiced, as if compensating for how she had sounded when I last saw her. She seemed to be playing a role of herself as she thought she ought to be.

"I was a fool and I know it," she said, holding herself with her back straight and her chin up. "But that doesn't mean what I have to say isn't true."

She made me swear that I would give the letter to Poppy unopened. I watched her leave the lot and made it as far as my driver's seat before breaking my promise.

What I couldn't reconcile was the disparity between the things Sophie described in her letter and the language she used to describe them. The letter was riddled with spelling errors and misplaced punctuation. She used words like *hugged* and *kissed*, I suspect, because she didn't have the vocabulary required for what had really happened to her.

I don't know what Poppy would have done with the letter. Perhaps toss it in the garbage. Freddy was one of the most popular leading men in Hollywood. Based on the price cuts Poppy gave me, a single interview with him was enough to pay a month's mortgage on my two-bedroom bungalow.

Publishing anything remotely critical of Freddy would be a declaration of war against FWM Studios. While FWM didn't have the powerhouse roster of MGM or Paramount at the time, the studio was still a formidable force, which Poppy couldn't afford to alienate herself from. Moral quandaries aside, it would be an economic nightmare for her.

Sophie, new as she was to the industry, had some idea of this, because she offered Poppy five hundred dollars to publish her article. That wasn't anywhere near Poppy's rate for potentially destroying her career—I, however, had no career to destroy. What I had was a dwindling savings account and bills that needed paying. I kept the letter.

. . .

The next day, I stopped by the writers' offices at FWM. I wasn't scheduled for any filming, so I went on the pretense of visiting my brother. After he was hired at FWM, Seb wasted no time getting out of my guest room and finding himself a place in the city—he ended up at the Garden of Allah with the other displaced intellectuals of Hollywood. I only ever saw him between the lots at FWM, where he was quick to dodge me.

To be fair, he was quick to dodge *anyone.* When I asked around among the screenwriters and production assistants, I learned that Seb took very little interest in film. He declined to go on sets unless he had to and preferred to spend his time with his typewriter. According to one screenwriter, Seb had recently spent the larger part of an afternoon debating between the adjectives *winsome* and *alluring* in a script that was already three days late.

Because of my stage name, most of the people at the studio hadn't realized we were family. I figured the red hair would do the trick, but no one took notice. Given my rapidly impending departure from the studio, it seemed clever to have Seb stay tucked away in the writers' office. I found him there that day; he was sitting in the windowless room with a typewriter and a worn-down copy of Theodore Dreiser's *Sister Carrie.*

"Who's the poor soul about to die in destitution?" I asked him.

Seb didn't look up. "A man named Rex Northrop? What difference does it make?"

I told him that Rex was one of FWM's primary dramatic actors—he was everyone's favorite person to imagine finally winning an Academy Award for the studio.

I sat down at a vacated desk next to him. Usually, the writers' office had a few men and exactly one woman, but never the same woman, typing and retyping. It was cleared out for the afternoon. On the desk, there were some scribbled notes and a long-since-watered-down drink. I checked the notes; they proved wholly uninteresting.

"I don't suppose you know where Rooney's gone to?" I asked him. Rooney Calhoun was one of FWM's seasoned scriptwriters. Years ago, they'd poached him from the *Los Angeles Times* because Brodbeck liked a film review he'd written. I wanted to know if he was still in touch with the newsroom there.

Seb shrugged and began flipping through *Sister Carrie*. "I think he had to go on a set. Someone was yelling something about someone's lines being off."

I repeated his words back to him in the hope that he might realize precisely how unhelpful they were.

"It was the loud one from the party," Seb said. "She jumped in the pool."

As I left, I took a good look back at Seb. He was chewing his thumbnail while reading over a page. It was the kind of gesture that made me forget where we were, as if we were back in the Boston apartment of our childhood with four other siblings in the next room.

I used to sit with Seb at the kitchen table each night and we would do everyone's school assignments for them. We were almost Irish twins—I was barely more than a year older than he was—and the oldest of our siblings. We'd divide everything up and work through mathematic equations and grammar exercises until I had to fix dinner. I'm confident we were the only reason any of our sisters made it through grade school. It was a pity none of them went beyond that. But we got out, Seb and I—we got out of that suffocating apartment, the floor space we'd shared with our younger siblings, the pantry that never stayed filled for a day, the constant repurposing of clothing and sheets—it wasn't ours anymore.

On reflex, I turned around and gave Seb's shoulder a squeeze. I had intended it as a gesture of comfort, but I felt the sharp point of his shoulder bone and immediately drew my hand back. I spent the elevator ride down trying to shake the feeling.

. . .

"Calhoun," I called between takes on a busy set. Rooney was rapidly flipping through a packet of typewritten pages. His hand flew between turning the pages and pulling at his graying hair.

"I'm busy," he said when he noticed me approaching. He explained that the woman who usually wrote Margy's lines had quit last week. "None of us can get her right."

I imagined the room of men upstairs, all trying to figure out how Margy would order a drink or answer the phone. Of course they were wrong. I held out my hand and gestured for him to give me the packet.

After reading a few lines, I spoke: "No wonder she sounds off; you're writing her like she's a New York socialite."

"She's playing a New York socialite!"

I shook my head. "It doesn't matter what accent she puts on, Margy Prescott is *always* a pageant queen from Kentucky."

I took the pencil from Rooney's hand and crossed out a few lines on the page. I set the pages down on a nearby card table so I could rewrite them as Margy would say them. Margy wouldn't ask for a drink, she'd demand it, and when she answered the phone, the first thing she'd want to know was why someone was bothering her.

I hung around while Rooney took the corrected pages back to the director. I was wearing plain clothes—a patterned dress with low heels—and no one noticed me. That's how it had been for the last few years: I could wander onto any given set with little to no question.

Across the lot, I saw Margy standing in an evening gown. The dress was her usual cut—silk with long, clean lines to accentuate her willowy figure. When she started at FWM a few years ago, she was always cast as a beauty. It made sense—the idea was that she could mostly be mute and, as long as she was mute, she'd be whatever her male counterparts needed her to be. It didn't work. It turned out that audiences liked the way she sounded and they wrote in, demanding to hear more of her voice. Augustan and Brodbeck started putting her in roles where she wouldn't be standing around at overcrowded parties, waiting for someone to talk to her—she'd be the one starting conversations.

On set that day, she was wandering around a fake patio, toying with the props and talking with the production crew. Her costar was her husband, Hal, who was sitting behind the cameras. While Margy chatted, Hal took no notice of her and appeared to be reading a book. With any other couple, their distance might have struck me as odd, but Hal was known for keeping to himself.

Hal had been put under contract in '32. FWM almost passed on him because he was too tall to be a romantic interest for most of their ladies. He was, without a doubt, a *physical* actor. He could define a scene by filling a doorway or lording it over some poor chump who dared to cross him. He didn't have the spry athleticism of Charles, or the homegrown charm of Freddy. Hal's characters often loomed in dark corners, emerging just in time to catch a lady from losing her footing.

In person, he was soft-spoken—I always suspected that it was an affectation to compensate for his imposing stature. Whenever he did contribute to a conversation, he sounded almost apologetic.

When the director called everyone back, Hal removed his reading glasses and got up from his chair. He joined Margy on the fake patio. She perched her chin on his shoulder as the director walked them through the script changes. They made for a handsome couple. Theirs was the rare marriage in Hollywood in which both spouses appeared genuinely to be friends. They had no need for theatrics or grandiose gestures of affection—they were content simply to be together.

"Since I've been so nice to you," I said when Rooney came back, "perhaps you'll do me a favor?"

Rooney frowned and scratched his stubbled jaw. "What do you want, O'Dare?"

"Do you still have contacts over at the *Times*?" I asked.

"Depends on what you need them for."

I explained that I had a story that wasn't quite Poppy St. John material. He wanted to know if that meant it was too boring or too scandalous, so I told him it was none of his business.

Rooney took a step back and examined me. "You're publishing on your own now? Should Mrs. St. John be worried?"

I assured him it was nothing serious. He then pulled a small notepad from his jacket and wrote down a name and a phone number.

On the drive home, I considered what to tell Sophie. I could say that no one would publish the story, and Sophie would never know better. It might be the kinder thing to do. Going up against a man like Freddy was an impossible task. Even with all the money and support in the world, Sophie hardly stood a chance. She had a right to know that.

I went home and hesitated by my telephone. I had Sophie's letter next to me; her number was just below her signature. I glanced through the letter; it was written in pristine cursive, the kind that schoolgirls take great care in perfecting. Once again, I was caught on Sophie's terms for what had happened to her. She simply didn't have the right words. The least I could do was give her the right words.

When I rang the number, a woman answered.

"Calling for Sophie? What is it now?" the voice yelled into the phone. I quickly learned that I was speaking with Sophie's aunt, who, I imagined, had been appointed as her unofficial personal secretary and was less than enthused about the job.

Sophie apologized when she got on. "We've gotten some odd calls the last few weeks."

I gave her the news up front: Poppy wasn't going to run her story. I was willing to try it at some other outlets if she wanted that.

Sophie's voice sounded different on the phone—she didn't pause or hesitate when she instructed me to go forward with the story.

.   .   .

I'd placed about a hundred anonymous tips before that day. Those were easy: You essentially just pick up the telephone, say something salacious, and hang up. Sophie's story was not the kind of thing that could be handled in a five-minute phone call.

The *Times* editor proved to be no help at all. As soon as I explained that I couldn't give him names up front, he laughed and told me to send it over to the *Inquirer,* a farce of a paper that made most of its money from people who mistook it for the *Examiner.*

I did call the *Inquirer.* I told an editor there that I had a story from a young actress who had been attacked by a top star from one of the major studios. I explained that the actress was going to press charges and, if they ran the interview, they'd have exclusive access to her side of the story. He said they could work with that.

Sophie wanted to meet at a soda shop, and I told her I wouldn't dream of it. The soda shops were usually littered with low-level publicity scouts, crowds of lesser Augustans across studios.

"One of them will recognize you before you could even say 'root beer float,'" I told her, tucking the receiver under my chin. "I've got a better spot."

In the past, I'd used a little tea shop a few blocks from the FWM Studios lots. Their sandwiches were terrible and their coffee was usually burned, which meant that hardly anyone ever went there on purpose.

"Your option isn't great," I said. I emphasized the singular *option*.

Sophie sat across from me. She looked like any high school girl in Hollywood; her hair was tied back with a ribbon and her face wasn't made up.

"But I've got an option?" She briefly caught my eye before looking away. I watched as she became very interested in a loose stitch on her cardigan. She began to pull at the stitch while I explained what the *Inquirer* had told me over the phone. Her story would run as an interview and she'd need to put her name on it. I was planning to use an alias for myself.

She was fine with it. She told me so in the same voice she had used on the phone—steady, unaffected. I told her that she was ending her career, and she said she was fine with that, too.

"Don't you at least want to wait until the film comes out?" I asked her. The premiere of *The Sure Shot* was in November, less than two months away. There was a real chance that audiences would be taken with Sophie. Even as she sat across from me in her plain clothes, she was unmistakably beautiful. I continued: "I know Augustan Charters; he thinks you're a real talent. You'll be offered a contract, I'm sure."

She looked at her glass of water as she spoke: "Why would I want to be under contract at the same studio as him?" She never mentioned Freddy by name. I wasn't sure if it was a matter of discretion or disgust.

She continued: "Before this all happened, Margy told me how everything works under contract. If they want to put me in a film with him, I'd have to be in a film with him. Margy doesn't even get to say who she wants to work with!"

Sophie was right. Seven years and I'd never picked out a role for myself. Not that I'd tried very hard—I didn't mind the succession of roles as someone's provocative best friend or madcap coworker. I was the empty vessel into which leading women could pour their innermost thoughts and feelings. I would tell them to *be careful about that man,* or *you'd be a perfect match!* Sometimes I got to have a husband or fiancé of my own, but mostly I was there to advance someone else's story line.

"If it's what you want," I said with shrug.

I took her letter out of my bag and told her to read it through again. When I held it out to her, she refused to take it from my hand.

"I know what it says," Sophie said, shaking her head. "You do what you want with it."

"So," I began, "you wish for me to publish your story for any-one in the country to read, but you don't want to look it over—that correct?"

When she didn't reply, I softened. I explained that if she wanted to publish, she might have only the one opportunity.

"After this, it's all going to be out of your hands. You understand that?" I asked. Sophie had the advantage of putting out the story first; she could at least control this part. Even if it was only the *Inquirer*, I wasn't willing to put any details in there that Sophie didn't personally consent to.

"It would be a disservice to both of us," I said.

She nodded.

I hadn't planned on opening my house to Sophie, but I couldn't bear the thought of making her recount that night with constant interruptions from a waitress who wanted to know if I'd like another cup of coffee.

When we arrived at my house, Sophie asked if she could sit on the floor. I tossed her a few pillows from the couch and told her to make herself comfortable. The small house was disorderly anyway—there were jackets and scarves flung on the chairs, shoes across the floor—what difference would it make if the already mismatched pillows joined them? With any adult, I would have apologized and felt embarrassed about the state of things, but Sophie didn't seem to notice. Or if she did, she was polite enough not to point it out. I left the letter on the coffee table and went into the kitchen.

"Does your aunt know where you are?" I asked as I brought in a cup of tea for myself and a glass of water for her. I sat down on the couch and removed my shoes so I could put my feet up.

Sophie shook her head. She sat cross-legged on the floor, with a pillow on her lap. The letter remained on the table, untouched.

"She thinks I'm on set," she explained. "She's supposed to go with me, but she was down with a migraine this morning."

"She knows?" I glanced at the letter.

Sophie nodded. She fussed with a tassel on the pillow as she spoke. "She tried to get me on a plane back to Ohio as soon I told her what happened. But I still have a shoot to finish. It's a small role, three scenes, I'm only playing someone's daughter."

She had declined any films after that, citing a need to be with her family for the month of December. Her father had agreed to arrange her legal aid on the condition that she leave Los Angeles as soon as the trial was over.

She shrugged. "I guess I'll go back to school and try to pretend none of this ever happened."

She wouldn't be able to do that. I should have asked if her parents were aware that she was going to the press, or even called them myself. I suspected the five hundred dollars Sophie offered wasn't coming out of her own finances. It wouldn't have been unreasonable for me to ask about it. Instead, I looked at the girl sitting on my floor—she was tracing a pattern on the pillow with her finger and I could almost see her practicing words in her head: "Try to pretend none of this ever happened." She'd spend the rest of her life rehearsing the role of an average girl. I took the letter off the table and put it out of sight, then asked her to tell me what happened.

What Sophie remembered from Brodbeck's party: There was no one in the dining room when she left the bathroom ("I thought maybe I'd been in there hours instead of ten minutes, that the party had ended somehow"). She was looking for somewhere to get a glass of water and ended up in a sitting room, where Freddy found her half asleep on a chaise. Freddy smelled like soap and starch when he carried her upstairs to an empty bedroom. She said she didn't want to take a nap, she wasn't actually sleepy, and he'd laughed at her. His voice was cruel. The door had a lock. He told her what they were doing was fine because he wanted to divorce his wife anyway. She would have kept the dress she was wearing that night, but it belonged to Margy, so she had all the stains removed. "My aunt was *not* happy with the dry-cleaning bill, and that's when I told her."

While she talked, I stayed on the couch. I thought I should have a pen and a notepad, but the gesture seemed callous—taking notes as if it were a school assignment. It didn't matter anyway; I couldn't have forgotten the things Sophie said that day even if I'd tried. When she finished, I offered her a ride home. She said she didn't mind calling for a cab.

"Don't be ridiculous," I said. "We're both about to be unemployed; let me spare you the cab fare."

She was quiet in the car and spent the entire ride staring at her lap.

At one point we were stopped in traffic due to a road blockage up ahead. I sighed and looked over at Sophie to make a comment about driving in Los Angeles, but then I saw that she was gripping the seat and her face was coated in sweat.

"Good Lord," I said.

Sophie remained silent, but I could hear her breathing in and out of her nose. Just as I reached over to her, she opened the car door and ran to the side of the road.

I pulled over, got out, and saw that she was kneeling on a patch of grass. She hugged her sides as she rocked slightly. I crouched beside her but refrained from touching her.

What I wanted to tell her: that she didn't have to do any of this and maybe she should take her family up on the plane ticket home. That she could just go back to the nice house in Ohio with the nice parents who loved her enough to hire lawyers for her. That if she was this overwhelmed talking to one person, a courtroom would only be worse.

But then she took a deep breath and stood up. Aside from some red in her cheeks, she looked fine.

"I apologize; I only needed some air," she said in a practiced tone.

. . .

The next day, I had to go back on set with Nell and Freddy for *Stars Over Calcutta*. A number of Freddy's scenes needed to be reshot because he'd missed his marks. Nell was furious—not that she would ever show it. I could only tell from years of learning her tics, the way she dug her fingers into her palm or bit the inside of her cheek.

It would be the last role I'd ever do for FWM Studios. Not the capstone I would have preferred. When Freddy appeared on set in his full military regalia, my pulse quickened. Nothing about him had changed and yet everything about him had changed. I could barely speak my lines because any air I shared with Freddy felt tainted, gaseous. At one point, it became so bad that crew members were ordered to fan me—they thought I was overheated from my costume.

For the next few days, I'd watch Freddy refuse to take direction, grab Nell without warning "to keep her on her toes," make lewd remarks to the crew. Repeatedly in my scenes with him, I would have to look him in the eye and tell him how happy I was to have him there. I would inform him that everyone owed him a great debt of gratitude for his services. Freddy would save the day, as he always did.

When I took off my costume on the last day, I stared in the dressing room mirror for a long time. The corset had left my skin red and pinched all along my rib cage and back—there was a time when great care went into dressing me to make sure that every garment fit correctly, but lately I'd been left to do it myself, and it was clear I'd done a poor job. There were shifts and petticoats that were meant to go in a specific order; I'd spent enough time with George in costuming to know that. I looked at the heaps of different fabric on the floor. My body had changed in seven years. Bodies change—it wasn't something I was ashamed of—and as far as they go, mine wasn't a bad one. But I didn't think mine could serve me for another seven years of fitting and refitting. I put on my plain clothes and left.

My first top-billed role was with Guy Campion in '34. It was a Maugham adaptation. I played the muse of a great man. Guy was the great man. My character would have affairs with many men and inspire them to make the kind of art that matters. I was twenty-two at the time and the most I'd known of any man was some drunken fumbling in the back parlor of a party or two. I'd had plenty of acting lessons by that point, so I gave it my best attempt.

Had the film been released six months earlier, I might have had a different career. But that summer, the Hays Code went into full effect and it was decreed by the Production Code Administration that half of the film had to be edited so that no American viewer would be morally offended.

I'll never know if I was meant to be a great seductress on-screen, and perhaps that's for the best. The film was released, and it barely made an ounce of sense after the edits. The studio had put money into the production and then more money into fixing the thing. They barely broke even. Everyone upstairs was irate about the whole ordeal.

As these things go, Guy Campion still had a great career, because when the film was recut, his character kept most of his lines. Mine did not. He received glowing reviews; I received none. If I wasn't for men, then, apparently, I was for nobody at all.

THREE

I had a standing lunch appointment with Poppy every other Wednesday. She had her own table in the back at the Formosa, where she'd sit for hours while her sources came and went.

The day the *Inquirer* interview ran, Poppy looked flummoxed. She wore her usual heavy makeup, and her eyebrows were drawn high on her forehead. She sucked on her lower lip as she stared at the table.

"I didn't realize people actually read this nonsense," Poppy said, and I saw that a copy of the *Inquirer* was tucked below her coffee cup.

"Well, sure," I said, taking my seat across from her. "But no one believes it. They buy it *because* it's ridiculous."

"Have you seen Freddy?" she asked.

I told her that Augustan had probably locked Freddy in some hotel room where he couldn't say or do anything the studio would regret.

Poppy didn't ask where Sophie was.

Sophie and I had timed things so that the interview would be printed after Sophie wrapped up her final shoot for FWM. It made the *Inquirer*'s front page and featured a picture of Sophie with the caption "He Attacked Me!" just below her. We selected a school photo, taken just months before she left for California. In the grainy printed photo, Sophie had a soft smile and was wearing a school uniform, complete with a ribbon tie and the school crest embroidered on her sweater. I'd told her to avoid using any of her FWM publicity photos because the studio could contest the rights, and frankly she looked too glamorous in all of them. Her press photos for *The Sure Shot* featured her smiling coyly in a tightly laced dress. That wouldn't do.

I was listed in the byline as Ash Copeland. A mistake on my part—I panicked when the editor asked and I gave the name of the protagonist from Sebastian's novel. His book was the first thing I saw sitting on my coffee table and I couldn't think of anything else.

I hadn't heard from Sophie, though I'd tried to call her a few times after I saw the paper. She hadn't paid me the five hundred dollars she had originally promised to Poppy. I worried that it might have seemed as though I were tracking her down for my money, when what I really wanted to know was whether or not she was okay. All I got was a curt message from her aunt saying that she was down with a cold and not taking any calls.

When I spoke with Poppy that day, she fidgeted with her silver-ware and napkin. She always picked at her food; she had odd hab-its, like consuming salads one leaf at a time. On most people, it would be off-putting, but with Poppy, it made one feel strangely protective of her. I've wondered if that's why so many of us sold secrets to her, some kind of pity.

Poppy explained that she wanted someone to go to the Palo-mar Ballroom and get a read on how the industry was reacting to the news about Freddy. She couldn't go herself; no one would dare speak candidly to her. I, on the other hand—"Well, people just *like* you, don't they?" There was a tone of bitterness to her voice that I hadn't picked up on before. It concerned me for a moment, before I remembered that Poppy was feuding with an actress at MGM who had recently called her a snob. I felt bad for Poppy. She was a lot of things, but rarely a snob.

So I agreed I'd get myself dressed up and sleuth around a nightclub.

· · · ·

I called up an old friend, Baird deWitt, to go with me. Baird had kept steady work as a character actor since the twenties. He usually had a neat little mustache that lent itself to twirling.

Baird was conveniently well liked in the industry and amenable to my borrowing him for a night here and there. He was one of my earliest allies in Hollywood. We'd played conniving best friends to Jeanette Manning in a comedy years ago when he was on loan from MGM. We spent most of the shoot off set, sharing a flask of whiskey and sneaking away to dark corners.

"Do I have to do any dancing?" was his first question. He had a rich voice with pseudo-British inflections to it, though I was fairly certain he was born and raised in Indiana.

I assured him that he did not, unless he felt personally compelled to do so.

He told me he'd be around to come get me in an hour.

I made myself a cup of coffee. My phone rang as I was going upstairs to change my clothes.

It was Augustan on the line. "Any chance you're going to the Palomar tonight?"

He never addressed my connection to Poppy; it was another game of ours to act as though he didn't know.

"I *happen* to be stopping by. Want me to keep an eye out?"

He did. After voicing a few choice thoughts about the *Inquirer* and the godforsaken rat who'd conducted that interview ("No one in this town knows an Ash Copeland; it's a made-up name!"), he explained that he wanted a list of which actors and actresses might give him trouble when the Freddy Clarke scandal inevitably began picking up steam.

I was surprised at how easily I handled him on the phone, knowing that I was the godforsaken rat causing him all this trouble. Cheerily, I told him I'd give him a full report.

For the next hour, I sat on the floor of my closet, taking slow sips of coffee while trying to figure out a dress to wear. I still had dresses from when I was put under contract at the age of twenty. For a short period of time—because I was new and exciting—designers would give me gowns to wear to premieres. I sometimes anonymously called the ateliers to ask for the prices and calculated how many steak dinners I could buy for a single garment from Lucien Lelong. Seven years later, the dresses didn't fit the same way. There were eyelet hooks that could no longer be hooked, and temperamental fabrics that refused to give way over my hips. Even so, I couldn't bear to part with the dresses.

Thankfully, I'd made a point of allying myself with the FWM costume department. George, the head designer, liked my figure, but he liked my propensity for gossip even more. I'd spend hours in the basement with him, trying on his variations of designs from Schiaparelli and Madeleine Vionnet while trading stories.

I found a dress designed by George for one of Nell's premieres— she didn't like the high cut of the neckline, but it suited me just fine. All George had to do was take out the hem for the four inches I had on Nell. He let me keep it in exchange for a dramatic retelling of one of FWM's actresses having a meltdown on set.

I always hated getting ready for parties in Hollywood. I could never pin my hair correctly, or I would select a lipstick a shade too dark for my pale skin. Clothing was something I could get right, though, when I had the resources to do so. I always mocked George for his insistence that he was the only person in the industry who *truly* understood how to tell a story—according to him, actors were phonies, directors were pigs, and screenwriters were drunken hacks. It was his belief that he could convey more about a character's inner life through a fabric choice and tailoring than any of the stars could hope to do with their diction or facial expressions.

George wasn't wrong: As I slipped on his dress, the rich silk fabric clinging in all the correct places, I felt like the sort of woman who could walk into a nightclub and talk to anyone.

Baird pulled up in a flashy yellow Packard. He greeted me with a kiss on the cheek after dashing around the car to open the door for me. I was grateful to have thoroughly pinned my hair, because the car didn't have a roof.

On our way, I asked him about his current role—a capricious European count who conspires to steal away a wholesome American girl from her entrepreneur fiancé. Against all odds, American ingenuity prevails.

"You ought to see the getups they have me in, all lace and ruffles," he said. "I was permitted to shave off the hideous goatee for a few days, so consider yourself lucky."

Baird had just divorced wife number three, who made a good run of it with three years and one kid. She left him for a baseball player out in St. Louis, so I imagined he was feeling particularly self-conscious about all the lace and ruffles.

I assured him that I'd never seen a costume he couldn't make marvelous. That night, he was looking sleek in a pin-striped suit. His hair had developed a gray streak, which gave him a nice gravitas. The entire look would photograph well for the papers and announce to the world that Baird deWitt wasn't the slightest bit worried about his divorce.

Most of the tables in the Palomar were occupied and the dance floor was crowded. The sound of brass and percussion filled the room; the floor throbbed with it.

I kept an eye out for somewhere to sit—Baird was frequently rented out to other studios, so he could fit in at just about any table. My search was concluded when I heard the loud laugh of Margy Prescott.

"Do you mind mingling with some of the outlaws from FWM?" I asked him.

"Yeehaw," he deadpanned back.

Margy gave me the once-over as I walked up to the table. She was seated with Hal and a few of FWM's other players—Victor Perez, Carla Longworth, and Grace Stafford among them.

Margy had on a cobalt dress that wrapped carefully around her chest, showing her collarbone and shoulders. A fur stole was loosely arranged around her arms.

"Is that gown an Adrian creation?" I asked her.

She crossed her arms, pulling the stole tighter around her, and sat back in her chair. "As a matter of fact, it is."

"Give us a seat, and I'll be happy to tell Poppy how lovely you look in it."

Poppy had still neglected to mention Margy in her column—in spite of Margy's efforts to give Poppy a good story, there was always someone else more exciting. I could see the desperation in her eyes when I mentioned Poppy's name.

She patted an empty chair to her right. There was only one, so Hal pulled over another for Baird.

Margy picked up her drink, a sidecar with sugar disintegrating along the rim, and gestured at me with it. "We had bets going, you know, for how long until Augustan or Poppy would send you over here," she said, her voice treacly. She laughed loudly and a beat too late. She had a habit of throwing her head back when she laughed, so her auburn curls fell away and exposed her neck.

"I'm an impartial observer tonight," I swore, willing my voice to steady.

Margy rolled her eyes. "Bull-*sheet.*"

Hal leaned into the table and gently placed a hand on Margy's arm. He made a noise not unlike the sound you make when trying to calm a horse.

As those at the table settled into their conversation, Hal sat back in his chair, his legs stretched out in front of him, as if the chair simply couldn't contain them. His hands were loosely clasped at his waist and he thumbed at one of the buttons on his dinner jacket. He was disengaged from the chatter; his eyes traveled around the room, looking for someone.

. . .

"No one at this table knew the girl," Victor Perez said to me with a dismissive wave of his hand. Victor mostly did accomplice or rival roles—he was typically an obstacle to be defeated. He was one of few actors who died more frequently than Charles.

"She only did two films," Grace Stafford added with a hint of excitement. Grace, barely older than Sophie, had done *five* films. She was one of Augustan's more recent discoveries. She had played Helena in a touring summer production of *A Midsummer Night's Dream,* and Augustan thought her photo in one of the local papers looked nice. After flying out to California at his request, she deferred indefinitely her first-year studies at Vassar. She was offered a seven-year contract with FWM shortly thereafter.

I looked over at Margy, who did know "the girl." Margy was rummaging in her clutch for a lighter, cigarette dangling limply from her lips. She caught my eye while lighting it and quickly looked down at her lap.

Around us, the band was switching over and the couples took a break from dancing, patting their brows with handkerchiefs and fanning themselves. Every moment or so, someone slowed down to inspect our table, looking for Freddy, most likely, and consequently disappointed to see only Hal and Victor.

"Look, we all think Freddy Clarke is a *swell* guy," Margy said, raising her voice above everyone else's. She smiled at me with her mouth clenched. "You can go ahead and print that for Poppy: 'Margy Prescott, looking *stunning* in an Adrian gown, says that Freddy Clarke's just the finest that FWM has to offer.' Isn't that right, everyone?"

The table went quiet, and the sound of a snare drum warming up overtook the room. I could barely hear Hal murmur Margy's name in a low voice. She ignored him. Across the table, Baird gave me a pleading look.

"Shoot," Margy said over a flare of trombones from the stage.

"Why don't we all toast to Freddy god-*damn* Clarke!" She lifted her glass with the same hand that held her cigarette. She set her jaw and gave everyone at the table a menacing look. They reluctantly raised their glasses as well. Next to me, Hal gently nudged my arm with his elbow, and I realized my hands were still tightly clasped in my lap. Everyone was staring at me, waiting for Margy to make her toast. I grabbed the glass closest to me—I wasn't even drinking that night—and held it a few inches above the table.

"To Mr. Clarke," Margy said. "Actor, husband, father, respecter of the female sex, all-around American hero."

Her eyes swept across each person at the table as they clinked glasses. Margy stared at me and it became clear that was the most I was going to get out of her. So I made my good-byes and left them.

After we walked away from the table, Baird laughed. His laugh was loud enough to cover the sound of me letting out the breath I'd been holding.

"Remind me again how much Freddy is worth," he said.

I told him more than that entire table combined.

He stopped mid-step, held up his hands, and looked at me. "I've just realized I'm starving."

We found an empty table up on the mezzanine, where the noise couldn't get to us. Baird ordered a steak for himself and a salad for me. He sat with his elbows on the table, his hands propped under his chin.

"So," he began, "you think Freddy did it?"

I smiled. "You, of all people, should be aware that I don't know, and even if I did, I wouldn't tell," I lied. It was a line I had practiced in my bathroom mirror during the days leading up to the *Inquirer* publication.

I had a rough time concentrating on poor Baird—my eyes kept wandering over the mezzanine, where I had a clear view of the dance floor and tables below us.

"But you were there!" he pleaded, his voice going up.

Downstairs, I could see Hal excuse himself from his table and walk toward the outskirts of the room. Margy kept everyone entertained; every few moments she slapped her hand against the table and laughed.

Baird gave our table a loud tap with his fingers and I told him, yes, I was at Brodbeck's party. "But do you think I was paying any attention to Sophie Melrose?"

"I stopped by the set for *Sure Shot;* she doesn't look sixteen," he mused. He shifted so his cheek rested against his hand and he stared off into the distance. His other hand circled the rim of his scotch glass. "Well developed."

"It's one of Rolf's films; what do you expect?" I retorted.

Rolf liked to direct a very certain type of woman. For years, he had a fixation on the actress Anita Carlyle, who cut a full figure and never minded having a button or two undone on her dresses. Then she made the unfortunate mistake of having a child, ruining that figure Rolf admired so much. For *The Sure Shot,* he was frustrated that he had to cast Nell, who was on the petite side, so the studio's compromise—as I understood it—was letting him put Sophie in whatever costuming he wanted.

Looking over Baird's shoulder, I saw Hal reappear on the mezzanine. He stood only a few yards away from us. He fidgeted with his jacket, smoothing down his lapels and tugging at his cuffs. He seemed fretful, as if waiting for someone. He kept glancing down below and then feigning nonchalance.

"Let's play a game," Baird intoned.

When I looked at him and raised my eyebrows, he held a finger up. "Before you protest—remember you owe me," he said, and then drained his glass of scotch. I held my hands up and let him continue.

"Let's say you wanted to ruin someone in this town. Who could you—*theoretically speaking*—dig up the most dirt on?"

"*You,*" I snapped. I tried to hold a straight face, but he sat back in his chair and laughed at me.

"I really thought we were better friends than that, Edie."

I shrugged and returned to tracking Hal.

"At least tell me who you're watching." Baird sighed. A waiter came by to deliver his steak and my salad.

"What do you know about Hal Bingham?" I asked.

Baird cut a piece of steak. "Hardly anything," he said after a moment. He gesticulated with his fork. There was a piece of meat on the end of it, which dripped onto the tablecloth. "The man's never said an ill word about anyone in this town. Keeps to himself."

"What about Margy?"

Baird chewed thoughtfully and said, "A different story. We all know Margy likes to run her mouth. Some folks said she married Hal because she was—well, *you know.*" As he spoke, he drew a round belly in the air with his fork. "If you ask me, she doesn't look it. I don't know, doesn't Poppy bribe the doctors around here, or is that another thing she's got you doing?"

She did bribe the doctors, but FWM's doctor on call was a man of either great principles or a greater salary.

When I glanced over Baird's shoulder, I could see that Hal was now leaning against the railing of the mezzanine and talking to someone who was facing away from me.

I told Baird I had to use the ladies' room and left my salad untouched.

I slowly walked past Hal and it took me a moment to realize that the man with his back turned was Charles. He was underdressed for the Palomar, which, I assumed, was why he was lurking on the mezzanine—it appeared he had thrown on a dark gray suit jacket over his regular clothing; he wasn't even wearing a tie. When he turned his face toward Hal, I saw that his hair wasn't slicked back; instead, it curled over his forehead, giving him a boyish look. There was something mischievous in the way he smiled at Hal.

Charles looked out into the crowd downstairs and Hal leaned toward him, one elbow resting against the railing, his other hand cradling a drink. Neither appeared especially serious or concerned. Hal laughed, loud and full, as Charles raised one arm and—as far as I could tell—threw a balled-up napkin into the crowd below. Presumably, someone noticed, because Charles ducked below the railing and Hal turned his back to the crowd, shaking his head and smiling. After waiting a moment, he gave Charles a light kick to summon him back onto his feet.

I watched Hal offer Charles a hand and then I darted away before he could notice me observing them.

True to my word, I did go to the ladies' room. I was stopped by a young woman who clutched my arm and wanted me to know that she was getting engaged to Hugo Zane (unlikely, given his marriage to actress Janet Tomlinson). As I was washing my hands, another woman, an actress at MGM, stared at me in the mirror. She asked if I had done her makeup for a film whose title I couldn't make out. When I told her no, she didn't listen, and instead looked at me intently and informed me that I had done a great job.

She looked back at herself in the mirror and said quietly, "It was the best I ever looked."

I nodded and left her with her reflection.

Hal and Charles were still talking while Charles continued to toss napkins at people below him. Someone called out "Zorro!" and Charles turned his head—the news about Edward Percival fracturing his ankle had broken in the midst of the Freddy Clarke debacle. Charles waved and then kept his head down, bashful.

At one table, Gary Teague was ostentatiously courting Olivia Newport—the two had recently signed on for a film with Columbia. Gary kept waving his drink around and commenting on how nice Olivia looked. At one point, he even asked his waiter if he wasn't the luckiest man in the world, to which the waiter politely nodded and said nothing.

And, in the midst of it all, Baird was quietly eating the remains of my salad by himself.

I apologized when I sat back down. It wasn't fair for me to leave him alone like that where people could see.

"No need for apologies," he said. "Just ask Poppy to tell everyone I danced with some young beautiful thing, would you?"

"You've got it," I told him.

"Unless you happen to be interested in becoming the fourth Mrs. deWitt," he said with a quiet laugh and a wink.

I shook my head. "You would *loathe* being married to me."

Baird raised his eyebrows as he thought about it. "What is there to loathe? I bet it'd get you back under contract."

"And what if I don't want to be under contract?"

"I'd say it's about time someone gave Poppy a run for her money," he said with a smile. He offered his arm as we got up from the table.

Downstairs, Hal had rejoined his table and Charles had disappeared.

The band started up with a fast tune. I watched Hal grab Margy's hand and pull her to the dance floor.

Audiences responded well to Hal and Margy. They believed their quick marriage was in response to their falling wildly in love on location. The fact that they had never worked together or crossed paths before *Afterglow* added to the allure. Their presence on-screen was refreshing—Hal was often stoic and Margy was effusive. Sometimes Margy overshadowed her male leads and audiences complained that she seemed brash or pushy. In Hal, the studio found a man Margy couldn't easily push.

It showed when they danced. Hal was surprisingly light on his feet, and when Margy tugged him, he tugged her right back.

. . .

As we were leaving, I looked at Baird.

"You do know I was joking about ruining you, right?"

He laughed and hooked his arm around me. "Oh, Edie, of course. I have so much dirty laundry out there already, you could sew it together and sail a ship with it."

On the drive home, an ambulance passed us in the opposite direction, followed by three police cars. I didn't pay it much mind until two fire trucks wailed in the direction of the Palomar.

"Baird," I said, and let the word hang.

He glanced at me and frowned, his eyebrows furrowed.

"I am not turning around," he said before I could ask.

I twisted in my seat to look at where the trucks were going— I could still see the lights from the Palomar. Another round of police cars flew by us.

"Baird," I said again.

He clenched his hands on the steering wheel and set his jaw. "I am tired, Edith, and I would like very much to go home."

"Baird."

"Whatever it is, it's going to be a mess!"

Behind us, a spotlight illuminated billows of smoke. Baird turned on the radio.

"Baird."

He glanced at me. "I want the top of Poppy's column," he said. "Baird deWitt steps out at the Palomar."

I nodded. "You turn around and you've got it."

Baird kept the car going steadily forward. "I want a good affair. Who's unattached right now?"

"Barbara Whiting just got divorced; how about her?"

Baird frowned and told me she was too old. I reminded him she was thirty-one. I tried again, ten years younger. "Olivia Newport?"

"Didn't we see her with Gary Teague?"

I waved him off. The sounds of the fire trucks were getting farther away by the minute. "Gary Teague's a rat! You're a gentleman!"

Baird shifted his hands on the wheel. "Olivia Newport," he mused. "I'll take it."

He twisted the wheel and the car swerved around, nearly throwing me into the door. Thankfully, no one was coming from the other direction, or there wouldn't have been a Baird deWitt to invent gossip about.

We couldn't get any closer than a block away from the Palomar, which was flanked with fire trucks and police cars. The streets were crowded with men and women in formal wear, the ladies clutching their stoles around their shoulders. They all stared at the building while officers cordoned off the road and demanded that they leave the scene.

I spotted Rooney, leaned out the car window, and whistled loudly to him. A number of FWM's screenwriters were regulars at the Palomar. He saw me and walked over to Baird's car.

"What happened?" I asked him.

He propped himself against the car door. "The place is on fire," he said. "It started in the kitchen and, from what I'm hearing, it's spreading. They took out three line cooks on stretchers."

"Who all is out here?" I asked, trying to get a good look at the individual faces in the crowd.

Rooney shrugged. "Goddamn, it's everybody."

In spite of Baird's protests, I began getting out of the car. I swore I'd only be a minute.

"You're welcome to go home; I'll find my way," I said before opening the door. "Or you could circle the block and find me in ten."

He grimaced as he looked out at the crowd.

"Olivia Newport," I reminded him. He put the car in drive and reaffirmed ten minutes.

· · ·

Rooney had been enjoying a drink with some of the boys when the bandleader abruptly stopped playing. Someone came up on the stage and took the microphone, told the whole place to evacuate. "It was a madhouse after that," he said.

Charles was in the bathroom when someone pushed the door open and screamed that everything was on fire. He confessed to me that fire was one of the only hazards that still got his heart racing. "Drowning, falling, getting shot, knifed, that's all fine. For chrissakes, don't burn me to death." He passed a rolled cigarette back and forth between himself and Hal as he explained.

Hal had been waiting outside for Charles. "Margy always wants to stay out till the sun rises. I'm too old for that," he said, exhaling smoke.

Next to him, Charles scoffed—Hal was just over thirty. He told me he was supposed to be Hal's ride back home.

Hal looked at me, and I noticed his eyes were red and he swayed slightly where he stood. With a wry smile, he spoke in an overly serious voice. "Perhaps you'd like to inform Poppy that Charles Landrieu is dedicated to serving Hollywood's elderly population." The two men exchanged a glance and held it. It was clear they were trying to see who would laugh first—Hal broke and Charles hit him on the arm.

I assumed Margy was aware of her husband's whereabouts until I saw her pushing through the crowd to get to us. She was only calling Hal's name. The surprise registered on her face when she saw Charles. I only saw it for a moment before she realized that I was standing there, at which point she smiled coolly. She was flanked by Victor and Grace.

They were among the last to leave the building. They thought somebody had been shot, assumed it was mob-related ("None of our business"). There weren't any more loud bangs after that first one, and Victor had just gotten a new drink that he didn't want to waste. It wasn't until they saw smoke coming from the back of the room that they started scrambling to find a way out.

"It occurs to me that we didn't pay our tab," Margy said slowly, staring at the smoke trails in the sky. "I suppose it doesn't matter much now, does it?"

Everyone eventually dispersed and went home. If I had been paying attention, I would've noticed that Margy didn't leave with Hal and Charles.

My phone rang as I was getting into bed.

"I'm *fine*," I said before Augustan could even announce himself. "You'll be happy to know that all of your stars are intact."

"Of course they are," he said. "It'll take more than fire to wipe any of them out. But how are they *doing*?"

I sat on the edge of my bed and fidgeted with the phone cord. "You'll want to keep an eye on Margy; she's contagious."

"Good contagion or bad contagion?" Augustan asked.

"For now? Bad," I said. "But I'm sure you'll find a way to turn her around."

Poppy wasn't happy about my deal with Baird and was even less enthused about putting Margy in the column.

"You've made quite the mess for me," she said over the phone.

I had half a mind to tell her to go the clubs herself, and while she was at it, she could also trawl the studio lots and the premieres and the after-parties. By that point, I knew how much Poppy was getting paid and I knew what I was worth. Her readers across the country might not have known it, but most of Hollywood was well aware that there wouldn't be a "Tinseltown Tattler" without Edie O'Dare. Poppy was right about one thing: People liked me. I only needed to find out how much.

Four

The petition was Thomas Brodbeck's idea. He declared it had to be a unified front: "Stars in support of Freddy Clarke." He'd loaned out Freddy a few times, so there were directors, actors, and actresses across the major studios who could all presumably vouch for him.

In the weeks between the *Inquirer* article and the premiere of *The Sure Shot,* the letters poured in, mostly from girls ages fourteen to twenty-five and women ages forty to fifty-five. Augustan let me read through the pile while he sat in his office making phone calls. "Mr. Clarke is a *GOOD MAN* and he would never do anything like that!!!" Some of them called Sophie a whore. They mostly discussed Freddy's heroic roles. "I saw how he saved Tilly Thatcher in *It's Heavenly,* and I know that's a man who cares for women."

Brodbeck might have created the petition, but it was Augustan who had the shrewd plan to make me collect statements across the studio. I was still technically an FWM employee, so he had every right to wring me out for the remainder of my contract. Throughout our history together, I'd always been game to do him favors and pass along information, but it felt different this time. Augustan took to being my supervisor with a little too much enthusiasm for my liking—as though this were something he'd envisioned before. During that final stretch at FWM, I showed up to the lots a few times a week, dressed in whatever I had around in my closet. I still took care in my appearance, made sure my hair was pinned and my stockings were straight, but I looked no different from any mid-level studio employee.

I was sitting in Augustan's office as he planned my going-away party in spite of my protests that a party was unnecessary; I never liked to draw too much attention to my friendship with Augustan. My last day at FWM would coincide with the premiere for *The Sure Shot* at the end of the week. Augustan insisted that we would have a toast in his office before everyone left to prepare for the premiere.

"Unless you'd like to stay, of course," he said, and gestured toward the desks outside his office, where the publicity staff members of FWM were typing press releases and scheduling photo shoots. It was a dull, faceless job, in which everyone operated under Augustan's tight control.

The whole idea had begun in jest, with Augustan making a remark that no one would notice if I began working in the publicity department: "Let's not fool ourselves; half of the studio thinks you work here already."

As my final day approached, I was struck by the urgency in Augustan's requests. His irritability began to show. I found myself bracing for impact every time I talked to him. The mere mention of Freddy could set him off, and he had forbidden anyone from saying Sophie's name. "I swear to God, I'll find whichever cretin thought it would be a good idea to put a millionaire's daughter on one of our sets and I'm going to—" (No one *really* needs to know what Augustan was going to do with that cretin.)

My contact with Sophie had been limited since she sat on my floor and told me everything that happened that night in August. The *Inquirer* interview was reported in every major paper: "16-Year-Old Accuses Clarke of Assault." The articles all ran amid updates on the war in Europe.

Poppy wasted no time setting up an interview with Freddy's wife. Bunny Clarke, just three years older than Sophie, was featured in Poppy's column with pleas that her husband was a good man, a good husband, a good father. He loved his baby and came home every night to tuck her into bed. He even sang her lullabies—"Wouldn't America like to know that Freddy Clarke can carry a tune!"

A date for a preliminary hearing was set for January, which meant that Augustan and Brodbeck had a few months to wrangle public opinion in favor of Freddy Clarke. Based on the letters and press so far, they had a relatively easy task ahead.

FWM director Gideon Wright signed Brodbeck's petition for Freddy with the accompanying statement: "Having worked with him on *Stars Over Calcutta,* I can say with certainty that Freddy Clarke represents the finest America has to offer, not only in film but in life. He has worked hard to build his career, and it is no coincidence that his roles show us courage, valor, and kindness on-screen, because he embodies those values in real life as well. I know that Mr. Clarke has many bright years ahead of him and so many more stories to tell. To tarnish his reputation in this way is an outrage and a disgrace to the entire American film industry."

Within the next few days, the entire roster of stars at FWM joined the petition, with one exception: Charles Landrieu. Filming for *Zorro* had begun, which meant all of Charles's time was packed between costume fittings and dance lessons. He used every opportunity to avoid me.

Augustan asked me to do some investigating. He supposed Charles had a petty grudge held over from when Freddy punched him at a party. "Either that or the man actually thinks he's some kind of vigilante folk hero."

Though Augustan was sitting calmly at his desk that day, there was something alarming in his tone when he asked me to check on Charles. "If he doesn't speak to you, I'll have to intervene."

I wondered what he would say had he known I was the one who helped create this mess for him in the first place. It was one of the stranger situations I'd ever found myself in—I bristled at the ease with which Augustan ordered me around, how openly he wielded his power in front of me during those last days. Even so, I still said I'd do it. I knew the kinds of things Augustan was capable of when someone didn't fall in line: unpaid suspensions, withholding roles, offering sordid anonymous tips to the papers. It mattered very little to me whether Charles signed the petition or not, but he deserved to know what he was dealing with if he refused.

Margy Prescott, who starred opposite Freddy in the films *Bells of Belmont* and *The Guests,* stated, "I've had the pleasure of working with Mr. Clarke on multiple occasions and found him to be nothing short of professional. In fact, he was beyond kind to me. My first role was in *Carnivale*—I had all of two lines and I doubt Mr. Clarke even remembers I was in it, but he took the time to pull me aside after my take. He told me if I really worked for it, I could be great someday. As I kept trying in Hollywood, I thought about that moment all the time. Still do."

I found Charles on set, where he couldn't duck away into another room or hallway. He was dressed as Zorro, wearing all black as he tore down tax ordinances in the town square and carved Zs into any unadorned walls. His eyes were visible through his mask when he glanced menacingly around him. A crowd of men in sombreros applauded him wildly.

When the director called the scene, I beckoned Charles over. He pulled off his hat and the mask covering half his face. His hair was oiled back and black kohl rimmed his eyes. Someone in makeup had darkened his eyebrows, emphasizing the arch in them.

"Augustan send you?" he asked me.

"I don't work for Augustan," I reminded him. He gave me an incredulous look. I had accepted that there would always be speculation about Augustan and me—and that if one of us was going to bear the brunt of that speculation, it would be me.

I continued: "I'd just like to know *your side* of this."

Charles furtively glanced around—everyone on set was pre-occupied with prepping the next scene, moving fake walls and tables. He furrowed his brow.

"My side?" he asked. "Have Augustan look me in the eye and say Freddy only took that girl upstairs so she could take a nap. I'll sign anything he wants."

He was right, though I couldn't say anything to that effect. Everyone at FWM was perfectly aware that Freddy hadn't per-suaded Sophie upstairs to tuck her into bed. At no point dur-ing those months did anyone seriously question whether or not Freddy assaulted Sophie. They only wanted to know when he could get back to work.

Charles shook his head. "I don't see why I'm supposed to go out of my way to pretend like Freddy Clarke is anything but a rat bastard."

The man did have a particular way with words.

Charles's history with Freddy had always been a fraught one. The two men were often pitted against each other for playing a simi-lar type. They overlapped when it came to swashbucklers, but Charles had the monopoly on cowboys and outlaws. Frankly, the real difference was that every one of Freddy's films passed Code without issue, while Charles's were frequently flagged for various indiscretions—a kiss that went on for too long, or a woman who looked at him with "impure thoughts."

"Someone is going to notice if you don't sign."

Charles's eyes went wide and he held his hands up. "Who? Poppy only writes what you tell her to write."

"I think you're overestimating how secure you are in this stu-dio," I finally said.

There were at least five actors in line to become Charles Landrieu and none of them would think twice about signing. They'd probably do it blindfolded.

"Am I? This film's projected for at least a million," Charles said.

If I had been feeling cruel, I would have noted that he was only leading a million-dollar film on a fluke.

"Look, it's not my petition," I reminded him. "If anything, I'm talking to you as a friend right now."

Charles laughed and put his hat back on.

"You have sources and you have enemies, Edie, but we all know you don't have friends," he said before pulling the mask back over his eyes.

He was called on set, where a tall black horse was waiting for him so he could go rob a few corrupt lawmakers at gunpoint.

After talking to Charles, I had planned on going back to Augustan's office; instead, I found myself walking to my car, away from the studio lots. I knew how it all looked from Charles's perspective—at best, I was mindlessly doing Augustan's bidding, and at worst, I was scrambling to stay in his good graces.

If anyone could speak out against Freddy, it was me. My contract was expiring; soon I would have no ties to FWM Studios. If I wanted to douse the place in kerosene and light a match, I could. But as long as I didn't have another job outside the studio waiting for me, there wasn't a way for me to do that without going down in flames myself.

Director Rolf Junger considered himself a close friend of Freddy—the two frequently went on fishing trips together, usually joined by women who weren't their wives—and had this to say about Sophie: "She's a beautiful girl. But we can't excuse this kind of behavior . . . this, this act of putting a man's reputation on the line for some publicity. Next thing, every girl who wants to become a star is going to go around saying '*He attacked me!*' It's a horrible thing."

. . .

My champagne toast was a small ordeal. A few stars from FWM crowded into Augustan's office—Jeanette Manning, Rex Northrop, and Nell among them. Freddy was not there; I assumed this was because he wasn't allowed at social events anymore. His absence was noted, but he was not missed.

Someone had informed the writers, so Sebastian and Rooney traveled up five stories from their windowless room. I found them standing in the corner of the office, eyeing Augustan's collection of high-end liquors.

Rooney raised his glass to me. "A big day for Ash Copeland—sorry, I meant Edie O'Dare."

I told him to shut it, and he and Seb exchanged conspiratorial looks.

Seb crossed his arms and narrowed his eyes. "The least you could've done was come up with an original name. I envisioned a lot of things for Ash, but taking down Freddy Clarke was never one of them."

"Good thing only two people have ever read your book," Rooney mused. I had the embarrassing impulse to insist that plenty of people had read Seb's novel, but before I could say anything, Rooney leaned toward me. He looked at Augustan, who was regaling the small group with the story of my contest entry into Hollywood. "What'll they do if I tell them, anyway?"

"You wouldn't dare," I said before Augustan or anyone else could hear us.

On the other side of the room, Augustan clinked his glass and called out for a toast. "To Edith O'Shaughnessy of Boston, Massachusetts, who won the trip of a lifetime!"

Nell left first; she had an afternoon of hair and makeup before that night's *Sure Shot* premiere. Everyone filtered out shortly thereafter, until it was me and Augustan in his office. I poured myself the last of the open champagne bottle while he took a phone call from the theater for the premiere. I kicked off my shoes and sat down on the couch.

Freddy had—to the best of the studio's power—been forbidden to attend that night. Sophie, on the other hand, they couldn't ban. The idea of telling an actress she wasn't permitted to go to her own premiere left an unsavory taste in everyone's mouths.

"There are already crowds outside the theater," Augustan said after hanging up the phone. "Big ones. I didn't even make this happen. Not that I *want* this to be happening, of course."

"Sure you don't," I mused, and finished my glass.

He joined me at the other end of the couch and I put my feet up so I was facing him. With a glance at the large clock on his wall, he announced that I had one hour and four minutes left as an FWM employee.

"What could possibly be next for Edie O'Dare?" he asked.

"What if I said I was planning to get married and have a houseful of children?" I replied, leaning forward so my elbows rested against my knees.

He shook his head. "I'd tell you that I know *exactly* how mediocre an actress you are and that I don't believe you for a second."

I kicked him with the flat of my stocking foot. I was taken aback when he took my foot and gave it a gentle squeeze—the gesture was intimate, even for someone I'd known intimately. For a moment, I thought he might try to kiss me. Instead, he stood up, brushed himself off, and told me he would be leaving shortly to prepare for the premiere.

"Security will escort you out of the studio if you're not gone within the hour," he said with a smile.

"Very funny," I replied, putting my shoes back on. With a parting kiss on the cheek, I saw myself out.

I had just arrived home when I received a call from Sophie. She wanted to know if I would mind stopping by.

"Your place?" I asked her.

Of course, the girl still wanted to go to her first major film premiere. She wasn't naïve enough to think it would be reasonable for her to appear in the open, where the press could see her. "Only for a bit," she assured me. "Ten minutes! The opening credits. I just want to see my name."

I told her I would give her a lift. "Be ready at six o'clock. I should be able to get you into the theater. You're on your own for a trip back home, though. Understood?"

Sophie dressed up for her debut. As she walked out of her house, she held her arms close, hugging her clutch to her chest. Her aunt was looking on through the doorway, staring daggers at me. Once the door was closed, Sophie eased up, revealing one of the more beautiful garments I'd ever seen.

Under different circumstances, she would've made all the papers: "Sophie Melrose wore a stunning gown from the House of Lanvin; the combination of white silk and elaborate colorful beading suited her beautifully."

Girls across America would have clipped photographs of Sophie in that dress and pasted them to their walls, invented sewing patterns to re-create it. But none of them could have matched the beauty of Sophie as she was wearing it now.

Instead, I was going to sneak Sophie through the back door of the theater, where no one would see her, let alone photograph her.

In the car, Sophie thanked me in a quiet voice. I glanced over and saw that she had carefully pinned her hair. She'd done her own makeup as well. Aside from going a bit heavy on the blush, she hadn't done a bad job.

There was a line of traffic leading up to the theater. I explained that I would drive into the alleyway behind the theater and park my car there. She was to sit in the car until I was sure the crowd inside had cleared away; then I could let her in through the back.

· · ·

It was chaos by the front doors. There were hordes of photographers hoping to snap a photo of Sophie, or find out if Freddy had shown up. Though I'd been going to premieres for years by that point, I was still overwhelmed by the sound of flashing bulbs and voices calling out the names of their favorite stars. I slipped through the crowd to get into the theater. After Sophie's phone call, I had switched my gown to something perfectly unremarkable—a simple navy blue number that could blend in with any crowd.

Inside, there was an eerie quiet. People huddled in small groups, talking in low voices about Freddy and Sophie. Every few moments, they'd all stop their conversations to check around themselves.

I found Charles standing with Nell at the back of the lobby. Per usual, when anyone asked them a question, it was Nell who leaned forward and answered.

As I got closer, I could see that Nell was wearing an off-white Mainbocher. It draped around her shoulders and was embellished along her neck and waist with heavy brass details. She'd paired it with a white fur, which echoed her pale blond hair.

Next to her, Charles was in a black tuxedo. I had it on good authority that all of his tuxes were tailored to make his shoulders broader and hide the fact that he was slightly underweight. He hadn't been permitted to shave his mustache for the Zorro film, so he looked particularly roguish that night.

I worked through a cluster of people and slid into a patch of empty floor next to Charles.

He spoke low enough that no one could eavesdrop. "I'm not changing my mind."

"Have any reporters asked you about it?"

He shook his head. "Not yet."

I tilted my head toward him. "Are you eager for them to?"

Someone from across the room called out his name, and he

smiled widely and waved. He turned toward me and said, "I'm just eager for this to be over so we can all quit talking about Freddy Clarke."

He waved again, this time to someone standing behind me.

I turned and saw the Marquess of FWM Studios, Ines Marquis. She was wearing a close-fitting gold lamé gown that managed to cover her entire body and still leave little to the imagination. Her dark hair was pulled back, showing off her broad cheekbones and square jaw. Her beauty was singular among the crowd of blond women with fine features.

She was accompanied by the actor Griffith Taylor—Augustan's doing, I assumed. Griffith was a popular romantic lead, usually involved in some form of tragedy. He had wide brown eyes and a face that always seemed to be wishing the love of his life farewell as she boarded a train with another man.

It was common knowledge that Griffith was a bachelor in perpetuity. Augustan naturally found a way to use it to the studio's advantage. Whenever the studio had an unattached woman who needed to make the rounds of parties and premieres but couldn't do so alone, there was Griffith, ready to be a charming date. He was good at his job on the clock, and discreet off the clock. As long as he smiled prettily for the cameras with whomever Augustan put on his arm, he was free to live his private life however he pleased.

Ines approached us and Griffith followed.

I grasped Ines's hand for a moment to greet her. She smiled at me, but there was something calculating in the way her pale eyes focused in on me.

"This is your first premiere, no?" I asked her. Augustan had been urging her to partake in public FWM events but had not been particularly successful prior to this one.

Ines nodded and Griffith spoke for her. "She's worried she might not understand the film."

Charles laughed and said something to Ines. I was surprised to hear French come out of his mouth—I'd known he could speak some French, having grown up with French Creole, but had never heard him in person. As he spoke, I only caught the word *idiot*. She smiled and spoke softly back to him, her hand grazing his arm.

"You can sit by me and I'll be *honored* to translate for Miss Marquis," he said. I swore I saw him wink at her as well.

Griffith sailed right over any subtext and thanked Charles profusely.

There was an announcement for everyone to begin taking their seats in the theater. Charles left with Nell clutching tightly to his arm. Ines and Griffith followed.

I waited behind and made myself scarce while I watched everyone file into the theater. The secondary players followed after Charles and Nell, along with a few members of the crew. The director, Rolf, and his wife kept a low profile—the two were probably getting exhausted from answering questions about Germany since war had been declared overseas. It was my understanding that his wife was a Jew. They had fled years ago and were in the process of becoming American citizens.

Augustan lingered at the back of the crowd. He looked worn-down—his hair was askew and his bow tie was coming undone.

"Wait with me for a moment, would you?" he asked after I caught his eye. Considering that I'd left Sophie sitting in the passenger seat of my car outside, I really had no choice.

Augustan motioned for someone to bring him a drink and proceeded to drain a glass of whiskey. He leaned back against the wall outside the doors and allowed his head to roll back so that he was staring up at the ceiling. He exhaled loudly, his eyes shut, before he straightened and looked at me.

"Would you tell anyone if I slept right through this whole thing?" he asked.

I rubbed his shoulder. "Darling, who am I going to tell? As of two hours ago, I'm officially nobody."

. . .

I told Augustan to go ahead without me into the theater and gave him some excuse about needing to use the powder room. I quickly went through the door to the concession stand, back into the small kitchen.

"Apologies," I said to the young man cleaning champagne glasses.

I looked at the door leading into the alleyway. It occurred to me that the thing probably locked automatically. I reached into my clutch and handed the young man some cash with instructions to let me back in when I knocked.

"And perhaps don't mention this to anyone," I added.

Sophie was waiting in my car. Her eyes shifted between looking out the front of the car to checking the side mirrors.

When I opened the door for her, I saw that she was visibly upset. My breath caught as I considered what could have happened to her in the short amount of time she'd been left in the car, but then I realized that the source of her concern was only that she had been sweating. As we walked back over to the door, she kept fanning herself. She touched her face below her eyes and asked if her mascara was running.

"Use a setting powder next time," I said, and immediately regretted my choice of "next time." It wasn't like she would be going to another film premiere.

I escorted her into the theater and made sure that when we went into the lobby I was the one on the outside in case any prying eyes were looking.

Inside the screening room, I took a seat in the very back row, with easy access to the door. I placed Sophie next to me, away from the aisle, where anyone might spot her in the darkness. She grasped my arm when her name appeared on the screen after Nell Parker's and Charles Landrieu's.

There was applause as the screen changed to a Technicolor

desert landscape. Someone let out a loud whistle when Charles's character appeared riding a horse over the horizon, chased by three men on horseback with guns aimed at him.

From there, it went the same way most Westerns go. Outlaw gets locked up; he makes inappropriate remarks to a beautiful young lady, who tells him off while clearly blushing and smiling (Nell's forte those days). Crisis befalls the town that the outlaw happens to be locked up in (Apaches this time). Outlaw lightly flirts with a naïve girl (Sophie was actually very arresting on-screen; she was capable of acting well beyond her years) and cajoles her into letting him out. She does and he runs away, even though he knows the town's in trouble. Beautiful young lady chases after him and begs him to stay (Nell with a very dramatic "We need you—*I* need you!"). He rides back to save the day, and then (in Charles's case) dies valiantly on-screen for three minutes.

I knew how the film ended—true love, destruction, tragedy—and I quietly left my seat, signaling to Sophie that it was time to go. I was sorry for her to miss the final shot, but I'd be more sorry if she were seen by the masses exiting the theater. She followed behind me as I went into the lobby. Under the lobby lights, I could see a smile on Sophie's face. Her makeup was ruined by that point; smudges of black lined her eyes. Not perspiration this time; she had silently cried through the entire film.

I had cried during my first premiere, too. It's already a strange thing to see yourself on a screen: Your voice never sounds right and you see your face from angles you didn't know existed. What I most remember, though, was the feeling of isolation. I'd been assigned a date—Ian Duncan, an early FWM acquisition whose contract had since been bought out by Paramount. He was perfectly nice, but all I could think about was that no one in my family knew I was there. I had no contact with my family in Boston by that point. I eventually told Seb, who was studying at Fordham at the time, and he didn't believe me until I mailed him a dollar to buy tickets at his local theater. I thought about the way Sophie reached for me when her name appeared on the screen. I wished I'd had someone to reach for.

With an arm around Sophie's shoulder, I ushered her to the back door.

"You'll be fine catching a taxi home?" I asked her, propping the door open. I handed her a handkerchief so she could clean up her face.

She blotted her cheeks and nodded. Just as I was about to step back inside, she hugged me. I nearly flinched before returning the embrace.

"Thank you," she said into my hair.

I planned to wait out the end of the film in the lobby. When I went back in, I saw Nell standing by the doors, smoking. Though I tried to act naturally, she raised her eyebrows when she saw me coming in through the concession stand.

"Edie O'Dare," she said, her voice soft, "I'd like to have a word with you later."

I began to protest, but she put up a finger. A moment later, applause broke out in the theater.

The doors swung open—people and voices began to fill the lobby. Nell pointed to me before disappearing into the crowd. Everyone pooled before the exit, waiting for an appearance from Nell and Charles. Glasses of champagne were distributed and then subsequently raised as the group made a space around the two stars. Someone yelled their names, to an eruption of cheers.

"Oh, thank you," Nell called out as loudly as she could. She clasped Charles's shoulder and looked up at him. He put an arm around her waist and swung her into a dramatic kiss, to ensuing clapping.

Before going back to my car, I stood by the theater exit and had a smoke. The crowd from inside filtered past me.

"No surprises coming from Rolf Junger—plenty of loud bangs and breasts."

"Would it be horrible if I said Mr. Landrieu is the prettiest thing in that film?"

"One of his best deaths yet."

"Nell Parker seems bored to me. Does she seem bored to you?"

"After seeing that, I don't think I can blame the man."

"I don't know any sixteen-year-olds who look like *that*."

"She all but hiked up her skirt for him."

We reached the point in the night when everyone would usually go to the Palomar—alas, there was no more Palomar to go to and people hadn't stopped bemoaning it as "the end of an era."

The party instead moved to a nearby nightclub that had been reserved for a select group of attendees from the premiere. Under the dim lights and live music, the crowd from the theater eased up. It helped that the guest list was tightly capped—no press, no extended crew members, no outside hoi polloi. People got a few drinks in them and started talking louder. Small groups formed around the little tables. Men and women coupled off to dance.

I found Nell sitting at a booth with Augustan. They leaned into the table and appeared to be having a heated debate.

"Edie," Augustan began, patting the space next to him in the booth. "Let me ask you this." He leveled his drink at my face. He began to speak, but there was a little whistle through his gap tooth and he paused, slightly embarrassed.

I raised my eyebrows and indicated for him to continue.

"Would you see a film about—what was it again, Nell?—about a lady doctor?"

I pulled a rolled cigarette from my purse and lit it. "I suppose it depends. Who's in it?"

Augustan laughed and waved his drink at Nell. "Apparently, she is!"

"Who else? Where's her ailing but charming patient?" I asked.

Augustan let out a heavy sigh.

"Now, now," I said, and handed him the rolled cigarette, "there's a lot of scandal in a hospital! Did you read *A Farewell to Arms*?"

Augustan set his drink down on the table and looked very seriously at Nell. He blew smoke. "Edie thinks I have time to read *books*."

Nell smiled darkly. "I suppose Edie has plenty of time for reading now, doesn't she?"

Augustan laughed and motioned for me to move so he could leave the table.

Augustan went to the bar, where Rolf and a few men were holding court, smoking cigars, and drinking whiskey older than half the people in the club. Some of the secondary players from *Sure Shot* danced together—the music was slow and nostalgic, with a French horn playing melodies of popular songs. At a table off the dance floor, Charles was sitting with Ines and Griffith, who appeared to be left out of the conversation. When the band switched to a quicker tempo, I watched Charles ask Griffith if he could borrow Ines for a dance. Charles and Ines danced with a respectable amount of space between their bodies, which somehow seemed more suspicious than if he had held her close.

Nell sat with her arms crossed, her elbows resting against the table, and she looked at me. Since arriving at the club, she hadn't bothered to seem interested in her fiancé. In the low light, her face was all soft lines blurring into the curls of her hair. It brought out the stark red of her lips. She could have passed for any age between eighteen and thirty, her skin was smooth and untouched, her hair lush. It was hard not to stare at her.

She asked if I was ready to talk now.

·   ·   ·

"Did you enjoy the film?" she asked me. She pulled a silver cigarette case from her clutch.

I shrugged. "It's a fine film."

She nodded. As she spoke, she lightly tapped the cigarette
case against the table. "They always have those little comment
cards after the premieres: 'What did you like about this film?'"
She laughed as she pulled a cigarette from her case and lit it. "I
always write, 'Nell Parker's immense talents are squandered on
this ridiculous production.'"

"And I'm sure no one suspects it's you writing that."

"One time, I paid Landrieu five dollars to write the same thing.
He wrote it on at least ten different cards. I think he still does it."

She looked over at Charles, who was dancing with Ines. The
song was slower now, the couples fewer as people began to trickle
home or to new venues.

"It's a fine film and he's a fine man. I know I could do much
worse," she said, "but goddamn if I don't know I could do much
better."

She didn't need to tell me she was tired of it. Tired of the studio,
of Augustan, of the endless roles where she needed to be saved.
She didn't want out; she wanted more.

In search of some form of creative fulfillment, she had tried
to do stage acting, but she was promptly told by an FWM lawyer
that any time she took off from film work would be tacked on to
her contract. "We're talking eight or nine years instead of seven,"
she huffed.

"Poppy's never done a thing to help me," she said, practically
spitting out Poppy's name. "And I've *tried*. I always send her flowers on her birthday."

"So does everyone in Hollywood," I said with a wave of my
hand. "Valerie McDonough gave her a diamond-encrusted bracelet for Christmas." That bracelet had earned Valerie four mentions in the column.

The corners of Nell's mouth turned down as she shook her head. "You could do something. On behalf of Hollywood, I'm begging you."

I explained to her that, for the most part, Poppy wrote whatever the studios told her to write. When she deviated, there were repercussions: studios denying her interviews or publicists ignoring her calls. Most of Poppy's authority came from omission, like her silence against Margy.

"So, consider every Margy Prescott that Poppy's ignored over the years," she said. "That's a lot of Margy Prescotts!"

"I'll think on it," I said. "I'd say that I've never written a newspaper column in my life, but—"

"You have," Nell retorted, confirming any suspicions that I was the person who wrote the interview with Sophie. "And I imagine that you'd rather Augustan not find out about that. All I'm asking is that you give it a shot. You could get a column easily. And not the *Inquirer*." Her voice softened as she looked at me. "You deserve better, too."

With a nod, I left her in the booth, smoking alone.

Statement from Nell Parker on Freddy Clarke, taken earlier that day: "Working on set with Mr. Clarke has been a revelation for me. This is an empathetic man who cares for his coworkers and his family. It saddens me to think that others would abuse his gentle nature to claw their way toward fame. Shame on them."

I walked past the bar and got Augustan's attention. It took little more than a nod of my head toward the exit for him to square up his tab and come over to me.

"For old times' sake, what do you say?" I asked him.

With a smile, he held out his hand and asked for my valet ticket. He hadn't driven that night, opting instead for a lift in one of the studio limousines. He went ahead to get my car as a courtesy.

As I was leaving, I saw Ines rounding a corner. She stopped in front of one of the mirrored walls to check her face. A few strands of her dark hair had come unpinned and her lipstick was smudged. She smiled at herself as she tucked her hair back and then carefully reapplied her makeup.

When she turned and saw me, her smile immediately disappeared. She darted away to the table where Griffith had been sitting alone for the last hour.

FIVE

first met Poppy St. John while I was on set for *The Lonely City* in '35. Like everyone in the country, I knew who she was long before that. Poppy's "Tinseltown Tattler" was syndicated by nearly half the major newspapers in the United States.

She had found me waiting on the lot. The stars had dressing rooms; I had a chair outside to sip coffee alone in. Just a few years into my contract and my roles were small—that time I was playing the vapid fiancée whom the film's protagonist would soon be leaving for a more compelling woman. The costume I wore had more character development than I did. I might have only had a handful of lines, but the elaborate fascinator pinned to my head had plenty to say.

Most studios allowed Poppy to wander around the sets, though it was clear she favored having other people do her investigative work for her. She had a handful of lesser actors and actresses across studios who sleuthed around for extra cash.

She stood next to me and told me I had a nice comedic edge. After I thanked her, she said with a small sigh, "But FWM has never done right by their comediennes."

I was well trained enough to neither agree nor disagree, but I listened as she told me about how Jeanette Manning had the potential to be one of the greatest comedic actresses. "If she landed at Columbia instead of FWM, she'd be a Jean Arthur who can sing and dance. Unstoppable."

Poppy had a habit of repeating words three times. That day it was, "Pity, pity, pity." She would sort of sing the words to herself.

She didn't ask me for any information, but the next time she came around the lot, I was happy to tell her about Hamish Daniels, the film's star, and the smell of alcohol on his breath each morning. I was just grateful for someone to talk to.

The morning after the premiere for *The Sure Shot*, I woke up alone. Augustan always made a point of leaving in the early hours to do whatever important work he was meant to be doing at the studio, even on a Saturday.

For the next few days, I kept to my house. I sat at my table and ate what food was left in the kitchen before fretting about the money to buy groceries. I read through all the fan magazines I had lying around and even finished reading whichever books Sebastian was foisting on me from his friends back east. I went days without putting on makeup, a first in over seven years. In the mornings, I threw on a lush costume robe over my dingy night-clothes and then stayed like that the entire day. My hair grew unruly and wild; I laughed at myself each time I passed a mirror.

One morning, after the sheen of unimpeded freedom had worn off, I took out a pad of paper and wrote down some figures: my savings, my last paycheck, my monthly payments on the house. I'd always been overly conscious of my contract money, even more so when it became clear I wouldn't be offered a renewal. Frugal as I was, I could last only so long on savings alone. I suppose I could've moved to an even smaller house or an apartment. Sold the car, or any of the gowns and jewelry.

The *Inquirer* had paid me a small sum for the interview with Sophie and then they had the audacity to tell me that it was their bestselling issue of the year. When they asked me if I'd like to write something else, I hung up the phone. Nell was right about one thing: I did deserve better.

When I finally left the house, I put on a dress with a matching jacket and tamed my hair back into something presentable to the general public. At the downtown library, I asked to look at the past issues of the *Los Angeles Examiner.* I received some odd stares from the plain-suited regular patrons in the reading room as my heels clicked against the tiled floor.

With a stack of papers next to me, I found every "Tinseltown Tattler." I searched for the other missing Margy Prescotts—the Hollywood stars Poppy had intentionally ignored for whatever petty grievances she had against them: Someone forgot to thank her for a mention in the column, she didn't like the way they smiled at her at a party, or they neglected to send her flowers on her birthday.

News of any major film announcements ran on the pages opposite Poppy's columns; it wasn't difficult to spot the discrepancies. I wrote out a list of names: Margy Prescott at FWM, Allegra Hart and Richard Silas at MGM, Lucille Davenport at Columbia, the brothers Quinn and Perry Kelly at Paramount. The list grew as I read through Poppy's columns from the last year and searched for every omission.

Some of them would be easier to access than others. FWM wouldn't be an issue; I could get Sebastian to let me back into the studio anytime. Baird deWitt was at MGM and always game to do me a favor. After ten years in the industry, Nell knew just about everyone in town, even if she didn't care for the majority of them.

I called Nell from a pay phone outside the library. She was at home that day and delighted that I was considering her suggestion to start writing gossip of my own. I could come over anytime that afternoon, she told me.

Nell had a party to attend that night; her hair was neatly pinned in little waves around her head and her face was lightly powdered. She looked spectral in a flowing mauve robe, which she clasped shut when she let me inside.

I had never been in Nell's house before—she lived with her former-vaudevillian mother, whose presence wasn't especially endearing the few times I'd seen her on set or in the commissary. It was well known that Nell continued to take most of her career advice from her mother. Standing in the foyer, I imagined Winnie Parker was hidden away in a backroom somewhere, rehearsing her old lines.

It was actually a nice home; the decorations were sparse but luxurious, much like Nell herself.

Nell led me to a plush velvet couch the same color as her robe and took a seat on a matching love seat across from me. She tucked her feet under her and asked if I'd like anything to drink. A small cup of tea was sitting on a glass table next to her. Before I'd finished saying tea would be nice, a maid with a dainty cup appeared beside me.

"Let's start with FWM," Nell said, her voice sounding breathless, as it always did. Even at home in her robe and slippers, she was poised. The sight of her made me self-conscious—how dowdy I must have looked in my crepe dress from last season, how unkempt I'd allowed myself to become since leaving FWM.

"I've got you and Margy," I said.

Nell bit her lip, considering. "You could get Freddy," she said. "He doesn't like how Poppy talks to his wife. Or, more likely I suppose, that she talks to her at all."

I shook my head. "I don't *want* Freddy." I had hoped to keep my interactions with the man as minimal as possible.

Nell told me to suit myself. "Every paper is going to be reporting on him and Sophie. You don't need me to tell you how much he's worth."

She looked over my list of names and told me she could get me in contact with the actors and actresses at Columbia and Paramount. "There are more than enough people in this town that Poppy has declared expendable at some point. I'll sort something out and give you a call."

Before I left, I thanked Nell for her help. She didn't get up from her place on the love seat.

"It's a role that I'm after," she said. "MGM is in talks about doing a production of *Marie Antoinette*. I want to be loaned out for it."

We both knew the unlikelihood of that happening. FWM was notoriously withholding of their stars. The only person the studio ever loaned out was Freddy, and he usually went for twice his regular salary, plus a cut of the profits.

"It's not something I can promise," I said as I went to the door. "I'll try, though."

I'll always remember the sight of Nell as I left that day: so neatly positioned on her love seat with her matching mauve robe and pillows, as if someone might come in to photograph her at any moment. I wondered if she maintained it all when no one was looking—a part of me wanted to swing the door back open to see if I'd find her sprawled on the couch, slippers strewn across the floor, pins coming out of her hair.

Over the years, Poppy had published less than 10 percent of everything I told her. Knowing that one star or another was having an affair, someone was seen pouring whiskey into their coffee, a young actress was trawling the jazz clubs—the point of it was power. Poppy couldn't afford to lash out at any given actor or actress who had a few vices—firstly because they all did, but more important because the studios wouldn't tolerate it.

Dolores Whitmore had a column two years ago with the *Times*. She had a steady start with a small selection of loyal sources. The studios welcomed her because they were getting exhausted with Poppy. Thomas Brodbeck regularly complained about Poppy's "monopolizing." (A rich sentiment coming from the man who ran a studio that would eventually be disbanded by the Supreme Court for monopolizing.) I remember Augustan off-loading a handful of FWM's stars on Dolores, hoping they'd garner the attention that Poppy had withheld.

Then Dolores made the error of crossing Kent Strauss at MGM. Out of all of Augustan's counterparts across the studios, Kent was a particularly vicious publicity chief. This was the man who helped build the careers of Joan Crawford and Norma Shearer. Dolores wrote that one of his rising actresses looked "matronly" at a party, which everyone took to mean "pregnant"—an issue, given that she was unwed. Kent cut Dolores off from MGM, and soon after all the other studios followed. She lost the column within the month.

No one said a word when Kent's actress went away on a six-month respite for "chronic migraines."

I asked Seb to let me into the FWM Studios lots. When I met him at the studio entrance, he looked out of place in the sun, using his hand to cast a shadow over his pale freckled face. His red hair stuck up at odd angles and his linen suit was wrinkled.

As we walked in, I asked him if he had enjoyed California at any point since he'd arrived months ago.

"The parties are swell," he said, "and I don't mind being close to the ocean."

I went with him to the commissary. While Seb got coffee, I picked out a table on the edge of the room. I was, by and large, unnoticed by the crowds in there—a few people paused to look at me, most likely trying to remember where they knew me from.

Seb took the seat across from me. He handed me a coffee and a letter from our sister Jillian. "The girls say hello," he told me. I knew that to mean the girls had actually said hello to Seb, because none of them had reached out to me in over seven years.

He continued: "They want to know if I've met Clark Gable." He dipped a biscuit into his coffee, and got distracted to the point where the biscuit almost disintegrated. He looked up and asked with genuine concern, "Have I met Clark Gable?"

I informed him that, to the best of my knowledge, he had not. As I spoke, I realized that my Boston accent—the one the studio paid loads of money to make disappear—had begun to creep back in. I was curious if our sisters ever asked about me. It was likely they only wrote to Seb in secrecy, considering our mother swore never to acknowledge either of us again. Throughout our childhood and adolescence, I had always been on thin ice with our mother, but I did us both in the day I told her that Seb had been accepted at Fordham; the idea of Seb leaving Boston for his education was intolerable, even if he was going on a scholarship.

When I asked him about our sisters, Seb told me that he had seen Jillian and Maeve a little over a year ago during a covert visit to Boston.

"They're both working the laundry circuit, picking up and dropping off around the city, but Maeve wants to take typing classes," he said. He continued on: Jillian was engaged to a good Catholic man and hoping to find an apartment nearby the family, but she would probably have to rent a bedroom somewhere. Kate and Em were working with our mother, cleaning houses. Seb had begun setting aside money to send to them—a part of me wanted to tell him to keep it for himself, as it was unlikely anyone from the family would accept our sullied Hollywood money.

As Seb spoke, guilt rose in the pit of my stomach. I remembered there was a reason I didn't often ask him about the girls. It was difficult not to imagine what I would have looked like alongside them, if I had stayed. I suppose I could have also had a job on the laundry circuit, or a man I found tolerable enough to share a bedroom with. Every detail of their lives felt like an indictment, proof that I had abandoned and failed them.

"You miss it all, don't you?" I asked. He quickly shook his head. Seb was a bad liar—we both were; we had the same angular kind of face that becomes easily pinched and betrays whatever we're thinking. The only difference was that I'd been thoroughly coached out of the habit. "Promise me you're not spiting my name every day that you're here."

He wouldn't promise it, but assured me he was happy. "I like and am very well liked in the Garden."

Seb was living in the Garden of Allah hotel, with the other writers and bohemians. The place was overrun with festivities every night, indulging every sort of sin. He never answered the phone when I called for him there—the only way I got him to meet me at the studio was to call the writers' room.

"You know it's where they're hiding Freddy, right?" he asked. "Your pal upstairs got him a villa." I could only imagine the fit Augustan had over trying to keep Freddy quiet and secluded.

When I asked if Freddy was behaving himself, Seb shrugged. "Depends on who you ask. I'll tell you that he won his boxing match last night." I raised my eyebrows.

Seb wanted to know how my unemployment was going. I told him I was exploring a new line of work.

He didn't ask any further questions, just smiled and said, "You know, if you need a job, I know a guy in the writers' room at this studio."

I asked him if he'd seen Margy Prescott anywhere ("The loud one," I reminded him). He shook his head.

"The big fella she's married to is on Lot Three," he said. "It's a Western. They tried to put me on the script, but what the hell do I know about Westerns?" With that, he got onto the elevator to go back to his windowless room and his typewriter.

I slipped onto the lot with no issues. The production crews recognized me enough to know that they'd seen me around FWM before, but not enough to remember that I didn't work there anymore.

The first voice I heard belonged to Rolf, who was directing. He was shouting something in a mixture of German and English. His large hands waved around him while he yelled to an audience that couldn't understand him. A few feet away, the young actress Grace Stafford stood idly on a set of a fake saloon. Hal was nearby, his hands on his hips, surveying the situation.

The issue, as I understood it from the two minutes I witnessed of Rolf's tantrum, was that Grace looked like a child next to Hal. The two stars were in costume: bonnet, petticoat, cowboy hat, chaps, the usual. They had given Grace a pair of risers that peeked out from under her dress, but she was still half a foot shorter than Hal and she had a small build. She looked sixteen, even though FWM had it on the books (they triple-checked) that she was of age.

A harried production assistant was tasked with listening to Rolf. The young man stood with a notebook and nodded dutifully as sweat formed around his hairline. He presumably also had the unfortunate job of telling Augustan or Thomas Brodbeck that Rolf was about to halt production until he got a more suitable female lead.

I stood by the makeup tables and let out a deep breath, catching the attention of one of the women working there.

I smiled at her and we shared a knowing look. "Where's Margy Prescott when you need her, right?"

The woman rolled her eyes. "In goddamn Kentucky," she said. "Studio let her go home, something about a relative getting baptized or christened or whatever it is they do in the South. We'll never hear the last of it."

While Rolf continued to yell, the woman in makeup leaned over to me. "The whole thing has been a mess for everyone here, don't you think? First they took Charles out to location, then they replaced him with Hal, and now everything's off."

I watched as Hal took a seat on one of the set's barstools. He leaned back against the saloon bar with his right foot propped on his left knee. He removed his hat and shook out his hair, which was damp from sweat. He had a sheriff's badge pinned to his shirt—if the role was supposed to be Charles's, it meant he was some sort of outlaw trying to go legitimate. By that time, Charles was far away in New Mexico to film *Zorro*. I could only imagine the mess Augustan sorted through to recast everyone, because I knew Hal had been scheduled for a screwball comedy.

I heard the woman again. "I don't think anyone in costuming has slept for the last three days; I'm worried half of them will go blind from all the stitching. And for what?"

She gestured at Grace, who appeared to be on the verge of tears. Grace paced the set, shuffling her feet on account of the risers.

Rolf got up, ready to leave the set entirely. He yelled at the production assistant: "You think you can give me a man and a *child*? I need a woman, a real one. How can I make a film with that?" He pointed to Grace as he yelled "that." He knocked over his chair and made for the exit. As soon as the door clanged shut, Grace erupted into tears. I watched Hal stand up and lead her away from the main stage to a corner where fewer people could see her. His arm enveloped her shoulders. All I could think was that he looked like he could be her father.

The woman next to me briefly touched my arm and told me that was her cue. She had a handkerchief in her hand as she rushed to Grace.

I called Hal over once he handed Grace off. He was unfazed by the screaming—he'd recently worked with Rolf on *Afterglow*. Hal leaned against one of the makeup mirrors and looked down at me, his arms crossed. His skin was lightly weathered, but the overall effect was becoming on him. He looked like he had spent the last few years riding through the deserts of Arizona or New Mexico; his skin was tan and his hair had tones of blond.

"Where's Margy?" I asked him.

"Nevada," he told me with a wry smile. He lowered his voice. "She was talking about wanting to get a quickie divorce, purchase some illegal substances, maybe see what killing a man or two feels like."

He then broke into laughter and told me she was back home in Kentucky.

"Aren't you funny," I said. "Watch yourself—you say something like that and someone might actually print it."

"Would that be you?" he asked.

I ignored the question. "I was hoping to talk with Margy," I said. "I think we have some mutual interests. I'm happy to talk to you, too."

Hal shook his head. "The last time I was in the papers, it was on a list of Hollywood's long-standing eligible bachelors. My mother saw it and got so worked up that she called me at four in the morning from Vermont. Listed five different girls I grew up with who would like very much to marry me. She was ready to buy any one of them a plane ticket out here."

He let out a deep breath and ran a hand through his hair. "So you can imagine I'd really rather not."

Hal was never on the "Best of" lists and he never seemed to mind. He received good reviews and kept steady work. That was enough for Hal. But I knew good reviews and steady work were not enough for Margy.

I told him to let Margy know I was waiting to talk whenever she returned.

As I was leaving the lot, a young man tapped my shoulder.

"Mr. Charters would like for you to see him in his office," he said.

I asked him if I was receiving a demerit and he laughed with the kind of emptiness that shows someone hasn't really been listening. We went into Augustan's building and took the elevator upstairs in silence.

The man delegated me to the small bench outside Augustan's office. I could hear Brodbeck and Rolf yelling on the other side of the door, so I inched closer on the bench to listen. Brodbeck was insisting that Rolf make Grace work, while Augustan rattled off the names of other available actresses.

I learned that Margy wasn't just in Kentucky—she had requested to stop working with Rolf altogether. The last film she was on with him was *Afterglow,* when she was starring with Charles and Hal. To my surprise, none of the men discussed further why Margy wouldn't go on set with Rolf or suggested persuading her to change her mind.

From what I could hear, they decided to swap Grace with Willa Markley, who was a respectable twenty-one years old and five feet, six inches tall. Grace would be moved over to the screw-ball comedy that Hal had just been pulled from. Willa had never been in a Western before and Grace had never done a comedy. No one seemed especially happy about it, but at least none of their actors would come across looking like predators.

As Brodbeck and Rolf were leaving the office, Brodbeck stopped and looked down at me. There was something suspicious in the look he gave. I gave him a little wave, but he did not appear amused.

Augustan was seated behind his large desk; he took a deep breath and leaned forward until his head was on his desk. I cleared my throat to let him know I was there.

"Edie," he said as he lifted his head. His hair had fallen forward and he slicked it back with his hand. As he recomposed himself, I could see that he was in a mood. When Augustan got cross, he'd put on this school principal act. He sat back in his chair with his hands clasped in his lap and examined me. He asked in a slow and measured tone, "What are you doing here?"

I stood by the doorway and reminded him that he was the one who had summoned me up here. He shook his head.

"I was having lunch with my dear brother," I said simply.

He raised his eyebrows and adjusted his round glasses. "I was unaware that you and your dear brother often have lunch on closed studio lots."

I tried again. "I wanted to catch up with an old friend."

He shook his head, slower this time. "Hal Bingham is not your friend. Hal has exactly two friends in Hollywood and their names are Charles and Margy."

He continued: "I'm well aware of what you're doing. Not that you're being especially subtle about it. Were you planning to walk from lot to lot until you found something to write about?"

"Something like that," I confessed. Given what I'd overheard about Margy refusing to work with Rolf, it wasn't exactly a failed plan, though I'd never say as much to Augustan.

"After giving it some thought," Augustan said, "I'm not opposed to it. Writing gossip, that is. Not trawling around my lots in secret."

"Before we get into this, I'll disclose that Nell is the one putting me up to it. She wants better press."

Augustan folded his hands, his elbows resting against his desk. "Let her have it."

"I mean that she wants better press for better roles," I explained.

"She is welcome to believe that's a possibility."

"I promised her that I would try, and now you're setting me up for failure," I said, leaning forward.

"No, I'm setting you up for a goddamn career," he said.

Augustan stood and poured two glasses of whiskey. After he handed one to me, he sat back in his chair with his legs crossed. He balanced his glass on the arm of his chair, his fingers grazing the edge of it.

"Here's what you're going to do," he began. He explained that the *Times* hadn't had a gossip columnist worth their salt since Dolores Whitmore took her chances at it. He told me I was going to call the *Times* and tell them who I was and what I knew.

"And what do I know?" I asked.

"That FWM actress Esther Brooks has been seen dancing in the clubs until the early hours and she hasn't been showing up for work." Esther had been popular with audiences for her witty retorts and low-cut dresses. The studio had trouble getting her to make those witty retorts and wear those low-cut dresses as long as she refused to show up for work.

Augustan paused and looked at me. "You understand, we've had her under contract for five years and she's got very little to show for it aside from an ongoing bout of public intoxication at Club Bali."

I nodded and sipped my whiskey. "You want me to take out every actor and actress you're tired of dealing with."

"Don't say it like we're *killing* them. All I'm going to do is send her over to the ranch."

The ranch, located in the desert an hour's drive from Los Angeles, was where FWM consistently produced B-list Westerns. They rarely changed the sets or costumes out there, and no one seemed to notice or care. Every film had a cowboy, a villain, and a woman in need of saving. The ranch films were bundled with FWM's top-tier productions and sold to theaters across the country for well over their worth.

Augustan then pulled out a press release from his desk. It listed what every notable star at FWM was working on, what events they would be attending, whom they were supposed to be attending those events with. He warned me that Poppy received the same releases, so I should be strategic about whom I wanted to write up.

"I'll see if the other studios can send you theirs as well," he said, jotting down some notes.

"Don't you think I ought to talk to them myself?" I asked, hoping suspicion wasn't creeping into my voice.

Augustan looked up from his desk and blinked his eyes. "I'm doing you a favor here."

The word *favor* hung heavy in the room. Augustan wasn't the sort of man to lock his office door and make untoward demands, but I could be assured that he wouldn't hesitate to remind me that he'd done me a favor somewhere down the line when he needed a glowing profile of an unlikable actress or a story to distract the public from one scandal or another.

I held out my hand as I stood up. We shook on it and I left Augustan's office.

I walked among the desks of Augustan's publicity team, where the men made calls across studios and the women frantically typed up press releases. They called whomever he told them to call and wrote whatever he told them to write. If Augustan decided one month that FWM's biggest star was going to be the Jack Russell terrier they used for screwball comedies, all those present would commit themselves to scheduling photo shoots for a dog.

As the elevator doors closed, I thought about how seamlessly I could have blended in with them.

Nell wanted to know why I hadn't mentioned that my brother lived in the Garden.

"I didn't think you knew I had a brother," I said over the phone. It turned out Seb was working on her script, and there were only so many redheaded men in Hollywood.

Nell insisted that we go to the Garden. "You want Poppy's expendables, that's where they are."

Poppy had never gone to the Garden of Allah. Poppy abhorred drug usage, gambling, the having of illicit affairs—all of which the residents of the Garden could accomplish before their noontime cocktails.

I agreed to go with Nell that night.

A cab dropped us off in front the hotel's neon sign—the GAR had gone out, so it only read DEN OF ALLAH. I had given Seb a call to let him know I'd be there. He met us at the entrance with a lit cigarette and an open bottle of wine. The irony that my brother had become my entrée to Hollywood's inner circles was not lost on me.

We sat at a poolside table, with the hotel behind us and the row of villas in front. It was one of the stranger groupings I've ever been a part of in Hollywood. I suspected that Nell considered herself dressed down for the occasion, which meant that she was wearing a bias-cut gown adorned with pink ostrich feathers. The staff immediately recognized her, and they swooped in at regular intervals to see that her needs were taken care of. She was given fresh wineglasses, napkins, and a tray of complimentary bonbons.

From the surprised expression on Seb's face, it was clear that the staff had never delivered him bonbons. He seemed unsure on how to conduct himself around Nell, whom he was used to seeing but rarely speaking to on set. He kept fidgeting with his lighter and chain-smoking. Finally, he looked at me, and I immediately recognized the devilish smile on his face as he turned to Nell. It was the same smile he used throughout our childhood, usually preceding some form of humiliating prank.

"Did you know Edie has always been a fan of yours?" he asked before I could intervene.

Nell laughed politely, but Seb kept going. "She made me learn the entire dance routine you did in *Sisters Perry*."

At this, Nell let out a genuine laugh. It was a film she'd made when she was first under contract in the late twenties and featured her tap-dancing with an equally young Carla Longworth.

Seb leaned toward her. "I swear to God, I still know it! Edie forced me to sneak into the local theater and watch that film a dozen times so she could draw out the steps."

I told him to stop, even though everything he was saying was entirely true. I couldn't control the blush rising in my cheeks. Before I knew it, Seb was making a bet with Nell that either he or I would do the dance before the night was over.

Nell eyed the bottle of wine. She turned to Seb and said, "We're going to need something stronger."

Among the things I remember from that night: The whole place smelled of sweat and smoke. An actress from Paramount was parading around the Garden dressed as a man, with trousers, tuxedo jacket, bow tie, but no dress shirt. Freddy, with only weeks until his preliminary court date, had cleared the furniture from his villa and was holding a boxing match, which he won, as he apparently did every night. A group of writers argued with one another about the literary merits of Henry James. A man with dark skin played the trumpet in another villa; the sound was sad and beautiful; I was told by Seb that he had only been invited into that villa and was not permitted to roam the grounds freely—while cocaine, marijuana, and every form of debauchery were widely accepted in the Garden, Negroes were not. Around every turn, it seemed someone was being pulled into a dark corner, to ensuing laughter and moans. At one point, Seb did grab a beautiful young woman and convinced her to dance with him; while I doubt he actually did the same routine from *Sisters Perry,* he danced well enough that they left together shortly thereafter. And I distinctly recall a man riding a horse.

The entire night, Nell stayed at my side. We spoke in low voices to each other and laughed at things only we seemed to understand. She took my arm, and I was close enough to smell her perfume—jasmine and rose. As we walked around, I felt cloaked in the warmth of her stardom. No matter how Nell acted, people treated her with adoration, and so when I was with her, they treated me with adoration. I forgot myself that night; every scrap of what I remember was bathed in the soft glow of Nell's presence.

I slept through the next day and awoke as the sun was setting. I had a full glass of water, aspirin tablets, and assorted handwritten notes on hotel napkins next to my bed. Though it would have been a terrible faux pas to take notes at a party, I'd had no qualms about recording everything the moment I left the Garden. How I had left and gone home was unclear to me. Based on my handwriting, it appeared some of the notes had been written in a cab.

Bleary-eyed and dehydrated, I checked the napkins and pieced together whom I had spoken to the previous night. Allegra Hart called Poppy a hag and told me that she had signed off on a relationship with Don Stroud that afternoon. Richard Silas was feuding with Giles Stanley. Quinn Kelly was vying for a role in an upcoming musical.

At the bottom of one of the napkins, written in a heavy hand and underlined, was this: "Sophie Melrose, SECRET SWEETHEART!! works on set with Rolf???"

Underneath it was an arrow instructing me to find him before somebody else could.

.   .   .

Though it was late into the evening by that point, I sat down at my kitchen table with a cup of coffee, along with a plate of scrambled eggs and toast. I laid out my notes from the Garden, Augustan's press release, and a few recent issues of the *Examiner* with Poppy's column. On a pad of paper, I began writing out the information I had, sorting it by how interested I thought readers might be.

I quickly adopted the first-person plural, which Poppy frequently employed. After a few hours, I became accustomed to the voice. "We were so happy to see Nell Parker looking lavish at the premiere for *Destry Rides Again*"—a premiere that I had not attended but saw on a press release and was confident in assuming that Nell had worn something lavish to. Soon enough, I was on my feet, wandering the house, commenting to myself in a royal we: "We'd love to include something about Margy Prescott, but she hasn't returned our calls!" I saw the sun beginning to rise and informed myself, "We really ought not to indulge in a nocturnal lifestyle!"

Eventually, I went back up to my room and set the alarm to go off in a few hours.

I called the offices at the *LA Times,* using the number Rooney had given me all those weeks ago. Because I wouldn't be using an alias this time, I eagerly dropped Rooney's and Augustan's names in addition to my own. I was put through to the Film and Entertainment desk without issue.

"Edie O'Dare?" a man said into the phone. "You know, I really liked your films."

I was about to find out if he liked them enough to hand me a column.

The editor at the *Times* had listened to some of my notes over the phone and requested that I type everything up and bring it to their offices the next day.

I had a typewriter that I'd borrowed from FWM for some task

or another given to me by Augustan. I felt a pang of nausea when I realized that the typewriter had a tag on it loudly proclaiming PROPERTY OF FWM STUDIOS. Given the conversation I'd had with Augustan earlier that week, it felt a little too prophetic.

The final result was eight pages' worth of material, which the editor told me was enough for three columns when I delivered it to his office. He did not mean it as a compliment. I had come from a world with an abundance of material—multiple takes, scenes to be cut, extra costuming—and it would take me a while to understand that the papers favored the succinct above all else.

He told me they needed to fact-check with the studios. After Dolores Whitmore, they were hesitant to take any chances. If my material cleared, they could publish it under their sporadically running column, "Notes from a Hollywood Insider," which featured guest bylines.

The next week, my name appeared in the paper across from a list of upcoming film premieres. "This week's Insider is Edie O'Dare, who has been featured in the FWM Studios productions *Funny Weather, She's So Lovely,* and the forthcoming film *Stars Over Calcutta.*" They kept my lines about Nell Parker's dresses and Allegra Hart's new relationship. I even included a nice bit about Margy as a gesture of goodwill.

I wondered if Sophie would see it. If she was reading the papers at all. The last time I'd called her, a strange voice answered the phone. I was informed that Miss Melrose had moved and declined to provide a forwarding address or phone number. I hoped that she was somewhere safe. I wanted to believe that she had people who cared for her—her aunt, whoever her "secret sweetheart" might be. I hated to think that she might be alone in all of this.

When I woke up one morning to the sound of my phone ringing, I was surprised to hear Rooney's voice on the other end.

"What kind of person forgets to give their phone number to the *Times*?" he asked, the irritation clear in his voice.

"I did?" I asked, rubbing my eyes.

"They called *me* at six in the morning," he said. "They didn't know to look for you under O'Shaughnessy in the directory. From what I understand, there are about a hundred tips from across studios and the secretary at the paper is getting tired of collecting them for you."

"Oh," I said.

"Oh!" Rooney echoed. "Call them. It would appear that you've got a column to write."

The last time I met with Poppy for our standing appointment, she did not look amused. She sat at her little table, enveloped in the cushioning behind her as she picked the crust off her sandwich.

"I wasn't sure if you'd show up," she said, her voice prickly.

"I'd like to part on good terms," I explained, taking a seat across from her.

"You've got only FWM—"

"So far," I added.

She looked down at her plate, and I watched the creases grow between her brows. She let out a heavy breath. "I would have offered you a job."

"I would have declined it," I said with a smile. I imagined what kind of title she'd have given me—part-time research assistant? Did she think I was going to sit with her in her office and do her copyedits? I might not have finished high school myself, but I'd spent enough years proofreading Seb's school essays to know what I was capable of.

"It's different, you know," she said slowly. She looked down at the table, and I realized she had my column in front of her. "When it's your name on the thing."

"My name's already been on plenty of *things*," I said.

She glanced up at me and let out a strange, awkward laugh. "Not like this, though." Poppy looked at me and said the same three words: "Shame, shame, shame."

∫ıx

Warren Bell was an assistant camera operator who had spent the last year working on films for Rolf. It was his first job out of high school, but he'd been apprenticing with his uncle since he was fourteen. He came to Los Angeles when he was twelve to live with his uncle and aunt—his own mother, back in San Francisco, had fallen ill and the family couldn't support six children. He liked working around cameras and didn't mind knowing the magic behind filmmaking; in fact, he thought that made it more magical. His favorite part of the job was traveling on location with the cast and crew. He'd already left California twice—once for *Afterglow* and then again for *The Sure Shot*. He asked if I knew there were real tumbleweeds in Wyoming.

"It's not something they made up for the pictures!"

He would have kept talking had it not been for Rolf hollering that he was needed back on set.

The kid was under the impression that I was a production assistant. It was his guess, not my lie. I'd returned to Rolf's set to investigate my note about Sophie's secret beau. Of the men working that day, Warren was the only likely candidate: He was young, good-looking, and he liked to chat—I'd gleaned his entire life story within five minutes of meeting him. His eyes were bright and he lacked the self-conscious compulsion to hide his excitement when he cared about something. If I were a sixteen-year-old girl on this set, I would've clung to him, too.

I wanted to leave before anyone else could see me. Rolf was busy coaching Hal and his new costar, Willa Markley, through a scene. Willa was in a tight corset—unlike Grace, there was no doubt that she was a grown woman next to Hal. Consequently, Rolf's yelling had stopped, though he was still curt and abrasive. Hal appeared distracted, and who could blame him? So did everyone else at FWM; the preliminary hearing against Freddy was two days away.

Every paper had its own profile of Freddy Clarke. They wrote about his roles as a hero, his sterling reputation for professionalism on set, and his lovely wife, his newborn baby. As a point of principle, I had ignored him in my column, which was not *my* column, per se. I was still writing under "Notes from a Hollywood Insider," but I'd been given a weekly slot as the "Insider" for the *Times*. The paper assigned a secretary to collect letters and tips for me. The Film and Entertainment editor had implied that if I continued to deliver good gossip, I might earn myself a desk in the *Times* offices.

If I told someone like Warren Bell about my career as an actress—the roles I'd played and the people I'd worked with—he would likely be impressed. I suspected that Warren and I were the same in that way; we liked to be around fame, even if we could only occupy the periphery.

As a regular ritual in those days, I'd attend matinee showings of films in some of the less fashionable theaters. It was easier to watch films properly there, without all the riffraff of premiere showings. I wanted to go to places where I could listen to regular people discuss the actors and actresses whom I personally knew. There was a running commentary in my head when I eavesdropped on these conversations—these people would never know that Baird deWitt hated going dancing, that Griffith Taylor's favorite hobby was chess, or that Jeanette Manning's preferred cigarette brand was Lucky Strike. I liked knowing these sorts of things, though I also feared that I could become someone blindly attached to a more exciting past, recycling the same stories over and over again, with nothing new to offer.

I wanted that desk at the *Times,* which was why I scribbled a note to Warren Bell, instructing him to meet me at one of the bygone bars near the studio. I wrote that I knew about his involvement with Sophie. Before I left, I had one of the actual production assistants tell me which jacket hanging on the wall was his, and I slipped the note in his pocket.

Three hours later, I was nursing a whiskey sour in a dimly lit bar. I had borrowed a dark overcoat from costuming before I left the studio. My demure plaid suit jacket wouldn't do for the night; it made me look like a high-end secretary, and I didn't want to look more conspicuous among the men at the bar.

In a quiet corner of the bar, I smoked a cigarette and tried to sort out what, exactly, my strategy was. I was curious to know about Warren's relationship with Sophie, particularly if he'd had any recent contact with her. A part of me hoped he'd been seeing her; I just wanted to hear someone else say that she was safe. As far as any illicit liaisons went, I had no intention of publishing anything that could harm Sophie—though I was certain my editor would have enjoyed that very much. What I really wanted was leverage. If Warren had been working with Rolf for over a year, it meant he'd been privy to every actor and actress whom Rolf had directed—Margy, Hal, and Charles included. Sophie might have been off-limits for me, but the three of them were not.

"Do you know who I am?" I asked when Warren appeared in front of my table. I didn't mean it as a threat, but the kid's face crumpled on the spot. For all I knew, he might've thought I was Hollywood's only lady detective.

"Edie O'Dare," I clarified, and told him I was a writer.

"Look," he said, his voice low, "I had nothing to do with Sophie."

He was awful at this. Not that there was any reason he should have been particularly good at it. When he was on the set of *The Sure Shot,* he probably thought he was going to have a brief flirtation with an actress and an exciting story to tell his grandkids someday.

I explained the kind of column I wrote; he asked if he could go get a drink. I gestured for him to do so. He nearly ran to the bar. I watched him fumble with his billfold as he ordered, his hands shaking.

He returned with what looked like straight vodka. "Are you going to print this?"

I wouldn't, but he had no reason to know that. "It depends," I said, willing myself to be steely. The only hard-boiled women I'd ever played on camera always ended up being farcical—in the event they ever pulled out a gun, a man would be there to tell them it was fake.

Not eager to be a punch line this time, I anchored my elbows to the table and persisted. "How far did it go?"

He looked up at the ceiling. His neck was exposed; I could see the spots where he had nicked himself shaving. "Hardly anywhere—she's a sweet girl, but she's a kid." His eyes traveled around the room, avoiding contact with me.

"How old are you?" I asked him, raising my voice.

"Just turned nineteen," he told me. "But nothing happened between us that the boys in the Code office wouldn't allow on an American film screen."

Warren's eyes watered as he told me that he thought of Sophie like a dear friend. He was the only person she felt comfortable talking to on set. "She left me notes in my jacket pocket," he said. "I thought that's what yours was. That she'd somehow sneaked back in and written to me again. I haven't heard from her in weeks." I could see the hopefulness in his eyes, his sheer earnestness.

He couldn't stand the idea of Freddy doing what he did to Sophie. He was one of the first people she told about it.

"It broke my goddamn heart," he said. "And I don't have any

illusions about Freddy Clarke. The man's a real bastard and he always has been."

He began to elaborate, but I told him there wasn't any need. After nearly a decade in Hollywood, I was well acquainted with whatever fresh terrors Freddy had wrought on others, from drunken brawls to public arguments.

Warren cracked at only the mildest suggestion that I would be more lenient if he had anything else to offer me.

"Here's the thing," he said eagerly. "I've been working with Rolf for months now. I was on location for *Afterglow*. They had us all sign nondisclosures, but what do I care if I get fined now?"

I had expected that nondisclosures were involved in the *Afterglow* shoot—everyone's stories had been too plain and too similar. By that point, my interest in actually publishing anything Warren might say was secondary to my selfish desire to know what Charles, Margy, and Hal could've done in Wyoming to merit nondisclosures.

Warren was willing to part with his knowledge of everything that had happened on location if I didn't leak his involvement with Sophie before the hearing. He wrote down his phone number on a napkin, with a warning that his aunt might be the one picking up. "Just say you're with the studio."

I told him I'd be in touch. The preliminary hearing against Freddy was only a day away, and I didn't want to talk to him until it was over.

I hadn't known that I was afraid of ladies' handbags until I tried to get into the courthouse for the hearing. As I pushed through the crowd, one bag swung into my gut and another nearly made direct contact with my head.

I began to regret my decision to sit in on the hearing as I elbowed my way to the front of the crowd. Nevertheless, I pushed ahead once the bailiff began allowing people in. I couldn't secure one of the few available seats in the courtroom, but I was standing toward the front of the crowd. A few reporters covering breaking news for the papers were across the room from me. They constituted the small percentage of men in the crowd that day.

Tracking down Sophie had proved impossible. Somebody was getting paid a lot of money to hide her in Los Angeles. And for good reason—the murmurings in the crowd that day were filled with vitriol. The women surrounding me in the courtroom called Sophie a liar, an attention-seeker, and a hussy.

"She ought to be ashamed of herself," a woman to my left said as the others hummed in agreement.

I did my best to blend in with the crowd—not a difficult task. I looked no different from all the women there to support Freddy. Standing among them, though, all I could think of was seeing Sophie on the side of the road the day I drove her home from my house. She should have been allowed to cry, to scream, to thrash against the world that had put her into this situation. But all she did that day was stand up, compose herself, and, of all things, apologize.

Every head and hat turned when Freddy was escorted by two lawyers through an interior door into the courtroom. The lawyers sat to his left and right—both were older men with pale faces and receding hairlines. I recognized one of them as Julian Schiff, who had handled the actor Kurt Dupree's hit-and-run last year, along with countless private settlements.

Freddy looked stiff in a dark blue blazer, complete with glasses that I was confident he didn't actually need. One got used to seeing him in billowing shirts and tight pants—I think half the room was disappointed that he didn't swing in from a rope tied to the ceiling while waving a sword.

The room went quiet after that. Sophie was still absent; I watched as everyone's heads went from looking at one door to the other, anticipating the moment when one of them would open and reveal the young actress. When one did open, a man walked out. He had a round, handsome face and couldn't have been over thirty. I had read that the Markham family hired Mr. Eric Yates, a graduate from Berkeley Law. He had practiced for only a few years but had established a formidable reputation as a representative for wronged women. Most of his cases up to this point had been high-profile divorce settlements: wives who claimed to have been abused and lied to. The Sophie Melrose trial was his first assault case.

He gave the courtroom a charming smile as he held the door open behind him. The rumor was that he was particularly gifted with winning over the women of the jury. But none of the women in this audience looked charmed when Sophie followed after him. He offered her his arm as she took the stand.

Sophie looked out into the crowd, her eyes wide. Her face had been done up in soft pinks—no lipstick, no shading around her cheekbones—and the effect was startling. The woman America had watched on-screen a few weeks ago at the premiere of *The Sure Shot*, the one who knew how to tilt her head and bat her eyes as she slowly looked a man up and down, was gone. In her place was a girl with her hair arranged into two neat corkscrew curls tied up with bows at either shoulder, wearing a demure dress in a rich creme crepe. They even gave her saddle shoes.

The room went quiet as Mr. Yates cleared his throat and asked Sophie to explain what happened on the night of August 2.

Sophie rested her hands in her lap and smiled at all of us in the courtroom, though her gaze carefully avoided where Freddy was sitting.

She explained that she had gone to a party at Thomas Brodbeck's Bel Air estate to celebrate the final day of shooting for *The Sure Shot* and the engagement of Charles Landrieu and Nell

Parker. Sophie was excited because she had convinced her aunt to let her go to the party with the actress Margy Prescott. It was the kind of night she'd dreamed about for years.

"Auntie Geraldine needed a rest anyway," Sophie said. "It wasn't fair to make her stay out late at a party."

Margy had been very kind to Sophie that night. She had even arrived early at Sophie's house so that she could help her pick out a dress. If Sophie hadn't known better, she might have shown up to the party looking like a fool in a cotillion gown.

At this point in Sophie's story, the judge expressed his disinterest in Sophie's gowns and he began gesturing with his hand for her to move along. Mr. Yates prompted her to tell the court what happened when she arrived at the party.

The girls got to the party late, which Sophie explained would have been embarrassing if she hadn't had Margy there with her. Thankfully, Margy was able to squeeze both of them into Freddy's table.

With a coy smile, Sophie stared down at her lap and confessed she'd been a bit starstruck at seeing Freddy.

"I know it's silly to say," she explained. Her voice had gone up higher when she spoke that day. "I'd been working with people like Nell Parker and"—she took a breath and fanned herself with her hand—"Charles Landrieu."

At this, she gave the women in the audience a knowing smile, the kind usually reserved for close friends at parties. When she let out a laugh, the women in the room snickered with her.

"Well," she said, and waved to quiet them, "you know." She recomposed herself, checking her posture like a schoolgirl might after being chastised by her teacher for slouching. "So I didn't think *anyone* could faze me. But then—there was Mr. Clarke."

The woman next to me nodded with an affirmative hum. I looked away from her just as she was trying to make eye contact with me.

Sophie explained that she had such butterflies in her stomach from being at a table with Mr. Clarke that she'd had to run off to the ladies' room at one point.

She made no mention of vomiting into the toilet or the red-haired lady who helped her. Or that the lady had left her alone in the bathroom. Didn't even notice she was absent from the party until hours later. In the audience, I grew nauseous and felt faint. I tried to suppress it before any of the women could try to comfort me.

I could only see the back of Freddy's head from where I stood. He didn't look behind him when the women began whispering and giggling at the first mention of his name. He had a pad of paper in front of him and appeared to be either writing or drawing pictures.

"Did you return to the party after that?" Mr. Yates asked.

Sophie shook her head. She had been on her way back to the party, she explained, when she was stopped by Mr. Clarke.

"I'd noticed him looking at me during supper and thought I was being downright delusional."

Mr. Clarke had said she looked unwell and ran to get her a glass of water. He then escorted her back to the sitting room, which was empty at that point because everyone else had gone outside. She had asked him if he didn't have any better places to be.

"He looked me in the eye and said the only place he wanted to be was by my side."

I could hear someone behind me let out a sigh with distinct tones of longing.

Mr. Yates paused for a moment and looked hesitantly over his shoulder at the crowd, assessing us. He turned back to Sophie.

"Were you aware at this time that Mr. Clarke is a married man?" he asked her.

Sophie nodded. "I assumed because he's married he would be safe." She spoke the word *safe* as if she were asking a question.

The woman next to me began clicking her tongue and shaking her head. I heard whispers throughout the crowd, none of which sounded approving. Not that any of the women in the crowd could pick out Mrs. Bunny Clarke in a lineup. For all I knew, that might have been part of Bunny's appeal to them—this faceless woman who had been wronged by a beautiful young actress. Many of the women had probably imagined themselves as a Bunny at some point.

Sophie explained that she believed Mr. Clarke was being kind in offering her a glass of water and a quiet place to sit.

"But then he suggested I go upstairs," she said. "And I wasn't so sure anymore."

She told the court that she had felt ill and thought her food wasn't sitting well with her—and, yes, she'd had some champagne. Mr. Clarke had insisted that having a place to lie down would do her a world of good. When she had asked him if she would miss the party, he told her that these parties went on for hours and she could come right back whenever she wanted.

Freddy shifted in his chair at this but didn't look up or make any noise; Sophie could just as well have been reading a grocery list.

"So," Sophie said, "I went upstairs."

As she spoke, she had a strange sort of smile. It was like in some of the older films when actors were coached always to smile, no matter the tone of the scene. There were still some movies coming out where an actor would be grinning like a madman while telling someone her son had just died.

Mr. Yates slowly nodded. He asked if her decision to go upstairs was of her own volition.

"Of course it was," she said with that smile. "I thought I was going to take a nap!"

.   .   .

Sophie continued: Mr. Clarke had led her to an empty bedroom. She had taken off her shoes but kept her dress on when she got into the bed. She thought Mr. Clarke was going to leave after that; instead, he sat on the side of the bed.

"Did that make you feel uncomfortable?" Mr. Yates asked. Sophie nodded, looking again at her hands neatly clasped in her lap. "If that made you uncomfortable, why didn't you leave?"

Sophie began to fidget with one of her curls as she explained that she'd tried to leave, but Mr. Clarke had pinned her down, insisting she needed to rest.

"I struggled with him." She stopped, faltered, and continued: "I struggled *against* him. When I got out of the bed, I fell to the floor. I bruised up my knees scrambling. He stood and went to the door. He was faster. He locked it."

As Sophie spoke, her eyes became unfocused, her mouth a bit slack, and she began clutching at her hair. I had seen that look before—blank, empty.

"Did you not yell out for help?"

"I didn't want to be embarrassed," she said, so softly that it almost sounded like a sigh. There was a fleeting look of surprise on her face, and I realized she hadn't meant to say that. Her mouth was slightly open and her eyes went wide. No one else in the crowd might've known it, but I'd seen enough actresses struggle with their lines to understand that she'd botched the script.

"That's why you didn't yell?" her lawyer slowly asked. The sound of his voice called Sophie back to attention. She quickly rearranged her hands and smiled again. There was a tightness in her smile that disappeared as she took in a deep breath. She explained in a clear voice that the band had started playing on the terrace downstairs—no one would have heard her.

She had told him to stop, but he didn't. He got into the bed with her.

When she described what happened next, the judge interrupted to tell her that she needed to speak louder.

. . .

Mr. Yates asked Sophie if she had ever gone on any dates before. She shook her head and explained that she'd never even attended a school dance.

"Had you known any men intimately prior to this encounter?" Mr. Yates asked.

Sophie shook her head again, her eyes set on the floor. She said she had expected to share that experience with a husband someday.

She explained that Mr. Clarke had left the bedroom shortly thereafter, and presumably went home, because Sophie didn't see him again. She then sat in the room for a while—she couldn't remember how long—before she got up and went back downstairs.

She had begun to feel very ill at that point, and Brodbeck's house was mostly empty as she wandered the halls. Everyone had gone outside and Sophie wanted to find someone to take her home, but she got lost looking for the doors to the terrace. She believed she exited the house through a servants' door, and she walked through the gardens for another indeterminate period of time. There were loud voices and lights by the pool, so she went toward them.

She swore that multiple eyewitnesses could confirm having seen her after midnight at the pool.

Eventually, a woman, Miss Ridgeway, had offered her a ride. In the car, Miss Ridgeway asked her what had happened and Sophie didn't know what to say. When they got to Sophie's house, where she lived with her aunt, Sophie found she couldn't get out of the car.

"I felt frozen," she said. "Like I was watching a film of everything that had happened that night, but I couldn't turn it off, couldn't leave my chair."

She didn't leave the car until she had told Miss Ridgeway everything.

. . .

"Did you have any contact with Mr. Clarke after the party?"

Sophie nodded. "He called me at my house a few days later and asked me if I loved him. I told him I hated him and hung up the telephone."

Mr. Yates sat and was replaced by Freddy's lawyer. In the interim, the room briefly went silent. I looked at the faces around me—most of them bore some resemblance to that of the woman next to me, who was now scowling and shaking her head. Every woman in the crowd had dressed up for the occasion; they wore their nicest dresses and skirts, and each had a full face of makeup. I wouldn't have been surprised if a number of them had had photographs of Freddy tucked into their handbags, on the chance that he might be able to do a few signings.

In the shuffle of people moving around the room, there were a few whispers. I heard a woman behind me whimpering that it wasn't fair Freddy couldn't talk during the hearing. "We ought to hear both sides," she said to whoever would listen. A number of women around her nodded.

Freddy's lawyer, Mr. Schiff, was very concise in his movements; he kept his pacing to a small square in front of Sophie. He rarely looked at the courtroom, focused instead on Sophie and the judge.

He began: "Miss Melrose, had you met Mr. Clarke before the night in question?"

Sophie said she had not—it was why she'd been so struck by seeing him.

"Now, you've stated that you had 'some champagne.' Could you please specify how many glasses?"

"I don't know," she said quietly. "There was an open bottle at the table and people kept refilling my glass before I'd finished."

"How about this: Could you walk in a straight line? Dance a two-step?"

Sophie said, "I didn't do any dancing, but I'm sure I could have. As for walking, I was fine."

"You said you went into an empty room after visiting the powder room. Was that room well lit?"

"If you're implying that I might have mistaken another man for Freddy Clarke, that's absurd," she said, her voice getting higher.

The judge raised his eyebrows, and Sophie quickly recomposed herself, smiling again.

"With all due respect," she said, "I've seen nearly every film Mr. Clarke has ever appeared in—I've been watching him since I was ten years old. I once wanted to dress up as Robin Hood for Halloween, but my mother told me I couldn't because I was a girl. I'd know Mr. Clarke anywhere. Even if it was pitch-black in the room, I'd know his voice."

Mr. Schiff asked how many films Sophie had appeared in ("Two that I had a big-enough part to be credited") and was she currently under contract with FWM Studios ("No").

"Miss Melrose," Mr. Schiff said, "did you discuss your film career with Mr. Clarke that night?"

"We didn't talk about it at all. Mr. Clarke wasn't in much of a talking mood."

"What do you think is the likelihood that you will be offered a contract with FWM?"

Sophie frowned at this and began to finger her hair again. "I was just in a film that's made plenty of money. And I saw it and I think I did a good job—but I also watched other people watching it, and they thought I did a good job, too."

The judge prompted her to answer the question.

"I know I deserve to be under contract," she said, her voice steady. "But I also know that putting a studio's top-billed actor on trial means that won't ever happen. And I accept it—that's how things are."

At this, I heard the smallest scoff from Freddy. Mr. Schiff

gave him a sharp glance from where he stood; it was the only time he looked back during the entire cross-examination.

The room went silent as Sophie left the stand. Her eyes didn't leave the floor while she walked across the room and took her seat. But when she sat, she was in clear view of Freddy's back and she stared directly at it.

I recognized Miss Ada Ridgeway from the party. When she took the stand, she told the court that she had worked in script supervision at FWM but had never seen Sophie before that night.

"I knew who she was, of course," Miss Ridgeway explained. She had been invited to the party by a friend who worked on production for *The Sure Shot*.

Miss Ridgeway proceeded to confirm that Sophie's account of the night—at least those portions that she was present for—was accurate.

"How did Miss Melrose appear to you when you offered her a ride home?"

"Unwell," she said. "And not in the way that girls who have a drink too many look unwell. I've seen my fair share of those. Miss Melrose looked unwell in body and mind. I can't speak to what happened in that upstairs room, but I know that, whatever it was, it wasn't right."

Before she had parted ways with Sophie that night, Miss Ridgeway instructed her to see a doctor as soon as possible.

Unbeknownst to me, Sophie had followed those instructions, because a Dr. Lydia Balfour took the stand next.

Dr. Balfour, an older woman with graying hair, had seen Sophie the day after the party. She said that she examined girls in Miss Melrose's condition frequently. That Miss Melrose had bruises on her wrists and thighs. That Miss Melrose seemed deeply unsettled. That the signs were consistent with those of rape.

.   .   .

At this point, we'd been standing for hours—a few people in the crowd had given up and left, allowing others to take their places. The air in the room felt thin; I struggled to take even breaths. Each time the doors in the courthouse opened, a chorus of voices swept through the room. The crowd outside was anticipating Freddy's departure from the building and would be sorely disappointed as soon as they realized there was a side door in the courtroom that he would most likely exit through.

A few, like the woman next to me, were still hell-bent on waiting until the end of the proceedings, possibly hoping that Freddy might turn his head at any moment and give them that wonderful crooked grin, show us all that he was still Freddy Clarke, here to save the day.

But instead, Freddy sat there with his back turned, doodling pictures on a notepad.

The officer who had first informed Freddy of the charges made against him said that when he went to Mr. Clarke's house, Mr. Clarke nearly shut the door on him.

"He looked me in the eye," the officer explained, "and said, 'That's a goddamn lie if I ever heard one.' Then he laughed—loudly. Woke up the baby in the next room."

That was it for the prosecution's evidence so far. Freddy wasn't going to speak unless the case went to trial. It was up to the judge to decide if there was enough information for that to happen—I'd been warned the process usually took a few days.

With the hearing finished, the room grew loud. I saw Sophie slip out the door she'd entered through, her lawyer shielding her as she went. I wanted to reach out to her, to make eye contact, anything. The crowd began pushing me toward the front of the room instead of filtering out the back. I heard the women reasserting how different it would be when Freddy got to tell his side of the story.

. . .

As the room eventually cleared out, reporters and photographers flanked Freddy. The remaining women in the audience were ordered to keep their distance, though many of them waved photographs at him and called out his name. I couldn't get through them to leave.

When the reporters got close to Freddy, he put his hand over his eyes.

"I'm just trying to make certain I don't even *look* at anyone under the age of forty-five!" he called out with a laugh.

The crowd laughed with him and he signed a few pictures before he was escorted away by his lawyer.

I waited outside the courthouse for an hour to see if Sophie would appear. She needed to know that there was someone on her side. Instead, an officer patrolling the courthouse stopped me. "I'm sorry, Mr. Clarke's gone home, and you probably should, too."

A few days later, I was reading the papers and waiting for Warren to arrive at my house. He refused to meet in public again, paranoid that people might see him in spite of my reassurances that no one had the slightest idea who he was.

I had spent an hour tidying and rearranging furniture. I didn't do very much entertaining—my modest home was primarily used for sleeping and changing outfits. I had four coats draped over the couch and an array of shoes that I'd kicked off around the front door. I threw all of them into a closet and shut it before anything could fall on me.

The papers were supposed to calm my nerves but, as they often do, had the opposite effect. Wedged between reports of war overseas was an account of the preliminary hearing and the announcement of Freddy's official court date—the judge had ruled that there was enough evidence to go to trial.

. . .

Warren was already sweating by the time he arrived. I directed him to the living room couch and gave him a cold glass of water to calm his nerves. I wasn't about to offer him booze. It was bad enough that I was leveraging information against a nineteen-year-old so he'd tell me about three actors being indecorous on a film set.

"Do you mind if I write this down?" I asked.

He nodded for me to go ahead. Looking at him sitting on my couch, I was reminded of where Sophie had sat. I felt a swell of anger at how cautious she had to be—every line carefully delivered, every gesture coordinated, every physical detail accounted for. Even when she was sitting on my floor with only me in the room, she'd been self-conscious.

As he talked, Warren let himself sprawl out more, so his feet extended past my coffee table. He stumbled on his words and corrected himself a few times. Once he eased into his story, there was a clear excitement in his voice.

It happened like this: Margy Prescott, Charles Landrieu, and Hal Bingham did a lot of drinking. Warren estimated that they might have been sober the first couple of days on location in Wyoming. After that, all bets were off. If Charles appeared intoxicated in any—by which I mean most—of the scenes from *Afterglow*, it's because he *was* intoxicated. Heavily, according to Warren.

"I guess the good thing is that they're all very nice drunks," he said.

Rolf had turned a blind eye to their misconduct because the three leads showed up to work on time, knew their lines, and followed his cues.

"If you're going to be unprofessional, might as well be professional about it," Warren said with a shrug.

When filming wrapped up for the day, they shared with the crew. Warren said he mostly saw liquor and reefer being passed around ("Not anything I'd try, of course!"), though there may have been a few pills in the mix. It seemed Margy, Charles, and Hal covered all manner of sins.

"Each night, they slept in one another's rooms. Didn't do a thing to hide it. Had breakfast with the crew the next morning like it was nothing." He swore he'd seen every combination of the three in different rooms—Charles exiting Hal's, Margy going into Charles's, and one morning he even found them all camping outside with a handle of bourbon.

It carried on like that for the nine weeks they spent on location. Someone must have tipped off the wranglers at FWM, because halfway through filming, a lesser Augustan showed up with nondisclosure agreements for everyone on the shoot.

"So when Hal and Margy got that quick marriage, we didn't have too much trouble putting together the pieces. One of the boys said that Hal and Charles flipped a coin to decide who would marry her."

When Warren stood up to leave, he looked like a different man. There was a lightness to him—it seemed to me that he wasn't just relieved to have gotten a secret out but that he was also reveling in his own wrongdoing. He smiled the way a schoolchild might after playing some nefarious prank on his teacher.

After Warren left, I drank two glasses of whiskey. If the studio knew about everything that happened in Wyoming—which meant Augustan knew—I'd have one hell of a time getting anyone to confirm it without resorting to blackmail. It was true that Augustan had happily let me take down one FWM actress, poor Esther Brooks, but Charles, Margy, and Hal were not Esther Brooks. The three of them consistently worked and they brought in money for the studio. I knew that scandalizing any of them could have severe costs; I also knew that scandalizing any of them could make me a household name.

The next day around noon, I heard a knock on my door. When I opened it, there was an envelope on my doorstep and Sophie was walking toward a car parked outside my house. I called her name and she turned to me. She was dressed in her regular clothes, a cardigan and a full skirt, and her face wasn't made up. Her outfit was essentially the same one she had worn when she first came to my house, but she looked entirely different now. Her face was drawn and washed-out. She was exhausted; it showed in her posture, the way her shoulders sloped inward.

"I was hoping you might not be home," she said slowly. She glanced at the envelope. "I'm sorry it's late."

I picked up the envelope and felt the heft of it—I didn't need to open it to know it was the five hundred dollars Sophie had offered months ago for publishing her interview. It felt wrong to hold it in my hands. More than anything, I wanted to give it back to her, but the moment I stepped forward with it, Sophie backed away.

"Please," she said, "I don't want to talk about it." When she said it, her voice was no longer practiced—the voice I heard that day was raw, hurt.

I was at a loss for words. The only thing I wanted was to comfort her, somehow. I looked at the car waiting for her; there was a driver biding his time up front and a woman in the back seat. I could hardly see her through the window, but from the flash of blond hair, I could only assume she was Sophie's mother.

"You did the best you could," I said quietly, the words directed more toward the ground than to Sophie.

"We're going to trial," she said. "If you can, I'd rather you stay out of it all. Let's be done with this." She glanced over her shoulder at the car, and this time I saw a gloved hand emerge from the window, beckoning her back in. From the brief glimpse I caught of Sophie's mother, she looked just like her daughter—rosy cheeks and bright eyes. She did not acknowledge me.

I nodded to Sophie. "Anything you need . . ." I said, and my voice trailed off. With nothing more to say, Sophie got back in the car, leaving me mute on my doorstep, holding an envelope of cash that I didn't know what to do with.

·   ·   ·

I sat in my living room until the late hours. My hand had drifted to the part of my arm that Sophie had grasped on to during the premiere of *The Sure Shot*. She hadn't been alone for that, and I shouldn't have left her alone for the hearing. How long she must have waited in that courthouse room before the hearing started. I imagined her listening to the tick of a clock, the voices growing in the next room, her lawyer informing her when it was time to go.

I wouldn't publish a story about her and Warren—but even so, I knew I had failed, and would continue to fail, Sophie.

There's another version of this where she gets to carry on with Warren behind the set, the two sending notes hidden in coat pockets, glancing across the room at each other. Where Sophie gets to have the career she deserved and become a lead, written up in the columns and admired by young women across the country. A reality where she isn't sitting in that courthouse.

∫EVEN

In the weeks that followed, Freddy Clarke had three FWM publicists with him at all times. They took turns making sure he didn't drink heavily, fight anyone, or sleep in a bed that wasn't his own.

They very nearly succeeded.

Nell wanted to meet with me in the FWM commissary. When I went in, the commissary was buzzing because one of the papers had published a leaked list of Academy Award winners, even though the ceremony wouldn't take place for another week. It was a sore subject with the FWM actors and actresses, none of whom had been nominated for an award since 1935. Every year, there was speculation about which of FWM's stars might distinguish themselves—three years ago, it was supposed to be Nell, then it was going to be Griffith, and that year it was Carla Longworth. But the only two nominees for FWM were Paul Eddington, the reigning art director on FWM's musicals, and Roger Moynihan for Film Editing in *Afterglow*. According to the paper, they would both lose to *Gone with the Wind*.

I found Nell sitting at a table, wearing a costume from her current project, a society drama in which she ends up swapping fiancés with her best friend after a few mishaps and revelations. She did not look pleased, and I could make a few guesses as to why. Since my bylines began adding up, Poppy had taken to maligning any

FWM stars in her column—the most recent one read: "Nell Parker refuses to sign autograph for ailing child."

"Ailing child!" Nell said over a coffee and biscuits. "He was twenty-five and about two minutes from coughing out a lung. Forgive me if I don't want to catch any diseases."

Nell's health concerns weren't unfounded: Edward Percival had five months added to his seven-year contract for fracturing his ankle, and the actress Margaret Fairchild recently had two months added to hers for having the audacity to be ill with pneumonia. Needless to say, they were not compensated during their suspensions.

"It's ridiculous," she said under her breath.

Later that day, I clipped Poppy's column on Nell and sent it over to Kent Strauss, who was handling publicity at MGM and was likely the man in charge of casting for *Marie Antoinette*. I attached an anonymous note that said, "She's not a queen of the people, but neither was Marie."

Charles had arrived back in Hollywood in time for the Academy Awards, but he was keeping a low profile. Augustan tipped me off that he would be on set for a publicity shoot and then he had to attend a charity benefit with his *Zorro* costar Josette Halliday.

I had spent the last few weeks leaving Charles out of the column, but the other papers were quick to draw conclusions about his refusal to sign Freddy's petition. Poppy questioned his moral vigor. The *Inquirer* started doing articles about a possible rivalry between Charles and Freddy. Most of their evidence was the fistfight at Brodbeck's nearly a year ago. The paper cooked up a whole scheme in which Charles was hankering for a rematch. Next to the column there were doodles of Charles and Freddy in boxing gear.

I was much more curious about confirming what Warren had told me.

· · ·

On a mostly empty lot, Charles was once again dressed in all black. A mask covered the upper half of his face as he stood holding a sword in front of a bright blue background with an orange tree beside him. I stayed on the outskirts of the lot until I heard the photographer say they were moving on to the next set.

"Thank goodness we have you here to protect us all from the dangers of citrus," I commented when he came over to me.

He kept walking toward a rack of clothing and motioned for me to follow. He pulled off his hat and mask, placing them on a table of props. A woman handed him a costume change—a light blue bolero jacket with floral embroidery and pants to match.

"It looks like I've been very busy lately," he said before disappearing behind a curtain. Someone must have shown him the various columns about him during his absence from Hollywood. "Don't suppose you have anything to do with that?"

I told him to take his concerns up with Poppy or the *Inquirer*. "Or you could release a statement for Freddy like everybody else!"

Charles came back out from behind the curtain, and the woman tied a silk cravat around his neck. He now had on a jacket cut close to his waist and fitted pants. It seemed that George and the boys in costuming had done some very strategic tailoring—Don Diego would be hard-pressed to do any sword fighting in that outfit, lest he rip a seam or lose one of the many jewels sewn onto his jacket. Nevertheless, Charles carried himself the same as he did in his cowboy clothes, even as another woman wiped the dark makeup from around his eyes and began coaxing his hair back into a neat wave. I'd seen him clean up in a tuxedo before; he was usually very handsome, but this was something else entirely. I don't know how else to put it: He was beautiful. I'd never noticed how long and dark his eyelashes were. I saw the definitive curve of his cheekbones and the softness in his lips, which were usually obscured by facial hair.

Josette, his costar in *Zorro*, appeared from the other side of the lot wearing a heavy ruffled gown, embroidered along the neckline to match Charles's jacket. Her dark hair was pinned up with flowers and lace. She was demure in her movements, looking coyly at the ground.

They stood together under the harsh lights as one of the house photographers adjusted his camera. He directed them to stand closer to each other, for Charles to brush his face against hers. He obliged, turning so that part of his neck was exposed and vulnerable. Charles placed an arm around her shoulder and she stared up at him. I didn't know which of them to look at.

After a few shots, Charles was handed a sword again and instructed to protect Josette. She partially buried her face in his chest, her eyes wide and frightened as he lunged at a nonexistent foe in the distance.

I waited for him to change back into his regular clothing. That day, though, his "regular clothing" was black tie. He asked me why I was still there.

"You're going to a charity benefit," I said. "I also happen to be going to a charity benefit."

He gave me a skeptical look before shrugging and lighting a cigarette. I walked with him off the set and asked how filming had gone.

Out of makeup—or mostly out of makeup, since none of them was ever entirely free of it—Charles looked worn-down. There was something genuinely sad in his posture and demeanor. If I hadn't known any better, I'd have suspected heartbreak.

When I asked what the matter was, he deflected.

"Why don't you just write that I'm still recovering after two months of being separated from the love of my life?" he said, his deep voice dripping with irony.

He was referring to Nell—the public always enjoyed reading about stars pining for each other while someone was away on location. I laughed along with the joke, but I couldn't help noticing that Charles seemed hurt. As I watched him walk away, my mind went to Margy.

. . .

He was taken to the benefit in a car with a handful of FWM's stars and their handlers, so I was left to drive myself. It had taken some careful maneuvering to get an invite to the benefit—the tables were selling for steep prices. I'd promised to include a mention in the paper, noting the hospital they were raising money for, and that did the trick.

In a room full of wealthy investors, I was placed at a table with a group of steel tycoons and their wives. One of them was short a wife, hence the empty seat that now belonged to me. The sole bachelor, middle-aged and overly tan, kept trying to drape his arm over my chair, so I kept moving the chair, until I was practically in the lap of the poor man to my left.

The benefit featured a recurring bit in which stars from different studios were given a sheet of questions from "average Americans"—otherwise known as publicists—and required to guess one another's answers.

Charles and Josette represented FWM Studios that afternoon, along with Griffith Taylor and Carla Longworth. I assumed that Freddy and his most recent costar were originally intended to be onstage but had been pulled from the event in light of Freddy's recently announced court date.

The questions proved dull: Where did so-and-so grow up? How tall are they? Do they have any hobbies?

Charles was asked if he kept a pet leopard on his ranch ("It's my understanding that that's illegal. I do own a large dog and could try painting some spots on him, but I don't think he'd appreciate it much") and Griffith was questioned on his marital status ("I haven't found the right girl!").

At one point, Charles read out a question for Josette about her age. He laughed and quipped that his mother had raised him right—he would never ask for a woman's age.

"Unless she looks under eighteen," he said under his breath, but loudly enough for the microphone to pick up.

The laughter in the room quickly subsided. The wives of the steel tycoons all raised their eyebrows and everyone exchanged knowing glances. There was an uncomfortable silence before Carla snatched the sheet of questions from Charles and moved on to the next one ("What does Josette eat for breakfast?").

It was the closest anyone from FWM had come to naming the thing out loud—their stars and directors had been coached by publicists to frame everything in a positive light whenever they could. Not "Sophie Melrose is a liar," but "Freddy Clarke is an honest man." Not "Freddy Clarke made a mistake," but "Freddy Clarke is an actor who continues to grow and has a great career ahead of him."

Before they left the stage, Josette quietly told the audience that she regularly ate porridge for breakfast.

In the interlude, I excused myself from my table and left, much to the disappointment of the single steel tycoon.

Charles was well aware of what he had done. He tried to avoid me as he was leaving the benefit. Although he could run faster than most actors and even vault tables if he had to, he wasn't about to be caught sprinting away from a gossip columnist.

Poppy wasn't at the benefit, but it was only a matter of time until someone told her. Then, somewhere down the line, the *Inquirer* would get ahold of the story. They'd add some vulgar headline: CHARLES LANDRIEU ATTACKS FREDDY CLARKE FOR CHARITY.

Charles walked with his hands in his pockets; Josette was nearby but pointedly ignoring him. He looked at me.

"Last year, they had me playing baseball for charity and that was swell," he said. He was famously the fourth hitter on the "Leading Men" team for an annual charity game against the "Comedy Kings."

He continued: "Don't know why I'm supposed to talk and ad-lib now."

I told him that it was probably in his contract. I pointed out that displaying professional conduct in any public setting was probably also in his contract.

He sighed. "I wish they'd just let me play baseball again."

At the top of the column, I wrote, "We noticed a few pairs of loose lips at the St. Bartholomew's Hospital Benefit last week—perhaps Charles Landrieu should keep some of his thoughts about his colleagues to himself. At least he's slandering for a good cause!"

I had to phone Augustan three times before he answered. I wasn't sure if it was because he was avoiding me or simply preoccupied. He had, of course, already heard about the benefit.

"We had Charles up for Gideon's next film—an epic set in colonial Australia," Augustan said. "Now we're giving the role to Danny Prior."

Danny was the first person in line to become the next Charles Landrieu. He was dark, handsome, and knew his way around both weaponry and women.

Charles, on the other hand, was going to be placed on three weeks' suspension without pay. The papers were supposed to frame it as a "well-deserved vacation" after going on location for two months to film *Zorro*.

Before I hung up the phone, I asked Augustan if I was still going to be his date for the Academy Awards. We'd made arrangements months ago. He had been my escort for the last two ceremonies; it seemed silly to break a tradition. I had also spent an embarrassing portion of my paltry finances on a gown months earlier. I wasn't about to waste a Madeleine Vionnet on a film premiere or social club.

Augustan agreed, on condition that I let him work in peace during the ceremony and keep my questions to myself.

"If you want to go nosing around the other studios, be my guest. I'd actually prefer it."

I promised to give it my best effort.

. . .

The Academy Awards were filmed for the first time that year. FWM had George Wynette personally approve every one of their leading ladies' dresses. Nell was refitted four times before he was satisfied. I had been warned that Margy would arrive in something "daring." The Marquess didn't understand why she was required to attend the event, but she was happy to be dressed in something shiny.

As long as no one was winning any awards, they could at least look nice.

FWM was selective about their invites—because *The Sure Shot* received no distinctions, the studio felt no obligation to invite the cast. It conveniently let them off the hook for disregarding Sophie Melrose.

I hadn't seen or heard from Sophie since she'd knocked on my door with an envelope of cash. I'd gotten word that her parents had rented an estate for the duration of the trial, but no amount of sleuthing turned up an address or phone number. I continued to ignore Sophie and Freddy in my column. I cited it to my editor as a conflict of interests because I had a film coming out with Freddy in the spring—a premiere I did not want to think about attending.

Afterglow received a nomination for Film Editing, which meant the trifecta of Margy, Hal, and Charles was invited as a courtesy. All three had agreed to attend months ago.

Standing alone in one's house wearing a couture gown is a uniquely ridiculous activity. But that's what I did while waiting for Augustan. I couldn't even sit, for fear of wrinkling the silk, so I paced the small space of my living room while admiring the movement of the dress. It was a lovely pink gown with silver embellishments at the waist. The color was especially nice against my red hair, which I'd spent another unreasonable amount of money having someone wash and tame that afternoon. I realized as I ran my hand over the soft fabric that it was the nicest thing I owned—at least the nicest thing that fit me properly.

Augustan was ten minutes late. I made myself a vodka and soda and drank the whole thing before my doorbell rang. "I hate this" is all Augustan said when I let him in. It was raining outside; he shook out his umbrella and left it by my door.

He continued before I had the opportunity to ask what "this" was. "I'm going to spit in Frank Capra's drink for demanding this whole ordeal be filmed."

Augustan had spent the last six hours okaying what the stars were wearing and where they were sitting. Someone had placed Freddy in the middle of the FWM banquet table, where he would be in shouting distance of Charles. When Augustan moved Freddy to the other end of the table, he was too close to Carla, with whom he'd had a tumultuous relationship a few years ago. Eventually, Carla's placard was moved to the end of the table with those of Charles, Nell, Hal, and Margy. Ines was placed in the middle of the table, hopefully to act as a cushion between warring parties. I wasn't about to tell Augustan that she might cushion too well— I had not forgotten her smudged lipstick at the premiere of *The Sure Shot.*

Augustan made it two minutes into the drive before breaking his own truce to keep me out of FWM business.

"Gideon is annoyed we gave him Danny instead of Charles," he complained. The director had never worked with Charles before and was very excited after seeing some of the early reels from *Zorro.*

FWM's other projects were equally disastrous. After being moved from Rolf's film to another one, young Grace Stafford proved that she had no comedic timing, and her costar, Rex Northrop, couldn't abide her general presence—the studio was trying to wrap up the film as quickly as possible and ship it away in a bundled package to theaters. FWM was usually strong on musicals, but with the temporary loss of Edward Percival due to his ankle injury, they had resorted to Spencer Greene. Spencer was still light on his feet, but his face was beginning to wrinkle and his hairline was quickly receding.

"Young men dancing is charming," Augustan said, making a sharp turn toward the Ambassador Hotel. "Old men dancing? Audiences start to worry they'll fall and break a hip."

Never mind that it was twenty-four-year-old Edward who'd recently fractured his ankle, while Spencer had been working for decades without injury.

Augustan drove around the block three times before he felt ready to go inside. I nearly had to grab the wheel from him so he wouldn't make another right turn. He stopped only when I threatened to cry if my dress got creased before I even made it to the ceremony. Moments before the valet opened his door, Augustan turned to me and unleashed a series of unprintable curses at all of Hollywood.

In the large ballroom, Augustan and I were tracked by a camera when we went to take our seats. I waved at the camera as I worked my way through the round tables at the back of the room, where some of the lesser stars and nominees were seated. It only took a minute for the operator to realize we were not particularly notable people. The camera moved on to the next couple entering the room.

The room was filled with so many tables that I could hardly see the floor. I nearly stumbled into someone's chair multiple times as I walked with Augustan toward the stage. In addition to a few cameras on the floor, there were at least ten set up in the balcony. Fake palm trees lined the periphery of the room, a string of lights set up between them.

On the stage, there was a pedestal showcasing the night's awards. I watched more than one actor make a joke of pretending to grab one from the table.

· · ·

FWM had a large banquet table at the front of the room, which began to fill quickly. As opposed to past years, when the tables had a degree of privacy, each of the major studios' tables had harsh lights fixed on them for the cameras. As people took their seats, the lights picked up every detail of their clothing and faces: the gold-threaded rosettes that were handwoven into the gauze of Ines's gown, the rust-blond color of Hal's hair, the way that Margy's dress draped precariously close to her chest under her mink stole.

My eye traveled between the different couples crowded in at the table. Margy and Hal were seated closest to the stage, the backdrop of a beach scene and the awards table behind them. Every few moments, Margy tipped her head up to look at Hal, laughing or smiling as she did so. He didn't return the gesture. Since my meeting with Warren, my perception of them had shifted. Before, Hal's reticence with Margy had seemed charming, but now I wondered if he wasn't just a man upset about the results of a coin toss.

Ines was once again paired with Griffith; the two of them were seated by one of the large fake palm trees, which Ines seemed happy to use as a barrier between them as she leaned in toward Margy's end of the table.

Freddy accompanied Jeanette Manning; they'd done a film together earlier that year. Bunny Clarke was understood to be "caring for the baby" indefinitely and would not be attending any events in the near future. Jeanette had been on the FWM payroll long enough that she'd follow any of Augustan's directives. She was old—by which I mean that she was the same age as Freddy—and didn't call too much attention to herself. She was essentially a babysitter for a very temperamental man.

That left two empty seats by Hal and Margy, belonging to Nell and Charles.

The other tables treated FWM with a certain degree of haughtiness that hadn't been there in past years, or perhaps I'd been too involved in the studio to notice it before. It had always been a running joke in the industry that FWM was Hollywood's premier studio for "style without substance." A friend of mine at Columbia had recently made an offhand remark that FWM would never be the same after the passing of Nico Marquis. Before Sophie went public about Freddy, one of the producers at RKO had been asking around about Freddy's salary. His contract would be up in two years, and I was certain other studios were counting down the days until they could make him an offer, trial be damned. George Wynette was being lured back to costuming on Broadway with promises of absolute artistic freedom. People had started asking after Thomas Brodbeck's health: "It's a demanding job and he's not the spry young man he was ten years ago."

I looked up and down our table. For a moment I saw what everyone else saw: spare parts.

Nell Parker wanted regal; Nell Parker got regal. She arrived late with Charles and overshadowed him the moment they walked into the well-lit ballroom. She was wearing a tightly buttressed silk gown sent from the designer Charles James and then tailored by George. It was the first time I'd seen any actress wearing a strapless gown to a formal event. Nell's hair was pulled back into an intricate series of curls atop her head, leaving her neck and shoulders exposed. She wore a choker necklace of rubies that dripped over her collarbone. The skirt of the dress contained yards of fabric, ruched into billowing sections so it didn't trail behind her. She carried it with grace, taking slow and careful steps.

Charles dutifully stepped away so a photographer could get a shot of Nell alone. She angled herself so she stood with her back straight, one shoulder pushed forward, her gloved hands clasped at her waist, and her chin held high. She had a soft, knowing smile on her face, the way women do in old portraits.

Charles then rejoined her and smiled for a few more photographs. The camera tracked them as they crossed the room. I watched several actresses from other studios narrow their eyes when Nell passed them.

. . .

As the only person present on FWM's publicity team, Augustan was obligated to sit near Freddy, which meant that I was also obligated to sit near Freddy. I was placed between Augustan and Griffith. Freddy was at the head of the table, Jeanette was across from us, next to Brodbeck.

Augustan kept the topics of conversation limited to only the most benign subjects. We discussed the type of champagne served that night, which led to a meandering discussion on who preferred champagne, red wine, or white wine. Everyone selected champagne and idled in silence while waiting for the ceremony to start. I tried to catch Augustan's eye—I could usually check his temperature with a single look—but he was fixated on his table setting.

Freddy sat with his cheek resting against his palm, staring enviously around the room. I caught him looking in Charles's direction a few times and then feigning that he hadn't. Freddy looked too big for the table, like he could give it a shake and the whole thing would topple over.

The other end of the table erupted into laughter every few minutes, Margy's laugh ringing above everyone else's. I saw her wave down a waiter and request another bottle of champagne. Nell was unamused; her arms were crossed and she kept sucking in her cheeks. Next to her, Charles maintained his composure. He wasn't taking his suspension lightly—the champagne glass in front of him was full, and I watched as he inconspicuously drank from a glass of water. He had unraveled his dinner napkin and gripped it tightly as he looked over at Hal and Margy. From where Ines was sitting, she had her pick of either conversation, and she chose Margy's. Her back was turned to Griffith so she could listen to them. She had a bemused smile as she watched Margy and the others take turns practicing British accents, supposedly "in honor of Miss Vivien Leigh."

. . .

"You've got to remember, the Brits replace their *a*'s with *e*'s," Carla explained.

"I'm just so *heppy*," Margy yelled.

"I really prefer a nice cabernet sauvignon," Augustan said to no one.

"*Heppy*," Hal said.

"Production's wrapped up on that one," the lone film editor said to Griffith.

"So we're letting them drink themselves stupid over there?" Jeanette mused.

"God, it'll be at least three months on *Zorro*. I've seen how many scenes there are to cut together. Lot of action sequences in that one. Who knows, maybe I'll actually win an award for it."

"*Heppy!*"

"I'd like to go to France someday."

"At one point, we had over five thousand carnations on set," the art director said. "*Real* ones."

"I mean, not today—certainly not anytime soon!"

"Selznick can keep his nominations. We had three of the top ten highest-grossing films this year."

"Ver-reh ver-reh heppy," Charles said when it was his turn.

"You know people can hear you, right?"

The technical awards were announced first. The FWM art director and editor, who had received nominations, were sitting near me. Both of them must have seen the article that predicted their respective losses. They clapped politely as *Gone with the Wind* swept nearly every category, including their two.

The FWM table grew loud enough that the presenter made a crack about cutting them off. Margy wasted no time in calling out in a thick southern accent, "Y'all can try!"

Everyone in the room laughed, though the laughter had a harsh edge of judgment. Across from me, Brodbeck was stone-faced. I could see Augustan anxiously twisting a signet ring around his finger—a tic I'd seen him resort to only a few times under extreme duress.

There was an intermission before the acting awards would be announced. Augustan quickly got up and went over to the other end of the table. He knelt next to Margy's chair, and I could only imagine what he was saying to her. In my line of sight, Nell whispered something into Charles's ear. He nodded with an air of seriousness.

Baird deWitt took Augustan's temporarily vacated seat next to me. Though he was not in any sort of a costume, he looked every bit the eccentric European count that night.

Baird leaned in close to me, and I could smell the gin on his breath. He said in a low voice, "Come on over to MGM's table, where people have some class, why don't you?"

I smiled at him and patted his shoulder. "No one is going to read my column for *class*."

I nodded in Margy's direction. She was gesticulating wildly, nearly hitting Augustan over the head where he perched by her. Nell seemed prepared to storm out at any moment. Next to her, Charles kept anxiously taking sips of water and glancing at Hal. Charles mouthed something to him, but I couldn't make out the words. Whatever silent conversation they were having appeared to be about Margy. I watched as Hal sat back in his chair and laughed into his hand. He tried to make it look like a cough. Charles shook his head and suppressed a smile before Nell could catch him.

Baird told me to suit myself. He went back to his table.

Across from me, Jeanette was quietly getting drunk and ignoring Freddy entirely. Freddy was now openly watching the other end of the table; his focus had shifted to Hal, who was opposite him.

Even though half the room had issued statements about Freddy's admirable character and professionalism, no one wanted to stop by and talk to him.

Augustan took back his seat and exchanged a glance with Brodbeck. He put his hands up in surrender.

He tipped his drink to me in a mock toast. "God save me," he said quietly.

A comedian took the podium to announce the honorary award for juvenile acting.

He smiled and looked at his notes. "There are about three jokes here that I don't think I'm allowed to tell."

Margy didn't yell this time, but most of the room heard her: "I bet I could guess 'em."

I watched half the faces in the room turn to Freddy and then immediately look down at their laps and then turn to see if anyone else had done the same thing, which, of course, everyone had.

There was some stilted laughter before Mickey Rooney took the stage to award Judy Garland for her work in *The Wizard of Oz*.

After Judy accepted her award, Charles stood and escorted Margy away from the table, his hand on the small of her back. He glanced back at Hal with an apologetic smile. Hal waited a beat, then followed them.

After a few minutes, Charles came back, but Hal and Margy didn't. Instead, their seats were taken by Spencer Greene and his wife, Lucia St. Vincent, a dancer who was under contract with RKO at the time. Spencer was a pillar of FWM—he was one of the most beloved singers of the early thirties.

With Spencer at the helm of the table, we were supposed to be reminded of the FWM Studios of yesteryear: dignified, consistent, appropriately sober.

I glanced over my shoulder to see where Margy and Hal had gone to—I spotted them at a small round table close to the doors. Our table quieted down after that, to the point where I missed Margy's laughter, which had now been replaced by stilted conversations and speculation about the forthcoming award categories, with everyone pretending as though the results hadn't been leaked a week ago.

When Hattie McDaniel won her award for Supporting Actress, she had to walk from a secluded table at the back of the room—the Ambassador had a strict "No Negroes" policy that Selznick paid his way out of. The people at every table clapped profusely after her speech, though half of them wouldn't allow her on their lots.

Given the staunch silence of the FWM group, I started to wish that I had taken Baird up on his offer. Across the room, those at the MGM table appeared to be having a very pleasant evening. Next to me, Augustan would only converse with me in scoffs, eye rolls, and exhales of smoke. I wasn't about to try my luck talking with Brodbeck, and certainly didn't want to engage Freddy, who had begun tapping the table loudly with the butt of his dinner knife.

Everyone clapped politely when Vivien Leigh accepted the last award of the night for *Gone with the Wind*.

There was a collective sigh of relief as we all got up to leave.

I coerced Augustan into going to an after-party in spite of his insistence that he would "rather eat hot coal."

"Maybe Capra will be there and you could spit in his drink?" I suggested. "Would that cheer you up?"

In truth, we both knew that Augustan didn't have a choice. Somebody had to watch the stars of FWM. They certainly weren't watching themselves.

The club was populated by at least half the attendees from the awards ceremony, with a few additions who didn't get an invite to the Ambassador but wanted to partake in the festivities afterward. There were assorted booths and tables, but the room was mostly open for dancing. A stylish four-piece band played on a small stage in a corner. The bar was crowded, and I could hear champagne bottles popping every few minutes.

I left Augustan to check on his various charges while I explored the room. There were too many partygoers for the tables and chairs, so small groups clustered throughout the room. Without the scrutiny of bright lights and cameras, everyone was a little more liberal with their voices.

There was a time when these parties frightened me. I didn't know how to move through them, whom to speak to. A few years into my contract, when it became clear to me that I wasn't going to be the focus of any party, I stopped trying. I realized that I could stand alone on the periphery of any group, listen, and no one would think twice about it. It was a skill I had honed over the years—as long as I could shirk off the fear that anyone cared enough to notice, I could see anything, hear anything, do anything. So I made myself invisible and joined the crowd.

Near the dance floor, I could hear Margy's loud laugh. Since being reprimanded by Augustan, she had not sobered up—if anything, it was quite the opposite. Hal was unfazed. He grabbed her hand and led her off to dance. Perhaps he was trying to wear her out. It worked; as long as she was dancing, she wouldn't be yelling offenses at anyone in Hollywood.

Jeanette had quickly disappeared from the party, so Augustan stayed near Freddy. It occurred to me that I had never seen the two men carry on a conversation with each other. I couldn't fathom what they would say. From the looks of it, nothing at all.

I searched the room for Ines and found her smoking in a corner while Paramount's latest leading man tried to speak with her. He inched closer and closer to her as he spoke, while she did her best to ignore him. Though I often struggled with the expressions on her face, this one clearly read as disgust. Eventually, she got up without saying a word, and I was later told she left the party with the matinee idol Tyrone Power.

.   .   .

Charles came over to me. I raised my eyebrows at him.

"I'm just covering my own hide," he said. "I thought I'd appeal to your gentler nature."

"I've got plenty of material that doesn't involve you," I lied.

He didn't seem convinced. He looked over at Nell, who was busy talking up the MGM crowd. He said, "Like I don't know that Nell would throw me over the minute she gets a chance."

If he was angry, he didn't show it. He mostly looked amused by the idea.

"Would you resent her for it?" I asked.

He didn't think about it, just shook his head and laughed. "Nell Parker is going to be working in this town until she's eighty. She'll be all wrinkles and drama. Probably win five different lifetime achievement awards."

He watched Nell for a little while longer—she held her chin high and smiled demurely when an MGM director spoke to her.

"At some point," he said, "you have to respect the hell out of it."

"And what about you? Are you going to work until you're eighty?"

He pulled a cigarette from his jacket and lit it. His expression shifted—there was something remorseful in the way he squinted as he took a drag. He considered his next words.

"Can I ask you something, Edie?"

I nodded.

"You work after the crash?"

It took me by surprise, but, looking at everyone around us, the question made sense. Half the people in the room had been gainfully employed as actors or directors in Hollywood when the market crashed over ten years ago. The other half—the Freddy Clarkes and Margy Prescotts—came from money; they didn't know a life without it.

"I worked when I could," I said. "It certainly wasn't steady for me."

· · ·

I suppressed visions of a cramped apartment in Boston, five siblings, all girls except for Sebastian. I dropped out of school at sixteen to look after them. I knew how to water down a soup to feed more mouths. I knew how to tell which day-old loaves of bread would still be edible after being discarded from the local grocer. I knew how to alter and mend dresses and stockings to be reworn by every girl in the family.

When it became clear that Sebastian would be the only one of us to graduate from high school, I forged a letter from the headmaster at his school to win him a scholarship to a university. I did so because I cared about my brother's education, but mostly because it meant he'd get square meals and housing for four years.

I didn't say any of this, but Charles nodded slowly.

"I figured," he said. "I don't know what it is, but you can always tell when a person's been hungry—properly hungry."

He continued: "I went to California a few years after the markets crashed. I thought I'd ride horses and shoot guns. You ever see the old Jesse James films?"

I told him I had. There had been a succession of them, all wildly popular. It was one of those franchises that was primarily built on explosions and wide shots of deserts.

"I got paid five dollars to jump off a moving train," he said. "They made me jump off it eight times before they got the shot right. Nearly broke my leg doing it. I still have scars because I couldn't get the whole mess stitched up properly."

I knew the scene he was talking about. Jesse, originally played by Archer Ward, climbs on top of a train to escape his would-be captors. His brother, the less famous Frank James, has already left the scene and is waiting for him with his horse. Jesse runs the length of the train and leaps onto the ground before swiftly mounting his horse for a speedy getaway. I'd seen it multiple times and hadn't known it was really Charles running down the train, risking injury, if not death.

He shifted and glanced uneasily around the room. "Every day I've been doing this, I feel like I'm running down a moving train again and I never know which jump is going to be the one that kills me. Honest to God, I don't know how I got here, and that's probably why I don't trust a damn thing to last."

We didn't get to finish that conversation, though, because Margy was yelling from the other side of the room.

In the days that followed, a number of people would claim that they saw Margy spit on Freddy—"A clear shot right to the cheek. You can't take the southern out of a southern girl." Others said that Freddy pushed Hal as he was walking by him, which caused Margy to then claw her way at him in anger. Either way, Hal caught Freddy in the gut and sent him rolling onto the floor.

Hal once explained to me, "One of the difficult things about being the largest man in the room is that there's always someone who wants to fight you."

Charles's face was petrified for a moment—he arched one eyebrow and his eyes went wide, an expression I recognized from many of his films—and he ran to the other side of the club without another word to me. He swiftly dodged between tables and chairs to get there, pushing through the crowd of people already gathering around Hal and Freddy. Charles grabbed Hal by the elbow and pulled him toward the door with surprising force. Margy followed closely behind Charles. As I watched them leave, I thought of Warren finding the three of them camped out together in Wyoming. That was the last I saw of any of them that night.

I joined the crowd building around Freddy. He tried to stand up quickly, but he wound up hunching over in pain. When he got his footing, he demanded to know where Hal had gone. A group of people had formed a circle around him, but no one answered. Augustan stood next to Freddy, offering a hand in support that Freddy wasn't about to take.

Freddy wanted to know why no one was looking for Hal or attempting to bring him back. There was a look of betrayal on his face as he processed that no one had any intention of going after Hal. Faces across the room stared at him. I heard hushed whispers behind me. A few partygoers held back laughter.

The party changed after that. Freddy wouldn't go home; he made rounds of the room so he could tell everyone how unfair Hal was to him.

"In all my years of boxing," he said to anyone who would listen, "I've never seen that kind of disrespect."

As he went from group to group, his voice grew louder. I saw circles of people check over their shoulders for him periodically, turning back quickly so as to not make eye contact. More than one group stood shoulder to shoulder to prevent Freddy from seeing an opening and joining them. An entire table vacated to stand at the bar so Freddy couldn't take the one empty seat.

I searched for Augustan, but he had left the room. I imagined him in a cramped phone booth somewhere, making frantic calls. Before I realized it, Freddy was at my side—I'd made the fatal mistake of standing unaccompanied.

"In all my years of boxing," he said again, "I've never seen that kind of disrespect."

There was an intensity to Freddy that I'd sensed before, but I had never felt it at this amplitude. As I stood next to him, I could feel the hairs on my arms stand on edge. The smile on his face was strange—not his usual signature grin; there was something more sinister in the way his lips were pressed together and his mouth upturned.

I was once bitten by a dog. It's the reason I avoid them to this day. The dog belonged to a neighbor; it went after me one morning when I was on my way to school. We lived on the top floor of our building, and as I went down the stairs, I saw that the neighbor's door had been left open. No sooner had I glanced inside than the dog came barreling out at me. It latched onto my scrawny arm, leaving gashes where there was no excess flesh to be found. Its owner ran to the door, screaming at me. Shortly afterward, my father came down the stairs, also screaming at me about a visit from the physician that we couldn't afford. After the dog had been pulled away, it did not struggle against its owner's grasp, but stood still, heaving, ready. It could have broken free at any moment. I'll never forget how that dog breathed.

Freddy was breathing the same way.

"Did you see Hal hit me?" Freddy asked me.

I told him I had.

"It wasn't right."

I told him it wasn't.

"This is an awful party."

I told him it was. And then, without giving the idea a second thought, I told him I was leaving.

When I looked down at myself, my dress had wrinkled and the pink fabric puckered. I was certain my hair had become unruly in spite of all the pins and sprays that had gone into it. It was a relief to go home.

On my way out, I saw Nell standing with a glass of champagne. She looked outwardly calm, but I could see her eyes darting around the room, both in search of another group to join and to make certain that no one saw her alone.

When I approached her, she let out a heavy breath and looked down into her glass.

"You know he didn't even check where I was before he left with those people," she said. The way Nell annunciated "those people," it was clear she was still reeling from Margy's earlier theatrics, and Hal's spectacle had only made things worse. Charles was nowhere to be seen. Nell frowned. "He probably didn't even think about me."

"To be fair, the circumstances seemed extenuating."

Nell took a slow sip of her drink. When she looked at me, her eyes were cold. "If you ever wanted to know who Charles Landrieu is fooling around with, you got your answers tonight."

EIGHT

I had been given a temporary desk at the *Times*. It was small and relegated to a cramped corner. The first time I sat down at it, all the men in the room gave me suspicious looks. I didn't entirely blame them—they'd worked their whole careers to write for the paper and, as far as they were concerned, I'd just been in some films.

When I started acting, I always had this fear that I wasn't doing it right, or that I didn't look good enough, or sound good enough. The studio had assigned me an acting coach, who would prod at me if I didn't stand correctly. Twice a week, I put on exercise clothing—black tights, a leotard, very little left unexposed—and went through a series of stretches with an older man. I stood in a room with mirrored walls while he coached me. I remember the way he jabbed at my back, the sensation of his hand tight against my rib cage when he would instruct me on how to breathe. Sometimes his fingers dug too hard into the soft part of my abdomen. On set, the directors were usually less invasive, but the message was the same: After twenty years on this earth, I could be inept at the most basic human functions. I was not an outright failure, but I needed to be corrected. For years, I was corrected.

Writing the column was a different experience entirely: I was *good*. I hadn't a doubt that I was good. Over seven years of waiting hours on sets so I could say three lines, hanging at the fringes of every premiere and party, listening to Augustan's and Poppy's tirades—when I sat down at that little desk to put together the week's column, I knew what I was doing.

Readers liked me. After all that time when I didn't have fan letters, I now had piles of *Times* readers who wanted to respond to the column. They would tell me that they really liked Nell Parker in *The Sure Shot*, or that Rowan Leo deserved more dramatic roles, and they agreed that Jimmy Stewart had the kindest smile. The letters went through the secretary and, on occasion, the Film and Entertainment editor. One letter, I happened to notice, had a portion circled: "I find such delight in Miss Edie O'Dare's columns. If she'll be contributing more to the paper, I'm all ears—do tell!" There was a red-penciled note: "New column title?"

In the lobby of the *Times*, I saw the latest issue in which Freddy's name appeared between photographs of the British army and a column on the Polish occupation: ACTOR FREDDY CLARKE ON TRIAL.

I wondered if it made him feel proud to hold the same editorial importance as a global catastrophe.

In spite of pressure from my editor, I wasn't going back to the courthouse for the trial. Part of my reasoning was that I could avoid writing about—and potentially damaging—Sophie that way. What it really came down to, however, was the fact that I had worn a pair of borrowed heels to a party the night before. It was foolish of me to do; I knew the shoes didn't fit, but I didn't own a pair that matched my dress, which I had also borrowed. The result at the end of the night was an unsightly, painful blister on the arch of my right foot. Just the thought of standing for hours in a courthouse was excruciating.

I arranged for someone from the paper to give me any notes on the proceedings at the end of each day. They had plenty of reporters to cover and transcribe the hearings.

For my part, I planned to use everyone's focus on the trial to find another story—Margy Prescott's.

The first day of the trial, I got dressed, bandaged my foot, and put on a pair of sensible shoes so I could take a bottle of George

Wynette's favorite sherry down to his office in costuming. When I arrived, he was in the process of pinning an evening gown on Carla Longworth. His eyes were fixed in concentration as he knelt by the hem of her dress. A roll of measuring tape hung around his neck and a pincushion was wrapped around his left wrist. I waited for him to finish, knowing better than to interrupt.

"George," I said with a wide smile when he saw me. I looked at the dress on Carla as she walked to a private changing room. It was floor-length, with three tiers of dark blue lace on the skirt. "It looks gorgeous. You're a marvel."

He thanked me and eyed the bottle. Once Carla was out of earshot, he took the sherry and clasped my arm. "Let's walk," he said. I hid the slight limp from my damaged foot and walked with him. It was our habit to wander through the aisles of costumes while George told me about everyone who'd been wearing them.

Poppy might have bribed all the doctors in Hollywood, but I had George, who frequently proved just as useful.

According to George: Charles was still underweight; Hal's shoulders were too broad, and thank God they wouldn't have to fit him for a tuxedo again anytime soon; Nell remained tiny; Griffith was insecure about his chest and had refused to wear an unbuttoned shirt in a poolside scene the other day; Carla had ideal proportions; Victor Perez hadn't actually requested that his pants be tighter for a fencing scene, but one of George's boys saw to it that they were ("The women of America can thank us later"); Freddy was wearing a costume adapted from a period film that originally starred matinee idol Peter Reynolds as a French courtier, and it turned out Freddy's arms were considerably longer than Peter's; and last week Margy needed an evening gown taken in around the bodice and waist.

"Do you happen to know if Margy needed anything taken *out* before that?"

"You know she prefers her own dresses loose on top," he said. "She had a corset for *Road to Santa Fe* last summer. We had to loosen it a few times; she said she was having trouble breathing." *Santa Fe* was filmed directly after *Afterglow,* while Charles was working with Nell on *The Sure Shot* and Hal was on *Sunday Market.*

George kept a file for each actor and actress with their measurements in case he needed to draw up custom designs and they were unable to travel down to costuming five times a week. Though he liked to talk about the stars in general terms, he was very protective of his actual files. I usually took his word—but I wanted to see it with my own eyes this time. It would cost more than a bottle of sherry.

I followed him to his office, half of which was taken up by a drafting table. On it, there were sketches of dresses for an upcoming film with Carla, Jeanette, and Tilly Thatcher as society women each vying for an advantageous second marriage. The designs were equal parts beautiful and opulent—yards of lace and silk sculpted to the female form, skirts that trailed and pooled out behind them, extravagant hats that could dip over their faces.

George was the rare person in Hollywood who was wholly protected by his talents. Most of America didn't know his name, but they knew his dresses. Good costuming is often invisible—an audience doesn't register most of the clothing in a film, not until someone like Nell appears in a doorway, silhouetted by the flowing lines of a perfectly tailored gown. For all the stories about actors and actresses being replaced by the year, George had no equivalent. In his off-hours, he could do anything short of murder and the studio would turn a blind eye.

"How much time do you have left on your contract?" I asked him, still ogling the sketch in front of me.

George looked at me over his spectacles and hummed. "Less than a year," he said with a smile. He sat down at his table and began inspecting the sketch.

"And you want to go back east?" I asked. He nodded with

another little hum, this one higher than the last. "What if you could go to another studio?"

I explained: "I'd petition for you—fashion spreads, mentions in the paper, the whole thing. Your work is too stunning and too unappreciated here."

"You're trying to package me off to MGM," he said. "Me and Nell, right?"

I told him that Nell's Academy Award dress was beautiful—but that he could do better on his own.

"Nell has a premiere coming up, with Freddy. It will be his first premiere since this whole"—I considered my next words and gestured with my hand—"*thing*. Everyone in the papers and magazines will cover it. You could make something stunning for her, and I'd make sure everyone knew it."

As George considered, it occurred to me that I hadn't once entertained the idea of Freddy's not attending the premiere for *Stars Over Calcutta*. In my head, it was always a given that he'd carry on with his life after the trial.

"*Marie Antoinette* would be a dream," he said slowly. "Jasper has never been suited to costume dramas." Jasper Thompson was MGM's head designer at the time.

"Show me Margy's file and I'll do everything in my power. You'll be up to your neck in French silk. Build the tallest wig you want."

He unlocked a cabinet and took out Margy's file. Her measurements for last May were "Hips: 33, Waist: 24, Bust: 34." At the end of July, they changed to "Hips: 34, Waist: 28, Bust: 36." Her most recent measurements had her back at "Hips: 33, Waist: 24, Bust: 34."

Margy came from the world of beauty pageants; she knew better than most actresses how to keep a trim waist. There were only so many explanations for why she would need a costume loosened.

I gave George a kiss on the cheek before leaving.

. . .

I visited Augustan's office. He was finishing an irate phone call when I walked in. Upon seeing me in the doorframe, his face relaxed. He waved me in and instructed me to shut the door.

I sat in one of his plush chairs with my shoes off so I could rest my foot while he complained to me about the Academy Awards. In the midst of Freddy's trial, the whole thing had actually blown over pretty quickly. There was only one mention of the incident with Hal in the papers, and it was presented as a blind item: "A little birdie told us that fists were flying at an Academy Awards after-party."

Augustan sat at his desk with his feet perched up on it. He massaged his temples as he spoke to the ceiling. "Griffith is the only person at that table who didn't make an absolute fool of himself. If I could suspend the whole lot of them, I would. I'd have this studio comprised solely of Griffith Taylor and a series of mechanical puppets."

Because the after-party was a closed event, the studio didn't have much ground to suspend Hal. Margy was let off with a stern warning for her drunken commentary at the ceremony, mostly because her current project, *The Idealist,* was only a few weeks into production—too late to recast her, and too early to wrap up her scenes. They couldn't afford to have Margy out of work for three weeks. There was also the small matter that Margy was set to be a witness for the defense in Freddy's trial. It wasn't in the studio's interest to damage her credibility.

It all left Charles on his own, suspended from working as more and more headlines cropped up about him. Though he was far from the only person who found Freddy abhorrent, he was the one who bore the burden for publicly disliking him.

Before I left, Augustan gave me a press release on Freddy's trial.

"What am I supposed to do with this?" I asked, feigning ignorance. Augustan was perfectly aware that I didn't want to write about Freddy.

He told me I was being difficult. I told him trials weren't gossip.

"I'm going to have to disagree with you," he said. "It seems to me most trials are gossip, only with state-mandated consequences."

I made a point of leaving the press release in his office, which I knew would only anger him. I had not forgotten how gleefully he'd ordered me around during those last weeks at FWM. On the elevator down, I relished the thought of him fuming alone at his desk.

In the offices of the *Times*, I received the day's trial summary in a tidy little folder. I'd already heard bits and pieces when I went to and from Augustan's office—it was all anyone was talking about in the FWM commissary and around the hallways. It seemed that most of the day had been spent on a rehashing of the preliminary hearing.

Sophie testified again. From the photos taken as she entered the courthouse, she wasn't wearing pigtails and bobby socks this time around. Someone had swapped the schoolgirl dress for a dark one with a high neck and frills along the hem. Her face hadn't been made up—now she looked not only young but also slightly ill.

When she was questioned by Freddy's lawyer, Mr. Schiff, he wanted to know about her desire for fame. He pointed out that the trial put her name in the papers and wondered if that wasn't a back route to stardom—to which she claimed that she was "on her way" before the attack happened.

I knew she wouldn't be able to get any FWM publicists to verify that, though, unless they wanted to lose their jobs. The standards at FWM were very clear: With rare exceptions, actors and actresses worked for the studio for one year before they could be offered a contract. Sophie was just shy of nine months with the studio. There was no way to confirm that she would have been offered a contract and not a chance that any FWM publicist would speculate on it. That was the kind of hold Augustan had on his team. With the trial, I wouldn't have been surprised if he coached them on every word, right down to the syllables.

Freddy's lawyer also asked Sophie if she'd had any intimate partners before Freddy, even though she had already testified that she hadn't. He asked her if she had any sweethearts.

"There are plenty of boys who are sweet on me, but, no, I don't think of any of them as sweethearts," she said, according to one of the court reporters.

As far as I was concerned, she wasn't committing perjury for not thinking of Warren Bell as a sweetheart.

When I went to sleep that night, I tried to convince myself that I had protected her. Because of me, she had the opportunity to tell her story before anyone else could do it for her. I could only imagine what the headlines would have looked like if I'd published the story of her and Warren's courtship—how eager the public would have been to call her a liar or a hussy. Though the honest truth was that they already had.

I couldn't stop the echo of what I'd said to George earlier that day: Freddy would be at his premiere in a few months. I didn't even hesitate to say it. He would be photographed, celebrated, free to do as he pleased. It was inevitable.

George's measurements for Margy were proof enough for me, but I wanted to hear from someone in the *Afterglow* trio. Of the three, Charles was the obvious choice. I found Margy too temperamental, and I suspected if I asked Hal about it, he'd only stand there and make wisecracks at me. Charles, however, had been entertaining my queries for a long time now. I felt certain he would talk.

When I called Charles to see if I could speak to him in person, I didn't think he would invite me to his ranch. I had assumed he was bored, but I didn't consider that he might be lonely until he offered to have me over.

I drove up toward San Fernando until I hit the turn for Charles's ranch. A mile in and I saw a few donkeys and horses, then the ranch house.

Charles didn't have any house staff, but he did have a groundskeeper, who told me when I drove up that Charles was with his horses. I had prepared for this to be the case and worn my worst shoes, an old pair of brogues that I was confident were originally made for young boys. My slight limp from the incident with my heels hadn't gone away, but the thick socks and flat shoes helped. I'd have clung to the walls for shame if I'd been anywhere else. But I suspected neither Charles nor the small herd of donkeys outside his house would be especially concerned with my outfit.

I found Charles sitting on a stool in an open barn. He was holding a horse by the hoof and using a tool to scrape dirt off it. A large black dog with wiry hair paced around him. I recognized the dog from Charles's film *Georgia Summers*. It had also made guest appearances in *Bait and Tackle*, *You're the One*, and *Barreled Over*. The ranch, I assumed, was the dog's retirement home.

"I forget you actually know how to do these things," I said, walking over to him and the horse. The dog began trotting toward me, its tail wagging, but Charles called it back to him with a whistle.

"Sometimes I think about how much I would pay to see Nell attempt to saddle a horse," he said, looking up.

"Good thing it's not her job to do that," I said. "It's not yours, either."

He let the horse go, and its hoof hit the ground with a satisfying clack.

"I don't have any other jobs to do," he said. "It's this or drinking 'til I can't see straight."

"Surely you have *someone* to keep you company."

"They all have jobs," he said.

"I can think of one person who doesn't." I raised my eyebrows. "Very wealthy, very French. Perhaps you know her?"

He laughed and shook his head before leading the horse back into its stall. Based on what he was wearing, he might as well have been in costume—his shirt was stained with dirt, as were his trousers. A blue bandanna was tucked into his back pocket; he pulled it out to wipe the sweat from his brow.

"Ines told me you saw her that night," he called over from the stall. "Thought it was very funny. She tried to get me over to le Château Marquis for dinner but I'm not about to have you and yours writing that I've left Nell to abscond with an heiress." He paused before shutting the door behind him. "Though I suppose Nell might actually enjoy that. That sort of thing gets your readers riled up, right?"

"Oh certainly," I said with a smile. "Something like that? It would be the scandal of the decade."

I went with him into the house, where a pitcher of iced tea was waiting on the kitchen countertop. The dog followed close behind and settled itself on a plush pillow by the door. His kitchen was open, with a clear view into the living room. Charles's ranch was minimally decorated. What furniture there was inside, I felt certain had been chosen by someone else to fit the idea of what a young Hollywood actor would want in his house. The styling was all very modern, with clean lines and simple shapes. When the ranch had been photographed for *Life* a few months earlier, it was staged with western blankets—a striped Pendleton was still draped over the couch—and Catholic crosses, none of which remained. So much for Charles Landrieu feeling a profound connection to his Catholic roots in Louisiana.

I glanced around as Charles busied himself in the kitchen. He didn't keep many photographs around—I've known plenty of stars who frame their film posters and even some of their glamour shots. Charles mostly had candid photos from different shoots. Because he usually worked on location, the pictures ranged from Arizona to Wyoming, featured his costars caught off guard, laughing and talking with the crew. I found pictures of both Nell and Margy in period costume with anachronistic details like sunglasses or a pair of galoshes under their gowns.

There was only one picture that Charles was actually in. It

was a small framed black-and-white photograph on a bookshelf facing the kitchen. He and Hal were in full cowboy attire for *After-glow*, properly dirtied up from whatever havoc they were supposed to be wreaking on that day's shoot. They both had scratches and bruises painted on their faces and arms, but they were sitting calmly—Hal was reading a newspaper with a pair of wire-rimmed glasses perched on his nose and Charles was drinking out of a tin mug. Hal appeared quietly absorbed in the paper, while Charles conspiratorially leaned his elbow against the armrest of Hal's chair. Charles rested his chin on his hand, about to speak to Hal. Only on closer inspection would anyone see that Hal's eyes were shifted to Charles, the way Charles's hand was gesturing to the camera with his mug, how they both were smiling.

"I know what happened on the *Afterglow* shoot," I said after he poured a glass of iced tea for me and we'd made a round of polite conversation.

Charles turned away. He opened a cabinet as if to get something out of it, but when he turned back around, he was empty-handed. He hesitated a moment before sitting down on a stool at the kitchen counter.

He put a hand over his mouth and stared at the empty space on the counter. When he looked back up, the corners of his mouth were upturned and he looked like he was about to start laughing. He finally spoke, his voice clear. "I'm not going to act like I know what that's supposed to mean."

I leaned against the wall, putting my weight on my good foot. "You know, I actually like you, Charles. As a person, I mean. I think we understand each other. Now, I don't like Margy nearly as much, but I'm giving you a chance to tell me what happened before I print it."

I watched him closely as he processed what I was saying. The man was not a strong improviser—he'd confessed as much to me after his debacle at the charity event a week earlier. Actors usually have one feature they rely on when they're performing. For

Charles, it was his dark, expressive eyebrows. Which proved useful, given that most of his roles required very little speech. His brow was drawn in tightly when I first spoke, then rose when I mentioned Margy.

"I have no idea what you're talking about," he said, his voice getting slightly louder.

I'd seen a lot of actors play the idiot with me before, but this was the first time Charles had done it. He wasn't especially convincing. But whatever he lacked in conviction, he more than made up for in intimidation. He sat with his elbows on the counter, squared up to broaden his shoulders. He didn't stand or even shift toward me; everything in his posture signaled a brute defensiveness.

I told him to call if he changed his mind.

As I drove away, he was walking one of the horses by a lead around an enclosed ring. It was an older one, marked by white hair around its eyes and muzzle. Charles was slow and careful as he walked with it. His dog trotted next to him, keeping close to his heels. I could imagine it enjoyed the outdoors after a life spent on studio lots.

We like to say that Clark Gable was a hunting aficionado, or Tilly Thatcher really did know how to fish. And I'm sure there was truth to those statements. But Charles was the only one I ever saw play his part off the clock. For whatever reason, it made my heart break for him.

In the FWM commissary, people were talking. The mood throughout the studio was somber; no one was certain whom they could speak to or what they could say, for fear of exposing themselves on the opposing side of one of their peers.

While waiting for Seb, I took a seat at one of the tables and drank a cup of tea. I feigned engrossment in a newspaper as people passed by me. Every voice in the large room was hushed, creating an otherworldly hum through the space.

"As if anyone's going to convict Freddy Clarke."

"They're putting Margy on the stand for him. One day she's spitting on him, the next she'll be swearing on a Bible that he's innocent."

"They asked Landrieu to testify and he told them to go to hell."

Freddy had been pulled off his shoot. Production was planned so all of Freddy's scenes would be filmed up front, in the event that he had to go to trial. If I went to the lot now, I would find only the film's villains and secondary players.

Seb looked pale. Both of us always did—with our Irish complexions, we were freckled all over as children—but we usually had a pink tint. When he sat down across from me, his skin was sickly.

"What, are you now living in a windowless room?" I asked him.

His meal was a cigarette and a black coffee. He was not amused by my jesting. "I've been trying to avoid going between the lots. If you haven't noticed, things are a little tense around here." His eyes shifted around the room.

"Can't imagine why," I mused, hoping to get a laugh out of him.

He shook his head. "It's unsettling. None of them can say *anything.*"

I explained to him that was how it worked. You go under contract, you say what they tell you to say.

"All the time?"

All the time. Early on in my contract, there'd been a scandal with an actor in a car crash. I'd been at the premiere he left before he barreled off a road at two in the morning with a woman who wasn't his wife. If reporters asked us about it, every one of us had been coached to say, "Geoff Whitcomb is an honest man who works very hard. I wish him a speedy recovery." We had to say it even after the woman he was with was pronounced dead.

"How do you bear it?" Seb asked.

I stared into my cup of tea and shook my head. "I don't work here anymore, remember? Augustan can send me all the statements he wants; I don't have to use them. I could toss every one of them into the trash."

"If that's true, then why aren't you writing an exposé about the terrors of Freddy Clarke?"

Even if he wouldn't admit it, Sebastian knew perfectly well that no one would print it. It was one of his most irritating traits—the man loved to moralize. Growing up, he was never the one who had to lie to our sisters' teachers about why they were missing school, or tell the neighbors that our mother was just out on an errand and that of course she'd never leave four children in the care of two teenagers for days at a time. We told our sisters the truth—we were poor; that was it—but Seb always wanted to know why we couldn't do the same for everyone else. He liked to tell me the world would never change if we weren't honest. I, for one, wasn't aware that we were trying to change the world when we were sixteen and fifteen years old, respectively. I was more concerned with not getting the lot of us sent away to child services.

"I doubt you'll believe me, but I'm trying to do some good here," I said. "If I get a column, then I'll say what I want."

"I hope you will," he said, though the flat tone of his voice betrayed how little confidence he had in me. He finished his coffee and went back up to the offices. I watched him walk away with his head down and his hands in his pockets. He stood out amid the crowds at FWM—his wrinkled linen suit, his lanky figure, his unruly red hair. I always felt responsible for putting him in this strange city, where he was so clearly misplaced. But that's how the two of us were: Anywhere we went, we'd always be a little misplaced. This way, I told myself, at least we could be misplaced together.

Ada Ridgeway and Dr. Balfour made their respective returns to the trial. This time around, the defense was ready for them. Ada, who had driven Sophie home that night, was accused of being a hard drinker with a vendetta against FWM Studios, where she had only been hired freelance. Dr. Balfour was discredited as a quack. It was heavily implied that Dr. Balfour performed illegal procedures on girls in "a similar predicament as Miss Melrose."

The mention of a "predicament" sparked an entire investigation into whether Sophie was pregnant. Dr. Balfour insisted that she was not and had never been, but the defense wanted a second opinion from a "more reputable" source.

After realizing that their request would prolong the trial—and that they had a film star who needed to go back to his job—Freddy's lawyers dropped it.

By my estimates, FWM Studios was losing a few thousand dollars for each day that Freddy was on trial.

The photos of Margy's appearance at the trial circulated. She was the only star called in, aside from Freddy himself. Someone had carefully dressed her down in a dark skirt suit with a sharp hat. She almost looked normal, if not for the impossibly beautiful lines of her face. In the picture used in all the papers, there was something haughty in her expression. She'd been shielded from the public since the Academy Awards—no more drunken outbursts, at least not where anyone could hear her.

When questioned by the defense about Brodbeck's party, Margy pled ignorance. As transcribed:

"Had you known Miss Melrose before that night?"

"We were acquaintances, but I didn't know her especially well."

"What made you decide to go to the party with her?"

"I was encouraged by the studio. And I know how difficult it is to start in this industry. I was hoping to be helpful."

"How would you characterize Miss Melrose's conduct that night?"

"I think she was in over her head. I don't think she knew how to act in that kind of place."

"Can you clarify what you mean by 'that kind of place'?"

"It's one thing to go to work on set and be given directions. But at a party like that, there isn't anyone telling you what to do. I think some folks just don't know what's appropriate."

"Miss Melrose among them?"

"Yes, like Miss Melrose."

"Did you see Miss Melrose after the alleged attack?"

"I did; I was swimming in the pool when she came back."

"Did she mention anything about having been attacked?"

"No, she said she had gone for a walk."

"Did you believe her?"

"I assumed she had gotten ill and taken some air."

"Do you believe Miss Melrose is lying about the attack?"

"Look, I was sixteen, too, not that long ago. It's easy to mis-construe these kinds of situations. A girl like Miss Melrose doesn't know about men like Mr. Clarke. At that age, you're used to boys, not men. I can't say what happened in that room. But I can imagine it's easy to overreact. I don't think Miss Melrose is a bad person and I don't think she means to defame Mr. Clarke— I do think it's possible she stretched the truth and put herself into this situation right now."

"Yes or no, do you believe Miss Melrose was attacked?"

"No, I don't believe she was."

When I went home each night, I sat on my couch and ate what-ever canned soup I had in the cupboard as I listened to the trial coverage on the radio. I could pick out every talking point that I was certain had been written by Augustan: "Mr. Clarke is a great actor because he understands the depths of human emotion. We are talking about a man who *cares*—about his career, his family, and the people he surrounds himself with."

I went over to my kitchen table and drafted a column about Margy's surprise elopement. In the background, the radio host was discussing Margy's "empathetic" testimony: "We've always known Mrs. Prescott is a good Christian, and today she showed us the very definition of grace."

I knew I couldn't directly state that she'd been pregnant out of wedlock, but there were plenty of ways to imply that kind of information.

As I wrote, the host went on a tangent about the importance of mentor figures like Margy in today's society. "Think if all girls had someone like Mrs. Prescott, the kinds of trouble that could be avoided!"

At that point, I stopped writing. If only he knew—some friend Margy was. She left Sophie alone and vulnerable at the party. Sophie was attacked and Margy testified that Sophie lied about the whole thing. If there was anyone there that night who had the power to turn the trial, it was Margy. All she had to do was describe how Sophie looked when she walked out of that garden, how everyone could tell that she was not okay, how we were all searching for an injury that we'd never be able to see.

While considering my phrasing, I settled on "Margy Prescott found herself in a predicament last spring after the filming of *Afterglow*."

After I wrote out a draft, I set the pages aside. I put a glass of water on top of them, as if they needed something to anchor them down. I told myself I would get a night's sleep before deciding whether to send them to my editor.

In spite of an *Inquirer* headline declaring BUNNY HOPS OUT OF CLARKE MARRIAGE, Bunny Clarke testified on her husband's behalf.

Bunny was usually seen in garish prints and heavy makeup to make her look older than her nineteen years, but someone had seen to her presentation that day. From the photographs, she looked equal parts approachable and pretty enough to hold the attention of a man like Freddy. Her hair was relaxed into soft curls and she wore a sensible dress in a solid tone. Her figure had filled out since becoming a mother—when she and Freddy were first married, Bunny was a wisp of a girl. I remember trying to get a quote from her after their wedding. I was hoping to sell Poppy a meaty paragraph or two—something I could get paid for—and ended up with ten dollars' worth of lines. I had asked if she was excited about the wedding, she said "Sure." I asked if she loved Freddy, she said "Sure." I asked if she thought Freddy would make a good husband, she said "Sure."

When asked by the defense about her marriage, Bunny said she was very happy. Freddy was a good husband and a dedicated father. The rest of it was predictable: Freddy loved his daughter, and Freddy was nothing short of gentlemanly when he courted Bunny, and she never once saw Freddy go astray from her.

"It's hard for him! Girls are throwing themselves at him all the time!"

But this is Freddy we're talking about and Freddy is an honest man. Bunny insisted that he wouldn't dare lay a hand on another woman.

I was at home, still staying off my wounded foot, when I received a call from Charles. His voice sounded rougher over the phone—I had to ask him to repeat himself twice before he switched accents completely.

"Look, I've got nothing better to do," he said. "What'll it take for you to tell me what you're writing about *Afterglow*?"

I told him that it wouldn't take a thing. I had always planned to run it by him; it was the whole reason I'd gone to his ranch.

In truth, I expected that he would deny everything—that there'd been any affair between either him and Margy or Hal and Margy, that Margy had been pregnant, that her elopement had been anything other than a love match. But I wasn't sure on which terms he'd deny it. I held the phone away from my face as I tried to level my breathing while running through the mental calculations of how he might react.

He said, "Tell me what you're going to say about Margy; you can leave me and anyone else out of it."

I steadied my voice: "It will be a little difficult to leave anyone else out."

"I trust you to try your best."

"Fine," I said. I paused and found myself fidgeting with the phone cord. "I heard a story from someone on the set of *Afterglow*, who said Margy might have had *a few* dalliances with *a few* different people. My source said she got in trouble after that and that's why she married Hal so quickly."

"Don't" was all he said to that.

I pulled the phone cord tightly around my fingers until my hand was shades of white and red. "Wouldn't you like to know who Margy was dallying with?"

"I really wouldn't," he said, his voice heavy. "You can't write that she got pregnant."

"And why not?" I pressed on.

"Let's say Margy was pregnant—where d'you suppose the baby went?"

I decided I could wait for him to answer his own question. My heart beat so loud that I was convinced Charles could hear it over the phone.

Finally, he said, "Write anything else, please. You can write that I'm about to run off with the Marquis family fortune, for all I care."

"Is that even true?" I asked.

"Does it matter?" he replied. "Go ahead, print it."

"You don't really mean that," I said, already envisioning a new headline.

"Sure I do. Scandal of the decade, right?" he said, and hung up the phone without saying good-bye.

When I put the phone down, I reflexively looked over at the drafted pages sitting on my table. Of all the reactions that Charles could have had, that was not one I was expecting. It was as if I'd threatened to set fire to his house and instead of grabbing water, he'd brought me a stick of dynamite.

Over a week into the trial, I saw an unexpected name on the list of witnesses: Warren Bell. My heart sank when I realized that he had been called by the defense.

Reading over the notes from his testimony, I understood why he hadn't warned me beforehand. They asked him to point out Sophie Melrose; he pointed out Sophie Melrose. They asked him if he had known her intimately; he said he'd known her intimately. They asked him if she had ever talked to him about becoming famous; he said all the time.

According to Warren, Sophie was only interested in making her own name in Hollywood. Their relationship began after she asked him about another actor on the set. She constantly requested that he tell her any gossip about the stars of FWM.

Warren claimed that Sophie dropped him as soon as Freddy made his advances. The last time they had talked, Sophie was cooking up a scheme that she swore would make her famous. Warren said he didn't want any part of it and she stormed off. That was the end of things between them.

After that, the papers had a new angle to write about Sophie Melrose.

Bret Young, in an op-ed: "Can any of us say that we're surprised? We all saw the truth on our film screens months ago. There's a scene in *The Sure Shot* where Miss Melrose visits Mr. Landrieu in jail—he's behind bars, asking for a cigarette. Let me tell you: The way that girl lights a cigarette? How about we agree that good midwestern girls don't know how to light up like *that*."

Or Alice Norton: "Girls of America: Value yourselves! You don't need to cheapen your self-image in pursuit of fame or money. Men will treat you just as well as you treat yourself. If you want to sell yourself away for mere pennies, do you think any man is going to offer you a dime?"

Hampton Gregory: "As many have suspected, Sophie Melrose's pigtails were deceptive. It seems that Miss Melrose's *worldly* knowledge far surpasses her sixteen years on this earth."

I sat on my floor with every major newspaper spread around me, the radio coverage playing, and my own proposed column on the coffee table in front of me. My foot was still bandaged because I had kept walking on it in heels to visit the *Times* office and it reblistered.

I knew better. I've had every bruise, blister, and rash a woman can get from years of fitting into tight costumes and wearing heels. For one of Gideon's films, years ago, I was required to wear a full eighteenth-century French rococo gown day in and day out for a month. I didn't have the heart to tell George that part of the boning of my corset had come apart and I was being punctured by it—I was worried he'd take offense, and he was such a dear friend. Because I didn't want to be a bother, every day when I took off that gown, I saw yellow-and-blue flesh under my left armpit. Sometimes it bled.

I always assured myself that I knew how to take care of the pain. It seems like such a simple thing—if a shoe hurts, you take it off. But then there's a part of me that always says the pain isn't so bad and perhaps it won't go on for that long. And in the moment, it usually isn't so bad. It's not until I'm looking at the thing hours later that I see what I've done.

I read over my proposed column for the next issue. Margy's "predicament" took up a subsection, right at the top. The rest was my usual prattling about premieres, parties, and whatever else the Augustans of Hollywood wanted me to point out.

I thought to myself, Perhaps Charles is in love with Margy, protecting her by offering up a bigger headline about himself and the Marquess. I told myself a story: There had been a coin toss that he had hoped to win and a baby that he thought was his. Everything came into focus—Margy's head against his shoulder when he danced with her at Brodbeck's, his covert meeting with Hal at the Palomar, his sadness when he came back from filming on location and told me he was reeling from being separated from "the love of his life." I knew he had been joking about Nell at the time, but that didn't mean there wasn't someone he genuinely missed.

I crossed out the section on Margy, but I kept the notes. I needed more time.

NINE

With less than a week left in the trial, a note appeared on my desk. It was attached to a clipping of Poppy's most recent column, which detailed "The Mistreatment of Mr. Clarke." Poppy reiterated that Freddy was happily married and the defamation of his character was unkind to his family. "What will he and his wife tell his daughter when she grows up? Why should we subject them to that humiliation? All of this because a young lady wanted some attention."

The note, written in my editor's red pencil: "You know the man; surely you can do better than this? Everyone's expecting it."

I knew I would get a note like this at some point—it only made sense that the paper would want to capitalize on having a writer with a personal connection to Freddy. Reading Poppy's column, I had no doubts that I could do better than that. The issue wasn't one of capability but of will. I had no interest in writing anything that was favorable to Freddy. It was a silent promise I had made to myself: I wouldn't harm Sophie. I knew that every major paper was running an op-ed on how foolish she was, that she had lied to become famous, that she was a ridiculous girl with too much time and money at her disposal. I wouldn't add to that.

I had made it so far with minimal involvement in the trial and had been hoping to keep it that way. There were only a few testimonies left, including those of Thomas Brodbeck and Freddy himself. Depending on how long the jury needed to deliberate, it could be over within the week.

Though I had promised myself that I wouldn't write about

Freddy, I took some liberties where I could. When discussing Baird deWitt in the column, I commented, "While Mr. deWitt might be frightful on the screen, in person, he's anything but! He's a gentle, kind man. It's funny how actors can sometimes be the opposite of their screen selves, isn't it?"

Two pages later, there was an advertisement for *Stars Over Calcutta* featuring Freddy Clarke, "The Hero We Need!"

The next day, Thomas Brodbeck begrudgingly took the stand for Freddy. As the head of Freddy's studio and the owner of the house where Sophie had been attacked, his involvement in the trial was unavoidable, no matter how important or busy he was.

When I went to the offices to collect the transcript of Brodbeck's testimony, the young man who was holding them for me gave me an odd look.

"Shouldn't you be testifying?" he asked. He was grinning, and not in a friendly way. The smile on his face was the same one men get before they hiss something obscene at a lady passing them on the street.

I tensed and shook my head. My voice was cold and indifferent when I replied. "If every person who'd been at the party testified, we'd have a months-long trial."

The man shrugged. "You're in it," he said, tapping the folder.

I snatched the folder from his hand and tried to walk away at a reasonable pace. Once I got into my car, I opened the folder and began skimming the text.

Two pages in, Brodbeck was asked if Sophie appeared inebriated that night. He stated that she'd been ill in the bathroom. "Miss Edith O'Dare attended to her, I believe. It was even in the papers that the girl had spilled her drink and made a fool of herself."

I knew, once again, that I was reading Augustan's words. Brodbeck had had little reason to pay attention to me that night, but Augustan did. He'd planted my name in the testimony.

. . .

When I called Augustan to ask him about it, he seemed to find the situation amusing.

"I thought that might get your attention," he said after admitting that he'd been alongside the team of lawyers coaching Brodbeck on his testimony.

"If you want something, there are plenty of other ways to get my attention," I said.

He ignored my grumblings. "Put Freddy in the column," he instructed me.

"I'm trying not to be involved," I replied.

"Well, now you're in the testimony. You're involved," he said. He spoke in a curt, disaffected tone. I suspected it was the same one he used to speak to his lesser Augustans.

I attempted to put my case a few different ways: There were reporters from the paper covering the trial; Poppy had already written about it; Freddy hardly needed anyone else to come to his aid.

"What Poppy did was useless," he said. "Need I remind you that you have a film coming out with him?"

And that was when I understood Augustan was angling for a marketing ploy. I remembered the look on his face when he found out the premiere for *The Sure Shot* was packed with spectators after Sophie's interview. He hadn't planned that, but he could plan for *Stars Over Calcutta*. It made no difference to him that he was using an assault trial for profit. Profits were profits and it would be easy: Freddy as the hero, redeemed amid a crisis.

"I have something else I'd like to write," I said. I waited for Augustan to respond. When he didn't, I simply said, "Thank you for your input." Then I hung up the phone, like it would burn me if I touched it a second longer.

Freddy hadn't yet said a word on the stand. He'd been present—wearing fake glasses and taking "notes" on a pad of paper, as he had in the preliminary hearing. Every day, a growing crowd appeared outside the courthouse to show support for him. Many of them brought signs with quotes from his most famous films.

Over a week into proceedings, it was finally time for Freddy to speak.

According to Freddy, Sophie had approached him at the party. He noted that she seemed very inebriated.

As transcribed by the court reporters: "Being a new father myself, I was worried for the girl."

So worried that he suggested she go upstairs.

"I had no intention of joining her, but she insisted I see that she was settled."

He swore that in the short amount of time he had spent with her, she incessantly reminded him that he was Freddy Clarke ("Trust me, I'm well aware who I am!") and kept asking if he would help her career. She had said that she wanted to be cast in a film with him more than anything in the world.

"By that point, I was so frightened for the girl's safety that I would have said anything. She wouldn't take care of herself, so I made some promises—I said if she went upstairs and had a glass of water, sure, I'd put in a good word for her.

"It came down to this: Did I want to see this girl both safe and far away from me, or did I want her to make a scene in front of everyone? I think anyone would choose the former."

The most important thing, though, was that Freddy didn't want anyone to take advantage of the young drunk girl. He didn't think that she would use his good nature against him like this.

"She's a sweet kid and I think she's gotten in a little over her head with this whole business."

When I glanced through the next day's papers, I saw that they all commended Freddy on his "calm demeanor." They said he conducted himself like a gentleman when anyone else would have been angry or frustrated. No one seemed to pay any mind to the fact that it was Freddy's job to please audiences and he'd been more than proficient at it for well over a decade.

I worked at home, my kitchen table overcrowded with papers, the typewriter, pages of notes. I was at a loss as to what to write. I made two lists: one detailing what I knew about Margy, one detailing what I knew about Charles.

I was angry at Margy—angry that she was willing to testify in public for a man she hated in private. She had her reasons: Charles had already been made an example of; he had spoken out against Freddy in public and doing so landed him with a suspension.

My position wasn't all that different from Margy's—I, too, had Augustan and FWM on my heels, asking for me to do a favor for Freddy. If I wanted to know whether I would've done the same thing as Margy, here was my chance.

I could be angry with Margy, write that she was pregnant and had rushed to the altar with Hal to cover it up. It would ruin her life.

Or I could write that Charles had been sneaking off with Ines behind his fiancée's back. It would be a scandal, but it might not ruin his life. He wasn't married, after all, and these things happened. The public had forgiven worse before—within the last year, Clark Gable had married Carole Lombard a mere three weeks after his divorce from his second wife.

If anyone was going to suffer the consequences of my slandering, it would most likely be Augustan, who'd have not one but two scandals to reckon with. That day, I really liked the thought of Augustan's life being difficult. I liked the thought that *I* could make Augustan's life difficult.

As I was reading the same page of column notes over and over again, taking in nothing new, my phone rang. It was Rooney Calhoun.

"It's Seb," he said. "He's in a bad way."

He gave me directions for a hospital downtown, and I hastily tucked all of my notes into a bag.

. . .

My hands shook as I drove over. There had been a hospital visit once before, when Seb was living in New York. I didn't learn about it until weeks after the fact, when a friend of his wrote to me, pleading for some form of intervention. That was when I began my campaign to move Seb to California.

I had told him he would have a job here. I thought it would be better than whatever contract copyediting he was supposedly doing back east. I could keep an eye on him. If he worked for the studio, I'd know that he was being paid and who he was with. I really thought I had done a good thing.

In the hospital, Sebastian was asleep on a white bed. His eyes were swollen. There was a trail of spit from his mouth to his pillow. He simultaneously looked both very young and very old, his skin so pale that it almost appeared translucent. My first impulse was to put a cold washcloth on his forehead and start praying the rosary, but then I remembered that I didn't own a rosary anymore.

A nurse explained that he had collapsed in his office. It appeared to be a combination of exhaustion and an empty stomach with a mixture of liquor and pills. It would be a few more hours until he would be in stable-enough condition to leave.

When I didn't move from my spot or say anything, the nurse gently took my arm and steered me to the doorway. She told me I was welcome to have a sandwich and a coffee downstairs.

In the hallway outside Sebastian's room, a group of nurses crowded around a small portable radio set. The trial coverage was playing.

I could hear the announcer: "Prosecution claims that Freddy Clarke was a known seducer of women, a 'Glamour Man' at large. They say that he made advances on a young woman, suspecting that she wouldn't tell anyone. There's no law that says she can't tell anyone—if anything, the law demands that she tell someone, according to the prosecution."

Sophie's lawyer had argued that the defense went out of their way to scandalize Sophie for "very normal adolescent behaviors." She had a sweetheart; she had a few drinks at a party—many young girls do, whether the world wants to acknowledge it or not.

The nurses made sounds of disapproval within their huddle.

"If my daughter *ever*—she would be sent to her grandparents in Idaho, no question. See how she likes that."

"You'd think these lawyers want girls to act out."

"Shame on them."

Rooney was sitting in the waiting room. His hat was on his lap and he kept tapping it. He looked half as bad as Sebastian did. I sat next to him and asked him how concerned I should be.

Rooney gave me a puzzled look. "I'm no psychoanalyst," he said. "I think it's just poor luck."

I had my doubts and assumed Rooney did, too. On subsequent hospital visits, Rooney and I would be listed as Seb's emergency contacts. Neither one of us was about to give voice to any doubts that day. Instead, we smiled awkwardly at each other. It was clear he wanted to be kind, so I let him be kind.

"If you need to go back to work," I began.

He looked at me and lowered his voice, with a furtive glance to the nurses by the radio set. "If I'm being honest, I'm not sure a hospital waiting room is much worse than FWM right now."

Though I didn't say as much, I felt the same.

He told me he'd keep me company for a few hours; he had asked the other FWM writers to cover for him in case anyone upstairs asked questions. If I'd been him, I wouldn't have wanted to go back to that windowless room, either.

Seb was discharged that afternoon on the condition that he would be housed with someone who could watch over him. Rooney lived in a single room across town, and I doubted he had much more than a bed and a card table in it. So I found myself driving back to my home with my brother half asleep in the passenger seat. He murmured nonsense while looking out the window. Something about the deserts being on fire and our mother crying.

I made up the guest room, clearing the bed and floors of my evening gowns and dress suits. I'd never dealt with someone in recovery and I wasn't sure what to give him, so I left a glass of milk and a plate of biscuits. It was still more than I'd ever been able to offer him when we lived at our parents' apartment.

"Sure you don't want to read me a story before bed?" he asked as I was leaving. It was the closest he had come to a full sentence in hours.

I told him that he was welcome to read any of the ten copies of his own novel that I had stacked under the bedside table. There were also three boxes in the closet—I'd bought out the stock at every bookstore in Los Angeles when it was released.

He laughed, his head rolling to one of the pillows. "You never told me whether you liked it."

I assured him that I did. It was a slim novel about a night clerk in a seedy hotel. Ash Copeland—the character whose name I stole all those months ago—spends the novel imagining the lives of the hotel's short- and long-term inhabitants.

"Even the Catholic bits?" he asked. The novel, of course, ended with Ash Copeland going to Sunday Mass. He sees one of the women from the hotel, who he presumes to be a prostitute, in solemn prayer at the altar.

"Could've done without those, but I don't blame you," I said. I was about to say more, but when I looked at Seb, he had fallen asleep.

While Seb slept, I went downstairs and wrote out a list of the worst things that could happen if I published what I knew about Charles and Ines. The Marquess was already the source of constant speculation, so I imagined it would have little impact on her. Charles, though, would be jeopardized. No matter the outcome, Augustan would be furious with me.

The reality of a life in Hollywood without Augustan was unsavory—I would have to show up to parties alone, forever too early or too late, and keep my most spiteful thoughts to myself. I would no longer have someone to ask for a second opinion and expect any kind of an honest answer. So much of my time was spent calibrating and recalibrating everyone's responses to sort through their personal agendas. Which isn't to say that Augustan never had an agenda, just that he was always open about it. For better or for worse, we understood each other.

Seb wandered into my kitchen a little after midnight. He saw me at the table and wanted to know what I was doing.

"My job," I told him.

He squinted at me before opening the fridge and pulling out assorted ingredients for a sandwich.

"You know," I said, looking over my notes, "I envy you."

Seb began arranging ham and cheese on a slice of bread and frowned. "Should I remind you that I've only just been released from a hospital for self-inflicted damage?"

I waved his comment off. "You get to invent your own truths. I have to reckon with the messy truths given to me."

He finished making his sandwich and sat across from me. He propped his chin on his hand and said, "I don't think you understand how writing fiction works." He then sat up and took a large bite.

"What I'm saying is that I'm trying to write about real people with real consequences."

With his mouth half full, he told me that he once wrote a character based on our aunt Midge for a short story in *The New Yorker*. "And now she won't send me money on my birthday."

"Aunt Midge has *never* sent me anything on my birthday," I told him. "Could you allow me five minutes of self-pity?"

We sat in silence while he finished his sandwich. After he put his plate in the sink, he didn't immediately go back upstairs. He stood in the doorframe, his arms crossed, and looked at me. I was a pitiful sight, but then again, so was he.

"Your five minutes is up. I know you like to say we were disowned and all of that," he began, "but the girls really do miss you. They told me they sometimes sneak out to see your films. *Funny Weather* is Em and Jillian's favorite, but Maeve and Kate prefer *A Marvelous Sight.* Soon enough, they'll be reading your column, too."

Just the sound of our sisters' names made my throat tighten. For a year or so after I was put under contract, I tried to send checks back home. Every one of them was returned to me unopened. My mother had gone through the trouble of placing them in another envelope, writing out my name, with no return address, no letter inside. More than anything, I was hurt by the idea that my mother would waste precious money on postage just to spite me.

If I could have gotten my sisters out, I would have. Instead, I got Seb. For all I cared, he could spend the rest of his days sleeping on the twin bed in my guest room—at least I would know that he was being sheltered and fed. I had kept him afloat for this long.

"I just wonder," Seb said slowly, "if your life back there was more salvageable than you think."

"I admire your optimism," I replied, looking at the pages on the table in front of me, "but there aren't enough Hail Marys in the world to make me an O'Shaughnessy again."

He smiled weakly. "Pray for us sinners," he said.

"You can do enough of that for the both of us," I replied.

"The sinning or the praying?"

"Well," I said slowly, "the prayers get a bit dull without some sinning, don't they?"

After Seb went back to his room, I made a pot of coffee and stayed up the rest of the night. I wrote more lists and threw them out. I fell asleep on my living room couch and didn't stir until I heard

Seb rattling drawers and cabinets in the kitchen, unable to find the coffee.

Given the low-grade disdain I received from the *Times* reporters, I had hoped to keep my interactions with the Film and Entertainment editor as minimal as possible. But my fretful night made it clear that this wasn't a decision I was going to make on my own. I had no one else at the paper to consult with. The department reporters would sooner die than speak with me as a colleague.

When I went into the editor's office, he was marking up a page. Without looking up, he asked if I had a column on Freddy.

"It's a bit more complicated than that," I explained as I sat down.

"How?" he asked. He put down his pencil and looked at me. He was a sturdy man in his mid-fifties—not usually angry, in spite of appearances, just very focused.

"I have something on Charles Landrieu," I said, and he grunted a word sounding like *good*. Talk of the rivalry between Charles and Freddy was still circulating. I fidgeted in my chair. "The thing is, I could lose FWM Studios over this."

"Why do I need to know that?"

"I haven't published anything like this before," I said. "If I'm putting my name on it, I want to know that I have the paper's support in case FWM retaliates." As I spoke, I thought of Dolores Whitmore, wherever she was, and her failed column.

"You pull in numbers, you can have support and any other goddamn thing you want," he said, waving me out of his office.

I went back home, where I could keep an eye on Sebastian and my colleagues couldn't keep an eye on me. While I sat back at the kitchen table with my notes and typewriter, Seb was asleep on my couch. The doctors had said to keep him away from any harmful substances, but I turned a blind eye to the glass of scotch on the floor next to him. He was too tired to drink it, so what did I care.

I thought about my conversation with Charles at the Academy

Awards after-party. How he knew hunger when he saw it. When I looked over at Seb, there was a definitive meagerness to him. He hid it well most of the time, but while he slept, I could see how bony his arms and shoulders were, the way his red hair had prematurely thinned, the sickly pallor of his face. I couldn't deny that my body was just as scrawny as his—hunger had shaped both of us.

Perhaps Charles had been telling me the truth that night. That he didn't know how he got here and he didn't trust anything to last.

The man had survived jumping off trains, falling from horses, countless duels. On-screen, he had been shot, knifed, strangled, drowned, and once, while playing a matador, he was stabbed by a bull. Offscreen, he survived Augustan and Thomas Brodbeck, a name change, speech lessons, hours of costumes and makeup, and his colleagues. He'd survived a global economic collapse and a childhood in the Catholic Church.

Surely he could survive Edie O'Dare.

The next day I submitted a column with the subheader "Robin Hood and Zorro." In it, I avoided praising Freddy by directing everyone's attention to the people who opposed him—namely, Charles Landrieu.

If Augustan wanted a marketing ploy, I realized I could easily give him one: Here was Charles, the Zorro of FWM Studios, attempting to dole out justice on his own terms. At the very top of the column, I wrote, "Have we all heard the tales about El Zorro? Like many of our readers, I've always loved stories of the masked hero who challenges authority. Since being cast in the upcoming film *The Mark of Zorro*, Charles Landrieu has proven himself FWM's very own vigilante folk hero. His target? Why, Freddy Clarke, of course."

From there, I detailed Charles's fights with Freddy, his offhand remarks, his refusal to show support during the trial. I painted him as a misguided masked bandit. "So what should we make of the fact that Mr. Landrieu was recently seen escaping to dark corners of the Trocadero with FWM's most famous heiress, Ines Marquis? Perhaps he's found a new pocket to pilfer."

The column concluded: "Does FWM have enough space for both Robin Hood *and* Zorro? I suspect we'll find out soon, dear readers."

When I handed in the completed column, my editor raised his eyebrows. I thought he was going to accuse me of being another Dolores Whitmore. I assured him Charles had told me everything willingly. If he wanted to call him up, Charles would confirm every word.

As I left the building, I had the embarrassing impulse to cry—as if someone had done me an unkindness. I drove home too quickly, perhaps thinking I could outpace the tears. When Seb asked me what was the matter, I insisted it was nothing.

The issue made numbers. A day after it ran, I received a call from my editor offering me the column, which would be renamed "Do Tell." I thanked him and asked if I could take the weekend off. I told him I would be visiting friends up the coast.

In reality, I was sneaking into theaters to watch double features with my degenerate brother. We consumed popcorn until our teeth began to hurt and watched every film available within a five-mile radius, from MGM to Columbia to Paramount to FWM. I didn't bother with makeup and tied a scarf over my unwashed hair. With each feature, Seb asked me to give him the real story on every actor and actress; I happily obliged. Most of the theaters were empty, so we talked and laughed our way through every film. We sat in the dark; for the time being, we were both nobodies.

In one of the theaters, I asked Seb if anyone at FWM was wondering where he'd gone. He hadn't been following the news and made a deliberate choice not to read the papers or listen to the radio. I had disconnected my phone line for the weekend.

He told me that Rooney was doing his edits for him—everyone

was too caught up in Freddy's business to notice that he wasn't there.

"Who knows," he said as we waited for the next film to start up. "Maybe I'll stay out of there. Write another book."

I went back into the office after hours. Before I left, I had lied and told Seb I forgot something at my desk. In the newsroom, there were a few lingering reporters. A radio played the news, with a passing mention of the trial, but there was little to report because the jury was in deliberations. It was suspected that there was one holdout on the jury.

On my desk there was a large stack of letters thanking me for my support of Freddy. I had anticipated that I would receive some comments about Charles, but I was taken aback at the level of vitriol in those letters. "I always had my suspicions about that man and I suppose you did, too, Miss O'Dare. He's a wretched person and now everyone else knows it." That was one of the milder ones.

I had a message from Nell, asking me to contact her as soon as I was able. When I phoned the villa, I heard a rough voice. I was put off by the sound of an older Nell Parker before realizing it was her mother.

"Put Nell on; this is Edie O'Dare," I said. I listened to shuffling and the sound of Nell's mother calling for her.

"It's taken you long enough," came Nell's breathy voice. "Here I was certain that you'd want the exclusive interview about my philandering fiancé."

"Perhaps we should give him a few weeks to recover," I said.

I heard Nell's laugh at the other end. "Edie, he's not going to *recover*. It's all anyone's talking about here."

She obliged when I asked her what she'd heard around FWM—Charles's suspension had already been extended and no one knew when he'd make his return to the studio. Augustan was furious. Everyone assumed he'd ordered both Charles and Ines to stay in their respective homes until he could come up with a strategy.

For her part, Nell was ready to deliver the final blow to

Charles's career. When the actress Sally Lockwood's beau was found cavorting with another woman last year, she garnered so much sympathy that she rose to the top of the charts and landed three successive roles as a domineering leading lady.

I told Nell I was taking some time until the trial ended but that I'd be in touch.

When I went back to my house, Seb was gone. There was a copy of the paper with my column in it and a note in his handwriting: "I don't know why I expected better of you, but I really did.—S"

I called Rooney to see if Seb had gone to his place.

"The kid's fine" was all he would tell me.

During this time, the jury had been deliberating. According to the court reporters, the first round came out 10–2, not guilty. The two holdouts were men. Of the six women on the jury, every one of them voted for Freddy's innocence.

I thought that as long as I'd seen where this whole thing began, I had an obligation to see how it ended. I got one of the boys in the office to obtain a press pass for me so I could go to the trial the next morning.

It was chaos outside of the courthouse. The crowd I had seen on the day of the preliminary hearing had tripled in size. There was one group of women all wearing sashes that proclaimed them "Freddy's Army." Why he should need an army, I wasn't sure—it wasn't as though there was anyone walking around with "Sophie's Army" sashes.

Poppy was there, wearing a pair of sunglasses as a disguise. We hadn't spoken since our last lunch. I'd stolen some of her sources, but they weren't really her sources in the first place. I was the one who had been contacting them all that time in her stead. The tone of her column changed—she had begun pontificating more. She started to read as the schoolmistress who wanted students to stop smoking cigarettes behind the gymnasium.

I caught her eye as I went through the crowd to the court-house doors and gave her a slow, awkward wave. She reciprocated with one of her own.

"You've certainly done it now, haven't you?" she said to me over the sound of the crowd.

There were questions I wanted to ask her, but instead I just said, "They gave me the column."

She looked at the crowd surrounding us, all the women yelling and chanting Freddy's name. Her mouth was smiling, but I could see how her painted brow furrowed above her sunglasses. "Good luck" was all she said before disappearing.

When I got inside the courthouse, there was a different kind of chaos. People were trying to get on with other trials and go about their jobs while a rogue film star was wandering around waiting for the final verdict. Every corner I turned, there was a group of people muttering about Freddy.

"He was just in this hallway," a young man said. "The real Robin Hood!"

I doubted that anyone was searching for Sophie, or that she would be wandering the halls herself. I could only hope that she had a safe, quiet room to sit in and someone who could sit with her. It ought to have been me. I could have carried on as Ash Copeland, writing her story for the *Inquirer*. There had to be people out there who understood.

It didn't take me very long to find Freddy. He paced the hallways, chain-smoking and telling anyone who would listen that he would be vindicated.

When he saw me, I couldn't read if the expression on his face was aggression or excitement. But then he grabbed my shoulder and called out "My champion!" to the entire hallway. He clasped my hand tightly; there was something manic in his smile as he looked me in the eye.

"That article! I ought to have it framed," he said before return-ing to his rounds of the building.

In '38, Freddy played a city councilman who stands up against a corrupt businessman trying to shut down the local general store. In the final scene of the film, he dons a suit and glasses to make an impassioned speech about the value of small towns. When he spoke to me that day, he used that same voice. I wasn't sure that he didn't have on the exact same pair of glasses, too.

As I left the courthouse, I saw a blond woman smoking alone by the doors. It wasn't difficult to recognize Sophie's mother, though I'd only seen a flash of her in the car when Sophie last came by my house. I was prepared to leave her be, but she caught my eye and nodded at me.

She stopped me before I could properly introduce myself, said she knew perfectly well who I was. "And don't bother apologizing now."

I didn't respond. It went against all my impulses not to ask questions or offer commentary, but I was beginning to learn that sometimes it was best to let people fill their own silences. Mrs. Markham wasn't walking away from me—she had something to say; I only needed to give her the space to say it.

I watched as she put out her cigarette on a windowsill. The sunlight caught her face—she was older than I expected; I could see the fine lines around her eyes and mouth under her makeup. She looked out at the crowd as she spoke to me. "Did she ever tell you it was her father who let her come out here? Four children, Sophie is our only girl. Do you know what her brothers are like?"

I shook my head; I didn't even know Sophie had brothers. Mrs. Markham had a soft, if not slightly sardonic, smile as she spoke of Sophie's brothers. "One's just finished medical school, one's at Harvard Law, and the other's studying abroad in England."

She continued speaking to the window. "Sophie's father told all of them they could be whatever they wanted. And why shouldn't he believe that? *He* got to be whatever he wanted. He's the richest man in Ohio." The mockery was clear in her voice when she said "Ohio."

"So," she said, "why shouldn't his daughter get to be a Hollywood star?"

I paused, unsure if I should respond. Mrs. Markham looked away from the window and back at me. I felt terribly exposed; my voice caught in my throat.

"Would you believe me if I said she could have been?" I asked.

Mrs. Markham sighed, the sound coming from deep in her chest. "I hope you realize what a cruel thing that is to say."

I left her standing there by the window as the crowd outside began chanting Freddy's name. Her parting words were "Be well." In my many years writing gossip, I'd have people hurl every variety of insult to my face; sometimes they would scream, sometimes they'd hiss, but nothing ever struck me so hard as the way Sophie's mother uttered those two words.

I was back outside when the verdict was announced. A wave of cheers went through the crowd when a young man ran outside and yelled "Not guilty!" People hugged one another and began to chant famous lines from Freddy's films. I scrambled for the edge of the crowd as various women began reaching for me to share in their celebration. I shook their hands away and moved against the crowd, which was pushing closer to the courthouse steps.

One of Freddy's cronies—I think it was one of his regular stuntmen, though I could never tell any of them apart—found me in the crowd. He leaned close to my ear and told me there was going to be a party for Freddy.

"Freddy himself requested you go," he said. "You know, as a thank-you."

Before I had an opportunity to decline, I was swept in the crush of the crowd. There was a hand on my elbow and I was steered toward the street by Freddy's stunt double. A car with another of Freddy's doubles at the driver's seat was parked nearby.

When I explained to the man that I had my own car, he laughed and looked at the growing crowd of people. "I don't think you'll be able to get to it now, sweetheart. We'll give you a lift back after the party."

I didn't have a chance to protest—I was shuffled into the car with the two Freddy doubles, a young woman I'd never seen before, and a lesser Augustan.

Ten

The house belonged to John Hewlett, who worked as Freddy's personal secretary. Hewlett hadn't testified for Freddy—the rumor was that Freddy's legal team didn't want him anywhere near the trial. If anyone knew the full extent of Freddy's misdeeds, it was Hewlett.

When I walked into the house, I was greeted by a young woman in a tight-fitting blue dress. She wore a large blond wig that was barely pinned to her hair, and her face was heavily made up. As she led me through a small crowd of people to the backroom, she spoke loudly and her words were unnaturally slurred.

"Issa beautiful house," she said. "A lovely party, no?"

I nodded and wished I could've brought someone with me—Augustan would have known what to do, how to react. In my head, I went over the things I would say to him and what he might be muttering under his breath at any given moment. We probably would have talked ourselves out of this nightmarish party within five minutes of walking into the house.

The woman handed me a martini without asking if I wanted it.

"Issa a nice drink," she said. She looked over at a man who was tending the bar. "Was that good?" she asked him—her accent was now a hard midwestern one.

The man smiled and winked. "That was perfect, Miss Melrose," he said.

I looked at the woman again and it all made sense. The blue dress, stained with dirt because she had fallen in the gardens. The makeup, too heavy so she would look older. The accent, slurred so she would sound drunk.

On the other side of the room, there was another "Miss Melrose," but this one was wearing a schoolgirl's uniform—pigtails and saddle shoes, as Sophie did during the preliminary hearing. The pigtailed "Miss Melrose" was also serving drinks and showing the guests around.

There was yet another "Miss Melrose," this one wearing a high-necked frock similar to the one Sophie'd had on during the trial. The woman had a trail of inky mascara running from her eyes down her cheeks. I met her eyes and she smiled at me, a discordant amusement in the way the corners of her mouth turned up.

I placed my drink on a nearby table and began to walk toward a side door that I assumed would take me out of the house. I had my hand on the handle when the man tending bar called out to me with a sharp "Miss!" He wanted me to know that the party had only just begun.

"Our guest of honor isn't even here yet!" he said.

Slowly, I walked toward him. He happily introduced himself as John Hewlett. His face was tanned to the point of looking leathered and his dark hair was streaked with gray.

"Those girls are something," I said to him. The contempt in my voice was thinly veiled, but Hewlett didn't catch a thing.

He grinned and shook a tumbler. As he poured more martinis, he explained that he'd found the girls outside the courthouse that afternoon.

"They told me they'd been there every day of the trial! Can you believe it?"

I could believe it.

"Anyway, I got this idea on the spot. Had a friend in costuming at RKO pull the outfits and bring 'em over. Offered the gals ten bucks each to dress up and serve drinks. Funny, right?"

I told him it seemed like a very funny idea. He handed me another martini without my having asked for one. He instructed me: "Everyone's out back. Go join them." I eyed my paths to the doors out of the house, both of which were in view of Hewlett. I could only go to the backyard. Before I could say anything else, I felt his hand on my arm and he walked me to the back door before returning to the bar with a smile and a wink.

In the yard, there was a large dollhouse on the patio, which I realized had been modified to look like Thomas Brodbeck's estate. There were dolls positioned around the house, one of them wearing a blue dress, another wearing a makeshift tuxedo.

Partygoers convened around the dollhouse; every few moments someone would pick up one of the dolls and laugh at it. The rest of the people milled around the pool, all of them drinking from martini glasses.

I overheard one man telling his circle, "We were going to pay one of the girls to seduce Freddy tonight and then say she's sixteen. But . . ." he said, and then trailed off with a sigh, to which everyone nodded knowingly.

"It *would* be a bad idea, right?"

I told myself that if I waited until Freddy got there, the crowd would be too fixated on him to notice my departure. I could slip back into the house and leave before another Sophie offered me a martini.

Although I recognized many of the faces at the party, there wasn't anyone I considered myself friendly with, even in the precarious way I was "friends" with many film stars.

Freddy's two stunt doubles were standing by the pool. They had already gotten their drinks and settled in. For a moment I thought they might be dressed as Freddy, but I supposed there was no need when the real Freddy would be making his appearance shortly. I watched two lesser Augustans scheming in a corner. Freddy's most recent costar, Linda Ogden, was with another FWM actor, Casey Lowell, who mostly did B-list Westerns. Danny Prior, the man who replaced Charles after he was suspended, was also making the rounds. I overheard a few people congratulate him on what would be his first leading role. They also expressed their good riddance to Charles, with a few choice words for him.

The only person I was remotely familiar with was Rolf, who was skulking along the perimeters of the party, unaccompanied by his wife (a common trend for this crowd). He and Freddy were good friends—they were known to go on yachting trips with a select group of young women, mostly models, with the occasional actress mixed in. On that basis alone, I was not particularly interested in making conversation with him.

I pulled a pair of sunglasses from my handbag and observed the festivities from a place on the back patio, careful not to make contact with anyone, on the off chance that someone would want to interact with me. The yard was fenced in and a group of people blocked the only gate out. I abandoned my second undrunk martini—I felt nauseous enough already. I considered whether Freddy might arrive through the house or the gate, which one would be better to make an escape. I gravitated away from the patio, heading toward the gate.

There was a round of applause when Freddy arrived. He came through the house and loudly let everyone know that they didn't have to go through all this trouble for him. He put his fake glasses on and squinted out at the crowd, one hand over his brow. He was still wearing his suit from the courthouse.

"None of you look *too* suspicious," he said. He put his hand down. "But don't think I won't be checking identification and birth dates for the whole lot of you!"

To Freddy's delight, everyone laughed at this.

Freddy discarded his suit jacket and fake glasses, then went around the party, accepting hugs and congratulations. He lightly punched Hewlett on the arm when he recognized the different Sophies.

"You dirty rascal!" he yelled out to Hewlett before putting his arm around the Sophie in a blue dress.

Someone had gotten ahold of one of the "Freddy's Army" sashes and given it to Freddy, who proudly posed with it on. He lunged at one of the Sophies while wearing it and called out, "We shall never be defeated!" It was a tagline from a film he'd done two years earlier, in which he played an American Revolutionary during the Boston Tea Party.

Wearing his sash and carrying a bottle of champagne, Freddy took a seat next to the dollhouse. He let out a bark of a laugh when he noticed the little dolls in the house. He immediately picked up the Sophie doll. He gave it a good shake and made a high-pitched crying noise. He tossed it onto a little bed in the dollhouse.

He then clapped his hands to get the attention of everyone at the party. He sat back in his chair with one foot propped against his knee.

"What would you all say to some dinnertime theater?" he asked.

There were whoops and hollers from the crowd. The energy of their cries was different from those at the courthouse. Those women had been chanting because they were angry—they felt they had a right to their anger on behalf of Freddy. The people gathered at Hewlett's weren't angry. They wanted to ridicule. They had won and they wanted to parade their cruel victory.

Freddy nodded to one of the lesser Augustans, who brought over the Sophie dressed in court attire.

Freddy played Freddy, the lesser Augustans played the prosecution and the defense, and the Sophie with tears streaked down her face played Sophie, with supporting roles from the other two Sophies. Hewlett narrated and acted as the judge.

I watched the spectacle from the periphery of the crowd. I wanted to be as close to the exit as possible. As I watched, I drifted closer to the back gate, my hand hovering over the latch.

In the center of the yard, the mock trial began. While Freddy and the Sophie in the high-necked dress reenacted the trial, the Sophie in a blue dress dramatized the "incident" with one of the dolls.

When trial Sophie said that Freddy had attacked her, party Sophie made a show of the doll in a tuxedo attempting to smother her. She held the doll to her face and shook it around her cheek.

"Oh no, Mr. Clarke," she yelled before giving the audience a suggestive wink. She playfully hit the doll. "You stop that right now, Mr. Clarke!"

Trial Sophie mentioned that she'd had a little bit to drink that night, and party Sophie mimed drinking heavily and stumbling around.

Freddy was nearly in tears from laughing. When it came his time to "testify," he could barely get his words out.

"Mr. Judge," he said, looking at Hewlett, "I'm only a man, aren't I?"

He glanced at party Sophie, who was now provocatively lifting the skirt of her dress. Freddy's mock lawyer stood by the girl and gave a wide flourish of his hand.

"Your Honor," he said. "We present Exhibit A."

Hewlett nodded slowly. "I think that about settles it, no? What says the jury?" he asked, looking out at the crowd.

The members of the party began to chant "Not guilty" in unison. They grew louder and louder, until Hewlett sharply clapped his hands in lieu of a gavel.

"Court adjourned!" he called out.

The actors all took a bow, with Freddy accepting an extended round of applause.

I unlatched the gate so hastily that I almost fell when it opened. I nearly ran down the street, not slowing down until I could no longer hear the loud cheering from the yard. It wasn't until I stopped that I realized the situation I'd been placed in— it was a residential neighborhood, without a single pay phone in sight. I slowed down to a walk, worried about how out of place I must have looked. I was coated in sweat and there was at least one run in my stockings. The thought of knocking on someone's door and asking to use their phone occurred to me, but I was overly conscious of being alone.

Finally, I saw a young woman pushing a pram down the street. She took one look at me and asked if I was lost ("You just have that look right now"). I nodded, hoping that she wouldn't ask how I had gotten there or what I had been doing. A part of me felt like a criminal, as if I had just been looting through people's houses in broad daylight.

"I was looking for a pay phone to call a cab," I said. My mind began sifting through explanations to offer her, and I had to stop before I caught myself in a lie I couldn't substantiate.

She pointed to a house down the block and told me I was welcome to use her phone. As I walked along with her, I avoided making eye contact. I knew I ought to make small talk, compliment her baby, ask what her husband did for work. I couldn't do it; my heart was still racing and the sounds of the party echoed in my head.

After we'd gone into her house and I'd called for a cab, she insisted I wait inside with her.

"You look very familiar," she told me after she'd set me up with a glass of cold water and a seat in her living room.

"It's the red hair," I deflected. A small headshot of me had run with every column I'd published so far. The chances of my being recognized were fairly high and, that day, I really didn't want to be recognized. I could feel everything I'd seen at Hewlett's sitting in my stomach, noxious and vile. It would take only the slightest provocation for it to all come spilling out of me.

So instead, I asked the woman about herself. I learned that she had been married to her husband for just over two years, he worked in accounting, she'd been trained as a secretary, and her baby girl was about to turn nine months old.

"Are you from here?" I asked.

She shook her head. "Fort Collins, Colorado. I didn't think anyone was *from* here. I've never met anyone from Los Angeles, have you?"

I'd lived in the city for enough years to know that, of course, there were people from Los Angeles, no matter how much we all liked to forget that this place existed before it became Hollywood.

I nodded at her baby, who was asleep in her arms. "I've met her. She'll be from here someday."

Out of the corner of my eye, I'd been watching the window for my cab and saw it pull up in front of the house. I thanked the woman for her hospitality and made my exit. I spent the ride back to the courthouse thinking about that baby, the little girl from a city that no one was supposed to be from.

~2~

Eleven

I don't take full responsibility for everything that happened in the following months. There might have been a time earlier in my life when I would have scourged myself more in the retelling, but it's been over forty years now since that party at Brodbeck's. As far as my role in all of this is concerned, I've done my best to be faithful to the events leading up to Freddy's trial in March 1940.

I will say this for myself: A large part of what I do is tell America what they want to hear.

Freddy celebrated his acquittal at the *Stars Over Calcutta* premiere. He was joined by Nell, who garnered an equal amount of attention on account of an extravagant gown designed by George Wynette. Neither attended the premiere with a romantic counterpart.

I reluctantly went to the premiere at the insistence of the studio. I initially threw my invitation in the garbage, but when a mid-level FWM publicist called, I agreed to go. Augustan had been particularly cold toward me after the column on Charles, and I was hoping that my attendance might help me win back his favor. He tolerated my presence there, but it was nothing like our old days—there was no snide commentary or exchanging of glances between us.

When my name showed up on the screen that night, I was reminded of how Sophie had grabbed my arm during the premiere of *The Sure Shot*. The thrill of seeing yourself larger, more exaggerated, than you could ever imagine being. It was a ridiculous role for me, and not one I was especially proud to call my last for FWM. My purpose in the film was clear: I was there to make Nell's character seem both sensible and desirable. And it worked—for a moment, even I forgot myself and began thinking how lovely Nell looked next to Freddy; both of them were so gorgeous and so golden.

For all the film's flaws and all my embarrassment at being involved in it, I realized I would miss acting. I'd do a few guest appearances as myself in the coming years, but that was the last film I ever properly acted in.

Stars Over Calcutta went on to be one of FWM's biggest successes at the box office, with talks of Academy nominations for both Freddy and Nell. Critics discussed how the role could be Freddy's transition away from swashbucklers to more serious work. Between the film and the trial, Freddy had displayed his humanity and shown himself capable of depth far beyond swinging a sword around. After everything that had happened, we were now in the dawn of "A New Era for Freddy Clarke."

A few months later, *The Mark of Zorro* had a mediocre showing at the box office. FWM had no choice but to go through with its press rollout in spite of the public contempt for Charles following my column. The fervor eventually died down, but Charles's standing in Hollywood was not improving. He disappeared from the columns and his fan letters dwindled. In the end, numbers won out: The cost of producing *The Mark of Zorro* was too great for FWM to do a quiet release.

The reviews were positive, though they mostly focused on the beauty of the costuming and art direction. The phrase "a feast for the eyes" was used more than once.

I didn't attend the premiere, which was in San Diego, but I did see the film on opening weekend. I expected Charles to excel at being a masked bandit because I had watched him on set excelling at being a masked bandit. Though I had seen him in costume, I was surprised at how naturally he took to being the foppish Don

Diego. His hair was left to its natural curl and his eyelashes were darkened. He wore a ruffled jacket embroidered with flowers and waved a handkerchief around while declaring his distaste for fencing. He performed a dance number with Josette and I half expected him to break into song.

When it came to discussing Charles, the film critics seemed at a loss. They wrote that he was "theatrical," "humorous," and "too charming." Any other actor would have been honored with that feedback, but the critics used an undertone with Charles— Charles Landrieu, the film cowboy, wasn't meant to be *theatrical*; he was meant to be *gritty*. The sheen of authenticity that had made Charles a star in his Westerns had disappeared the moment he became Don Diego.

When Nell confirmed to the world that Charles was an unfaithful liar, she made every headline, including mine. I sat with her for an exclusive interview, in which she detailed her suspicions that Charles had his eye on Ines Marquis. She waited until *Zorro* had been given a generous run in the theaters, probably at the direction of someone from FWM. The engagement was broken— though I noticed that Nell kept the Cartier engagement ring the studio had bought for her.

Nell's fan letters tripled and then quadrupled, half of them detailing a different tale of infidelity across America. Every woman who felt she had ever been slighted by a man became a devoted fan of Nell Parker. They wrote that Nell exemplified dignity and grace while dealing with a grave injustice.

I started speculating in the column about which men in Hollywood were worthy of helping Nell heal her broken heart. She would never end up with any of them, but the American public didn't need to know that. Candidates included Cary Grant ("someone handsome and stable"), Griffith Taylor ("a nice young man who loves his mother"), and Baird deWitt ("Sure, he's older, but doesn't Miss Parker deserve a man with some self-knowledge?"). Those articles were some of the best things to happen to her career since she got her breakthrough cracking one-liners in *Sisters Perry* at the age of fifteen.

While I was running columns on Nell's romantic future, there was an overnight outrage over Bunny Clarke's filing for divorce. That outrage was quickly quelled by the knowledge that Freddy Clarke had fallen in love with Nell Parker while filming *Stars Over Calcutta*. According to them, they felt drawn to each other from the first day of the shoot but kept their feelings hidden—a fact that I corroborated at Nell's request. I obtained exclusive rights to their engagement announcement, which prompted twenty more newspapers across America to syndicate "Do Tell."

I was profiled for *Screenland*, with a headline proclaiming me THE MOST FEARED WOMAN IN HOLLYWOOD. I had to laugh at the accompanying photo. When I went in for the shoot, they styled me in a Chanel dress suit with a jaunty little hat. I was told ahead of time what the tone of the article was and that I should act accordingly, but after all those years of strict training from FWM, I wasn't someone who knew how to pose without smiling. When the article ran in the magazine with the photos, I thought I looked perfectly friendly. In the close-up, my head was turned over my shoulder, as if I had just been writing something salacious at my desk and someone called my name. My hair was cropped short, just below my jawline, and a few loose curls framed my face. My smirk gave the whole picture an air of mischievousness.

The profile detailed my history as an actress and very gently avoided the fact that I was not a success in my time. The writer claimed that I had "a greater calling beyond the screen." My work as an actress gave me a unique edge as a gossip columnist and I wasn't afraid to use it. My editor at the *Times* was delighted with the publicity.

From that point onward, I became Poppy's more vicious counterpart. Actors and actresses across studios were warned not to cross me. Charles was made an example of: "Offend Edie O'Dare and she'll make you the next Charles Landrieu."

No surprise when the role of Marie Antoinette opened up for Nell. MGM made the announcement for Nell shortly after she broke her engagement with Charles. I heard rumors that she was loaned out for three times her usual salary. The next day, the papers announced that George Wynette had been hired as the head costume designer for MGM—*Marie Antionette* would be his first major project.

I think that, of everything that happened, what sent Augustan over the edge was the loss of George Wynette to MGM. Charles had proved replaceable—there would never be a shortage of willing and able actors in Hollywood—but as a costume designer, George was a different story.

For the last decade, FWM had been sustaining itself largely on its costume and art departments. There were plenty of studios that used striking visuals to distract from shoddy scripts or overworked actors; FWM just happened to make that the cornerstone of its enterprise. The consequences turned out to be brutal. George couldn't take his entire staff with him, so FWM was able to keep some of his expertise through the two young men from Broadway who had studied with George. However, George's replacement, a designer from New York, wasn't nearly as talented, and it showed on the screen.

I visited Augustan's office shortly after George's departure. Our conversation that day was stilted and withholding.

"Are you well?" I asked him.

"Do I look well?" he retorted.

He didn't. His hair was thinning and his pale skin looked puckered. He looked at me with scorn—it was the kind of look he usually reserved for his actors and actresses when they threw fits on set or got into drunken brawls. I had never been on the receiving end of that look before.

He had every reason to be unwell. FWM Studios was now dependent on the success of Freddy and Nell, with supporting actors like Hal, Margy, and Carla to keep them afloat. And everyone's costumes looked cheap and ill-fitting. Their primary stockholder, the remaining *M* in FWM, was avoiding scandal after an onslaught of speculation about whether or not she had allowed one of the studio's lead actors to seduce her for fame. We both knew very well who in that room was responsible for the onslaught of speculation.

FWM began production of *Fifty Grand* in January 1941; it was the studio's first film of the year. Sebastian adapted the screenplay from the Hemingway story. Incidentally, it was the last one he completed for FWM Studios.

Freddy was cast as Jack Brennan, the up-and-coming all-American boxing champ. Charles played his opponent, known as Walcott in the story but changed to Lopez in the film. The role had been written for Victor Perez; however, Charles was swapped in a few days before shooting began—an executive decision from Thomas Brodbeck.

It had to have been the easiest marketing job anyone in FWM ever had. The ads in the magazines and on the posters across town all said "CLARKE VERSUS LANDRIEU." Only on second glance would anyone notice that the names "BRENNAN" and "LOPEZ" were below their real names.

The film left no doubts about whom the audience ought to be rooting for. Jack Brennan was a hard worker and devoted father. Roberto Lopez was a drunkard who verbally abused his wife. In the film, Brennan becomes tied up in some unsavory business fixing boxing matches. While Brennan battles with his morals, Lopez gets into bar fights and cheats on his wife.

Audiences were livid. They went to see the film in droves, many for repeat screenings. It became a popular activity for audience members to yell at the screen whenever Charles's character appeared.

At one point while the film was still in theaters, Charles had a glass bottle thrown at him as he was leaving one of the clubs. Though he was rarely seen going out prior to that, he became completely absent from the public eye afterward.

Charles still had time left in his contract, and the studio wasn't going to quit profiting off him as long as it had the opportunity. He was exiled to the film ranch an hour outside Los Angeles, where his days were spent putting on the same cowboy costume and saving the same two women or getting shot trying. After *Fifty Grand,* Charles made six Westerns, most of which are barely watchable.

Against the best efforts of a team of lawyers, Ines Marquis put her shares of FWM Studios up for auction, where they were bought in full from an investment firm in New York after a bidding war with an eccentric millionaire. The millionaire was purportedly attempting to buy the studio so he could give his daughter a clear road to Hollywood stardom.

Having a few million in cash wasn't enough for Ines to buy her way back to a war-torn country. Accepting that she wouldn't see Paris again anytime soon, she settled into the Château Marquis and began spending her time inventing new ways to spend money. Oddly enough, she started following the footsteps of her late uncle, Nico. She threw extravagant parties with unconventional guest lists, mixing Hollywood stars with writers, artists, and the occasional academic if they were tolerable. I heard strange stories about her around the studio lots and at after-parties. One month she was dedicated to purchasing racehorses and the next she was collecting modern art. Everyone shared these stories with a shrug and a laugh: "If that's what she wants to do with the money, fine!"

When I asked Augustan about the studio's new ownership, he put his head in his hands. Augustan was working overtime to promote FWM's rising stars—Danny Prior, Grace Stafford, and Delilah Baker among them—and find new faces for the studio. I'd heard reports that Thomas Brodbeck was getting more and more irritable by the day, to the point that the new stockholders wanted to oust him.

"I think it might be best if we don't talk," he said.

"Talk about the studio?"

"No, talk at all."

He didn't look at me as I left.

The only person I apologized to during that time was Augustan—nearly every visit I made to his office was preceded by my saying "I'm sorry" so many times, the words lost all meaning. Each time, his face remained unchanged from a disdainful scowl. Even after he requested I stop speaking to him, I found myself muttering apologies as I looked over his press releases and memos.

I never did apologize to Charles in person. Perhaps that makes me contemptible. Charles knew that I needed to write something daring during the Freddy Clarke trial, and he told me what to write. He was well aware of the impact it could have. I doubted an apology would do very much beyond assuage my own conscience.

Out of everyone, I wanted, very badly, to apologize to Sophie. And I tried. I looked her up all across Ohio, hoping to find an address or phone number. I even went through her father's company to see if I could contact him. I talked to a chain of mid-level to executive managers at Markham Auto Parts, but I found nothing. It was as if the girl disappeared from the face of the earth.

Through all of this, Hal and Margy remained married and on the FWM payroll. They were dependable leads and they were versatile. They went from Westerns to comedies to society dramas. I was informed that they maintained their friendship with Charles but kept things discreet—every week or so his car could be seen parked in their driveway. I never contacted any of them, and they certainly didn't contact me. In the column, I'd include generic references to Hal and Margy, mostly things the studio sent over. Otherwise, I ignored them.

Nell received her first Academy nomination for *Marie Antoinette*. She would go on to lose to Ginger Rogers.

When the attack on Pearl Harbor happened, Margy and Hal were throwing a brunch party to celebrate the purchase of their new beachside home. They had invited many of their favorite people in Hollywood—Jeanette Manning, Victor Perez, Carla Longworth. I heard that Charles even made a brief appearance to congratulate them.

As the story was explained to me, Margy and Hal had not yet unpacked their radio set. The entire group was unaware of what had happened until Rex Northrop arrived late and flustered. He had to break the news to everyone over the dessert course of mango sorbet.

Nell was on location in Missouri for *Oregon Trail*. She spent the day consoling the young men and women on the crew, and I know this because the photographs of her consoling the young men and women on the crew were widely circulated.

Freddy was visiting his mother and father back east. He was scheduled to make an appearance at his alma mater in Michigan the next day. His guest lecture was canceled indefinitely.

To the best of my knowledge, Ines Marquis was alone in the château. Her country had already been at war for more than two years, so I imagine it made little difference to her.

I was having an early lunch with Sebastian. He was done with Hollywood society after *Fifty Grand*. The film left a bad taste in his mouth. "These aren't the kinds of stories I want to tell," he said to me. We were sitting outside, next to a fence by the sidewalk. A man ran down the street, stopped by us, and grasped the railing tightly. "It's happened," he said, out of breath. "We've been attacked." He then kept running. Alarmed, Seb went inside, where the restaurant staff had turned up the radio.

. . .

The next day, the United States made an official declaration of war. Many of the men in Hollywood had already been preparing to enlist—Jimmy Stewart was flying planes, Hal began telling stories about his father serving in the last war, and others were envisioning photos of themselves in real uniforms—and they got their opportunity.

In an odd case of serendipity, I heard about only two actors who were barred from enlisting: Charles and Freddy. Charles had a weight deficiency, which could be remedied if he put some effort into it. Freddy's issues were never officially disclosed, though I was told he had a heart murmur and a list of venereal diseases.

The last time I talked with Charles Landrieu was in the spring of 1942.

He looked exhausted that day. I had been surprised when he called and asked if he could stop by my house. He seemed out of place in my dowdy living room and refused to take a seat, opting to pace instead. I was caught off guard by seeing him out of costume; he wore a patterned knit sweater that looked too large for him—the sleeves were rolled up his forearms—and a pair of brown work trousers. When he removed his sunglasses, his eyes—usually a striking blue—were bloodshot, lined with dark circles.

After months of halfheartedly turning out low-budget Westerns, there wasn't a single studio in Hollywood willing to offer Charles a new contract. We both knew that it was largely my fault. I was prepared for him to deliver a speech or some form of admonishment, and perhaps he did have one ready for me. Instead, he told me that I had gotten everything wrong.

"Everything?"

Everything.

There were only so many things I could have been wrong about. When I listed them in my head—Charles and Margy, Charles and Ines, Charles and Freddy—he was the one common denominator.

"So join the army," I said. "You'll come back a hero and everyone will forget about this." He laughed at that and explained he'd already tried—too underweight.

At that point, he stopped pacing. I'll never forget the silhouette of him as he stood against the evening sun coming through my window: the way he sunk his hands in his pockets and stared at the floor, the errant curls of hair that fell over his forehead, how even when he was standing still, his posture always indicated that he was ready to run full sprint at a moment's notice. I heard a quiet sigh as he shook his head. He didn't have anything more to say to me after that; he just left.

When Charles was officially released from his FWM contract without renewal, he gained those ten pounds—while training for *Fifty Grand,* he became friends with a professional boxer who knew a thing or two about changing weight classes—and joined the air force.

Actors across every major studio enlisted, and the women of Hollywood began supplementing their workdays with war efforts. All the social clubs went dark as various actresses took turns hosting USO shows, and later the Hollywood Canteen. It was some of the best publicity they could ask for. It also meant that they had to redouble their commitment to a job that already demanded most of their time.

Freddy stayed in Hollywood, where he was the obvious choice to play the hero in any of the war films FWM was now churning out. What was more, FWM could loan him out for triple or quadruple his going rate—during the early war years, Freddy was borrowed by MGM, RKO, and Columbia. He played admirals, colonels, privates, and generals. On-screen, he flew planes, shot rifles, dodged bullets, and gave impassioned speeches. When he left the set, he went back to being Freddy Clarke, free to do whatever he pleased.

TWELVE

There was a possibility that I was only invited to a party at the Château Marquis in the fall of 1942 because Ines had finally exhausted all of her guest lists, which were now constricted by the number of men enlisted. Among those invited to the château before me: Nell, Augustan (exempt from service due to exceedingly poor eyesight), Grace Stafford, Victor Perez (not an American citizen, it turned out), Margy, and—this was a nice touch—Sebastian (who was serving through writing recruitment scripts).

When I arrived at the château, I was told by a member of the staff that Ines was by the pool for a "boat race." I'd brought an overnight bag, in the event that this party carried on through the night, as the late Nico Marquis's parties once had. A woman dressed in black wordlessly appeared by my side and took the bag from me before disappearing up a staircase.

A butler led me through the main foyer and down the same series of hallways I walked when I'd been in the château many years ago, back when Nico was the one hosting parties. I was a favorite of Nico's, not for my acting talents, but because I could hold a conversation with any person he might seat next to me at the dinner table. I once listened to the ambassador to Luxembourg describe variations on the dish *Bouneschlupp* for nearly an hour. After that, Nico would tease me before throwing me into any dull conversations: "I hope you're in the mood for *Bouneschlupp*."

The château had since been transformed. The decadent tastes of Nico Marquis were gone: no more gilded furniture or ornate tapestries. It appeared that Ines had tossed everything into a ware-house somewhere, or sold it all off. Some of the rooms were now furnished in a sparse contemporary style, which felt discordant with the frescoed walls and high ceilings. Other rooms remained empty, save for a few defining items—a lone painting easel in one room, a medicine ball and weights in another.

I heard whooping and hollering outside; the voices all sounded female. When I went onto the back veranda, I was offered a chilled drink. The first person I recognized was Ines, who stood by the pool. She was wearing a floor-length gown and had a sailor's hat perched on her head. She held a copper megaphone in one hand, a lit cigarette in the other.

"*Allons-y! Allons-y!*" she called out. A large black dog sat at her feet and barked when she yelled. It leaned toward the water, but Ines swatted her hand to keep it from jumping in.

In the pool, there were two women and two wooden sailboats. One of the ladies was paddling behind a boat and splashing at it, trying to create waves. The other was treading water and making large fanning motions with her hands.

I heard a familiar voice next to me. "They're trying to get their boats across the pool, but the rule is that they can't touch them."

I turned and saw Margy. She was wearing a gown, slightly damp along the neckline, where it clung to her skin, and she had a towel wrapped around her head. She pressed her hand, palm up, below her eyes to stop any mascara from running down her face.

"Last time it was herding kittens," she said as she watched the pool. One of the boats was now veering to the side of the pool. "Ines had them brought over special for the occasion."

I wanted to know if Margy had been to any of Nico's parties during his prime. Of all the times I had attended with Augustan, who was another favorite of Nico's, I couldn't recall ever having seen Margy there. She was a bit young for his parties, but I knew

Charles had been to at least one, so it stood to reason that Margy would have as well. There was a time when the two of them went everywhere together.

I considered asking her outright if she had ever gone with him, but I had the whole night ahead of me. I was fortunate enough that Margy had spoken to me at all after everything that had happened with Charles.

Below us, the woman who had been paddling and splashing let out a loud cheer as her boat knocked against the side of the pool.

"Mademoiselle Stafford! *Très, très bien!*" Ines called out.

The winner lifted her arms in the air to a round of applause. Without all the water splashing around her, I recognized her as the young actress Grace Stafford. She pulled herself up onto the side of the pool and was given a crown of flowers to wear.

"Do you all *want* to be chasing boats?" I asked Margy.

Margy smiled. "Chasing boats this afternoon has been the singular joy of my week," she said.

In addition to Margy and Grace, I recognized Carla and Jeanette from FWM. There was also the costume designer Minna Davidson from Paramount and Kay Wilson, the newly appointed head of film editing for RKO. Margy informed me that the woman who just lost the boat race was FWM director Gideon Wright's wife, Paisley. She was still treading water midway down the pool and offering her congratulations. Paisley had been quietly doing her husband's job for the last two months while he was in Washington, D.C., working on a "secret government project." None of the other women had registered my presence so far and I wasn't sure how they'd react when they did.

Grace and Paisley each went into a dressing room to put their gowns back on.

I asked Margy if she'd won her round. She gave me a pageant-ready smile and asked, "What do you think?"

The war had been great for Margy, professionally speaking. She was permitted to keep her southern accent on-screen and shifted into roles that focused on her as a "real American." She was old enough now to play wives instead of fiancées or sweethearts, though she still played a number of those, too. Her most recent film featured her as a wife who manages her husband's general store while he's overseas. She took the number-eight spot for most popular actress that month, outranked only by women like Bette Davis, Nell Parker, and Ginger Rogers.

Ines waved me over to the side of the pool. Everything about her face and posture should have indicated that she was happy to see me, but something in her eyes told me she wasn't. A few of the women around the pool glanced at me before immediately pretending to be doing something else.

"Afraid I didn't bring anything to wear," I said, gesturing to the pool. The dog sniffed at my feet, and I took a step away from it. Ines took no notice and allowed the dog free rein.

She laughed at me. "You're not playing today. It's nearly suppertime." She paused. "Unless I think of a game for after supper."

As we walked up to the veranda for drinks before dinner, I greeted all the women, even those who seemed disappointed at my presence. Paisley was suspicious of me—fair enough, I had called Gideon's last film "unremarkable" and didn't realize until afterward that she had directed half of it, uncredited.

A few months ago, the idea of a table of women having a dinner party would have struck me as odd—usually the only exclusively female spaces I encountered were dressing rooms in department stores. Sitting on the veranda of the château that spring evening, though, it seemed the most natural thing in the world.

It was standard practice for me to be invited to large social events—film premieres, award ceremonies, themed parties—but when my column became the second-most syndicated in the country, I discovered why I was shut out of smaller, more intimate gatherings. No one trusted that some offhand remark wouldn't end up in print the next day. I missed lazy postdinner conversations after people had had a glass or two or three, or sharing a knowing glance across the table when discussing someone everyone disliked. In those early days of the column, my life lacked a certain rapport. I started to understand Poppy's social awkwardness and worried my own skills would somehow atrophy—like I would wake up one morning and no longer know how to talk to a stranger.

I sat next to Ines, as she and Margy were the only people who had addressed me so far and Margy was preoccupied with mixing herself a drink. While I listened to the conversations around me, I kept thinking of different ways to contribute and found myself muted by my thoughts.

Ines was considering setting up a card game for after dinner. "But we can't play something dull. No bridge, no hearts."

There was an intensity about her that I'd never noticed before. I suspected part of it was getting accustomed to wealth, the ease of making demands and seeing what it would take to get anyone to say no.

Pacing around the table, Margy explained how excited she was to wrap up production on a comedy in which she played a woman learning to outswindle a swindler. It was a break from her rotation of dramas. "I know there's a war going on, but people still need to laugh, don't they?"

Propped on the side of her chair so she could speak to Margy, Jeanette complained about playing the mother to "every man left in Hollywood, apparently." She mused that it was only a matter of time until someone cast her as Humphrey Bogart's mother (she was seven years younger than Bogart).

Grace usually ran with FWM's younger set of unwed actors and actresses. Under different circumstances, she would be spending her time in the clubs, stirring up speculation about whom she might be dating. Instead, her off-hours were dedicated to selling war bonds. At the table, she was hesitant to talk with the other actresses and stayed close to Ines.

I watched Margy toss her head back and let out her loud laugh. It occurred to me that she probably had no idea what Charles had done for her before my column on him, that he had run his career right into the dirt for fear that I would publish that she was pregnant out of wedlock.

And what if it had been Margy instead of Charles? Impossible that she'd be at that table right now, laughing and drinking. She certainly wouldn't have her surprise appearance on the "Best of" lists. Depending on what people believed happened to the child she never had, she might not even be in Hollywood.

Margy hadn't been particularly warm toward me. As far as she was aware, I was the woman who'd severed her and Hal from a dear friend and possible lover. I wondered how she might act if she knew the truth. It was hardly more than a flip of a coin that left Charles in exile and Margy in the spotlight.

Ever since the story on Charles, there had been an expectation that I would go after someone else next. I came close—at the request of Kent Strauss at MGM, I turned readers sour on a burgeoning relationship between two of their stars that had not been studio-approved. The alarming thing was how effective I was. All it took was a single line about the twenty-year age difference between the two stars and I had readers demanding they find more suitable partners.

The paradox of becoming "the most feared woman in Hollywood" was not lost on me; I was terrified all the time. Even the most innocuous of observations on my part could cause the end of someone's career. As Poppy's source, I wasn't paid much mind. I was selling information, sure, but I wasn't the person publishing it. With my column, people noticed me in a way they hadn't before.

While sitting quietly among the women having their evening cocktails, I felt my presence, discordant among the group, practically vibrating.

Dinner was served inside. I hoped to be seated near Grace, who seemed the easiest ally in the room, but found myself between Jeanette and Margy, across from Paisley. I nearly laughed when I realized that Ines had placed me in an FWM trifecta.

Jeanette looked at me. Her most striking features were always her dark eyebrows and high cheekbones, and I felt their full impact as she arched an eyebrow and appraised me. "It's the Academy Awards all over again," she said flatly.

I smoothed the napkin in my lap. "A few key players are missing, don't you think?"

"I suppose we could do a reenactment," she said. "The only question is who'll play Freddy and who'll attack Freddy." She took a long sip of her wine. "And which one of those people you'll decimate in a few weeks' time."

So, there it was. I had been expecting some blowback for a while now. Regardless of how I'd made it look, Charles was well liked by his peers.

While my column was doing very well nationwide, I lost a few of my local contacts to Poppy. Most FWM interviews were now redirected to her. A few weeks earlier, I had paid a visit to Nell on the set of *After Hours* and I was followed by a lesser Augustan in and out of the studio. I was tempted to ask what the fuss was—Charles was far away at boot camp; there wasn't much slandering I could do there—but I understood.

It wasn't that it was Charles I went after; it was that I did so without the studio's permission.

I can't say what FWM's plans for Charles originally were, before I published the column—probably just the suspension and a stern warning—but I'd foiled them. And the rest of Hollywood took note. Actors and actresses were tight-lipped around me; a number of them simply had their studios send over a press release in lieu of any interviews.

The upside was that an emerging generation of actors and actresses was ready to take full advantage of any empty column space I might have. Danny Prior, who had replaced Charles in *The Convict Ship,* sent me a bouquet of flowers after I did a brief interview with him. Delilah Baker was more than eager to stand next to me at parties, slipping in a rumor or two about her colleagues. They knew perfectly well what they were doing.

Jeanette wryly nodded at me before plunging her fork into a piece of salmon on her plate and eagerly cutting away.

At the head of the table, Ines was watching us with an absent-minded smile on her face.

I turned to Margy and asked her how Hal was doing.

"Boot camp's only a few more weeks," she said. He was in North Carolina with the air force. "He has to come back here to wrap up a few scenes for *Holidays,* but then . . ." She made a motion with her hand like a plane taking off.

I'd heard Hal would most likely be cleared for cargo delivery or radio communications. Between his age and his standing as a Hollywood actor, he wasn't going to the front lines anytime soon.

Margy answered my next question without my having to ask it: "Charles's with the air force, too, but he's somewhere in Arizona." Charles was under twenty-eight and had no current standing as a Hollywood actor to shield him from potentially seeing combat.

Margy continued: "When they got some *extra time* on their hands last year, they both took up piloting. Don't suppose you knew that."

I didn't.

Margy turned away from me and began talking with Carla.

I asked Paisley what she was working on.

"Finished a drama with Victor and Tilly. He's supposed to

have fled Italy for the States before the war. Marries Tilly, fights fascism. That kind of thing. I think you'll find it's a rather *remarkable* story."

After that, I turned my attention to my meal and quietly listened to the others at the table.

"It's a shame that Nell doesn't go out more."

"She used to be entertaining."

"I suspect Griffith will enlist next. People have started talking."

"It's a popularity issue. If you refuse to go, it'll look like you're afraid or you think you're too good."

"Or you lack a necessary American fervor."

"And when Jimmy Stewart is demanding to fly directly into the Third Reich, everyone else starts to look a little skittish."

"They just want the photo ops at boot camp."

"Yes, but Freddy doesn't go out, so Nell doesn't go out."

"How do you think she stands him?"

"By not going out, that's how."

"Those are good photo ops. I swear some of them oiled up before removing their shirts."

"Carla!"

"Is he even divorced yet?"

"I think Bunny's having second thoughts."

"She never even enjoyed being in the spotlight."

"I mean, God, at least enjoy it."

Ines was quiet for most of the meal, preferring to listen to her guests. Her expression was one of concentration—she had a habit of pouting her lower lip when she was listening—but every so often, her mouth would shift into a smile, or she'd nod slowly.

After my column on Charles, the press was deeply invested in Ines. Stories began circulating about her cavorting and having secret trysts with Charles. I received a tip that his car had been parked at the château for a week straight before he started production for *Fifty Grand* ("I don't think he's out there *just* admiring the Marquis family zoo!").

As always, there was a quick distraction for any speculators. Publicly declaring her love for Freddy might've been the nicest thing Nell could have done for Ines and Charles. Most of the columnists gave up on their pursuit of details about Ines's love life in favor of stories about Nell and Freddy.

There was very little talk about the Parisian heiress after that. The parties of Ines Marquis were primarily known to the social circles of Hollywood. They took on a mythical quality—all of which served to make an invite to a Marquis party more enviable. But I never heard a word about boat racing or kitten herding prior to that night.

Once dinner was finished, it was too late for anyone to drive home. Nor were most of the attendees in any fit state to drive an hour back to Los Angeles.

By this point, Margy had gone through a few glasses of wine. Her face was flushed and she had a dreamy look. I asked her if she had been to the château when Nico was still alive. She nodded.

"I went with Charles once, years ago," she said. She sat with her elbows on the table and rested her chin against her palm. "That's when I met Hal."

It was my understanding that Margy hadn't officially met Hal until they filmed *Afterglow*. I had also suspected that was a story invented by Augustan to promote the film and their subsequent marriage.

I turned toward Margy and asked her to tell me more. She did.

Sometime in 1938, after the successful premiere of their film *Georgia Summers*, Charles and Margy were invited by Nico to the château. Margy maintained that there wasn't any romantic agenda in their going together.

"I liked going places with Charles because he always felt very safe," she said, her gaze drifting off. "I don't know if it's because he sounded like some of the boys I grew up with. But I felt like I never had to, you know, worry around him."

The other actors in attendance were intimidating to Margy— among them were Claudette Colbert, Spencer Greene, and Baird deWitt. She said that Charles naturally gravitated toward Hal, so much so that she assumed he already knew him. She was shocked to learn they'd just met over cocktails that night.

"I don't know how to describe it," she said. "When they talked, they didn't explain anything to each other. There was no need. It's like how it is with some"—she paused here and cleared her throat—"*people,* I guess, when they just always know what the other person is thinking."

The three stole a crate of wine from the cellar and slipped away to the indoor pool, where they discarded their formal wear ("Quite the scandal, right?"). There was singing, laughing, and one swim race across the pool, which Hal won. They drank until Margy couldn't swim anymore. She loudly announced that she would be going to bed, but neither of the men seemed to pay her any mind. She left Hal and Charles in the pool with a few bottles of wine bobbing in the water. She wasn't sure how late the two stayed there; they both overslept the next morning and missed breakfast.

They didn't know they would all be starring in *Afterglow* until a few months later, but Margy's theory was that Nico had to have seen the three of them together and suggested the casting.

"Isn't it a shame that's the only film Charles and Hal will ever do together?" she asked slowly. She looked like she was about to speak again, but stopped.

"Can anyone sing?" Ines asked the women at the table. "Or play the piano?"

Margy was the first to shake her head. It was well known that she couldn't carry a tune. Carla had done one musical during her long tenure in Hollywood and she was dubbed over for her solo.

Jeanette was a very exceptional singer, so much so that she wasn't likely to perform for free. Grace raised her hand.

We moved into one of the many parlors in the house. This one had two couches and a few scattered chairs. A piano was stationed in the corner of the room. Grace calmly took a seat in front of the piano and ran her hand over the keys. She had seemed out of place for most of the night, but once she began to play, something settled in the air.

She began to sing "I Don't Want to Set the World on Fire," with a slow piano melody. The words spilled from her mouth, every syllable heavy, like a drop of rain. The room quieted, each of the women receding into her own corner to listen. There was no impetus to make conversation—no talk of the war, of petty qualms between studios, of new roles and opportunities. A calm settled over everyone.

It was a moment that I did not wish to pass. For the first time that night, I didn't feel the need to justify my presence. I didn't realize how tense I had become until I let my shoulders drop as Grace sang. In the dim light of the parlor, she almost looked like Sophie—she hadn't redone her hair or makeup after swimming in the pool, so there was a certain softness to her facial features and her loose blond curls. My heart sank as she crooned the final lines and then placed her hands in her lap. There was a brief silence before Ines asked if Grace knew anything up-tempo. She began to play a quick tune with no lyric accompaniment. As she played, the members of the party began to speak with one another, first in soft voices, then progressively louder.

I stood next to Ines as she lit a cigarette. Her face had changed since Brodbeck's party years earlier. Her features were fuller, most likely from an unlimited diet of whatever foods she could possibly want, and her broad cheekbones had a rosy glow.

I asked her, "Any chance you'll tell me why you invited me here, or shall I just amuse myself with guessing?"

Ines took a drag of her cigarette before responding. "I thought you might enjoy the company."

The black dog I'd seen earlier had returned and was now sitting by Ines's feet. I realized that I knew the dog—it was Charles's, the same one he'd adopted from the studio. When I looked at the dog's face, there was something downcast in its whiskers or the roundness of its eyes.

I asked Ines if she'd seen Charles before he left for boot camp.

She smiled and told me she had. "His car was outside the château for one week, remember?"

"What did you talk about for a week?"

She narrowed her eyes and said, *"You."* Then she let out a loud laugh and briefly touched my shoulder. "I am only making a joke. He mostly stayed in the east wing of the house. Wanted someone to make certain he kept sober."

I looked at the bar cart in the parlor and considered the liquor cabinet, along with the large wine cellar. The château seemed an unlikely asylum for anyone who wanted to be free of alcohol.

People began to break away from the group. Margy, Paisley, and the costume designer moved back outside for a late-night swim. The editor asked Ines to let her use the screening room. Jeanette was on the divan and began to drift off to sleep every few moments. Carla sat nearby her, staring out the windows and occasionally talking to Ines. Grace kept playing the piano—she seemed relieved to have a break from making conversation, grateful for the task.

I sat and feigned interest in the music, but it wasn't the same as that first song. I was once again conscious of my presence in the room, even if no one else seemed to be. I was frightened of being the first person to retire for the night—I envisioned whispers and sighs of relief among the women at my departure up the stairs. I waited until Grace seemed tired of playing. She said she was going to her room and wished everyone a good night. The group dispersed shortly thereafter.

. . .

On my way up the stairs, I heard hushed voices in the hallway. One had a pronounced twang to it; the other was soft and practiced. I paused at the top step, where I could hear Margy and Carla below.

"They want to put me back with Rolf," Margy said. Her voice sounded different—there was something taut in the way she whispered to Carla.

"How long is the shoot?"

"At least ten weeks. More, depending on how the action scenes go."

"Who's with you?"

"It's Casey."

"That's no help," Carla said. "Can't you get Hal to come back for a little while longer? I'm sure the war will still be waiting for him."

"I doubt it. Augustan's set on Casey."

"At least it's not Freddy."

"Might as well be."

Casey Lowell had joined Danny Prior as one of Freddy's protégés. The young men frequently joined Freddy on his infamous boating trips, along with a rotating cast of actors and directors—Rolf Junger among them. Casey had made his start in FWM's B-list Westerns. He didn't enlist in the army, which led to his taking some of the roles vacated by Hal and the other enlisted men. He was on his way to getting top billing, and a role opposite Margy would certainly help him there.

I took the rest of the stairs gingerly. There was a hall of bedrooms, which brought back memories of years ago, when those rooms would all have been filled. Usually, if I was discreet enough, I could track who left their rooms in the middle of the night. Augustan and I used to have a tradition of comparing notes at breakfast the next morning.

I checked all the open doors, until I saw a room with my suitcase laid out on the bed. I ran my hand over the plush bedcover, the soft fabric patterned with bright florals. It was a beautiful room, the kind that I couldn't even have imagined when I was growing up. The bedrooms in the château were the size of my parents' entire two-bedroom apartment. I'd spent my childhood and adolescence sleeping on a broken wire-spring mattress that I shared with my younger sister Jillian. As the only boy of the family, Seb was given a makeshift bed in the living room. My youngest sisters were still sleeping on the floor by the time I had left for Hollywood. My stay in the hotel provided by Miss Appleton's was the first time I'd been in a room by myself for the night. Even though I tried to take up as much space on the bed as possible, I still found myself curled on the rightmost side when I woke up in the morning, making space for Jillian. It's true to this day.

Though the bed in the château was terribly comfortable and the temperature wasn't too hot or too cold, I couldn't sleep. I'm sure there's a psychoanalyst out there ready to inform me that I was feeling residual guilt. But I was plenty used to people being angry with me and familiar with the feeling of being morally in the wrong; I'd never lost sleep over it before.

I convinced myself the château was haunted, and that felt more comforting than my current reality.

The next morning, breakfast was served on the terrace. It was a Saturday, but Carla and Jeanette had already left for early shoots, as had the editor, costume designer, and director. Margy and Grace were still there, quietly drinking sugarless coffee. Ines sat sideways in her chair, the morning paper propped on her knees, her feet dangling over the armrest. The dog sat next to her; she mindlessly tossed it a bit of sausage from her plate. She looked up when I walked onto the patio.

She lifted the paper. "Baird deWitt marries Barbara Whiting in secret?" she asked. It was yesterday's column of "Do Tell."

"Can you blame the man for feeling shy about his fourth marriage?"

Margy narrowed her eyes. "I thought you were friends," she said.

"We are," I told her. "Baird knew it was going in the paper. I trust you know a thing or two about the power of putting an elopement in the gossip columns."

Margy scoffed and shook her head. Mocking her staged elopement with Hal was a low blow, even for me, but she appeared too tired for any sparring that morning. Ines raised her eyebrows and returned to reading.

I took the seat next to Margy and asked her what her next film would be. She sighed and explained that she had been cast for a Rolf Junger film.

"*Afterglow* was quite the success, wasn't it?" I asked her.

At the mention of the film title, her face went blank. She looked into her coffee cup and remained silent for a moment.

"It was," she said slowly. She then quickly lifted her chin and smiled widely. "But I'd like to work with some different directors," she said in her pageant voice. "Like Paisley. I think she'd be swell to work with."

We ate the rest of our breakfasts in an amicable quiet, but there was something unsettling about Margy. It stayed with me even as I drove home—the way she'd switched so easily to her pageant presentation when I asked about Rolf.

When I arrived home, I called up Nell.

"How's Freddy?" I asked.

"How should I know?" she responded flatly. There weren't any large events that week, so she hadn't any reason to see Freddy. "He tried to take me with him on a boating excursion and I told him to leave me alone. For all I care, he can sail that boat clear into the Pacific Ocean."

"I'm curious about something," I began. Nell was my primary source of information about FWM by then. I could contact Freddy, but I never wanted to, and getting him on the phone was a nightmare anyway. Whenever I did have to speak with him, he had a tendency to go off on twenty-minute monologues about things he swore he didn't do. Nell and I had a more pleasant rapport.

"Go ahead," she said breathily into the phone.

"Why doesn't Margy want to work with Rolf?"

"Good God, none of us wants to work with Rolf," she said.

I knew the stories about Rolf's directing methods. I'd seen them up close that day when he yelled Grace off the set for looking too young. It was not an anomaly for him. He was particularly opinionated on the costumes and demeanors of his leading ladies, but he otherwise distributed his anger evenly over everyone on his sets. Charles once told me that while working on *Desert Sands*, Rolf regularly refused to let the cast and crew break for lunch until six or seven at night. He stopped only after one of his actresses fainted while climbing a ladder. Rolf wasn't the kind of man anyone wanted to argue or negotiate with.

"But you never work with him," I said to Nell.

"I did my time," she said, exhaling loudly. "The year *Sure Shot* came out, I had already been on three films with him."

"And Margy hasn't?"

"Margy just renewed her contract. She hasn't got any leverage." As long as the studio wasn't worried about her leaving, they could put her in whatever films they wanted. Had this happened a year ago, Margy wouldn't have had a problem.

Nell, on the other hand, had two years left in her contract and was already being courted by MGM for a generous new salary. She was well aware of the kind of power that afforded her—she could work with any FWM director she wanted.

I had no events scheduled for that night. No parties, no film openings, no social clubs. The clubs were all shuttering their doors anyway—not enough clientele. The studios were also scaling down premieres—it seemed too lavish, unless it was for a war film. Party invites, as I was well aware, were becoming scarce where I was concerned. Now that I could afford to buy my own dresses again, I had no place to wear them.

It was too quiet, so I put on the radio. I made it through five minutes of listening to coverage of everything happening overseas before the voices on the radio were too loud, so I shut it off. I tried to read a book and then I tried to read the paper. I wanted someone to call, or a place to meet people. I needed to hear a voice that wasn't my own. I stayed up half the night for no reason at all; I couldn't overcome the feeling of restlessness.

Thirteen

Standing in the back of a dark theater, I watched as Sgt. Rocky Carlisle ran between two tanks with a rifle in his hand, a battlefield sprawled behind him. In costume, Freddy looked equal parts haggard and determined to save the day. Though he was wearing a helmet and fatigues, he was unmistakably Freddy—wide crooked grin, bright eyes, cocky determination. One of his fellow soldiers cautioned him against going into active fire, but he swore he'd do whatever it took to keep his brothers alive.

Having been in there only a few minutes, I hadn't the slightest clue what the plot of *Glory at Dawn* was, but I suspected it didn't matter. All those in the audience needed to understand was that their sons, brothers, husbands, et cetera, were fighting as valiantly as Sgt. Rocky Carlisle was.

I left the screening room right as Rocky went running into the line of fire, staccato blasts of drums and horns playing in the background and fading as I shut the doors behind me. In the quiet of the theater lobby, tables were being set up while a handful of actors and actresses milled about. I had been commissioned to sell bonds with the Victory Committee. A young woman with a clipboard offered me a complimentary cup of coffee and showed me to my station. I had done a few bond sales before and quickly understood that most people wanted to talk to the real actors and actresses. I was only there to work the tables and provide amusing anecdotes.

While waiting for the film to finish, I went outside with my coffee for a cigarette. Anywhere I stood, I was next to a poster featuring Freddy in *Glory at Dawn*. The illustration showed Freddy positioned with a rifle in hand on a battlefield. Presumably there was some form of explosion or disaster looming out of frame. The illustrator forwent a helmet for Freddy, so he was running bare-headed into battle in all his handsome glory.

As I fumbled with my cigarette and lighter, a familiar voice called my name. I looked up to see Baird walking toward the theater.

"Why hello, love," he said. He came over and lit my cigarette for me. Baird had been loaned out for *Glory at Dawn*; he played a commanding officer to Freddy's young hero. Freddy was too high-profile to do daytime bond sales, but Baird wasn't.

"You might be the only person in this town who's ever excited to see me anymore," I said bitterly.

"It can't be that bad."

"I assure you that it is," I said. I nodded at the poster of Freddy behind me. "The way I'm treated, you'd think I was the one who had gone on trial for some horrific crime."

Baird exhaled loudly. "God, find me someone who will put that man in his place. We'd all be better for it."

I laughed, but Baird continued: "Go to one of his sets and you'll see. He acts as though he nearly perished on the beaches of Dunkirk. We should all be so honored that he would ever grace us with his venerated presence."

I'd always known that Baird was one for dramatics, but the spite in his voice sounded very real that day. Baird regretted not having enlisted—his father was a decorated veteran of the last war—but he'd been heavily encouraged by MGM to stay in Holly-wood. The United States government thought that might be best, too. I assumed that participating in events like this was some form of atonement for him.

Shortly after we went inside, we were met with a flood of people coming out of the screening room. Most of them flocked toward Baird; their faces lit up with the surreal joy of seeing someone who had just been on the screen appear before them in the flesh. Baird spoke to every person who approached him, smiling and graciously signing autographs.

From my table, I watched those in the crowd, which was primarily made up of women and older men, pull out their checkbooks. Every person Baird spoke to purchased bonds.

At his request, I joined Baird for lunch. He wanted to thank me for putting his elopement with Barbara in the column—they'd both received a generous bump in fan letters since the announcement. At an inconspicuous restaurant by the water, we ate salads with scant servings of chicken.

Baird mostly wanted to voice his complaints about working with Freddy, whom he found to be egomaniacal and cruel.

"And it doesn't help that his entire studio is practically operating just for him," he said.

I started to point out that FWM still had people like Nell, but as soon as he shook his head, I realized he was right—Nell would almost certainly be leaving FWM for MGM. FWM's other stars had had only fleeting successes of late, like Margy's surprise debut on the "Best of" lists that year.

"I don't see FWM holding up much longer. Certainly not since . . ." he said, and then trailed off, gesturing toward me. I waited for him to finish his sentence, but he began fidgeting with his cutlery instead.

"Are you suggesting I ruined the studio?" I asked, resting my elbows on the table and leaning in.

Baird leaned back and put his hands up. "I'm only saying! Charles, George, Nell—that's a high body count for one gossip columnist."

I relaxed my shoulders and smiled. "You flatter me. Let's get you back home to your wife."

Baird dropped me off by the theater, but I didn't immediately go back to my car. Another showing of *Glory at Dawn* was letting out. There wasn't a bond sale for this one; no actors or actresses were stationed outside. I lit a cigarette and stood by the doors. As moviegoers filtered out, I waited for them to mention Freddy—his pending divorce, his relationship with Nell, anything. I wanted to see if the public was as annoyed with him as Hollywood was. I didn't hear his name once; instead, every person who walked out of the theater talked about husbands, sons, and nephews away in England and France.

I had been hired by *Photoplay* to do a piece on the opening of the Hollywood Canteen—it was Hollywood's answer to the Stage Door Canteen, where Broadway performers served members of the Allied forces. Nell was among the star-studded list of actresses on the committee, so I asked if I could talk to her while she was setting up.

A few days before the grand opening, I followed Nell around the mostly empty canteen. It was unclear what she was actually doing aside from nodding approvingly at the placement of tables as others moved them around.

"Look, they told me to be here, so I'm here," she said after we'd sat down at the serving counter for a brief chat. The room had cleared out by that point, as the rest of the committee moved on to the kitchens.

"And we thank you for your service," I said. I smiled, but Nell wasn't amused.

"You know I'd prefer to have something *real* to do," she said defensively.

I asked if she meant something like Freddy was doing—running through battlefields with a loud rallying cry. At the mention of Freddy's name, she exhaled loudly.

"I said *real*," she hissed.

"It's not as though you can wake up tomorrow and start flying planes." I stopped myself before the conversation could proceed to its logical end point—the fact that Charles would soon be piloting on active duty and we'd both had a hand in making that happen. Nell and I never discussed Charles. It does strike me as odd that I received all the flak for his fall from grace when Nell was the one who had happily confirmed every unsavory rumor about him.

"I don't know how much longer I can hold up with him," she said after a pause. She'd often complained to me about Freddy, but usually she did so with her dry, quiet humor. Just the other day she'd been calmly fantasizing about strapping him to a missile and launching him toward Japan. This was different.

"Why, is there someone else?" I asked, only a little facetiously.

Nell looked at me and raised her eyebrows. She didn't miss a beat: "There's always someone else, and that someone else is *me*."

When Nell had originally mentioned inventing a relationship between her and Freddy, my first question was whether the studio would sanction that. She promised me that Augustan and Brodbeck had given her the go-ahead. I should have known that wasn't true, because, no matter how irritated he was with me, Augustan would have told me himself.

I ran the column, complete with an interview with Nell, and didn't give it a second thought.

The day after I published it, I received a phone call from Augustan. "If there are any other relationships you'd like to invent for us, by all means, tell me now," he yelled into the phone, and then hung up. Frankly, I was just excited that he called me at all.

I couldn't say I was shocked that Nell had changed her mind and wanted to return to the one relationship that had always mattered most to her: herself and her career.

"Surely you have enough information on him by now to do some damage," she said in a low voice.

"Doesn't matter," I said; "he was acquitted."

She instructed me to find something new. "You were asking about Rolf. They're on those ridiculous boating trips every weekend now that no one can go on location anymore."

"You understand that I can't publicly flay Freddy Clarke," I said, as much to remind myself as Nell.

Nell leaned on the counter, her hands clasped under her chin while she stared at the wall. Her hair was pulled back into neat rolls. She favored hairstyles that draped and curled around her face; it was unusual to see her fine features so exposed. Nell's beauty was never something I could get used to—it struck me anew every time I saw her.

"Just do *something*," she said, not looking at me. And I wanted to, I really did.

Nell was still sitting at the counter when I left the canteen— I had a rare lunch appointment with Seb. He had befriended a "patron of the arts" in Santa Monica and spent the last two months in her guesthouse, writing a book and neglecting his job at FWM. Though I explained that every week he took off would be added to his contract, he didn't seem to care. "Sometimes I send Rooney a page of dialogue and call that working," he had explained to me.

Sebastian had tried to convince me to meet him for lunch at the Santa Monica mansion, but I wasn't about to have some wealthy mistress floating around while I tried to talk to him. I arranged for lunch at a place nearby the canteen.

He showed up in a car that had to cost at least a year's worth of his FWM salary and smiled at me from the driver's seat. It had been weeks since I'd last seen him—he looked healthy and restored. At his best, he always had an impish handsomeness to him.

"Her father owns half the orange trees in California," he explained, holding his hands up. He paused. "Or something to that effect."

I crossed my arms and feigned disinterest as he got out of the car. I assumed his patron of the arts had a pool, because his arms and nose were red with sun. I mocked him as we walked down the street.

. . .

Sitting across from Seb, I thought of Baird's comments about Freddy on set. Baird had wished that someone would put Freddy in his place, and it occurred to me that someone almost certainly had: Charles.

"What happened on the set of *Fifty Grand*?" I asked Seb after our waiter took our order and cleared out.

"What happened was, Thomas Brodbeck let two men who hate each other engage in a fistfight for three months. You already know that."

"I think there's more to it than that," I said. Seb frowned and wrinkled his nose as if smelling something foul—it was a habit we both had when we were feeling stubborn. "For chrissakes, I'm not putting my own brother on the record. Just talk to me, would you?"

Seb leaned back in his chair, pushing the front two feet of it off the floor, and sighed while staring at the ceiling. "You know how Freddy likes to make jokes about people. He thinks his jokes are funny. With Charles, it was talking about his weight. That's how it started." He sat back up, his chair hitting the floor with a clang.

He paused when the waiter delivered our drinks, then waited for him to leave before continuing. "Then, whenever Freddy saw him, he'd ask him these ridiculous questions about his boxing weight class. When Charles wouldn't answer, Freddy settled on featherweight. He went around the set every day complaining about the inaccuracy of having a heavyweight boxer up against 'the featherweight.'"

I crossed my arms. It was obnoxious, but not remotely surprising.

"So, Charles beat the hell out of him. The production was set up so they'd do their own stunts. It wasn't difficult for Charles to get real punches in there. Most of the time, he didn't even bother pretending it was an accident," he told me. "They paid everyone on set a stipend to keep quiet on it. Didn't want to conflict with Freddy's illustrious legacy as a semiprofessional boxer."

He paused and stared at the wall behind me. "If Charles hadn't already wrecked his career, that alone would've done it. At least he went out swinging." He stopped to laugh at his joke.

We filled the rest of the lunch with empty chatter while Seb avoided all my attempts to discuss his neglected job at FWM. I asked what he was writing and learned he was planning to skewer Hollywood in a novel.

I raised an eyebrow. "Am I in this one?" I asked.

Seb smiled. "That's the issue, isn't it?" he asked. "Even if I promised you that you weren't, you'd probably try to find yourself anyway."

I paid for lunch and Seb stopped me before I got up from the table.

"Look, there isn't anything you could say that would make me want to go back to the studio," he said.

"You signed a contract; they can sue you. Your mistress might lend you a car here and there, but do you think she'll pay for a lawyer?"

I had explained it many times before, that he could lose everything he had and that no novel profits would cover it, no matter how good the novel, but Seb didn't seem to care. He didn't want to write scripts anymore.

As we left and walked down the street, he insisted that thinking about the script for *Fifty Grand* made him nauseous.

"Even I know the public wasn't especially keen on Charles," he said, "but, goddamn, no one was trying to assault him before *that* film premiered. And I'm not innocent here. I wrote those lines, made that character. We all knew how people would react. It was poorly done. I might as well have thrown that bottle at him myself."

I had heard a few different reports of what happened; the consensus was that a man had thrown a glass beer bottle at Charles as he was leaving Ciro's. The bottle struck Charles's shoulder and shattered. Aside from some bruising, Charles was physically unharmed by the attack. One source was certain that the man who threw the bottle also yelled a slur at Charles. In spite of his French last name, Charles had become subject to speculation that he was Mexican or even mulatto. People hadn't asked those kinds of questions about him before *Fifty Grand*.

As Seb got in his car, he looked at me.

"See, that's where we're different," he said. "When something I write hurts a person, I *stop*."

It was a discussion we'd had before. Seb hated that column on Charles and Freddy. After he left my house that day, he refused to speak to me for weeks. I got reports from Rooney that Seb was alive and doing "fine," which was far from comforting. I spent the entire time imagining the two men going on benders, Seb back in the hospital with that awful pale look on his face.

I had finally gotten through to Seb after bribing a receptionist at the Garden of Allah. I had arranged to meet him in the hotel bar and he had said it was below me to write "unsubstantiated garbage." When I told him it was *very well* substantiated, he told me that wasn't the part that should have upset me.

Eventually, he ran out of funds to put himself up at the Garden. I had given him the money on the condition that he complete one more script for FWM. I didn't know that the script would be *Fifty Grand*—yet another thing he could blame me for.

Seb drove off in his borrowed car before I could explain that he had the privilege of stopping: Sebastian O'Shaughnessy would always write another book, get another wealthy patron with a mansion on the beach, make another move across the country if he had to. Seb was never the person who would worry about getting sued over his contract, because he'd always had someone to do his worrying for him. For most of our lives, that someone had been me. No matter how bad things got, Seb would be taken care of.

A few nights later, I was scheduled to be at the grand opening of the Hollywood Canteen. I was about a thousand names down on the list of volunteers, but I had been given a press pass for that night.

When I arrived, I saw that a set of bleachers had been set up across the street from the canteen so that people could pay to sit and watch the opening. The bleachers were already full of spectators, some of whom had even brought binoculars and opera glasses. Every few moments, one of them would grab his seatmate by the arm and point excitedly at someone famous entering or leaving the building. There was a line of servicemen curving around the block, waiting to go inside. The doorway was jammed with people.

I was searching for another way to get into the canteen when I heard a voice calling my name from the other side of the building. Margy's head poked out from a window—her auburn hair was pinned back and she wore a little military-style hat made from paper. She waved me over. When I asked her where the door was, she shook her head and pointed to the window she was leaning out of.

"This is your door," she said, gesturing for me to climb through the window.

I begrudgingly did so, checking behind my back to make certain no one could see up my skirt. I was keenly reminded of how much slimmer the cut of ladies' styles had gotten over the last year when I tried to swing my leg over the windowsill. I felt a man's calloused hand at my wrist and looked up to see Hal.

I was pulled into a small, sweltering kitchen populated by Hollywood celebrities. Hal, along with the other men in the room, was wearing an apron and a matching hat. Without saying a word to me, Hal returned to his post at the grill, flipping burgers. He was joined by Rex Northrop and Gary Teague, all three men sweating through their shirts. A few actresses held serving trays, waiting for their orders. Some of them stood by open windows or before electric fans as they drank ice water and wiped the sweat from their foreheads.

There was live music in the next room and loud conversation. Men in uniform ate their meals or danced with the actresses. The mood in the room was positive—people laughed and crowded close to one another. I realized how long it had been since I was in a place where people were simply having a good time with one another, given the closure of most of the clubs in town. The space was entirely transformed from a few days earlier.

Among the actors and actresses enjoying themselves, there was one exception: Hal. The other men were working at the grill with the lighthearted acknowledgment that they were not cooks. I listened to Rex and Gary laugh loudly as one of them tossed a few burned patties in the garbage. Hal, however, was stuck in deep concentration on his station. His mood was so solemn, I could feel it from across the room.

The last time I had seen Hal was at a premiere for *Our Year of Abundance,* a comedy in which he played a penniless young bachelor from Montana who lives in his wealthy aunt's Manhattan penthouse apartment while she travels around Europe for a year. High jinks ensue.

He hadn't spoken to me at the premiere. Margy had attended with him and continued to acknowledge me with a tolerable degree of derision. But Hal excused himself from any conversation as soon as I showed up. Though I occasionally praised him in the column, it made no difference. Ever since Charles joined the air force, I had received nothing but pointed disdain from Hal.

As I stole a glance in his direction that night, I saw something else. It was in his tense posture, the unusual sharpness of his voice, the way he loudly hit his spatula against the grill—the man was furious. If he was trying to hide it, he wasn't doing an especially good job.

I asked Margy if I could shadow her for the night and she agreed, with the tacit understanding that it would earn her a nice line in print. She collected a full tray from Hal and walked it into the dining room. It was difficult to follow her, with all the people in the canteen—I bumped into three actresses and nearly knocked over a serviceman's glass of water.

As we waded through the room, Margy turned to me and spoke closely so I could hear her. "Don't mind Hal tonight; he's in a rotten mood." She lifted the tray above her head to let another actress pass by her.

She continued: "We got word earlier today that Charles has been stationed across the Atlantic. Hal's completely guilt-ridden about the whole thing." There was something affected in her tone when she spoke to me; she overenunciated the words *rotten* and *guilt-ridden,* as if she were practicing a line read on a new script.

Across the room, Nell was standing by the door, smiling and greeting young servicemen as they came in. She was very gracious that night, giving each man as much time as he wanted to speak to her. She didn't even withdraw when one of them touched her arm or shoulder.

Because it was the opening night and the space was small, none of FWM's newer stars were there. Every major studio's most iconic celebrities had signed up for the night—Bette Davis stood a few feet from Nell, Spencer Greene was entertaining a table of troops with a story, Olivia Newport readied herself to perform a piano number, and John Garfield meandered through the room.

Back in the kitchen to reload Margy's tray, I saw a man's foot, followed by part of a leg, struggling to get through the window. I looked at the other people in the kitchen, all of whom were suddenly fixated on what they were doing. Margy took one look at the shoe and then shook her head.

With a graceless thud, Freddy landed on his feet through the window. He brushed himself off with a dangerous glance at everyone around him. Rex wordlessly threw an apron to him. He put it on and loudly said hello to the room. Everyone responded by continuing what they'd been doing before.

Freddy saw me and a smile spread across his face. He walked over and put a hand on my shoulder; he asked if I knew where Nell was. I recoiled at his touch and gave Margy a pleading look as he began walking me out of the kitchen with him, steering me with a firm grip. Margy held up her empty tray in lieu of an explanation.

After pushing through the crowd, Freddy took his place next to Nell by the door. He grasped her elbow tightly and repositioned her so that he could shake the hands of the servicemen first. I stood nearby, unsure of whether or not to return to the kitchen. But when I turned to go, Freddy called my name and asked if I was getting everything.

To appease Freddy, I took out a notepad and wrote down some arbitrary words.

I spotted Augustan on the outskirts of the room, standing against a wall, doing his best to recede from the crowd. When Freddy wasn't paying attention, I sneaked over to him.

"Not so fast, O'Dare," Augustan said flatly. He crossed his arms and didn't turn to me.

I leaned into him. "I know you've got a flask in there," I said, pointing to his jacket. The canteen was strictly forbidden from serving alcohol. I pulled a rolled cigarette from my clutch. "Just one walk around the alleyway, for old times' sake."

He looked around the room—all of the people under his charge were preoccupied.

"You know Nell won't let Freddy do anything foolish on her watch," I whispered, and cocked my head toward the kitchen.

. . .

In the back alleyway, I lit the cigarette and traded it with Augustan for his flask. I took a swig and felt a pleasant burn in the back of my throat.

"It's been ages since I had a good whiskey," I said with a sigh.

He coughed and said between breaths, "You're drinking from Thomas Brodbeck's personal collection."

"How is Tommy?" I asked.

I hadn't seen Brodbeck in months. The popular rumor was that he was being eased out of operations at FWM. A friend of mine at RKO was convinced that Brodbeck was angling to start his own production company—he had been asking around town for any potentially available directors and writers. It was difficult to imagine a future for FWM without Brodbeck. The man had been the studio chief since the late twenties. He was appointed by Nico Marquis himself, plucked from lower management at Paramount. But with the Marquis family out of the picture entirely, Brodbeck's standing with the studio could be challenged.

"*Tommy,*" Augustan repeated, exhaling smoke, "needs a hobby."

"Has he tried boats?"

"For chrissakes, no one is buying boats for pleasure right now," he said, waving a hand in the general direction of the ocean. "I beg you not to say anything like that inside."

"Sorry, I don't know what other things the extraordinarily wealthy like to do. It's not as though *Freddy's* been deterred from seafaring."

Augustan passed me the cigarette and I gave him back his flask. "Freddy won't be deterred from anything."

"So I've heard," I said.

"His most recent quirk has been asking me if I've seen George anywhere. He keeps demanding that George tailor his suits. He knows very goddamn well where George is."

I kept quiet on that front. Not that it was my fault that George had absconded to MGM, but I wasn't entirely free of culpability.

George's replacement had gone from bad to worse—no one's costumes looked right. There was a particular devastation in watching a cowboy try to get onto his horse while wearing oversize chaps.

"To think you could've pawned him off on Columbia or Paramount," I said. A year ago, Freddy had received competing offers for his contract, but FWM matched them, and then some. It wasn't as though they had much of a choice—they had one of Hollywood's strongest leading men during a time when many were being shipped overseas. A large portion of the studio's profits was coming from a single man.

Augustan took a long swig from the flask. "Oh, I tried. Brodbeck wouldn't even entertain the idea, though. You give it a year and I swear Danny or Casey could take on any of Freddy's roles and we'd all be happier for it."

Given everything I'd heard about Freddy's protégés, I wasn't sure that we would.

"I suppose you already know Nell is trying to distance herself from him," I said.

He scoffed. "Right now, Nell might be the only thing anyone here likes about Freddy. But he's ours for another six years."

I looked at Augustan. "You know you can always ask for my help."

He mulled that over as he took the cigarette back from me. He paused. "What, do you think you could take down Freddy?"

I bobbed my head, feeling the immediate effects of the cigarette and whiskey. "You're talking to 'the most feared woman in Hollywood,'" I said in a low voice with an exaggerated air of danger.

"Watch out," he warned the empty alleyway, "Edie O'Dare is here!"

Augustan walked slowly down the alleyway and I caught up to him.

"How about this," I said. "I'll stop mentioning him for a while. See what happens."

He sighed. "Fine, go ahead."

We shook on it and went back to the canteen. Before we climbed back in through the window—the door was still overcrowded—I asked Augustan if I could call him again.

"Please," I said. "You're the only one who's any fun to talk to."

From the way he freely complained about Freddy, I had the sense that he felt the same way. Working in a studio could be suffocating, and I had always been confident that I was his outside air.

He nodded and swung his leg over the window. He had already disappeared into the crowd by the time I got through after him.

Hal was still flipping burgers, even though Rex and Gary had long since departed and been replaced at the grill. I watched as Margy urged him to leave—he responded by leveling the tray in her hand and placing another burger on it. She promptly handed the tray off to another actress and grabbed Hal's arm, pulling him over toward the supply closet. By design, there weren't any dark corners or private rooms for people to sneak away to in the canteen, so anyone in the kitchen could catch the gist of Margy and Hal's argument.

From what I heard, Margy told Hal that if he wanted to go to war so badly, he ought to get it over and done with.

"We all know they're only going to give you a job for show," she said. "By all means, enjoy the photo op."

As I listened, I tried to hide myself amid the foot traffic going in and out of the kitchen, though it was clear I wasn't the only person whose attention had been caught. One of the actresses raised her eyebrows as she refilled her tray, a man at the grill whispering in her ear.

Next, I heard Hal's voice perfectly clearly over the sounds of the kitchen: "We logged the exact same hours. If *he* can fly a plane over there, *I* can fly a plane over there."

My breath caught. Everyone in that room knew exactly which "he" Hal was referring to. There was too much noise coming from the next room for the kitchen to go silent, but there was a marked change in the air. I watched as Margy shook her head and mouthed something to Hal, but I couldn't make out the words. For a tense moment, the two of them stared at each other.

I heard someone whispering behind me. "I never took him for the jealous type."

Margy looked over her shoulder, the distress barely concealed on her face as she realized she'd been made into a spectacle. Everyone in the room either dispersed or invested themselves in a task, but I wasn't quick enough. Margy's eyes were fixed on me, and it wasn't long until Hal's were as well. He looked as if he were about to speak.

In that moment, I understood. I couldn't put words to it—it would be years, if not decades, before I had the right words—but I saw the expression on Hal's face.

For a long time after that night, I tried to see what everyone else in that kitchen saw: Hal was a man with an inferiority complex, who wanted to join the air force to prove a point to his wife. Most everyone believed Margy and Charles had been lovers at some point. It was an easy story to tell.

The look on Hal's face, though. It was as if he had been laid bare. His mouth was slightly open as he took slow breaths. There was terror in his eyes when they met mine. Immediately, he blinked and looked away. His shoulders hunched forward and he clasped his hands together, his elbows drawn close to his waist. He held on to his own hand tightly while Margy looked on coldly with her arms crossed. It's a strange and sad thing to watch a man of Hal's size try to make himself small.

It occurs to me now that I probably looked just as bewildered as either of them. Before any words could pass between us, I surrendered myself to the flow of the crowd and disappeared from the kitchen.

Back in the main room, nothing had quieted down: The line was still out the door, new musicians came in, and some of the stars had swapped out. The air smelled like a mixture of sweat and grease. And yet everyone was content to have a task at hand, to eat, to talk.

I could have reveled in the joviality, a respite from the harrowing headlines and photographs of everything happening overseas. I was happy for everyone who did lose themselves in that night, but I felt a tightness in my chest, a reminder that all of this was nothing more than a distraction.

Freddy still held his post at the door. Next to him, Nell had a fixed smile on her face, her jaw clenched. It wasn't like when she was with Charles—they had maintained a platonic comfort with each other's bodies. It was always true of Charles on set; I'd heard stories from other actresses that he was in the habit of telling them his stage directions before every scene in which he had to grab or hold someone. It seemed much the same when he was with Nell after hours.

I watched as Freddy placed a hand on Nell's shoulder, his fingers curling toward her collarbone. If I hadn't been looking for the way in which she drew her arms closer to her body, I would've missed it. I'd been in the same position with Freddy just an hour earlier, as had countless other women before. When Nell thought no one was looking, she swatted his hand away from her.

All at once, the noise became too loud for me. The faces of everyone around me dancing and laughing seemed distorted, wrong. Without a word, I left the canteen.

FOURTEEN

In the spring of 1943, I found myself standing on a windy strip of tarmac, preparing to leave California for the first time since I'd arrived over a decade earlier. I waited with Jeanette Manning and Spencer Greene—we were among a long list of notable Hollywood figures invited to join the Victory Caravan tour to raise funds for the army.

Staring up at the plane that would take us to Philadelphia, I grasped my bag so tightly I thought I might lose feeling in one of my hands. Spencer paid me no mind, but Jeanette noticed. She placed a hand on my shoulder.

"Don't worry," she said in her low, melodic voice, "I won't tell anyone that I know what the most feared woman in Hollywood is afraid of."

I'd agreed to join the Victory Caravan because they had written an interlude sketch for me as "the most feared woman in Hollywood." When I originally spoke with one of the coordinators, I was told I would be taking a train across the United States with the rest of the ensemble. No one had mentioned a plane. I felt ridiculous for not realizing that I'd have to take a plane out to the East Coast and even more ridiculous for being frightened of planes in the first place. Seb had assured me multiple times that I had nothing to worry about ("Look, it goes up, it comes back down"), but that did very little to abate my anxiety.

I had left my secretary with a detailed list of notes and lines for the column during my absence, with the promise that I would telephone with news. I bought a new suitcase and dresses for the occasion. I even purchased a few travel books and pamphlets for each city I was visiting with the Victory Caravan—why I should need to know where the best golf courses of Cleveland, Ohio, were located was beyond me, but I took an odd comfort in the information. I suspect it had something to do with knowing that Sophie Melrose had returned to her home there. Flipping through the pages of popular restaurants and attractions in Ohio, I was able to construct a life for her, to imagine that she had an existence beyond the trial transcripts and headlines. If I'm being honest, wanting to see that life with my own eyes was part of why I agreed to get on that plane in the first place.

I climbed the stairs to the plane with a hand on both railings as Jeanette trailed behind me. After everyone had filed on and I'd taken a seat by Jeanette and Spencer, Grace Stafford pushed through the door, out of breath. She was hastily dressed, with her stockings bunched up and her hat askew. Jeanette raised her eyebrows at me and exhaled loudly through her nostrils. When Jeanette wasn't looking, I gave Grace a smile as she searched for the remaining empty seats on the plane. Jeanette thought the girl was foolish, but she'd endeared herself to me ever since she'd played piano for us at the château.

Just when I thought I'd calmed my nerves, there were loud noises coming from under us. As the plane began to move, Jeanette handed me an old scarf of hers ("Sometimes it helps to have something to hold on to"). But I ended up holding on to Spencer's arm. He was a good sport about it.

After hours of my nearly bruising poor Spencer, we landed in Philadelphia. I could barely stand up; Spencer offered me a hand and walked with me off the plane. We were bused to the train station so we could store our bags and change our clothes.

While everyone sorted out their luggage, I left to find a phone booth and some solitude. I had to explain to one of our handlers that I had proper business to do. It wasn't until I showed a man my press badge that I was led to a small quiet room in the train station. I checked that Faye was ready with the next day's column and gave her some lines about the tour. I tried calling Seb at the Santa Monica mansion. When I was finally put through to him, I could practically hear the liquor in his voice as he answered the phone over the din of loud conversation in the background. He insisted he could talk.

"It's fine," I said. "I just wanted you to know that I landed safely."

He asked where, and I realized he had already forgotten I was traveling at all. I told him I'd call again when he wasn't clearly preoccupied.

In my years of acting, I'd only ever performed for a closed set, where I had the leisure of multiple takes and the freedom to slip up with little consequence. The appearance with the Victory Caravan was my first live audience and there'd be no second attempts. I found myself thinking of Charles, back in his days doing stunts, running down the length of a moving train. How one misstep could foil an entire production. I was overwhelmed with anticipation to the point where I could hardly breathe. It didn't help that after our rehearsal, Jeanette gave me a sincere look and asked if I wasn't a little concerned about being out of practice.

When the show began, I stayed backstage. Based on how much noise the crowd made, I assumed it was a full house. From the wings of the theater, I watched as a large troop of girls did a dance number while Evelyn Highsmith sang. A young man with a dark face played the piano and sang very beautifully. A brother-sister duo tap-danced in perfect harmony.

Before my bit, Grace took the stage and read out letters from the troops, thanking the audience and the American public for their contributions to army and navy relief funds. Her hair was pinned back and she wore a modest suit with a skirt and jacket in muted green tones, but she still had an understated beauty.

She was doing well with audiences lately. She had flailed after being forcibly recast by Rolf in that debacle with Hal and sent to do a comedy. Initially, she wasn't suited to humor. In some of the early reels, her sincerity on-screen made her seem dim and caused the other actors to appear malicious instead of funny. But with a bit of coaching, she refined her wide-eyed confusion into a charming coyness. That same sincerity led to her being cast in a romantic drama for her next film, where she came across as devastatingly endearing. She quickly gained a devoted base of fans.

Onstage, she had that same charm. The paper shook in her hands as she read, but her uncertainty won her sympathy from the audience. When her voice grew steadier and more confident, the whole room was rooting for her.

She finished by leading a rousing chorus of "America the Beautiful."

When I heard my cue, I walked onto the stage and various cast members feigned terror at my presence. I was instructed to carry a notepad and pen, which I would point threateningly at people. Then the stage cleared and it was just me.

Staring out into the crowd, I was unsure how to move or to speak but knew I had no choice but to do so anyway.

"It's my supreme pleasure to bring my column 'Do Tell' to life tonight," I said into a large microphone before thousands of faces. I fixed my eyes somewhere in the mezzanine and tried not to think too hard.

I assured the audience they were in for a treat with the next act.

"Jeanette Manning is a lovely singer and dancer," I said.

At that point, Jeanette appeared from the wing to the right of the stage and talked into another microphone. "Do you suppose she left out *actress* on purpose?" she said with a wink.

I wildly shook my head, nearly causing my hat to fall off. The audience laughed when I checked that it was still pinned to my hair.

Jeanette made a headline gesture. "Breaking: Edie O'Dare doesn't think Jeanette can act."

I tapped my microphone to get everyone's attention back. "Spencer Greene is one of Hollywood's classic stars," I said.

Then Spencer appeared from the left wing—to great applause—and said, "Translation: Edie O'Dare thinks I'm *old*." The crowd laughed with him.

We went back and forth like that a few times: I'd say something, and Jeanette or Spencer would comment on what I really meant.

I took a bow and left the stage to Jeanette and Spencer, who then transitioned into a song and dance. Though I had seen glimpses of them performing on set, I hadn't seen either do a full number live. From backstage, I could hear their voices, clear and robust, fill the auditorium. I was reminded that both of them had experience on Broadway—Spencer had been discovered there in the mid-twenties and Jeanette made periodic appearances—and knew how to handle an audience. They received a standing ovation.

In the wing of the theater, I felt my body shaking—from relief or fear, I wasn't sure. I couldn't sit down, so I paced during the other performances. I didn't even register when Cary Grant walked past and feigned terror at the sight of me until he was halfway down the hall.

The show closed out with a large-scale performance of "You're a Grand Old Flag" that included a troop of young women in matching costumes. The applause went on for nearly twenty minutes after they were done. We all went onstage in turns for a final bow, the sound of clapping never ceasing.

Afterward, we stayed in the lobby and promoted war bonds. Most of the crowd wanted to see Cary or Bing Crosby. I stayed close to

Jeanette, while Spencer drifted away from us. I had the pleasure of standing quietly as people talked to Jeanette, though I was surprised by the number of audience members who sought me out to tell me they enjoyed reading my column.

"I think you have the right idea about things," a woman said before handing me a copy of a newspaper with my column to sign. I looked at my little headshot next to the column and tried to see myself as this woman did: an ever-smiling face with an endless supply of quips and witticisms.

Everyone was quiet from exhaustion on the bus back to the train station. I settled in next to Jeanette, who was leaning against the bus window, half asleep. Spencer was across the aisle from me, still alert. He smiled at me; he had removed his stage makeup and I could see the years on his face.

Jeanette and I weren't old enough to recall the last war, though I'd heard plenty of stories and had no doubt that she had, too. The specter of it loomed over my early childhood—I was hardly five years old when we went to war that time. But Spencer was well aware what it was like: He was barely too young for that war and barely too old for this one. He didn't say very much to his traveling companions, mostly sat in his seat, fumbling with the hat in his lap.

Back on the train, the group was plenty loud during our midnight dinner. People spoke over one another as we passed plates and drinks between us.

While I was finishing up my sandwich, Jeanette told me she had some decent liquor in her bunk. A few of the girls would be there, if I wanted to join them. I was surprised by the thoughtfulness of the gesture.

Sitting on the train bunks, Jeanette, Grace, and some of the dancers were exchanging a bottle.

Grace smiled. "It feels like school, doesn't it?" she asked.

Grace grew up in Connecticut, and it was well known that she was plucked from her boarding school to go to Hollywood after performing with a touring Shakespeare troupe for a summer.

I told her I wouldn't know, having barely scraped through primary school myself before being called away to raise my other siblings.

I took a drink. "But I'm happy to take your word for it!"

"People are saying that you've already been defanged," Jeanette told me when the girls weren't listening. She pulled a hand-rolled cigarette from her clutch and lit it next to the open train window. The train thundered below us.

"I can still be plenty mean," I assured her.

But there was some truth to it. I hadn't really gone after anyone in Hollywood since the column on Charles. For all the good that did me—a large portion of the industry was still angry with me in spite of my attempts to make nice. It did make a girl wonder what the point was.

"Anytime you want to tank Clarke, you let me know," she said, handing me the cigarette. "He's been insufferable since that goddamn trial."

I didn't want to explain to her that I was in the early stages of doing exactly that—though "tanking" might be taking it a step too far.

"I don't know why *I* get all this spite for Freddy," I finally said.

Jeanette arched an eyebrow. "You did a lot for him. And it seems to me you didn't have to do a lot for him."

"Neither did any of you, but that didn't stop you from signing his preposterous petition, going to parties with him, handing out statements."

"As if any of us had a choice," she said, taking back the cigarette. It was a fair point—Augustan told them what to say and do, and most of them said or did that. Charles had been the exception, and now he was at the mercy of the United States Army Air Forces.

But still, I continued: "If I recall correctly, plenty of women managed not to go to the Academy Awards with Freddy."

Jeanette let out an unkind laugh that had a quality similar to a dog barking. "With all due respect," she said, "I don't think you have any idea what you're talking about."

I left shortly after that. I recognized that I had an ally in Jeanette, if only a precarious one, and I didn't want to say something I'd regret. By that time, I was aware that most of the Jeanette Mannings of Hollywood were done with me. They'd written me off as Poppy's second-rate counterpart, but I made the same deals as anyone else in the business. Most of my sources traded me information for mentions in the column, but sometimes it could be more complicated than that—actresses who wanted a little more control over their public images, people vying for new kinds of roles, trying for a career breakthrough. No one should have been surprised: I learned it all from Poppy.

The next morning, Grace slipped into the seat next to me on the bus to downtown Cleveland. There were plenty of extra seats; Grace had been deliberate in selecting one next to mine.

"How can I help you?" I asked Grace.

She smiled and said, "I wanted to say thank you for covering the Victory Caravan. It's important that people know about it."

"That's sweet of you," I told her. I knew Jeanette was only a row away, happily judging me and Grace. I tried looking out the window, but Grace was persistent.

"You know I'm playing Nell Parker's kid sister when I get back," she said.

I did know that—they were both starring in *This Proud Heart*, a Pearl S. Buck adaptation featuring Nell as sculptress torn between passion and family.

"I think this could be something big for me," she said, her voice low. "If I could get a little help, I'd be happy to pay back the favor, let you know what's happening on set."

She mentioned that she had heard Nell's relationship with Freddy was on the rocks and offered to keep an eye on them. "I can tell you when things really start to go south for them," she assured me. I didn't mention that they already had and I was well aware of that fact.

I sighed. "Nell's a close friend, if that's what you mean," I explained. I didn't need to have someone leaking Nell's where-abouts to me. "Who else do you have?"

"Paisley's directing," she said. I shook my head—I had no inter-est in going after a woman working in a man's field. I had plenty of sympathy for that myself. She hesitated, then said, "Danny's the male lead."

Of course, Danny Prior, the replacement Charles Landrieu, was playing Nell's love interest.

"Let me know how it goes," I said. I gave her my card and she briefly squeezed my arm and smiled before taking it.

I phoned Faye to include a few sentences about how charming Grace was onstage: "Grace Stafford could very well be the face of American women today. She began her act unsteady, perhaps unsure, but her willingness to persevere made her performance all the more compelling. Readers: Keep an eye on this one."

We had the afternoon to walk around Cleveland, so I convinced Jeanette to lunch with me. She had very few other options—I was objectively preferable to the group of twenty-year-olds. A pack of them went to get hot dogs and sodas. I knew Jeanette would want to sit down and be civilized.

"What if I proposed a trade?" I asked Jeanette.

We sat in the corner of a small restaurant, where no one noticed her. She had a scarf tied around her head and wore an oversize pair of gold-rimmed glasses to read her menu. Usually I would've mocked the gesture of a disguise, but Jeanette did have one of the more distinctive faces in Hollywood, all cheekbones and eyebrows.

She looked at me over her glasses. "Information, I suspect?"

I nodded. I added that it was only out of curiosity—I wouldn't print anything she told me.

"Sure, that worked out nicely for Charles Landrieu," she said, pretending now to be immersed in the one-page menu. There were only three options on there, but I'll be damned if Jeanette wasn't giving them her undivided attention.

"Charles told me that on the record," I said. "You can ask him."

"I guess I'll call up the U.S. Air Force?"

I leaned into the table. "We've got three hours to pass. Indulge me, won't you?"

Once our food arrived at the table, she asked me why Charles would ever let me write that about him. I told her that I knew something else about him, and that he had used the story about his affair with Ines as leverage.

Then it was my turn. "Why don't the women of FWM want to work with Rolf Junger?" I asked her.

She chewed her food slowly. "The young ones do."

I asked her if they knew any better. She said they didn't. Then she said that was more than one question. She wanted to know what I knew about Charles.

"He was a little friendlier with Margy than they let on," I said simply. It was close enough to the truth.

Jeanette scoffed at that. "Why don't you try asking Margy about Rolf?"

I told her that I had and that Margy gave me a nonanswer—I still remember her pageant voice that morning at the château after I brought up *Afterglow*. To which, Jeanette shrugged and said she was tired of this game.

"That's fine," I said, "but I was hoping you could do me a favor."

She let out a sigh and adjusted her glasses. Before she could refuse, I told her, "I'll give you a full profile. You'll be the most patriotic woman in Hollywood."

"Edie," she said after a pause, "I'm already famous. And I like *exactly* how famous I am, not a bit more, not a bit less. I don't need to sidle up to you on the bus and ask for your business card."

"In that case, with no hopes of being able to repay you, could you tell Augustan that things went well out here?"

Jeanette's face softened—it was as close to pity as I'd ever seen from her. As much as my friendship with Augustan was common knowledge, so was our falling-out. "Sure, I'll do that. Sure."

While we were walking from the restaurant to the auditorium, Jeanette stopped and told me she needed to make a brief visit to the post office. She reminded me that she had a five-year-old boy back in Los Angeles—she liked to send postcards when she traveled.

I waited for Jeanette outside. On the steps, I watched people going about their days. A woman walked by with three young boys, one small enough to be in her arm, one skipping behind her, one tugging her toward an ice-cream shop. Two men in uniform walked into a restaurant down the street.

Then I saw her on the opposite side of the street: a young woman, around nineteen or twenty, wearing a sleek pastel blue dress. Her long blond hair was pinned back around a military-style hat, the same shade as her dress. She was pushing an expensive baby carriage. She looked healthy; her cheeks were round and her red lips were plump.

I got off the steps and started walking in the same direction on my side of the street. I kept a close eye on her. She was alone, except for the baby. She waved at a few people passing by and stopped to make conversation.

I imagined that they were her friends. That she hosted afternoon tea for them. I imagined that she finished school. That she got high marks and enjoyed her classes. That she'd changed her name back to the one her parents had given her, that they were excited to have her back home. That they only discussed her time in California as a passing phase, the same way some adolescent girls develop obsessions with hobbies like horseback riding or volunteering with the Junior League. I imagined that there was a wedding ring on her finger. That she'd found a nice young man with a steady job and a calm demeanor. I imagined that she loved that baby.

But mostly, I imagined that Sophie Markham of Cleveland, Ohio, was happy.

When Jeanette called out my name, the lady pushing the baby carriage turned her head. I had a clear view of her and my heart sank when I saw that the face was all wrong—her eyes were too wide and her chin was too sharp.

Jeanette joined me and we walked to the auditorium.

"You don't have kids, right?" Jeanette asked me as we went down the streets of Cleveland.

"Sebastian and I practically raised each other," I explained. "And you can see how that turned out."

"You know it was *months* before any of us figured out that you'd planted your brother in FWM Studios," Jeanette said. "Shrewd, even for you."

"If I were truly being shrewd, I would have planted him in MGM. Now he's gone into an early retirement that he can't afford. I suppose I did all I could for him . . ." I said, and my voice trailed off.

I considered how much worse off Seb would be if he broke the contract I'd gotten him into in the first place. My concern must have shown on my face, because Jeanette briefly placed a hand on my shoulder.

"Isn't it so exhausting?" Jeanette asked, retying her scarf so it hid her hair. "All that caring?"

Waiting backstage before the show, I thought about Sophie. For all I knew, she could be in the audience at that very moment. I imagined how she might react to seeing me onstage—whether she would be angry or surprised. Then I realized how ridiculous it was to believe she'd think about me at all when I was sharing the stage with some of the most famous names in Hollywood.

We had over ten thousand people in Cleveland. The second time around, I felt looser in front of the audience. By the time I took the stage, people had been laughing with Bob Hope and Cary Grant for an hour—they were happy to be there. So when I wanted the audience to pay attention, they paid attention. When I wanted them to laugh, they laughed. I understood why a number of Hollywood actors and actresses took sabbaticals to perform onstage, even if it meant their contracts would be extended: it was the purest expression of power that I'd ever experienced.

We ate our late dinner on the train, everyone sitting around a piano installed for the express purpose of rehearsing for the show. People took turns singing and playing. We all crowded around the piano, until half of us ended up sitting on the floor or sharing chairs.

A girl sat next to me with a copy of my column, syndicated in the Cleveland *Plain Dealer*. I recognized her as one of the line dancers for the finale number. She was young, with a round face and light red hair.

"I just love your column," she said to me.

"I suppose you want to become an actress," I said, feeling equal parts bored and sympathetic.

She nodded and began telling me a story about school performances and how jealous her friends back home would be when they found out she was in the same show as Cary Grant.

I stopped listening to her about halfway through her monologue and then politely excused myself. If the girl was lucky, someone would tell her outright that she didn't have a chance.

Before the performance in Detroit, I called up my office to dictate "Dispatches from the Hollywood Victory Caravan." Reading from notes scribbled onto napkins and scrap paper, I fed Faye a new column and hoped she could translate it into coherent English.

I asked her if I had any messages waiting for me and was surprised to hear that Augustan had called.

"Did he say what it was about?" I asked her.

"He wouldn't tell me," she said, resentment in her voice. "Said it was for your ears only. Wasn't especially polite about it."

When I tried his office, I got his secretary, who trusted me about as much as Augustan trusted Faye.

On the way to the Chicago stadium, I went with the motorcade instead of taking the bus. After all the film premieres I'd attended, I wasn't fazed by large crowds cheering or the burst and crackle of flashbulbs. But sitting on the back of the car alongside Jeanette and Spencer felt different. People wanted to be near us, to get our attention, to show us affection. Members of the crowd cheered and tossed flowers to us. They'd go back to their homes and tell their friends and family whom they'd seen from afar. It would probably be the highlight of their day, if not their week. After months of isolation, I felt warmed by their attentiveness. In short, it was intoxicating.

Before the show, I sat with Jeanette on the floor backstage. She held a flask and appeared a little looser than usual. She hadn't finished her makeup for the night, so her face was powdered but not rouged. The effect was odd and made her seem ghostly.

She handed the flask to me. "To assuage your guilty conscience," she said.

I took a drink and then I took a few more drinks.

"It takes some nerve," I said to Jeanette. She smiled, as if this was all amusing. "You think I don't remember who invited Freddy to be her plus-one to Brodbeck's that night?"

"Don't be absurd," she said with a wave of her hand.

I remembered it clearly: Back in August 1939, I had asked Freddy whom he'd bribed to get into Brodbeck's mansion for the *Sure Shot* party. He said he hadn't bribed anyone and then pointed to Jeanette. I saw them sitting next to each other at dinner. There wasn't anything romantic to it—both of them were married to other people at the time—but it was cordial.

"You did, though," I said. "He wasn't supposed to be there. Why'd you let him?"

"I didn't *let* him do anything," she said. "He asked if he could tag along with me. I thought—I thought it'd be funny."

"Which part?"

"What?"

"Which part was supposed to be funny?"

Jeanette frowned. "Look, I'm admitting defeat here—aren't you happy, Edith?" The tone of her voice was no longer melodic as she continued. "I was wrong. Freddy was wrong. That *ridiculous* girl was wrong."

She paused for a while and shook her head. She leaned back against the wall and lit a cigarette. "I don't know what any of us are supposed to do about it now."

I was worried I'd just ruined our bit for the night, or that Jeanette was too drunk, but the moment she appeared onstage, she was alert and ready.

It was the biggest audience I'd seen yet. They paid rapt attention to our every word, every move, every note. When I took the stage, I felt buoyed by their enthusiasm, as if I could forgo food and water if I had their unwavering support. For the first time during the tour, I felt a deep sadness when I went back behind the curtain. I couldn't even watch Jeanette and Spencer's number. I left early and missed the final bow.

After the Chicago show, I slept in a hotel for the night. The Victory Caravan was scheduled to continue on, but I had been allotted a few free days before I had to return to Los Angeles. It was the first time I'd been alone for days. I slept so heavily that I nearly missed my alarm the next morning.

When I went to the train station, no one gave me a second glance, though I kept anticipating a moment when I would be recognized. The station was populated by men in uniform, along with their families and loved ones. They exchanged embraces and heartfelt good-byes. I watched as a young woman reached up to one of the windows of the train and grasped an anonymous hand.

I boarded the train as a perfectly normal civilian. For all any-one in that station knew, I might be departing at any of the stops between Chicago and Los Angeles, returning to a life with a hus-band and two children in Des Moines or Omaha. If someone had asked that day, I'm not sure I wouldn't have lied and invented an entire story for myself and my nonexistent children, right down to their food preferences and favorite classes in school.

By Hollywood standards, I should have been on husband number two at my age. I'd had plenty of opportunities—Baird used to propose to me during the intervals between each of his marriages—but there was always something else I was meant to be doing. First it was acting; then it was moonlighting for Poppy, or some imperative task given to me by Augustan. Years had passed and all I had to show for them was a gossip column with my name in bold letters on the top of it.

Even that was tainted: Charles had told me I was wrong about everything. The one thing I'd managed to build for myself was predicated on falsehoods. It's easy to fool oneself into thinking there's a lot more control with a lie. I was reminded of working on set with a director like Gideon, who was known for his fas-tidiousness, and how many takes he demanded to oversee every detail. He once required a reshoot that went on for days because he'd noticed in his daily reels that someone had moved a clock on a mantelpiece in the background and he couldn't abide its inex-plicable disappearance from scene to scene. We all hated him for it at the time, but to this day, I can't stand catching inconsisten-cies in films.

I suppose it's why I never left Hollywood for all those years—it was a city that promised reshoots. You could tell a lie over and over again, until every variable was accounted for. As I sat on the long train ride home, I'd told myself I'd try again.

Fifteen

When I returned to my office, I had a message from Augustan on my desk. It simply said "His fan letters are down."

Weeks had passed since I'd agreed to stop mentioning Freddy. I thought Freddy would have noticed by now, but I also suspected that he didn't read the papers unless someone told him to. Augustan certainly wasn't telling him to.

For the next day's column, I wrote out a list of casting requests from readers. Things like "Miss Vera Bennett of Billings, Montana, would love to see Baird deWitt as a romantic lead." Most of them actually came from readers, though I occasionally did some inventing.

That morning, I decided that a nice young woman from Kansas City really wanted to see Grace Stafford take on more leading roles.

I tried to tell Augustan that I would be visiting FWM, but when I called, I couldn't get past his secretary, who scheduled someone to escort me in and out of the studio.

I was met at the studio gates by a young woman—another secretary, I assumed. I told her that I had business with Grace Stafford, but she didn't seem to believe me. She kept looking down at a notepad, which I imagined contained some mixture of instructions and warnings about me.

"Take me over to her lot; she'll tell you it's true," I said.

With an anxious look, the young woman agreed. We walked to Lot 7, where Grace was on set with Nell and Danny. My escort made me wait outside the door while she went in. I watched peo-ple filter in and out of the different lots. In the distance, I saw a tall man in contemporary riding garb walk a horse around the alleyway. The man's careful gait was unmistakable: It was Hal.

Although Hal had come back from boot camp only long enough to finish production on a film, the studio kept finding reasons to prolong his stay in Hollywood long after the shoot wrapped. At this rate, he wasn't getting deployed. Something sim-ilar had happened to Grant Hastings—he had logged his hours to become a pilot nearly a year ago but was deemed too valuable to Columbia's own war efforts.

I whistled loudly enough to get the horse's attention; Hal's fol-lowed shortly thereafter. He shook his head and continued walk-ing the horse along. I was reminded of how Charles used to ride them around between takes. It wasn't difficult for me to catch up with him as he slowly led the horse.

Hal looked at me and stopped walking. I hesitated as I stood next to them, feeling particularly small beside the imposing com-bination of Hal and the nine-hundred-pound beast he held by the reins. I remembered how he had looked at me that night at the canteen and my voice caught in my throat.

When I didn't speak, Hal let out a heavy sigh. "Don't know what you're bothering me for—Freddy's over that way," he said, pointing toward a lot down the alleyway.

I crossed my arms and looked up at Hal. Even when I was wearing heels, I had to crane my neck to see him. He was clean-shaven that day and his dark blond hair was combed back. He had developed a charming crease at the corners of his eyes; it added to the effect of the uncertain squint he gave me.

"I'm not here for Freddy," I said. I softened my voice. "Between you and me, I've had about enough of him for now. The war-hero act starts to look a little ridiculous when you realize what it's like for the people actually fighting over there."

I didn't dare to say Charles's name. I watched Hal's face closely, waiting to see if he would be upset at the implication. There was a slight twitch around his mouth, but otherwise he maintained his composure. He tightened his grip on the horse's reins when it tried to nuzzle my shoulder. He pulled the horse away from me and clicked his tongue.

"A belated revelation, don't you think?" he said curtly.

"What if I wrote something nice about you?" I offered. "Wouldn't you like the public to know that you toiled away making burgers and fries for servicemen?"

He exhaled loudly out his nose. "The whole goddamn point is that the public doesn't know I toiled away making burgers and fries," he said. The agitation was clear in his voice. "Can't a man just do something good for good's sake?"

"Of course," I said. "I'm only trying to do something good myself."

I tried to read his expression. Hal's anger with me no longer came as a surprise. Plenty of people in Hollywood were angry with me on a regular basis. Compared with some of the looks Jeanette had given me over the last few weeks, Hal's might even have been considered friendly. But the way his eyes drifted away from me—that wasn't anger. There was vulnerability there—something I hadn't seen in so long, I barely knew how to name it.

"Christ," he said in a voice so quiet, it was almost as if he were whispering to himself, "when have you done any of us an ounce of good?"

He laughed quietly and there was something pained in his smile. He ran his hand over his face and I could have sworn his eyes were watering.

Before I could respond, Hal refocused himself and nodded behind me to my escort. "You're making your handler nervous," he said. "Spare me and go do good deeds somewhere else, Edie."

My escort had reappeared and was beckoning me to the lot with Grace. I glanced back at Hal, who had fixed his attention back on his horse and begun leading it away from me. I watched him walk slowly amid the crowd.

. . .

The young secretary held her post by the door while I sat with Grace on the outskirts of the lot. On the soundstage, Nell did a scene with Danny, directed by Paisley. Paisley looked sharp sitting in her chair; she wore a pair of neatly tailored trousers and had her hair pinned back in a tight chignon. When she paused a scene, she went out on the set and spoke to Nell and Danny in soft conversational tones and thanked them when she was done.

I turned to Grace, who was outfitted in a two-piece dress suit—by this point in the film, she was supposed to be fumbling her way through a secretarial job while Nell's character made a choice between marriage and her passion for sculpture.

"They want me to go on the yacht this weekend," Grace said in a low voice. "They," I assumed, meant Danny and Freddy.

"Do you *want* to go on a yacht with them?"

Grace looked over at the set, where Nell was grabbing Danny's shoulders while proclaiming that she wanted to be an artist. Paisley motioned for her to give it more *oomph*. I saw Grace's expression shift as her eyes tracked Nell's movements on set.

"I can go on a yacht with them," she said without looking at me. I saw the determination in her eyes.

I sighed. "That's not what I asked you."

I tried to tell myself that I wasn't the girl's mother. Grace was all of twenty-one years old, though she could play younger roles, and if she wanted to go on a yacht, she could go on a yacht. It didn't stop my stomach from churning at the thought. The image of Sophie rose to my mind, her blank expression that night as she sat on the diving board, her bare feet dangling in Brodbeck's pool. I knew that Grace was older than Sophie. She was as old as I had been when I was cast in my first starring role. At Grace's age, I had been put in flimsy nightclothes and instructed to seduce men on-screen—no one gave it a second thought; no one asked if I was okay with it. I hadn't been hurt in the process. I told myself many times over the years that I hadn't been hurt.

. . .

Before I could voice any misgivings, Grace was called back on set so she could walk in on a quarrel between Nell and Danny. I saw the way Danny looked at her as she got up from her chair—hungry. Grace turned to me and assured me that she had a great memory for details.

"I graduated at the top of my class," she said. "I don't forget a thing."

Her entire demeanor changed as she walked toward the set: She held her head higher and set her jaw.

Before my escort could start leading me toward the exit, I asked her if I could go see Augustan.

"By all means, call him up," I said when she hesitated. I watched her face as she did the mental calculations—risk bothering Augustan with someone he very possibly didn't want to talk to, or upset an impulsive gossip columnist.

One phone call later, I was on the elevator up to Augustan's office.

"Tell me about Grace Stafford," I asked Augustan.

Out of habit, I sat in my usual chair in his office. I was mindful not to put my feet up or appear too comfortable in there; instead, I sat with my legs crossed, back straight. Augustan was sitting at his desk with his hands neatly clasped in his lap.

"You know, she could very well be the face of American women today," he said, feeding my own words back to me. His face relaxed into a smile. "I did appreciate that line."

I leaned forward, so my elbows rested against my knees. "I thought that you would."

In the likely event that FWM lost Nell Parker to MGM, Grace was poised to take many of her vacated roles. Grace's hair was a few shades darker than Nell's signature white-blond, but that's what bleach was for.

. . .

Over a glass of whiskey, Augustan and I discussed Grace, Nell, Freddy, and anyone else at FWM. He was still treading carefully with me. He was forthcoming with information about Freddy, but when I asked about Freddy's mentees, Danny and Casey, Augustan turned tight-lipped. If our scheme worked out, those boys would be the ones taking Freddy's roles.

The conversation wasn't unlike trying to get a knot out of one's hair. I started combing at the ends and hoped to work my way up to teasing out the thorny bits. Given everything that had happened over the course of the last year or so, Lord knew Augustan and I had some thorny bits.

"Do you ever wonder what Sophie Melrose's career might have looked like by now?" I asked him after we'd made a dent in the bottle of whiskey on his desk. Due to wartime scarcity, I hardly drank anymore. It wasn't long before I could feel the looseness in my jaw and a slight numbness in my cheeks.

"I don't think about it at all," he said calmly.

"You can't mean that," I said. By that point, I'd removed my shoes and put my stocking feet up against his desk. Augustan's secretary had called for him a few times and he'd ignored her.

"If it weren't her, it would be somebody else. After nearly twenty years of doing this," he said, and gestured to his window overlooking the studio lots, "it makes little difference to me."

He stood up and continued, his voice flat as he paced his office and spoke. "Before Freddy Clarke, it was Archer Ward. Before Danny Prior, it was Charles Landrieu. Before Edward Percival, it was Spencer Greene. And before Nell Parker, it was Thelma Conroy. In five years, I'll probably tell you that before Grace Stafford, it was Nell Parker."

I took my feet off his desk and sat up in my chair, feeling the whiskey as I did so. "You *do* care about some of them. I've seen you!"

"You and I, we can't afford to care about them," he said. He took slow and deliberate steps around his office as he spoke, occasionally gesturing with his glass. "Not properly care, anyway. You could have written a hundred columns about how wronged Sophie was, and you know what? The outcome would still be the same. I can't think of any deviation of events that would lead to justice for Sophie Melrose. America is a country built for men like Freddy Clarke to prevail and he is *always* going to prevail. People like us ought to be smart enough to make a profit off it if we can."

I shook my head too vehemently; I could feel the pins coming loose in my hair. I began to feel ridiculous. "I tried, you know. To help her," I said. The words came up like bile in my mouth. "I was Ash Copeland; I published the interview."

Augustan stopped pacing and looked at me carefully. "And you saw all the good that did."

All the times I'd imagined telling him the truth—I had expected resentment, I had expected surprise, I had expected him to throw me out of his office and swear never to speak to me again. I had not prepared for his cruel indifference.

His secretary rang again and this time it was urgent; he was needed on one of the lots. As he gathered his jacket, he looked perfectly composed, not a detail out of place. He told me I was welcome to finish my drink in his office but that he wouldn't be returning for some time.

I put my shoes back on and sat up in my chair. I felt disheveled and humiliated. When I stood up, I stumbled and quickly realized that I was too drunk to drive myself back home. There was a couch in Augustan's office that I knew he took naps on, but the entire space suddenly felt cold and sterile to me. I used his phone to call myself a cab. It wasn't until I caught a glimpse of myself in the mirror on my way out that I realized my face was streaked with wet mascara.

I had promised *Photoplay* a piece about women in Hollywood training to be nurses, and they finally scheduled some actresses for a photo shoot at a local hospital. With a throbbing headache from the evening before, I retrieved my car from the FWM parking lot and drove out to Pasadena for the shoot.

In an empty cordoned-off hallway of an otherwise busy hospital, Carla Longworth was joined by Olivia Newport as they smiled and wrapped bandages around a young man's head. Both women were dressed in demure green suit dresses and the man wore a service uniform. They took turns smiling at the camera as they went through step-by-step instructions for properly stanching a head wound.

As they did so, I asked them for some quotes about why it was so important for young ladies to take an interest in nursing.

"Because we'd usually care for our husbands at home," Olivia explained, "but while they're serving their country, we've got to take care of the young men here."

Carla unwound the bandage from the man's head. She spoke with a fixed smile. "He could be someone else's husband, father, brother, or son."

She then stood by and offered the young man support while Olivia fashioned a sling for an imagined arm injury. They were professional about it, but it was clear they were both amused by the whole thing. I didn't miss the sardonic wink Carla gave the camera while presenting the man's sling.

"Don't you feel lucky, having such beautiful women here to attend to you?" I asked the man. He looked twenty years old at most.

"Happy to be in good hands!" he said. He told me he would be deployed in a few weeks' time. "None too worried about it!"

As I left, I went through the hallways of the hospital and maneuvered around gurneys that held wounded men.

I caught Carla smoking outside the hospital. A lesser Augustan was waiting nearby to shepherd her back to the studio.

"I haven't seen you since our *fête des dames* at the château," she said, and offered me a cigarette.

I leaned against the wall, blowing smoke toward the top of the building. Around us, people were going in and out of the hospital with varying degrees of urgency. Every few moments we were interrupted by the loud wail of an ambulance.

"I'm sorry not to have made the cut for an invitation back," I lamented.

Carla waved me off. "Oh, neither have I—Ines hasn't had any parties lately. Says she's busy. My bets are that she's writing anti-fascist propaganda to mail to France. Margy thinks it's illicit love affairs."

Anywhere else, someone would have stopped and recognized Carla, but the staff and patients were too preoccupied to pay her any mind.

The lesser Augustan loudly cleared his throat, which I took as my cue to leave. I went to my car and she followed him to a black Cadillac waiting among the ambulances.

When I went back into the office that week, there was a message posted from Grace, asking me to call as soon as I had a chance. She had spent her Saturday boating with Freddy and company. As I stared at the little card with her message, I went through a mental inventory of all the worst things that could have happened on that yacht, just as I had the night before when I couldn't sleep. It had been a long night; every time I tried to relax, I had visions of Sophie sitting by the water—the grass, dirt, and debris coming off her feet as she submerged them in the pool.

When I called Grace, she didn't want to talk on the phone and asked that I meet her somewhere. There wasn't a hint of fear in her voice. If anything, she sounded excited, talking in short, hushed bursts. I then realized this was fun to her. When I suggested meeting at her home, she was adamantly against it. She lived with a few other girls, all of whom were terrible eavesdroppers. She requested that I meet her at the boardwalk.

Grace was standing against a railing on the Venice Beach boardwalk, looking out at the water. She wore a dowdy housedress and had a scarf tied around her hair. She had never done any spy films, but based on her dedication to being covert, I suspected it was an aspiration of hers.

"I very nearly didn't go," she said as we walked. "I got to the boat and it wasn't only Freddy and Danny; they had Rolf, too."

I resisted reminding her that no one—and most especially not I—made her go. This was Grace's own scheme, I just happened to be the person who might expose some of it. I asked if she'd been the only woman on the boat.

"There was another girl, Theresa," she said. "Around my age, but she could be younger. A model. She does catalog work and some retail at the department stores."

Grace required no prompting. She explained the entire trip in detail, from the moment she got on the boat to her departure late in the evening. She had been offered drinks throughout the excursion, but she kept tossing them overboard when no one was paying attention ("I learned my lessons about all that back at school"). Theresa had not. As a result, she became heavily intoxicated. The men, on the other hand, were all regular drinkers, and if they felt the effects of the alcohol, they didn't show it.

She told me there was a photographer on the boat as well. He claimed he was working for *Life*, though Grace doubted it. Theresa had never seen him before, and she swore she knew all the important photographers. The photographer had staged some pictures of the girls pretending to fish. They'd brought their own bathing suits, but the photographer asked them to change into some spare ones left on the boat ("Not the kind of thing I'd pick out for myself").

Two years ago, the actress Rose Stanley very nearly signed a contract with Fox—the papers were printed and everything—when it leaked that she had been photographed in flagrante delicto in her late teens. The photographs were never found and the story was never published, but it was enough for the producers to tear up her contract.

I had no doubts that a girl like Grace knew Rose's story; if she didn't, she knew plenty of similar stories. Though Grace was only slightly older than Sophie, and bore a lot of similarity to her lookswise, there was a sharpness in her tone and the way she glanced around her that was more reminiscent of Nell. That sharpness had only become more pronounced since I saw her crying on Rolf's set years ago.

I asked her how it was being on a boat with Rolf, given their history with each other.

"Oh, that's nothing personal," she said with a brave face. I caught the way she adjusted her voice as she said it and remembered how she'd looked that day when she was removed from the set by Rolf. She was fortunate that the incident hadn't ended her career.

As we walked, the occasional crowd of servicemen passed us. The boardwalk had regained some of its lost popularity when it became a destination for troops stationed on the West Coast. A year ago, most of the dance and music halls had been practically abandoned, but now they bustled with people and noise.

I watched some of the gentlemen coming out of the halls give Grace the once-over—even in her drab clothing she was clearly very beautiful. One of them stopped to tell her she was pretty enough to be in the pictures.

"Well," she said in a low voice to me, "wouldn't that be nice?"

She thanked him and continued walking.

"Rolf wasn't interested in either of us," she said. "Said we were good-looking but not his type."

"Did he say what his *type* was?" I asked.

"From things I've heard, it's tall, southern, and married to Hal Bingham."

I asked her where she'd heard that and she said she'd had it confirmed by Danny, Victor Perez, and possibly even Margy herself.

"Something about being on location for *Afterglow*—he became enamored of her. Or she of him. I'm not so sure which."

She didn't know anything more than that, and even those details were hazy.

When I asked her about Freddy, she scoffed.

"I'm not about to let him tell me that I need to go upstairs for a *nap*," she said. Her tone was not dissimilar from that of a schoolgirl offering up the correct answer only seconds after the question was posed by her teacher. "Or belowdecks, as the case may have been. Theresa, though? I think she was sitting a little close to him, but they never went anywhere that we couldn't all see them."

"Did you catch the girl's last name, by any chance?"

Grace shook her head. "They didn't care about our last names. Or first names, for that matter. They kept calling us 'Gracie' and 'Tessie' interchangeably; I guess everybody had to have an *ie* sound at the ends of their names. Freddy, Danny, Casey . . ." she said, and trailed off.

She gave me a description of the girl: dark brown hair, green eyes, pale skin, around five foot five, had a beauty mark on her left cheek ("A real one—it didn't come off in the water").

No last name, but no matter: There could be only so many catalog models named Theresa in Los Angeles.

I thanked her and told her I'd do a nice write-up for *This Proud Heart* when the film came out. I thought that I might be able to secure a fashion spread in *Photoplay* for her but couldn't make any promises.

"Well, if there's anything I can do to make you feel a little more certain," she said before we parted ways, "you let me know."

"A last name," I said. Grace frowned—it clearly wasn't the response she'd hoped for. When she sighed, I gave her a serious look. "Did you see *Marie Antoinette*?" I asked her.

"Of course I did," she said, the exasperation creeping into her voice. It was one of the highest-grossing films the year it came out; everyone and their mother had seen it twice.

"Nell's a very talented actress, but you and I both know that she didn't get that role on her own," I said. "Now, I want you to think: What is your *Marie Antoinette*?"

Grace pursed her lips and looked at the ground, probably visualizing a string of leading roles, parties to attend, a gown to wear to the Academy Awards. "Fine," she said, "Tessie's last name. I'll try my best."

In my office, I scoured the fashion catalogs for a Tessie or a Theresa. I even checked the phone books. It was a losing battle—if she were under eighteen, she wouldn't likely be listed anywhere. Chances were, she lived with a relative, like Sophie had.

I had sent Faye out to the newsstand with a long list of magazines that morning. As I went through the stack, I laughed to myself when I saw that she had purchased a copy of *Harper's Magazine* instead of *Harper's Bazaar*. My laughter stopped as soon as I noticed Sebastian's name on the list of that issue's contributors.

He had written a satirical farce of Hollywood. A world-renowned composer moves to Los Angeles to pursue his creative life after falling on hard times, and no one in the city has any idea who he is. He's hired to compose jingles for animated cartoons. He pays for prostitutes so he can play his original compositions for them. The prostitutes fail to understand.

I tried to get Seb's explanation. I was, in particular, curious about the red-haired publicist who seems to torture the composer throughout the story. But when I called the Santa Monica mansion, he was nowhere to be found.

I started on Wilshire Boulevard, going from store to store. I kept my eye trained on the girls modeling outfits. When anyone asked me if I needed help, I told them I was perusing or that I was waiting for a friend. On every floor, there was a new group of young girls to show me the latest jackets, dresses, and trousers. They wanted me to see the slimmer cut of their skirts—intended to save fabric—or the latest cork-heeled shoes.

In the eveningwear section of Bullock's, there was a young girl with dark hair. She was showing a floor-length gown made from a shiny bronze lamé. She swung a matching shawl around her, pulling it over her shoulders and then removing it.

"Perfect for your next party," she said to me as she walked by. There was a beauty mark on her cheek. "Lamé is the fabric of the future."

"Pardon me," I began, catching her eye. "Have you considered working in the pictures?"

She smiled and shook her head. I told her she had the right look for it and that I worked in the industry. It was usually a speedy way to get someone's name.

"Ma'am," she said, her voice steady, "I don't need to work in the pictures. I'm perfectly content here."

She walked away, careful to let the dress sway with her as she walked so customers could see how it billowed. I watched as she told another woman that it would be perfect for her next party.

"Did she happen to work at Bullock's?" I asked Grace over the phone.

Grace sighed and told me she really didn't know. "Isn't there something else I could help you with? Why her?"

"For Freddy, of course," I said. "What if something happened to her?"

Grace told me that if something happened to the girl, it was up to her to do something about it.

"It's none of our business," she said.

I told Grace that I would put her at the top of the column if she just went with me to the department store and confirmed that it was Theresa.

"I'll bet Nell Parker never had to put up with anything like this," she said, sighing into the phone. I was tempted to say that all Nell had to do was hand me a shovel so I could bury Charles

Landrieu's body, but that hardly seemed appropriate, given the circumstances.

"Don't respond to that," Grace said before agreeing.

At first, Grace was amused by the idea—she delighted in the shop-girls' flattery of her and took a few pieces into a dressing room before I reminded her that we had to move on.

"We're doing a piece for *Screenland*," Grace assured the girl arranging some outfits for her in the dressing room.

"I don't write for *Screenland*," I said to Grace in a low voice. "It's either the *Times* or *Photoplay*. Please don't tell people things that aren't true."

Grace looked at me before going into the room. "That's rich, coming from you," she said, and shut the door.

By the time I beckoned Grace out of the dressing room and escorted her to the evening gown section, I was worried that Theresa might not even be there. I'd have to go through the whole ordeal with Grace again another day.

"Tessie!" Grace called out. The same girl from the other day was walking around the sales floor, this time showing a crepe gown with a floor-length cape.

"Gracie!" she called back. The two girls clasped hands. They walked arm in arm around the shop floor, leaving me behind. Their voices were hushed as they talked.

I caught Grace's eye and she shook her head slightly to indicate that I shouldn't interrupt them.

"I don't think she'll want to speak with you," Grace told me in the tearoom afterward. I bought her a coffee and some biscuits for her trouble.

"Did you find out how old she is?" I asked her.

Grace shrugged. "She's old enough to make up her mind," she said. She slowly sipped her coffee and then leaned on her elbows, her chin propped on her hands. "Do you think any girl is going to see what happened to Sophie Melrose and think she'd like to try that out as well?"

"But if it's the right thing—" I began, but Grace stopped me.

"Trust me, she's not going to talk. Go sniffing somewhere else," she said. "If you can't take down Freddy, why not try Rolf, hmm?"

As I drove home, I considered the story I'd never published. A young actress: former pageant queen from Kentucky, devout Southern Baptist, unmatched with any of Hollywood's eligible bachelors. In the spring of 1939, she goes on location with two handsome actors and one temperamental director. No one working on the set is allowed to talk about what happened; everyone has an eerily similar script. On the return trip to Los Angeles, the three actors make a detour in Nevada for an impromptu wedding. All evidence points to an accidental pregnancy, and yet: no child.

$\int$IXTE·E·N

I don't go to the houses of actors and actresses uninvited. It is unethical and also horribly impolite. But I made an exception when I drove to Hal and Margy's beachside home.

Standing outside the house, I heard a dog barking. When the door opened, I saw the same black dog from the château—Charles's dog. After I gave my name, a housekeeper told me Mrs. Prescott was out on set but that Mr. Bingham should be available.

While I waited in the foyer of the house, I carefully checked the dog's collar. The dog cooperated and, to my relief, didn't move or lick me when I searched for its information. Its name was Jack and the address on the tag belonged to Hal and Margy.

"Ines watched him while I was at boot camp," Hal explained from down the hallway. "He didn't care much for the château, I think." The dog ran up to Hal and leaped at his feet, whimpering. Hal gave me the once-over—there was that uncertain squint again, the kind he usually reserved for his cowboy films when his character was debating whether or not to shoot an approaching horseman. I imagine the terror must have shown on my face, because he relaxed and reached for a jacket hanging by the door.

"How about a walk?" he asked.

Though I was unsure if the question was posed to me or to the dog, I obliged.

From Hal and Margy's home, it was a short walk through the dunes to the shore. That day, the sky was overcast and the weather felt cold for Los Angeles. The beach was mostly deserted. I found myself hugging my thin jacket to my chest against the ocean breeze. I still felt the chill in my neck and ears. Hal was wearing thick trousers and a rain slicker over a patterned knit sweater. He looked picturesque with the rough waters, like he could have helmed a whaler in another century.

The dog happily ran along the water, always circling back to Hal. Its tail wagged as it showed Hal a stick, begging him to be proud. When Hal tried to wriggle the stick free from the dog's mouth, the dog refused to release it, opting instead to run to the edge of the water until it found a different, presumably better, stick.

I tried to ask Hal if he had heard from Charles, but he gave me a dark stare before I could finish the question. There wasn't a day that went by when I didn't see new reports of death and injury overseas. Even if I didn't see the reports, wars were being acted out on every lot of every major studio. Hal's face was drawn and there was a hollowness in his cheeks that I had never noticed before.

"You have to know I'm sorry for what happened," I finally said. "I never thought things would get as awful as they did."

Hal made no response and continued to walk along the water. I caught up to his long strides, though my heeled shoes were entirely unsuited for walking on sand. Grains of it began catching in my stockings and shoes, chafing against my skin as I kept pace with Hal.

"That's why I'm here," I pleaded. "I thought I knew everything that happened in Wyoming. It's been made clear to me how mistaken I was."

Hal paused. "Tell me what you *thought* happened, why don't you."

I explained: I had told Charles that I had a story on Margy. A cameraman for *Afterglow* said that the three primary stars were cavorting with one another. There were strong implications that Margy was pregnant, either by Hal or Charles, which warranted a quick marriage between Margy and Hal.

"Did he also say we flipped a coin?" Hal asked. The edges of his mouth curled upward; if I wasn't mistaken, he looked slightly amused at the idea.

I nodded.

"Well," Hal said slowly. He tried to maintain his composure but then let out a laugh into his hand. "That all sure would've been complicated."

"Was it Rolf?"

Hal nodded. "Margy says it was her worst mistake. Though I'm not sure *mistake* is the right word. We all know how Rolf is."

He continued walking slowly along the beach while the dog ran and circled him.

It made sense: Even if he'd wanted to, there wasn't any way that Rolf could have gotten a divorce before Margy started showing. And I couldn't fathom what a divorce would have meant for Rolf's wife, who was a Jewish refugee. So Charles and Hal covered up Margy's predicament by offering to marry her. Because it was only ever going to be a marriage of convenience, they flipped a coin.

"There weren't any coins," Hal explained. That particular rumor had cropped up organically among the film crew, and the three of them did nothing to stop it from spreading. "Really, we just agreed it would be better for me to marry Margy. Stop you and yours from wondering too deeply about why I wasn't married yet."

"What happened to the baby, then?" I asked him.

"She didn't get rid of it herself, if that's what you're asking. I think her exact words were 'I'm not going to hell like the rest of you lot.' I take it you'll have no trouble figuring out who 'you lot' are." He stopped walking and looked at me.

"It was a miscarriage," he said. "One week before the party at Brodbeck's. I told her not to go, but she did anyway."

"Why wouldn't you go with her?"

"Not my kind of scene," he said. His voice was steady, but his face betrayed a contemplative sadness. "I knew Charles would keep an eye on her."

The way he spoke Charles's name was soft, tender.

Hal walked with his hands sunk into the pockets of his trousers, stopping every few moments to pat the dog or throw it a stick.

After a period of silence, he spoke. "You know, he talked to me after you went to his ranch that day. I told him you were bluffing and that he ought to keep his mouth shut. It turned out he's more paranoid than I ever was. He thought Margy would turn on us if she caught wind of what you were writing about her."

The way Hal said "us" was habitual. It became clear to me that there had been an "us" for quite some time. An "us" since they went for a night swim at the château. An "us" when they traveled to Wyoming. An "us" when Margy inevitably found them out—Hal left me with no doubts that she knew, that she accepted but did not approve. An "us" when they met covertly at the Palomar, sharing rolled cigarettes and making jokes that only they could understand. An "us" at the Academy Awards, the terrified look on Charles's face when he rushed across the room to see if Hal was okay. An "us" when Charles was ruined and became one of the most publicly disliked figures in Hollywood. And an "us," fractured, when Charles was stationed across the Atlantic, risking his life in a war that Hal couldn't fight with him.

I couldn't tell if Hal was even aware he had used the word. The man was wrecked and wrung out from bearing a heartache that couldn't be named out loud beyond that one word: *us.*

I remembered how Charles was the day I went to his ranch, how he tensed up and silenced himself as soon as I'd mentioned *Afterglow.* All that time I'd spent believing he was willing to sacrifice himself, his career, for Margy's reputation. I thought the act had been selfless, but now I saw the stalemate they were all trapped in: Charles and Hal knew about Margy's pregnancy; Margy knew about their relationship. The three of them were bound for life.

Charles had so much to lose that day. Then I looked at Hal

in front of me. He'd lost everything that mattered because every-thing that mattered was Charles.

I wasn't sure how long we walked in silence. "He was very distressed by the whole thing," I said uselessly, if only to have something to say. I added, "Frankly, I thought he was in love with Margy."

Hal let out a "huh" and whistled for the dog to come back to him. The dog nuzzled its head against Hal's thigh and he scratched its ears in return. He turned around and began walk-ing back toward his house.

"It wasn't Margy he was protecting," I said softly as we reached the front door.

Hal shook his head. "It was and it wasn't," he said simply.

Without further comment, he went inside with the dog.

When I walked back to my car, it wasn't quite raining, but I was coated with a fine mist. I tried to dry myself off with a scarf, but the condensation was everywhere.

I had a favor to ask of Ines Marquis.

"I was hoping I could borrow your screening room," I said over the phone.

My relationship with FWM used to be strong enough that I could ask to use their screening rooms, but I didn't want to try my luck and waste any favors from Augustan. None of the other studios had access to the archive of FWM films. But the Château Marquis most certainly did.

Ines hesitated and then spoke: "Tell me which film and I'll have it ready."

"*Afterglow*," I said.

I had attended the premiere of *Afterglow* in the summer of 1939. The summer heat found everyone retreating indoors; the early-evening premiere was sweltering.

Hal and Margy had eloped months before and arrived together. Margy had been sporadically linked to a few men in Hollywood, Charles among them, but Hal had evaded the usual romantic speculation. Everyone was still getting used to seeing him with a partner—he was very sweet about the whole thing, if not a little unsure. When asked to pose for a photo, he chastely kissed Margy's cheek.

From everything Augustan had told me, I knew that Charles was cycling through quitting and unquitting drinking. That was an unquitting night. He went to the premiere with Nell. It was their first public appearance together, as they were in the midst of filming *The Sure Shot*.

Like many others in Hollywood, Charles was a high-functioning alcoholic. However, after a certain period of time, I've learned most every drinker's tells, from lightly slurred speech to clumsiness to red cheeks. With Charles, it was slipping accents. It wasn't that he sounded too southern but that he grew self-conscious and overcorrected his accent to the point where he sounded like he was doing a poor impression of Cary Grant. I could hear it clearly that night as he greeted people before the film started.

I hadn't paid much attention to the film itself; I had seen plenty like it before. I left the theater before the film ended and caught Hal and Charles in the lobby. There wasn't a large crowd outside, so the two went unnoticed. I presumed that Margy was still in the theater. Hal leaned against the back wall, smoking. Charles was sitting on the counter of the concessions stand with one foot propped on the edge, his elbow resting against his knee. They were taking turns drinking from a flask. It seemed like they had been out there for a while.

"Edie," Charles called out. He held his hands up in disbelief. "Don't you want to know how it all *ends*?"

I walked over to them. Their faces were a little flushed—I assumed from the liquor—but they otherwise looked put together. Both men were in tuxedos; Hal's cropped rust-blond hair was combed neatly, while Charles's thick curls were strategically tussled to keep them out of his face.

I acted as though I were mulling it over. "I'm guessing that he"—I pointed to Hal—"shoots you," and I pointed to Charles.

Hal made a *tsk* noise with his tongue. "You'd better go back in," he said.

Charles shook his head and laughed. He turned to Hal, caught his eye, and asked solemnly, "You'd never do that to me, would you?"

I noticed that when he spoke to Hal, his accent returned to its natural southern inflections.

"I'd sooner die myself," Hal said with a hand over his heart. He patted Charles's knee and quickly drew his hand away when Charles broke out in a fit of drunken snickering.

At the time, I thought they were having a little fun with me. I later learned from a synopsis of the film that it was Margy's character who shoots Charles.

When I arrived at the château, Ines handed me an open unmarked bottle of wine, no glass, and instructed me to enjoy the film. She had a knowing smile on her face that I'd seen many times before and still never knew how to interpret.

The château was empty, except for Ines and her staff, and I couldn't imagine what she was doing by herself with all that space. While I was walking down the grand entryway, I pictured her riding a bicycle through the halls or doing dramatic readings of Greek tragedies for the miscellaneous animals in her zoo.

I glanced back and saw her walking toward the family library before I was led by one of her maids to the screening room. In the dark room with its plush chairs and carpeted floors, the film had been set up for me.

Afterglow opens with Hal's character, Ned, tossing wadded paper across the room. The camera pans down to Charles's character, Bo, asleep on the floor with a bottle of whiskey and a pile of wadded-paper balls that have bounced off him. He wakes up angry, muttering under his breath, and then sees Ned, sits up, and his face relaxes into a wide smile.

Charles was only twenty-three in the film, and I couldn't help noticing how youthful his face was, even when lined with stubble. There was a softness in his features. Though he was playing a drunk, the joy in his voice and movements was unmistakable.

"Well, if it ain't the sharpest shooter in all of Texas," he says, shaking his head in blissful disbelief. Ned extends a hand and pulls him up off the ground.

"That may very well be true," Ned says, clasping Bo's hand tightly, "but I still need the fastest rider in Texas."

From there, the two men cook up a scheme to rob a train. They ride horses together and spend a lot of time staring at moving trains. At one point, they have a competition to see who can shoot more rabbits—Ned wins. They take an unfortunate man's horse after one of theirs runs away. They sneak aboard a train and meet Margy's character, Annabelle, a prim daughter of a successful gold prospector. Annabelle quickly guesses what they do for a living and is fascinated with their scheme. She wants to leave her sheltered life behind. They learn that she has actually run away from home.

In a covert conference at the back of the train, the men debate over what to do with Annabelle, who has become persistent in her desire to work with them. Both appear to be angling to be alone with her—Margy's tall, angular physique was well suited to costume dramas and she looked particularly striking in this one—and Ned eventually convinces Bo to let him distract Annabelle so that Bo can implement their plans to rob the train undisturbed.

Little does Ned know that Bo has plans to double-cross him. (At this point, Charles's interpretation of Bo becomes significantly more sober on-screen.) While Ned shows Annabelle how to commit petty thefts, Bo is breaking safes and shoving cash and gold into a knapsack.

When Annabelle asks Ned if he would ever make an honest living, he tells her his dream has always been a small house on the river, a herd of cows and chickens, maybe a kid or two. He catches himself in the middle of his reverie and wonders how silly that must sound to a wealthy woman like Annabelle. She smiles and tells him he'd be surprised.

Ned is showing Annabelle how to shoot a gun from the back of the train when they realize that Bo is riding away with their loot. Annabelle, in a fit of surprise, takes a shot at Bo and winds up hitting him square in the back. He falls from the horse, gold slipping from his bag.

In a scene that many other actors would have played as a triumph, Hal crumbles for a moment as Ned. While Annabelle grasps Ned's shoulder, shocked and proud of what a good shot she's turned out to be, Ned's face goes blank. It's clear this isn't how he would have settled things. He jumps off the moving train and runs to Bo. Annabelle follows shortly thereafter. Though he never goes so far as crying, there is a brute sadness to the way that Ned kneels down to look at Bo's lifeless body while Annabelle watches on. The train disappears into the distance as Ned places a hand on Bo's cheek. He doesn't have a shovel to provide his friend with a proper burial, so he covers him with a blanket, tucking it carefully around his body so it can't be blown away by the wind.

The film ends with Ned and Annabelle riding away, gold in tow, presumably to find that small house on the river.

I sat in the dark when the reel ended. I listened to the click of the projector for a long time before the young man running it cleared his throat and asked me if I wouldn't like to leave now.

On my way out, I stopped by the library to thank Ines. I found her sitting sideways on a plush leather chair with a book in her lap. She was wearing what appeared to be men's pajamas in a fine silk pattern with a matching robe.

She looked up at me and gave me that enigmatic smile. "Care

to explain why you're watching cowboy films that came out years ago?"

"It's a point of personal interest," I said slowly, trying to read her expression.

"If you say so." She sat up in her chair and put her book aside. I followed her gesture to take the seat next to her.

She looked at me with her elbow perched against the arm of her chair, her chin propped against her hand.

"You knew, didn't you?" I asked her. She smiled and nodded. "How long?"

"Since I tried to seduce Charles Landrieu in the coatroom at the Trocadero," she said simply. She held her stare for a moment before laughing. "For a very perplexing minute, I thought he really might have been with Nell. He was so flustered that he told me everything, right there in the closet. Then I came back here to tend to my wounded pride. I ended up watching all of his films."

"I suppose you had the time," I said without thinking.

She receded back into her chair, pulling one of her knees up to her chin. She looked away from me, into some corner of the library. The bitterness was clear in her voice as she spoke. "That year was hell. It seemed like a cruel joke, to be given all the money in the world and I could do anything but go home. Instead, I had to sit here, powerless, while the fascists invaded my country. Every day, I had to learn about a new atrocity in the papers. And then I was told that I was expected to go to *parties*. They wanted me to dress up and act like the war didn't exist—just like the rest of you were doing."

Ines looked at me again. "So, yes, I had time to watch films."

She might have been in love with Charles. Or, more likely, she found him the most tolerable person in a sea of intolerable people. From what Ines told me that day, she developed a certain fondness for him, and maintained it even after realizing he would never return that fondness. They remained close friends. When he told her he was thinking of giving me a story about a secret tryst that never really happened between the two of them, she offered to pay out his contract in the event of his termination.

"He refused," she said. "Fair enough; I suppose he didn't want to feel like a kept man. I tried again when he planned to join the air force. I said I could pay off his house and he could spend the rest of his days riding horses around a field if that's what he wanted."

We both knew that wasn't what he wanted.

I left Ines sitting alone in her library, her bare feet dangling off the side of her chair. She would never return to France—not permanently anyway. After the war, she would move to New York and become a formidable presence in the art world there. She would be the largest private collector of works done by American women in the abstract modernist style.

The château would go up for auction and be sold to the state of California. It's a museum now. Curators restored it to the way it looked when Nico lived there in full opulence. I take the tour sometimes, and I always linger when we get to the indoor pool. It's easily the most beautiful part of the house—the floors and ceilings are all tiled in emerald and turquoise; it creates the most wonderful reflections. When the tour guides say it's time to move on, I pretend not to hear them so I can stay a little longer. I know the tour guides hate this and worry that a geriatric woman is about to slip into the pool. But I like to stand by the water's edge and imagine a night in 1938 when three beautiful young people stole a crate of wine and went for a swim. It's not a story anyone tells on the museum tours because it's not a story that anyone knows to tell.

On the drive home, I took a longer route along the seaside. It was a nice day, the kind that made me feel slightly guilty at having spent a portion of it in a dark screening room.

Halfway back to Los Angeles, I was stopped by a man in uniform who told me the road was closed for pilot testing. In the distance, a plane took off and flew over the beach, creating ripples in the water as it sped up into the sky.

I turned my car around so I could take another route back, but when I was safe distance away, I parked at an overlook. I'm not sure how much time I spent watching the planes take off. I imagined the young men flying those planes, how it must feel the moment when the wheels left the ground, when the ground ceased to be ground and turned to water. It seemed such a lonely, frightening thing, to fly a plane into that expanse of blue.

SEVENTEEN

I couldn't sit alone with what I knew. In fact, I couldn't sit alone at all. For the next week, I invented assignments for myself that would require me to drive around town, visit studio lots, pay house calls. I stayed late at the office, typing up notes, which Faye tried to help me with. I wound up giving her the week off so I could have more to do. I found myself echoing the urgency of the reporters in the building, which I understood was ridiculous. They were reporting on a war with thousands of lives at stake; I was writing about how Edward Percival looked in a pair of eighteenth-century breeches while filming his latest musical.

I finally called Augustan. I still felt the sting of his cruelty from our last conversation, but I couldn't shake the hope that he and I could talk things through. When he answered the phone, his tone was unchanged, as if nothing had happened. He told me I was allowed to come by the studio anytime.

When I arrived at FWM, I was still escorted up in the elevator by a secretary and I received some odd looks in the hallways, but it was an improvement.

Augustan was finishing a phone call and motioned for me to sit down. While he talked, I fiddled with my notepad, hoping to look busy. I eavesdropped on his call and could hear Brodbeck's voice on the other end. With the phone held away from his mouth, Augustan pulled faces and made a circular gesture with his hand while waiting for Brodbeck to finish speaking. I couldn't help letting out a stifled laugh.

"If it's that bad, I'll go on set and let you know," he said before hanging up the phone. He looked at me and frowned. "I'm not telling you which set and you're not coming with me, that clear?"

I nodded with a false air of seriousness before leaning in and asking, "Can I guess?"

"It's not Freddy," he said briskly. "For the first time in *weeks,* it's not Freddy."

"Is it Margy?"

"No," he said too quickly. I held my stare, but he didn't waver.

"Can I ask you one question about *Afterglow*?" I said as he was gathering his jacket to walk down to the lots. I stood an arm's length from him, making certain that wherever he went in the office, I was between him and the door.

"Do you not have better things to be doing?" he asked me. "Has no one told you there's a war happening?"

"I'm well aware," I replied, sighing. "Please, I'm not going to print any of this. I just want to know."

He agreed, though it might have been only because I was now partially blocking his doorway.

"Did Margy marry Hal to cover up an affair with Rolf?"

"It's been *years*," he said. He stepped forward and waited a moment, but I didn't move from my spot. "Yes, okay?"

"Why didn't you say anything?"

"You never asked me," he snapped. "Did you expect me to fact-check via telepathy?"

He pushed past me into the small waiting area outside his office and I followed, unprompted. We waited for the elevator in silence.

Augustan instructed me to remain silent while he visited the set that I wasn't supposed to know about. It was Lot 8 and I had to wait outside; I couldn't even catch a glimpse of who was working on the set.

I lit a cigarette and leaned against the wall, watching various

FWM employees going between the lots. I saw the back of Rooney Calhoun's jacket and whistled to get his attention.

He turned and walked toward me, shaking his head. "What did you have to do for them to let you back in here?"

I narrowed my eyes. "Light espionage. A handful of murders."

He laughed and asked me how Seb was doing.

"I was going to ask the same of you," I said.

Rooney held up his hands. "I've hardly seen him around here since *Fifty Grand.* He mails us pages every other week or so. They're not good."

"He's sitting poolside in Santa Monica, claims he's writing another novel."

He ran a hand through his graying hair and frowned. "Well, is he?"

"I'm sure you read his latest in *Harper's,*" I said, and Rooney let out a disapproving grunt. "He's not writing scripts, that's for certain."

I looked at the door next to me. "Do *you* know who's in there?"

Rooney didn't miss a beat: "It's Margy and Casey. Production was supposed to be on location, but no one could spare any trucks; we can't get our equipment out there. Rolf nearly lost his mind over it. Says it's an offense to his craft. He's been fuming since."

"Is that the only issue?"

"It's the only one I'm telling you about," Rooney said with a smile.

The door next to me opened with a bang so loud that half the people in the alleyway cowered on reflex. Margy stormed past me. She was in full costume, swinging a large petticoat around her ankles as she walked. She pulled her bonnet from her head and tossed it on the ground after her.

Augustan ordered a young woman to go after Margy and quickly shut the door behind him. He leaned against the back of the door and let his head roll back so he stared at the cloudless sky. The woman ran toward Margy, picking up the bonnet on her way. Augustan looked at me, exasperated.

"Rolf didn't like how she was saying the word *caravan*," he said.

When I glanced over to where Rooney had been standing, he had disappeared. I saw a flash of his jacket in the midst of foot traffic.

"So much for being secretive," I said with a smile. Augustan was not amused.

I sat outside Augustan's office while he spoke with Margy. I always wondered what, exactly, Augustan said to his stars when something like this happened. When I was an actress, I never had the misfortune of sitting where Margy was now. I imagine that he reminded them of their signed contracts and the things that would happen should those contracts be broken. Or he would tell them exactly what they were worth to the studio, down to the penny, and how many other people would be willing to do their jobs. Charles could have been made an example of in that regard—I'd heard that Danny had the same measurements as Charles; the costume department didn't even have to make alterations to swap him in.

At one point, while Augustan was speaking with Margy, I could have sworn I heard my name and understood that I might be a part of a threat being made to Margy.

After ten minutes of muffled back-and-forth arguments, Margy came out of the office. She was still wearing her ridiculous costume with a hoop skirt—a poorly constructed one at that—and her hair was in corkscrew curls. She stared at me. Her face was contorted; all those sharp angles that made her so beautiful now looked wrong.

"Whatever you think you know—" she began. She inhaled sharply and shook her head.

I leaned back on the bench and looked at the ceiling, refusing to meet her eyes. I said in a level tone, "Go back on set, Margy. Do your job." Augustan still hadn't come out of his office.

Margy crossed her arms and fumed. I had seen Margy worked up before, but something about this felt different. For years, I had been everyone's favorite designated emotional punching bag—I absorbed people's secrets, their sorrows, their rages—but in that moment, every part me wanted to be sealed off from Margy. I couldn't name what she was feeling, and perhaps that was why I found it so repulsive.

"I know you were lurking around my house," she hissed, willing me to look at her.

"Then you might want to ask your husband what we talked about," I said flatly. I motioned for her to leave. With her bonnet in her hand, she went to the elevators, giving me one last stare before getting on. She caught my eye that time. I had anticipated anger from her, but the expression on her face read closer to betrayal.

I invited myself into Augustan's office and took a seat.

"Am I often a part of your threats?" I asked him, crossing my legs and smoothing my skirt over my lap.

"It's usually the *Inquirer*," he said calmly. "As we both know, they'll publish any variety of nonsense. But you were more convenient just now. Thank you."

I held up my hands to indicate that I wanted no further part of it. "I only came here to tell you that none of my readers have asked about Freddy for a month now."

Augustan leaned onto his desk, resting his chin on his palm. "I suppose that's promising."

"What if I started writing against him? All it would take is a mention that he doesn't seem as *valiant* offscreen."

He shook his head. "These are still my films you're talking about. I might not like the man, but he's got a film coming out every three months through the end of the year. I do have to turn a profit."

It was the use of the first person that caught my attention— usually it would've been "The studio needs to turn a profit." However invested in his job he may have been, Augustan did historically have some form of boundary between himself and the studio. Now that there were murmurings about Brodbeck leaving, it seemed that boundary had begun to blur.

I shifted in my seat and let out a sigh that I thought was small, but Augustan caught it.

He leaned forward on his desk and said, "Do you know how much money we actually lost the last time you decided to make some noise?"

"I can't believe you're still angry about *Zorro*," I said. I made the mistake of drawing out the name Zorro, the sarcasm clear in my voice. Augustan stood up and placed both hands on his desk.

"Projected for well over a million!" he seethed. "It was supposed to be our biggest film of that year. We barely earned out because you have an inexplicable fixation on Charles Landrieu."

I remained seated. When I spoke, my voice was level and clear. "A price to pay to end the tyranny of Poppy St. John," I countered. "Look me in the eye and tell me it wasn't worth it."

As soon as I spoke the words, I realized it was a question that I didn't want to hear answered. I left before Augustan could say anything else.

I went to my office to check over the next day's column before I filed it ("We're looking forward to Nell Parker's turn in *This Proud Heart;* pairing her with the work of Pearl S. Buck feels like a match made in heaven!"). Faye was still away on the vacation I'd demanded for her, visiting family somewhere in Utah.

Usually the offices would be emptying out at that hour, but wartime had changed the rhythms of publishing. As I left the office, many of the desks were still occupied by men, some of whom gave me condescending looks as I passed.

More than once in the last year someone at the paper had made a compelling argument to remove the gossip column. They said that I was wasting valuable space with my inane chatter. It would be a service to global democracy to shut me down. Each time, I'd been saved by my readership. The world could crumble; people would still want to hear about Olivia Newport's engagement to Rex Northrop.

There was a car parked outside my house. It was too fashionable for my quiet, unfashionable street. At first I thought it might have been Seb, but as I walked up to the driver's window, I saw a woman wearing sunglasses and a scarf.

"I'll have you know I've had enough of actresses putting scarves over their hair and thinking that's a clever disguise," I said, leaning toward the open window.

It was Margy this time. Coming over to even the score, I supposed. She pulled off her sunglasses and scowled at me.

"Who did you think was going to see you?" I asked, gesturing around the empty sidewalks. The residents of my neighborhood were disproportionately elderly.

"It's not what I imagined," she said, looking past me to my house. "I guess I always figured you lived in some fortress built from lies."

I sighed. "It's a two-bedroom bungalow, built from bricks, to the best of my knowledge. Would you like to come in?"

I offered Margy a cup of tea while she sat down in my living room. She asked if I had anything stronger, so I brought her whiskey. She was out of costume and makeup, no more petticoats and corkscrew curls, but it was still strange to see her sitting there. I had become so accustomed to her wearing long, sleek gowns that I was taken aback at her casual attire. She wore a pair of loose trousers in a rich maroon fabric with a pale pink silk blouse; the patterned scarf she had been wearing over her hair now hung limply around her neck.

"So Hal told you everything," she said.

I cleared away a pile of dress jackets from my armchair and sat down across from her. "I've learned not to take the word *everything* at face value. You'll have to be more specific."

"Augustan said you knew about Rolf," she said. She sat with her legs crossed and her glass balanced on her knee. "I have to assume you know the rest."

"There's nothing I can do with it all, if that's your concern," I assured her. "Contrary to any of Augustan's threats, I'm not about to publish that you had an affair years ago. Is that even the right term?"

"Affair?" she asked, her voice going up. I saw the tendons in her thin hands as she clasped her glass tightly. "Of course it was. A stupid one, at that."

"You're one of the only people in Hollywood I'll ever say this to: Your secrets are safe with me."

"And Hal?"

"Not a word from me," I said, sitting back in my chair. We both knew I'd done more than enough damage to a perfectly undeserving man.

Margy stared into her glass. "There's a part of me that loves him," she said slowly. Her posture softened as she finished her drink and set it on the table. "Not romantically, but, you understand, right?"

I nodded. "I never doubted that you did."

She repositioned herself. After removing her heels, she sat with both feet on the couch, as a child might. "It's not enough to keep going on like this," she said. "I want a family someday. And call me old-fashioned, but I'd like to be married to the father of my children."

"So you get divorced," I said with a wave of my hand. Margy wasn't Catholic; I was sure that being a Southern Baptist, she'd survive a divorce. "You'll be in the good company of most of Hollywood."

"Hal's contract is up in a few years. I have no idea what the world will look like then. I do know that if Charles isn't back in it, Hal's going to quit." As she spoke, she fidgeted with a delicate gold necklace, a small cross dangling at the end of it. Her gaze drifted away from me, toward the window behind me. The sun was setting, turning everything in my house shades of purple.

"It would be a shame," I said, calling her back to the present. "I watched *Afterglow* after I spoke with him. You're right: It's a loss that's the only film they'll ever do together."

When she smiled, there was a remorsefulness to it. "One review said the two of them make a fine team. It scared the daylights out of Charles. He thought that was it and everyone knew. He signed an agreement with Nell almost immediately after. I should have known the same thing happened when he let you write all that nonsense about him and the Marquess."

She still had no idea what Charles had done for her, that the only reason he'd given me a false story was so I wouldn't publish hers. I watched her sitting on the couch, her lanky figure drawn tightly together.

I should have told her then and there. But in the years to come, Margy became one of my most loyal sources. When she would go on to divorce Hal, I would run a series of very popular columns speculating about husband number two. She was beautiful that day, but she hadn't even reached her peak. After the war, she would become a favorite of the director Lucian Gasper, known for his decadent, moody films. Pictures of her in costuming from Edith Head still circulate today—though I don't know if people remember her as Margy Prescott, or as just another beautiful woman with a small waist in a flowing gown.

I usually remember her as she was on that night in August 1939. I see her in the moment right before she leaped into Thomas Brodbeck's pool, the dangerous smile she gave us all as she threw her glass and plunged into the water. How her dress turned the color of arsenic when it got wet. The effect she had on those around her, how easily she summoned half the party to jump in after her. Some people get to bend the world to their will.

. . .

Hal had told me that Margy thought he was going to hell for whom he loved and how he loved. I considered my own family. If my mother knew even half the things I'd done, she would drag me to the nearest church and lock me in a confessional booth until I was prescribed a thousand Hail Marys. She hadn't spoken to me in nearly a decade—she was not and had never been a kind woman— but there was a time when she properly cared for me and Seb. Until I grew old enough to cradle and feed my sisters, she did. If anyone asked her if she loved me, I doubt even she could have said no.

There was so much I'd never know and never understand about what happened during those nine weeks in Wyoming with Hal, Charles, Margy, and Rolf. Margy and I never talked about it after that day.

It was dark by the time Margy finished her next glass of whiskey. I got up to turn more lights on, which she took as her cue to leave.

I was settling into bed when I got a call from someone with a voice I didn't recognize. It was a woman's voice, raspy.

"She's in hysterics; you've got to come quick," the voice said.

"Who?" I asked. The voice kept talking, something about how she wasn't listening, and how fast could I get there.

"Get *where*?" I nearly yelled.

She gave me an address that I recognized. It was Nell Parker's villa.

Nell's mother opened the door when I arrived—it was one of the rare times I saw Winnie Parker. Her face wasn't made up, her hair was hidden under a silk cap, and she wore a thick terry-cloth robe over a nightgown. Her eyes were rimmed with red, contrasting with her pale skin. She wordlessly led me into the sitting room of Nell's house.

All six feet, 180 pounds of Freddy Clarke was collapsed on the floor while Nell shook him to keep him awake. Both were muttering a colorful variety of expletives at each other. On the floor was a very lovely brass candlestick. It did not take me very long to piece together that Nell had hit Freddy over the head with it.

"Good Lord, you need a doctor," I said. I surveyed the room and saw that, in addition to the candlestick, there was also at least one broken glass on the floor.

"Go get her some water," I ordered Winnie, in part because I suspected Nell needed it but also to get Winnie out of the room. Winnie's thin lips shaped themselves into words, but no sounds came out of her mouth. She disappeared into the kitchen.

I instructed Nell to take deep breaths and explain what had happened.

It turned out that Nell had been paying Bunny not to sign her divorce papers. Nell thought that was a fair scheme to keep Freddy from getting any ideas about marrying her. It also meant that Bunny had a stash of untaxed money that no divorce lawyer could get to.

Freddy figured this out—Bunny wasn't one for keeping secrets and, as long as they were still married, he had primary control over her finances. The man wasn't sharp, but he could do basic math. He stormed into Nell's house, demanding answers. He asked Nell why she wouldn't want to marry him. Then he began guessing reasons why ("Horrible, awful, unthinkable things—and my mother was in the next room, listening to all of this"). When he became aggressive and started moving toward Nell, she panicked and threw a glass, but she missed. This only served to enrage Freddy more; he grabbed her shoulders and she was able to shake him loose. But Nell, small as she was, knew that she was no match for him. So she grabbed the candlestick.

Nell then calmly told me a story about how she had once done a scene in which she had to make it look like she hit Griffith Taylor over the head with a glass bottle. Though she never actually hit him with it, she had learned what degrees of damage she could do with a heavy object and a man's head.

"I only nicked him," she swore.

· · ·

Freddy was half-conscious as Nell explained everything to me. His face was pale and his blond hair was damp with sweat. I had never really considered how large he was until I saw him prone on the floor, like an animal injected with tranquilizers. He mumbled obscenities, his head rolling against Nell's lap. She held a towel to the back of his neck—he was bleeding. The towel could only absorb so much blood; it had begun to seep into the mauve fabric of Nell's robe and tinted her hands.

"He's probably concussed; you've got to get him to a hospital," I said in a low voice, though I wasn't sure whom I was whispering for.

Nell protested, worried about what people would say. The word *career* was used.

"It's not as though you need to worry about the press finding out," I said. To my shock, Nell laughed, the melodic sound of it echoing through her living room. I very nearly laughed with her.

Winnie returned with a glass of water for Nell and a fresh towel to place under Freddy's head. Nell carefully removed the soiled towel, setting it down on the wood floor next to her. The new towel began turning red. I knelt down next to Nell and Freddy.

"If you don't call for an ambulance," I said, "I will."

Nell held up her hands and told me to wait. Freddy began to slip back into sleep, his head dipping without Nell's hands there— she caught him with a little shake.

"You drove here," she said to me abruptly. "I'll find his keys; his car's out front. Can't we drop him off somewhere? Then call?"

It was a ridiculous idea and I told her so. Freddy was conscious. He was well aware of what was happening and would no doubt be able to relay the series of events to the authorities, should it come to that.

"Can you call Augustan?" I asked. I'd never personally seen him resort to it, but I knew he had a handful of police officers working under his discretion.

Nell shook her head; she didn't trust Augustan. She looked at Freddy.

Nell instructed Freddy in a clear, level voice: "You're going to stand up, Freddy. Then we're going to get into your car and I'm going to drop you off by Ciro's. When the ambulance arrives, you're going to tell them that you were struck by a hooligan and you couldn't see him because it was dark."

Freddy called her a harpy.

Nell didn't waver. "You're going to do this, because if you don't, I will personally go to every paper across this country and I will have you decimated." She carefully pronounced every syllable of the word. "And I won't do it tomorrow—I could do it weeks, months, or years from now. You cross me at any point and your legacy will be statutory rape and venereal diseases. That is a promise. Do you understand?"

Before realizing what I was doing, I stood and backed away from her as she spoke. I was standing with Nell's mother as we watched her deliver the strongest performance of her career.

Nell fumbled through Freddy's jacket for a set of keys. When she found them, she forcibly pulled him up onto his feet—I assumed the shock of what had happened had given her some extra strength—and led him to the door. He clasped the towel to the back of his head. With his other arm draped around her neck, he stumbled alongside her. I could hear him protesting under his breath.

Nell snapped at me to drive behind her and bring Winnie with me. I took it that she didn't trust her mother to be alone in the house.

Winnie hadn't moved from her spot in the living room, where she was fidgeting with the knot in her bathrobe, untying and re-tying it. I gently guided her toward the door.

Nell didn't put on shoes or slippers. I watched as she walked barefoot to Freddy's Ford coupe, which was parked haphazardly in front of her house. Nell held Freddy by the elbow as her robe billowed out behind her. The moonlight caught her pale blond hair, giving her an ethereal glow.

In the car, Winnie found her voice again. I attempted to drive steadily, following Nell's erratic turns and blatant disregard for speed limits.

"She's going to be ruined," Winnie muttered. "This is it. I told her. I told her not to let him in."

I assured her that Nell would be fine, but I wasn't entirely confident myself.

"I've seen men like that before," she said. "There's no reasoning with them. I told her."

Nell pulled Freddy's car into an alleyway nearby Ciro's while I waited on the street. I watched her maneuver Freddy out of the car and deposit him next to a wall. By this time, people were beginning to leave the club, wander home. None of them paid any mind to what was happening by the alleyway.

Nell got into my car and instructed me to find the nearest pay phone. I drove until I found one. She ran out of the car—as best she could, as her feet were still bare—and made a call. She let out a heavy breath as she got back in.

"What are you going to do when someone notices that Freddy wasn't seen conscious anywhere near Ciro's all night?" I said to Nell, though I couldn't see her over Winnie, who was now wedged between us. Winnie's mutterings had become background noise by then—"I told her," she said every few moments.

"He planned to stop by for a late drink, but he never made it," Nell said without hesitation. She rolled down the window of my car and was taking deep breaths of air.

Nell made me go back into the villa with her and sit while she chain-smoked in silence. She was perched on a chair, her legs crossed and her foot erratically twitching. Her hands were still red; she smoked with one and was wringing the tie of her robe with the other. The stains on the robe were beginning to turn from a bright red to a rust. I offered her a rolled cigarette, but she refused: "I'll just fall asleep."

"Why wouldn't you want to fall asleep?" I asked. The sun would be rising in a few hours, and I was keen on getting home myself.

"I just have to think," she said without looking at me.

I woke to the sound of someone arriving through the back door of the villa—Nell's household staff, I presumed, from the low chatter in the kitchen. Daylight was breaking through the windows; the glow of the early sun washed everything out. I had been sleeping on Nell's plush love seat. When I got up, my legs were cramped and my clothing was wrinkled.

Nell was nowhere in sight. I had no interest in finding her.

As I slipped out the front door, I considered the scene I was leaving behind me. The broken glass, the dark stains on the carpet, the discarded bloody towels. The candlestick was gone, which gave me a vision of Nell burying it in the yard sometime during the night. Closing the door behind me, I wondered what Nell would tell her staff. Then I saw the nice cars that Nell's maids or cooks had parked in the driveway; I understood that Nell wouldn't have to tell them anything at all. They would never dare ask.

I drove home in a daze. I could feel the exhaustion in my neck and willed my eyes to stay open while I drove. The thought of taking a detour to where Nell had left Freddy crossed my mind. I didn't know if an ambulance had arrived or not. For all I knew, he could have bled out in the street.

Freddy never once died on-screen. His characters came close enough to make an audience tense. He was nearly hanged as Robin Hood. Once while playing a swashbuckler, he was stabbed in the gut and made a remarkable recovery in the arms of the woman he loved. He could run through fires and explosions, dodge bullets and arrows, and still make it to the end credits mostly unscathed.

As I drove, I let myself believe he was gone. I turned onto my street with the incandescent belief that I was now inhabiting a world that didn't contain Freddy Clarke. We would never again have to bear his suffocating presence, his cruel humor, his domineering attitude. It would have been a fitting end for all of us who hated the man—that he should die alone and humiliated.

But, in practice, where would that have gotten any of us? He'd become an icon, mourned widely across the country. There would be special screenings of his films. Everyone would start quoting from *Robin Hood* again. He would accrue new fans and the women who had first loved him when he began his career would grow nostalgic. I could already hear Augustan's voice in my head, urging me to write something elegiac in his foul memory.

EIGHTEEN

Film Daily made a note in its issue the next day that Freddy was out for "an injury to the head" and had been taken to the hospital. After that, there was a column in the *Herald* demanding justice for Freddy and answers about who had attacked him. I received letters expressing concern for Freddy's well-being. The *Inquirer* took the opportunity to rebuke Freddy ("Why bother focusing on one man's head wound when there are thousands being injured and killed overseas every day!"). Poppy wished him a speedy recovery.

Augustan called, asking me if I would do some clarifying about Freddy's condition. He had orders from the FWM stockholders to assure the public that Freddy was recovering and would be back to grace their movie screens shortly.

"I don't know why you sound so put out," he said when I protested. "It's nothing you haven't done before."

I told myself that it would be the last thing I'd write about Freddy. People were welcome to speculate about why I held a grudge against him. For all I cared, I could get blacklisted from every studio in Hollywood, incur the wrath of any publicist. I didn't want to write another word about the man.

I wrote a sterile note about his anticipated release from the hospital.

A few days later, Freddy nobly decided not to make a criminal case out of his ordeal. When he was released from the hospital, he gave a public statement that the world had more important issues to deal with than a late-night attack from a ruffian. He claimed that he'd been unable to see who hit him. Of course, his words did nothing to abate speculation about the incident, or burgeoning efforts to identify his attacker.

"It saddens me that there are people who would do something like this," he stated to the *Herald*. "But I believe that this act of violence was merely misplaced anger at what's happening in the world right now." He then reminded everyone of the importance of supporting the Allied forces' efforts and contributing however they could.

I imagined Augustan somewhere around the FWM lots, feeling very proud of himself for having written those lines.

I came back from the office one day to find Seb sitting on my front stoop with a suitcase. He was leaning against the railing and appeared to be half asleep.

"You could have called," I said, and he jerked awake.

As I got closer to him, it became clear that he'd been living out of hotel rooms. From the scent of him, they weren't particularly nice ones. Though he'd made attempts to tidy himself up, his suit was wrinkled and his overgrown hair had accumulated a few days' worth of grease.

"I was waiting for you," he said; his voice was weary. "You never called."

I didn't mention that I had called, a number of times; I'd tried the Santa Monica mansion, the Garden, and the studio, to no avail. Instead, I offered him a hand and was surprised at how much of that hand he needed—he pulled hard on my weight to get himself up. Not that he was ever heavy; neither of us could put on pounds after our meager childhood. He had the same pallid look as the day I saw him in the hospital.

"I'll fix you something," I said as I let him into the house.

· · ·

It turned out that the Santa Monica heiress lacked an appreciation for high-concept satire. She'd tossed him out when she discovered the *Harper's* story a few weeks earlier.

"I *explained* to her," he said, staring into a plate of eggs and toast I'd prepared for him. "It's a parody of a parody."

I nodded slowly. His eyes were bloodshot, and I was impressed he was putting down food at all. Of course, I'd be cleaning it all off the floor of the guest room in a few hours' time. That night, I went through his things while he retched in the bathroom. I found the pills and the flasks. Another person would've flushed them all, and I suppose that's what I should have done. It's what a good mother would've done, but I wasn't his mother. I was only doing the best I could.

He stayed with me for a few weeks that time. After years of living alone, I took comfort in having someone there to eat meals with, another presence in the room while I wrote or read. Seb even talked me into attending Sunday Mass, though I confessed my suspicions that I might burst into flames upon entering a church. I sat quietly in the pew when he went to take Communion.

He left after he was offered an advance from a publisher for a book based on his *Harper's* story. It seemed the people of Alfred A. Knopf's publishing house did understand what a parody of a parody was.

I made a call that I'd been putting off for weeks.

Poppy St. John was in her office and didn't seem all that shocked that I was contacting her.

"What do you say to a peace treaty?" I asked her.

She agreed to meet me for lunch the next day.

I arrived at the restaurant early so I could request a private booth, only to realize that Poppy had done the same five minutes before me.

I was shepherded by a waiter to a quiet corner at the back of the room, where Poppy sat with a cup of tea. She looked up at me with her sharply drawn arched eyebrows. I could see the creases at the corners of her eyes as she smiled at me.

"So, you've won back FWM," she said to me after I had taken the seat across from her and ordered a coffee.

"For whatever that's worth," I responded with a shrug. We both knew that FWM was on shaky ground. We had an unspoken agreement about how to divide up the studios. At that time, Poppy held most of Paramount and RKO, from their stars to publicists to studio physicians. We had shared custody of Fox, MGM, and Columbia.

I got to the point—it wasn't as though Poppy and I had a wide variety of small talk to make—and asked her if she'd like to do any trading. Not of information, but of sources.

"Who did you have in mind?" she asked.

"I'd like to give you Freddy," I said.

Her face soured. "Why are you giving up Freddy?" We both knew how much he was worth. Given his recent press, it would be a major loss to my readership and my finances.

"You can pick any of a hundred reasons why someone wouldn't want to talk to that man. Consider it an offering, an acknowledgment of my debts to you as a mentor, hmm?"

A waiter delivered a sandwich to Poppy, who began immediately to deconstruct it. Wordlessly, she picked away at a slice of cheese. After popping a corner of it into her mouth, she spoke.

"Fine," she said. "Fine, fine."

I ordered another coffee and we did some bartering. I had been angling for Lana Turner. Poppy tried to get Margy for Lana, but I refused—after my conversation with Margy the other day, I figured that she was mine for life. I gave up Delilah Baker, FWM's latest rising star, for Lana, a trade that proved to be in my favor in the coming years, when Delilah would quit screen acting in favor of marrying into European aristocracy and spend the rest of her days somewhere on the French Riviera. Poppy also handed over a handful of MGM's young stars, whose cavorting she found distasteful; among them was Ava Gardner, who was still doing bit parts at the time.

That's how it went with Poppy and me until she retired in the early sixties. Once a year or so, we'd have a cup of coffee together and do some rearranging of Hollywood's moral standards. It was mostly cordial. Things would get a little tense during the Red Scare years, when Poppy was prepared to join the FBI and out every Communist in Hollywood. There was good money in Communist hunting, and Poppy had a retirement fund to save for. We balanced each other out that way—I would tell Poppy to stop persecuting liberals, and she'd tell me to stop romanticizing everyone's vices.

Everyone loves a rivalry, and ours was one of the best. The way people have written about us over the years gives the impression that we couldn't be in the same room with each other without some form of attempted murder via pen or pencil. In an odd way, it's the closest I've ever come to an arranged studio marriage—an arranged lifelong rivalry. It's not something I would have envisioned for myself when I was a young girl. Poppy was certainly not the good Catholic husband I thought I'd have. But, that being said, I've never excelled at planning things for the long term. Living through an economic depression and two wars will do that to you, I suppose. I've only ever known how to grasp at the opportunity in front of me and wring it out as best as I can for all it's worth. It's my good fortune that I found an opportunity I could wring out for decades.

Augustan wasn't one bit happy with my trading away Freddy. I visited his office, where he was sorting through the details of Freddy's official return to the studio.

"You can't be serious," I said when I read through the various statements Freddy would make over the next few days. Every one of them pivoted to patriotism, a love of country over self.

"Well, it's none of your business now, is it?" he said with a smile. The spite in his voice was spirited. It was a tone that might have frightened me earlier in our relationship, but I didn't wince.

Without looking up from the papers, I assured him that Poppy would handle the story just fine.

"And what about Nell?" he asked me. "She still yours?"

"I've got a handle on Nell," I said, keeping my voice level.

"No more surprises?"

I assured him: no more surprises.

In the coming years, I wouldn't visit Augustan in that office anymore. The stockholders would vote out Brodbeck sometime in the mid-forties, leaving Augustan a clear path to becoming FWM's next studio chief.

His new office would be on the top floor, accessible by a private elevator. On the occasions when I did visit him there, I marveled at the view. All of the studio lots were laid out below him, like little dollhouses. FWM had a few open lots with fake streets and storefronts. It was so strange to watch them from up there and see every moving piece at once—two actors walking along a sidewalk, film extras perfectly coordinated to make the street look busy, set crews pulling and rearranging details just out of the frame, a camera being pushed along a dolly, an actress poised on her mark to bump into one of the actors. I don't know how Augustan was supposed to get anything done in that office; I would've just sat and watched it all for hours.

Freddy's injury coincided nicely with a press campaign for his next film. The posters all featured him as a brave officer in the army, weathering through his injuries for the greater good. In one of Augustan's more deft moves, he had Freddy attend an early premiere for the film with his head in bandages, which I wasn't sure he still needed. The premiere was open only to the families of those serving abroad. The orchestration of the event was brilliant—here was Freddy, with his tidy bandages and his handsome face fully intact. Everyone could take their minds off the idea of their men coming home with battered bodies and fragile minds, or any of the things they'd read about in the papers. When they imagined their sons facing unknown terrors in faraway places, they could imagine Freddy. When they imagined their sons coming home someday, they could also imagine Freddy.

The film went on to be one of the studio's highest-grossing pictures of all time.

I received letters from readers speculating about what had happened to Freddy. Some of them suspected that Bunny had hired out a hit man—the logic was difficult to follow, but I think they believed that Bunny would rather be a widow than a divorcée. Many of them found a way to blame foreigners. Specifically, they were of the belief that he had been attacked by a gang of Mexicans. One very detailed letter laid out a plot in which Charles was not actually serving his country somewhere in Europe, but still in California, and still fixated on a years-old feud. Quite the imagination.

Most days when I went into the office, the only person I would speak to was Faye. On occasion, the Film and Entertainment editor wanted a word or two, but I was otherwise ignored by my colleagues. Imagine my surprise when one of the film reviewers came over to my desk and pulled up a chair. He crossed his arms over his chest and smiled.

"We've got to know," he began. "Who took down Freddy Clarke?"

He gestured behind him at the desks of reporters and explained there was a betting pool going.

"How should I know?" I asked as innocently as I could. Faye was listening, try as she might to look engrossed in her work.

"Because you're Edie O'Dare," he said. He exaggerated my name when he said it, drawing out the O and emphasizing Dare.

I leaned forward on my desk and rested my chin against my palm. "Who did you place your bets on?"

"The ex-wife," he said simply.

"How about this?" I began. "You get your lot over there to act a little more cordial to me. I'm not talking about drinks with the boys or weekly poker games—I'll take a civil greeting in the mornings. You do that and you can tell them all it was the soon-to-be ex-wife."

Making a pact with one reporter didn't substantially improve my standing in the offices of the *Times,* but it was a necessary start. I would lose subscribers when Poppy began publishing exclusive interviews with Freddy. It helped to have some allies in the office. To them, though, I was always Edie O'Dare—the way the reporter had said it to me that day, drawn out, caricatured.

No one made a note of the fact that Freddy's current paramour had not once visited him in the hospital or appeared at his side when he made his statements. Nell's name was conspicuously absent from the news. She remained out of the papers until she signed a contract with MGM to begin in the new year—another Edie O'Dare exclusive.

Augustan might have been angry at me for lying to him about "no surprises" when it came to Nell, but, if he'd been paying attention, it shouldn't have been a surprise at all.

He had once told me that we'd all say that "before Grace Stafford, it was Nell Parker," and on that score, he was horribly wrong. I watched many actresses burn out, develop addictions that they were led to believe were their fault, age out, defect to television, or quietly retire. They were promptly replaced with newer versions of themselves. But Nell Parker had no successor.

Nell would be nominated for seven Academy Awards during her decades-long career. After signing with MGM, she'd win Best Supporting Actress in 1950 for *High Tides,* and Best Actress in 1954 for her portrayal of Amelia Earhart in *That Open Sky*. Two years before her death, she would be awarded an Academy Honorary Award "for her unique portrayals of women throughout history and contributions to the art of screen acting."

In the days after Freddy's attack, I met Nell for lunch. If she was shaken, she didn't show it. Her hair was neatly pinned back and she wore light makeup. She didn't even look like she had lost sleep.

She still remained bent on tearing down Freddy, even though he had technically met her terms from that night.

"What do you want me to do, Nell?" I had asked her. "He's got a bucket of letters wishing him a speedy recovery. This isn't like it was with Charles—no one will be on your side."

"Then don't let anyone know it was you or me," she said. "Make something up. Do a blind item."

A blind item would never be published. Nell didn't find cause or means to follow through on her threats from that night. Whatever blows Freddy's legacy would take in the coming years— divorces, bankruptcy, lawsuits—they wouldn't come from Nell.

That day, she looked down into her lap. "Please," she said. I remember how different her voice had sounded; it had lost its breathy quality. There was something rough in how she spoke, raspy, like her mother. It occurred to me that might be what Nell Parker actually sounded like.

Nineteen

would call this a resignation letter, but I haven't written a column since 1975—I have nothing to resign from. And God forbid I begin feeling Catholic in my old age and call it a confession.

When I published the last of "Do Tell," I bought a house on the ocean. I am told that my neighbors are very famous, but I haven't bothered to figure out who most of them are. A young woman from down the street knocks on my door periodically and brings me coffee cake. I believe she does it mostly in the interest of confirming that I haven't slipped on my bathroom floor sometime in the night. She's married to an action star, who is rarely seen around the house.

I invite her in on the unspoken understanding that, although she knows who I am, we don't talk about the Golden Age. In exchange, I don't ask about her very famous husband. We talk about the weather and we talk about books and we talk about the ocean. Sometimes she brings along her little dog and I pretend not to be afraid of it. Having the company is nice. Over the years, I acquired two ex-husbands and two sets of stepchildren, who I don't think rank me very highly among the women they've been required to call "Mother." One of them still writes me and sends photos of her children, but otherwise I'm on my own.

I've outlived most everyone. I expected there to be more satisfaction in it. Mostly what I've got is time. No social calls, no family reunions, only time. I had a young man install a large television in my house, and there's a channel that plays old films. I'm not wretched enough that I spend all my time watching them, but I like to have them on when I take my dinner.

I keep anticipating the day when I'll turn on the television and see *The Sure Shot* on the screen. Not that it's a great film with a great story—there are dozens like it and I've watched them all a hundred times over. But it would be an interesting test of memory. It's like looking at childhood photos of someone you've known well only in adult life. You want to see the inklings of who they would become. I would have liked to see Nell before her renaissance, whether she carried that same quiet power that would earn her so many awards. Or if there were signs of what Charles was going through when he rattled off those one-liners. It would have meant a lot to know that Sophie was out there, somewhere, playing a role that she believed was her breakthrough. I would have liked for her to be remembered outside of the court documents and news headlines.

Instead, I've gotten repeat viewings of *Robin Hood*. Because even ten years after that man's death, he still gets to swing his sword around and save the day into eternity. Whenever his crooked smile appears on my screen, I turn off the television.

My suspicion is that *The Sure Shot* is among the lost films of FWM. When the Supreme Court demanded that all of the major studios divorce their production and distribution, most of them survived—MGM, Paramount, Fox, and others still stand today. FWM did not. The studio library was sold for television rights in 1954, but their preservation methods were faulty—not everything made it. The lots went to MGM a year later and the studio was officially shut down shortly afterward. Never one to retire early, Augustan packed up and took a job with Paramount, where he remained until lung cancer took him in the late sixties. FWM's stars were freed from their contracts and allowed to work with other studios as they pleased.

A year or so ago, a number of FWM films were found in some neglected property of the Marquis family. An archivist wrote me a letter informing me that an early film I had appeared in was now back in circulation. I was invited to a party to celebrate, which I didn't attend.

I wrote back to the archivist, asking if there was a need for Hollywood artifacts, because it would seem I'd accumulated more than a few. He put me in contact with an entire team. A group of young men and women in white gloves descended on my house and sorted through papers, letters, invitations, and whatever else I set aside for them. They took all of my letters from various film stars, including Nell and Margy, and a schedule and flyers for the Victory Caravan. They even wanted my early notes scribbled on Garden of Allah cocktail napkins. It was enough material to garner me my own subsection of a preservation library in Los Altos.

That wasn't my first brush with archivists. I lost Sebastian to an overdose when he was forty-two. He was still living in Hollywood, moving from place to place, occasionally staying with me when I could convince him, which wasn't often. He did write another novel—two of them, actually. His Hollywood farce, *The Bad and the Beautiful,* sold pitifully when it was released, though, based on the royalty checks I receive, it seems it's quite popular these days. I discovered his last manuscript when I was willed his things, so I contacted his old editor to tell me if it was any good. It was published posthumously and won a few awards that the editor assured me were very fashionable among the literati.

I was left to arrange the funeral on my own. I had my doubts that Seb would have wanted to be laid to rest in California, but I had limited options. He gets to be in Hollywood Memorial Park—even if it wouldn't have been his first choice, I have to imagine he'd at least be amused by the company there. None of our family was able to attend. Jillian sent a bouquet of flowers that had wilted by their arrival. The last few times I visited his grave, I found discarded screenplays. When I mentioned it to the estate lawyer in passing, I learned that my brother had apparently become the local patron saint of abandoned projects.

Before I moved into this house, I offered Seb's letters and manuscript drafts to the library at Fordham. They wasted no time sending someone to pick through whatever was left of my brother. Perhaps it sounds insensitive on my part, but what he wanted was a legacy, and that was one thing I could give to him.

A publisher in New York has put together a little book of my writing. I received a draft of it, tied together with twine and sent in a neat package. It's a nice collection; they included some of my favorite interviews, along with a few of my more incendiary columns, including the one on Charles and Freddy. They asked me to write an introduction to it. I wrote this instead. I'm unsure what to do with it now.

For decades, I dictated the public lives of the stars. I made heroes and villains and nothing in between. In the gossip column, things were either good or bad, or they were not fit to print. When I was wrong—and I was often wrong—I usually knew it. Sometimes I knew in the moment that I was wrong, deliberately and unapologetically. Sometimes, though, it took years, if not decades, to understand the breadth of my wrongs.

I know the kind of introduction they would like me to write. Poppy published a cheery autobiography a few years before she passed. It is filled with anecdotes and witticisms. There are stories about playing pranks with Mickey Rooney and having dinner with the cast of *Mary Poppins*. At one point, she sternly advises Judy Garland against "living a fast life," whatever that's supposed to mean.

In my equivalent, I would write about how Margy Prescott was a hoot at parties and what about that time she was nearly kicked out of the Academy Awards ceremony! Or that Freddy Clarke liked to "pester" his costars. I could provide a hundred charming stories about Baird deWitt and readers would eat every one of them up.

If I didn't perpetuate these stories, someone else would. It's easier to reinforce versions of what people already know than to fill in the gaps of what they don't.

I take an evening cocktail on the back porch every day. I have a nice dining set out there that I've never once filled with people. My young neighbors often go for runs on the beach, so I like to raise my glass to them. I always make certain I sit there long enough that someone passing by in the neighborhood has seen me, alive and functioning. I'd hate to become a topic of gossip myself.

Inside, I can hear my phone ringing, but the only person who ever calls is an editor with the publishing house in New York, wondering where the introduction is. I usually ignore it, though sometimes I answer and make the editor state his name repeatedly, as if I don't know who he is. He always gets exhausted and says he'll send me a letter instead. I figure if I keep this up long enough, they'll presume that I've gone batty and hire someone else to write the introduction. For what I lacked in children, I more than made up for in protégées. There are over a dozen gossip columnists from over the years who could write a thousand pithy words about my contributions to this odd form of journalism and thank me for my tutelage.

The phone keeps ringing and I toast another toned couple in spandex jogging along the waterline. They wave back, only a little confused. The water is clear and the temperature never gets too high. It's not a bad way to carry out the rest of one's life.

TWENTY

The last time I saw Charles Landrieu, he wasn't in Los Angeles. He was in an Off-Broadway theater. It was closing night of a sold-out play. I pulled every contact I had in New York to secure a ticket and even then I ended up paying quadruple the original price to a friend of a friend of George Wynette. I put a month's salary into flying out to New York, booking a decent hotel, and seeing the play. It was something I felt I owed to Charles.

Charles had served in the air force until he was released from active duty in 1945; he was awarded a Bronze Star Medal for his war efforts. He returned to Los Angeles and tried to resume his old life, with little success. He worked freelance and made appearances in some low-budget Westerns. He was listed as a technical consultant on a few pictures in which he had helped out with the horses and machinery, though I suspect his position was largely a token of pity from directors who had liked working with him in the past. From what I understand, his life was a quiet one during that time. He mostly stayed on his ranch and adopted a few more animals that the studios no longer had use for.

Meanwhile in Mississippi, a playwright named Owen Tracy Smith had a grand vision for a southern quartet: four plays, each corresponding to a season, which would take place over the course of twenty years of a man's life. He needed one actor who could pass between twenty and forty years old, who could speak with an authentic southern accent, and who would be available for the entire run of the four plays, which could take years.

It was the accent that proved to be the trouble. Some of Broadway's greatest auditioned and no one met Smith's standards. Smith was insistent.

In various interviews, Smith claimed that he found the solution to his problem after rewatching the film *Georgia Summers*. Produced in 1938, it was the first film that Charles and Margy did together. The premise is that Charles and Margy play childhood friends from a small town in Georgia. Margy's character believes she has escaped her podunk town when she gets engaged to a rising political star in Virginia, but she returns home to find that she's still in love with her childhood beau. Both Charles and Margy were permitted to use their natural accents, slightly modified for general American audiences. It was one of the only contemporary films Charles ever did.

It took weeks for Smith to track Charles down, and when he finally did, Charles refused to audition. The story is now common folklore. Smith, who had never gone west of the Mississippi River, flew to Los Angeles with the scripts for each play. He showed up at Charles's ranch and begged him to read it. Charles stalled for two days, distracting Smith with a tour of the ranch, anecdotes about every animal who lived on it, and frequent meals. Each night, Smith went back to his hotel in Los Angeles and fielded angry phone calls from his early investors about what he was doing with their money. On the third day at the ranch, Smith pulled one page from the first script. It was a monologue delivered by the protagonist about his first love. He asked Charles to read it out loud and Charles relented. Smith offered him the role on the spot.

Smith flew back to New York that evening. Charles took a week to put his affairs in order: he hired his groundskeeper's entire family to manage the upkeep of the ranch and its creatures, and he vacated California indefinitely.

·   ·   ·

I was told that Charles nearly quit multiple times during rehears-als for the first play. It was difficult for him to adjust to the city, both its climate and its people. There were a few Hollywood cast-offs in New York City around then, but none whom Charles would have acquainted himself with. He found himself alienated from the other cast members, most of whom had studied at various prestigious East Coast academies. He was keenly aware of how many of them had auditioned for his role, only to be passed up for an out-of-work film cowboy. A younger version of Charles might have weathered it, but the war had changed him the same way it changed all of those men. It was a lonely existence, and the one person who might have improved it still lived on the other side of the country.

Smith knew what he was doing. While I don't believe that casting Charles was necessarily a ploy, I can't deny that it worked incred-ibly well as one. By the time the play opened in 1948, everyone still remembered Charles's scandalous departure from Hollywood. They were eager to see if a man who had spent his career shoot-ing guns and riding horses would fail at delivering serious lines onstage.

And then he didn't. The reviews were glowing. The play was hailed as the next great southern literary drama. A month into the run of the first play, *Autumn Rose*, Smith had enough investors to fund the next three plays. After the initial reviews, *Autumn Rose* sold out nearly every performance of its first run. The next play would premiere on Broadway, as would each subsequent install-ment of the quartet.

That night, I sat in the mezzanine of the crowded theater, close enough that I could lean against the railings, with a clear view of the stage to my right.

When Charles appeared on the stage, I had the embarrassing impulse to turn to the person in the seat next to me and inform whoever it was that I actually knew him. He looked different—his face had sharpened, bringing out the lines of his cheekbones and jaw. He could still pass for a man in his early twenties, just not the man he had been in his early twenties.

It all changed when he spoke. His baritone voice filled the theater as he began to tell us a story. There was a collective loosening as everyone eased into their seats while he talked. Smith had been clever in giving him something to do with his hands—Charles alternated between whittling a piece of wood and telling the audience about his family. The story he was telling was, of course, Smith's: an alcoholic father, a former beauty of a mother, three sisters who wouldn't act right.

As Charles stood center stage to deliver his final monologue, I watched his eyes settle somewhere in the audience. I don't think anyone else would have known to look for Hal Bingham among that crowd. He was sitting four rows back in an aisle seat. In the darkness, I could see that he had dressed up for the occasion. It wasn't an appropriate moment for him to smile, but the corners of his mouth turned upward and his eyes were shining.

Hal's departure from Los Angeles had been very discreet. After he and Margy divorced, most of the public's attention was focused on Margy. When Hal's contract was up, he declined to renew. His mother, who lived on the East Coast, had been diagnosed with late-stage cancer, and his official statement was that he wished to move back home to spend more time with her. He divided his time between his hometown in Vermont and New York City, where he sporadically lent his voice to radio plays and enjoyed seeing shows.

The monologue Charles delivered that night wasn't his most famous. That would come later, when the final play of the southern quartet was adapted into a film, *Elegy*, and earned Charles Landrieu an Academy Award for Best Actor in 1961. It was the first film he would do after his failed return to Hollywood in 1945 and it would be the last in his career. Charles is now best remembered for his acceptance speech—he took to the stage wearing a tuxedo with a pair of cowboy boots, stared at the golden statue, and calmly said in his low drawl, "Look, I'm just as surprised as y'all are." He received such a long round of applause for the quip that he was unable to properly thank anyone except Smith and Hal. The papers noted that Charles had thanked his "good friend."

Hal never remarried and Charles never married at all. Nobody speculated much about them anymore, but all any good gossip columnist would have had to do would be to look up their real estate purchases. Hal owned two properties: a house in Vermont and an apartment in New York. Charles eventually sold the California ranch to his groundskeeper and bought an apartment in New York. Same apartment building—one lived on the eighth floor, the other on the ninth, a fire escape between them. They stayed there the rest of their lives.

When Charles fixed his eyes on Hal in the audience, I understood that this happened every night—he knew exactly where Hal would be sitting and he knew to look there. The monologue was about his character's first love, a girl who died from Spanish flu when they were both seventeen.

He spoke of their courtship, sneaking away for long walks at night, beyond the watchful eye of society. The promises they made to each other for a future that would never happen. He described the months they spent together as suspended in time.

Charles's voice softened while he spoke of their last meetings: "As spring turned to summer, the world was ours."

And so it was.

ACKNOWLEDGMENTS

To booksellers. It's not an exaggeration to say that this novel was forged in the early hours before my bookstore shifts, during my lunch breaks, and anytime I was awake enough after store hours. I'm so grateful to the communities I've found at independent bookstores—from the people who took a risk and opened up these stores; to the amazing, creative, brilliant booksellers who keep everything running; to the readers who support their local bookstores. This is a weird little corner of the retail world, and I'm so happy to be in it with you all.

To Parnassus Books, in particular. I am so grateful for the support I've had from the booksellers at Parnassus. It's been such a joy to share this whole journey with you all—there's no group of people I'd rather cry and eat a pint of ice cream with.

To my teachers. In some sort of chronological order: Rika Drea, Zana Previti, Thu Nguyen, Janet Hahn, Louise Brennan, Kevin Barr, Sergei Lobanov-Rostovsky, Ivonne García, Kim McMullen, Karen Snouffer, K. Read Baldwin, Kristen Van Ausdall, Alyson Hagy, Mark Ritchie, Rattawut Lapcharoensap, Joy Williams, and Brad Watson. You've all mentored so many incredible students and I'm humbled to be among them.

To the University of Wyoming. Thank you for the time and resources to undertake not only this novel but also the failed projects I needed to try before I could figure out how to write this novel. Thank you to the University of Wyoming library for letting me check out way too many books on Hollywood history (and thank you to the authors of those books: Otto Friedrich, Jeanine Basinger, William J. Mann, and Karina Longworth). Thank you to my fellow writers at Wyoming, especially my cohort—Jenny, Francesca, and Tayo, y'all are the best.

To my early readers. Thank you, Jenny Tinghui Zhang, Alyson

Hagy, Mica Cohen-Fuentes, Sarah Arnold, and Aly Plasterer, for your time and feedback.

To my agent. Thank you, Andrianna deLone, for reading my book in a day and sending me an email that changed my life.

To my editor. Thank you, Carolyn Williams, for being an early supporter of this book, a generous and thoughtful editor, and a wonderful guide every step of the way.

To the team at Doubleday. Thank you to Bill Thomas, Tricia Cave, Lindsay Mandel, Emily Mahon, Studio Martina Flor, Maria Carella, Kathleen Cook, and Lorraine Hyland for ushering this book into the world.

To my family. Thank you for making sure that I was always sheltered, fed, and (mostly) sane. And thanks for finally getting me a dog.

To Peggy Satterlee and Betty Hansen. I don't know much about your lives outside of the trial documents and press coverage of the 1940s, but I believe you.

About the Author

Lindsay Lynch is a writer from Washington, D.C. A longtime indie book-seller, she currently lives in Nashville, Tennessee, where she works as the book buyer for Parnassus Books. Her work has appeared in *The Adroit Journal, The Rumpus, Electric Lit, The Atlantic, The Offing,* and *Lit Hub,* among other places. She has been a participant in the Tin House Summer Work-shop and the Napa Valley Writers' Conference. She holds an MFA in fiction from the University of Wyoming. *Do Tell* is her debut novel.